REIGN OF MAGIC

The Fairy Tale Enchantress Book 3

K. M. SHEA

REIGN OF MAGIC
Copyright © 2019 by K. M. Shea

Cover Art by Deranged Doctor Design
Edited by Jeri Larsen

All rights reserved. No part of this book may be used or reproduced in any number whatsoever without written permission of the author, except in the case of quotations embodied in articles and reviews.

This is a work of fiction. Names, characters, places, and incidents are either the product of the author's imagination, or are used fictitiously. Any resemblance to actual persons, living or dead, or historic events is entirely coincidental.

www.kmshea.com

ISBN: 978-1-950635-06-1

Read: 09/25 LD Unit xix

For me,
Because this book was so difficult to write,
I would never wish it on anyone else.
Angelique, I feel your pain.

MAP OF THE CONTINENT

CHAPTER 1

"Why am I doing this? Because it's the right thing to do." Angelique paused, testing the truth of her words. "Yes, that's a fine enough reason to be going back to the same place I stormed out of just a few weeks ago."

Against her better judgement, Angelique was riding to the Veneno Conclave, the fortress which housed the organization all good mages, fairy godmothers, and enchanters belonged to... including The Council.

Six enchanters and enchantresses sat on the Council, overseeing the entire Conclave. And only a few weeks ago, Angelique had shouted at them rather colorfully for dragging her in for every minor rule she broke and for questioning her about nearly every spell she cast.

It wouldn't have been so annoying if they actually listened *to me and took me seriously when I tried to tell them all that has troubled the continent. But they seemed more upset with any minor infraction of mine than the fact that, over the last few years, a suspiciously high number of our world's royal families have experienced curses or vicious attacks by black mages.*

Pegasus shortened his stride and took a curved path, giving a wide berth to the farmer and his two oxen pulling a cart of dried straw—likely the last of the harvest. This late in autumn, the cold breath of winter was already frosting the world at night.

When he had put a sufficient distance between himself and the farmer, Pegasus picked up the pace again. Sparks hissed at his hooves, and the glittering stars that were buried in the blue-black swirls of his coat glowed brighter.

Angelique crouched lower on his neck, taking comfort in the heat that radiated from his mane—which wasn't so much hair as it was flickering blue flames. *At least I'm going to the Conclave voluntarily. With luck, I can duck in and out quickly. I just need to catch Blanche and Rein before they leave.*

Blanche and Rein were a pair of master weather mages. In the summer, they had agreed to look in on Ringsted—the southernmost country on the continent that had been cut off by storms created by a sea witch. Unfortunately, they already had an assignment at the time and were unable to look into the matter when Angelique first made the request.

It was late fall now, but they were finally free and had sent Angelique a letter that caught up with her when she and Pegasus were traveling through Loire. It informed her they finally had the time to check in on the isolated country, and they planned to leave in a few days' time to do just that.

I didn't intend to dump the whole mission on them. Perhaps I can accompany them and help in one manner or another. And I'd like to check in on the Selkie Princess whose voice I altered at the beginning of summer.

Soon, the glittering fortress of the Veneno Conclave appeared on the horizon, perched on a tall hilltop, looking stately with the backdrop of tall mountains that stretched due west of it.

Even from this distance, she could make out the spires of Luxi-Domux, the Veneno Conclave magic academy.

Angelique gently tugged on the reins, pulling Pegasus from a full gallop to a slower canter that kicked up far fewer sparks.

The constellation huffed, but he slowed enough that the

stinging wind no longer threatened to pull tears from Angelique's eyes.

She adjusted her dress, thankful for the heat charm spelled into the cloth as the gown shifted colors from a bright gold to a pale yellow.

When they reached the base of the hill on which the Conclave was perched, Pegasus slowed down to a trot—which was still faster than Angelique could run.

The fortress gates were open, and as Angelique and her mount approached them, two figures riding shaggy mountain ponies emerged from the shadows of the gatehouse.

Angelique blinked in surprise, then slapped on a smile. "Mage Blanche, Mage Rein!"

Rein was easily recognizable with his brilliant blue hair. He swiveled in his saddle and rolled back his shoulders when he caught sight of Angelique. "Apprentice Angelique, greetings," he said.

Blanche pulled her pony to a stop and adjusted the fur stole that was settled across her shoulders. "Did you not receive the message we sent?"

"No, I got it. It caught up with me when I was riding through Loire." Angelique smiled, feeling more than a little windblown. "I'm glad I made it here before you left. I cannot thank you enough for looking into the storms surrounding Ringsted."

"Of course," Blanche said. "It is our duty as master weather mages."

Perhaps, but it has taken the Veneno Conclave months to approve sending a mage out to check on the storms.

Angelique elbowed the frustrating thought aside. "I would like to come with you—that is, if it's not an inconvenience. When I was last in Ringsted, I was in a bit of a hurry and was unable to be as thorough in my actions there as I would have liked."

"That's not necessary," Blanche said.

Angelique shook her head. "I recognize that—and I appreciate that the two of you are looking into the situation. But accompanying you is the least I can do."

"Oh, um," Rein awkwardly said.

"That is very...kind...of you," Blanche limply said.

The pair looked at each other, but Angelique could read the alarm in their expressions. Rein's blue eyebrows slanted down in a sharp V, and he pulled his placid pony in an unnecessary circle. Blanche's eyes widened, and she bit her lower lip before dropping her gaze to the ground.

Ah, I see. Angelique's spirit sank. *They don't want me to come with them. Out of fear.* It was a jab to her heart, but a pain she was exhaustively accustom to.

Angelique was the first war mage to ever be trained as an enchantress. While she hadn't made the position yet—she was only an apprentice—the amount of power she had at her disposal and the particular strain of her war magic—the ability to control anything with a sharpened edge—made her feared among most mages.

In fact, if Lord Enchanter Evariste hadn't stepped in and taken on Angelique as his apprentice, her magic would have been sealed years ago.

The thought of Evariste produced a pang in her chest, but it was the way both Blanche and Rein uncomfortably held themselves and refused to meet her gaze that made her droop in her saddle.

Given that her power was really only good for bloodshed, and that she had a massive amount of this unsettling magic, Angelique couldn't blame the mages for their apprehension.

But it still hurts to face near-constant rejection and to be a person fellow mages fear. When I last met them, Blanche and Rein didn't seem afraid of me, but I suppose it's one thing to speak to me within the walls of the Veneno Conclave and another to journey across the continent with me.

"That is to say, we appreciate the offer, really. However, we have no need of aid," Blanche said, having regained some of her equilibrium.

"Yes," Rein piped in. "We'll have to sit around and observe the storms for a while before we even start to use our magic."

That is not why they don't want me coming with them.

"I see," Angelique slowly said. "If that is so...is there any other way I can thank you?"

"Nah," Rein was quick to say.

Blanche's posture eased with the threat of Angelique's presence fading. "We are weather mages, Apprentice Angelique. It is our honor to help Ringsted in this time of need." She offered her a slight smile.

Angelique nodded once, then twice. "I understand. In that case, my well-wishes go with you, and I look forward to hearing of your success." Though her tone was cheerful, the words tasted like dirt in her mouth.

They won't let me do anything at all to help?

Rein's flashed a grin. "Yep. We'll show that sea witch you heard about who the *real* masters of the wind and rain are!"

Blanche slightly shook her head, amused with her friend's antics. "Take care, Apprentice Angelique."

"Thank you." Angelique raised her hand in farewell and watched the mages and their mounts march out.

She rapidly blinked when she finally lowered her hand. "I suppose this is what I deserve," she told Pegasus. "For *shouting* at the Council and bucking rules." She sighed deeply. "But...something tells me even if I hadn't done that, they still wouldn't want me along."

As she watched, Blanche and Rein reached the bottom of the hill. Rein said something to Blanche that made her laugh, and they turned their ponies south.

More than their rejection, that sight made Angelique cringe in pain. For before he had been captured, Angelique and her master

—the young and handsome Lord Enchanter Evariste—had traveled the continent together.

Pegasus stretched his neck and bared his teeth, making a clacking sound when he ground his molars. He tossed his head and pranced a few steps.

"Easy," Angelique soothed the constellation. "I know it's been a frustrating few years, and you miss Evariste, too."

Pegasus stopped his carrying on and instead tucked his head and twisted so he could clamp his teeth over her shoe.

He didn't bite her through the slipper, but he did squeeze a little to voice his discontent.

Angelique patted his shoulder. "I know," she said. "I know." She fussed with the reins, trying to distract herself.

Lately, it seemed like everything in the world was working together to remind Angelique of her missing master. Though he had been captured years ago, Angelique still found herself turning around to say something to him, only to remember he was gone and she was alone.

Evariste had been taken by black mages. He had used his magic to send Angelique off to safety while he was hit with a spell that was originally aimed at her. In the scuffle that followed, the mages managed to overpower and take him.

Though Angelique had spent the last few years combing the continent in her search for him, she had very little to show for it. A one-use-only spell revealed he was being kept in a magic mirror, but she did not know where.

It was her search for Evariste that had taken her south to Ringsted, where she met the Selkie Princess.

Angelique tipped forward until she was splayed across the crest of Pegasus' neck. "Why can't anything be simple, Pegasus?"

The constellation snorted, making his mane crackle.

Angelique sighed. "I suppose at least now we can continue searching for magic mirrors and the like. Or perhaps we ought to head back to Loire to speak with Prince Severin and Princess Elle."

Pegasus gave her no reply but to paw at the ground.

Angelique wearily sat up and ran a hand through her loose hair, cringing when she realized it was her true hair color—a dark brown. (The darkness of her hair combined with her eerie silver eyes did very little to convince other mages she was harmless. Rather, it made her look a shade intimidating. As a result, she used illusion magic to color her eyes and frequently altered the shade of her hair. She was forever searching for the appearance that would net her the fewest suspicious looks, but thus far hadn't experienced much success of any sort regardless of whether she was a strawberry blonde with green eyes or a chestnut brunette with eyes of baby blue.)

"I should have taken time to change it this morning." Angelique pulled on a wisp of her magic and twisted it between her fingers, then combed the spell through her hair. Slowly, her locks shifted from the dark shade to a more copper-toned color of brunette.

She leaned forward to thread her fingers through Pegasus' flaming mane. "Yes, I think we should head south and go back to Loire for now. We can stop at an inn for the evening and decide what to do after that." She adjusted her skirts over the saddle and waited for Pegasus to move.

The constellation lifted his head and slightly arched his neck.

Angelique tucked a strand of her hair behind her ear and almost took a dead leaf to the face when the wind picked up. "Pegasus?"

The mount pricked his ears, but his gaze didn't stray.

Concerned, Angelique leaned to the side so she could peer around his head.

Off in the distance, she saw a glowing...orb.

It hovered at about chest-height off the ground, drunkenly zigzagging back and forth.

Is that...magic? Angelique squinted as she watched the orb—which glowed a cheerful yellow—slowly roll closer.

She turned in her saddle to peer at the tall, imposing walls that enclosed the Veneno Conclave fortress. *It must be meant for someone inside. But I don't know that I've ever seen a message passed along in this manner.*

She pressed her leg against Pegasus so he sidestepped for a few strides before settling back to watch the glowing orb.

The orb passed them and rolled closer to the fortress gates, stopped, then abruptly backtracked. It lazily drew closer, continuing on even after Pegasus bumped it with his muzzle.

The orb rose higher into the air until it was about eye-level with Angelique and hovering above Pegasus' neck.

"I know this magic." Angelique cocked her head as she identified the strong but good-humored feel to the spell. "Isn't it... Stil's?"

Stil was a craftmage whom Angelique and Evariste had found when he was a mere street urchin. They enrolled him in Luxi-Domus and had kept tabs on the boy and frequently visited him. He was an adult now—though mages aged a little slower, it was only the enchanters and enchantresses like Evariste and Angelique who aged as slowly as the elves—but Angelique still thought of him as something of a little brother.

Something warm stirred in her chest. *Maybe he uncovered news about Evariste?* Angelique extended a finger and cautiously tapped the orb.

The magic popped like a bubble, coating Angelique and Pegasus in yellow dust, and dropping a letter.

Angelique caught the letter midair but sneezed violently from the powdery dust. *This is probably why I've never seen a message passed along this way before. Leave it to Stil to attempt it, though.* A chain of four sneezes ripped from Angelique's nose, nearly pushing her over Pegasus' side before she caught her balance and could finally see.

She rubbed her nose, then did her best to straighten the sheet of paper she had crumpled during her sneeze festival, and unfolded it.

Angel,

Angelique laughed. "Yes, this is definitely Rumpelstiltskin. No one else besides Evariste and he call me that."

I'm being followed by a being of dark magic, so I'm stranded in Verglas. I'd appreciate your help when you get the chance,
Stil

Angelique's good cheer died immediately, and she warred between rolling her eyes at the unnecessarily polite tone of the letter and clenching her teeth in worry at the contents of it. *He's being followed? Do black mages mean to capture him as they took Evariste?*

Her heart beat faster, but she took a moment to breathe deeply. *No, wait. As long as he's in Verglas, he's safe from black mages. Anything with black or twisted magic can't cross Verglas' borders with the Snow Queen's magic forever guarding the country.*

Angelique folded the note into a small square. "Pegasus, there's been a change in plans."

Pegasus snorted a few times, and she barely grabbed onto the saddle in time before he shook like a dog. She coughed in the newly stirred puffed of dust, getting some of it in her mouth.

Gross.

She brushed the powder off her clothes, then noticed Pegasus was twisted uncomfortably so he could rest his chin on her foot.

She sneezed again, then settled into the saddle. "We're going to Verglas!"

"MASTER," Angelique said, annoyance lining her voice. "You cannot buy me an elven blade."

"You're right." Evariste leaned over a gorgeous sword wrought with pink gold. It was beautiful, but the blade was so big it would be unwieldy for Angelique. "Emerys will give it to me for free."

"You're awfully cocky considering your promise hinges on my generosity." Emerys scowled and used the sleeve of his shirt to polish a finger smudge on his bow.

Angelique took a deep breath—as she did whenever she tried to calm herself if she found Evariste's ideas particularly stupid. That and the adorable cheek twitch she occasionally got were her tells for annoyance. "It's inappropriate for a mage to carry a weapon," she said, changing tactics.

Emerys laughed outright. "You hear that, Evariste? She thinks you care about being appropriate. Hah!"

Angelique smiled so hard at the elf king, Evariste wondered if her teeth were cracking. "No, you're right," she muttered to herself, barely audible over Emerys' laughter. "How could I ever think Evariste is appropriate? After all, he's friends with you."

Evariste almost dropped the delicate dagger he had picked up for closer inspection, but doing so would alert his student that he had heard her comment, which would make her clam up in an instant.

Watery grayness started to invade his peripheral vision, a familiar and unwanted presence.

He cleared his throat and tried to look past it. "If you don't want a dagger for yourself, Angel, I suppose that's your choice. But perhaps you ought to pick one up for Stil? When he leaves his master and becomes a traveling craftmage, he ought to have a weapon with which to defend himself."

Angelique's expression changed from tight to pensive, and she cast an appreciative glance at the swords. "He mentioned he was learning how to use a spear for basic self-defense." She walked away from the table of shining blades and ambled toward the elven spears leaning in racks against the wall.

Evariste grinned playfully at her back, ignoring the grayness which crept into the room like fog. "Wonderful," he said. "And as his parents, we really ought to provide for him."

Angelique turned around with the stiffness of a puppet. "Master," she said in a voice full of exasperation.

Evariste laughed, but the grayness grew thicker until he couldn't see Angelique or Emerys. Steeling himself, Evariste tried to hold onto the memory, but it slipped through his fingers.

As the sweet memory drifted away from him like a wisp in the wind, Evariste held perfectly still.

He didn't shift, didn't crack an eye open; he didn't even groan. He kept his body limp and in the uncomfortable, folded position he had dropped into when the pain of having his magic drained from him had knocked him unconscious.

Over the past few months, he had started recovering faster from the vicious drainings.

It was a mixed blessing, for the only time the wretched, all-invasive grayness of the mirror couldn't pry into his sight was when his magic was violently ripped from his soul and his memories cocooned his mind in an effort to protect him. As soon as he awakened, it was to the yawning grayness of the inside of the mirror, which seemed to slowly chip away at his sanity.

But Evariste had come to realize that his captors were unaware he was starting to recover faster. This gave him an advantage—one he hadn't yet figured out how to use, but if he had anything it was time. He would find some way to implement it into a plan.

Evariste strained his ears, trying to listen. Funrus—the black mage who had just drained him—didn't seem to be around. (The man plodded everywhere he went, and the stillness of the empty cavern where Evariste and his mirror were tucked meant it was unlikely the mage was still around.)

Even so, Evariste didn't dare move. *Just because Funrus is gone doesn't mean the room is empty. Even if that's the most likely case, it's not worth moving and potentially sacrificing my only advantage.*

Footsteps that sounded far away slowly drew closer. It was Liliane, the vile leader of the black mages who held him captive. He had learned to recognize her dainty steps and the tell-tale swoosh of her skirts fairly early in his capture.

She sat down in a chair of some sort and tugged on what sounded like a wooden stand.

Her easel.

Liliane had a rather unusual sort of magic Evariste had spent months mulling over. She could paint a living creature on a canvas, and her magic transported it to her.

Based on what he had observed, her magic was limited to creatures—no humans or objects—and the painting had to be well done. (A crude stick figure would not bring a troll to her side.) Moreover, she didn't create the creatures—they already existed. She could only summon them.

I don't understand how the Veneno Conclave is unaware of her. She said she attended there as a student, but mages with teleportation magic— even with limits like hers—are so rare.

Evariste would know. He had a particularly useful brand of magic that let him make transportation gates, allowing anyone passage to whatever location Evariste desired.

I suppose I don't know how old she is. Though she has an adult son nearly my age, she is powerful. It's possible she has the lifespan of an enchantress if she has enough magic.

Time slowly ticked by.

Evariste held still—even though he was getting a cramp in his neck, and the spot between his shoulder blades pinched uncomfortably.

In the suffocating silence of the mirror, Evariste could make out the steady stroke of Liliane's paint brush.

He made himself remain motionless, even when he heard her magic click into place. Shortly after, the cavern was filled with the squawks of angry harpies—creatures that were a twisted combination of vultures with humanoid faces.

"You're to go to Baris," Liliane instructed.

The harpies hissed.

"I don't care if the royal family is hunting your forces down," Lilaine started. "You must keep up your pressure there, or Baris will realize what's going on. If their distraction is bought with blood, so be it. *Go.*" The orders sounded *wrong* as Liliane's voice was warm and bright.

More squawks, the rustling of feathers, and the click of talons on stone grew louder, then faded as the harpies stalked from the cave chamber.

Liliane was still present—Evariste could hear her fussing with her completed painting.

I guess now is about time for me to "wake."

Evariste groaned loudly and opened and closed his clenched hands.

Liliane's approach was marked by her footsteps as Evariste drew out his performance. *Though my chest feels like someone has been carving at it with a dull dagger, I now wake up relatively alert. But I'd rather have them think I'm as helpless as a lamb.*

He opened his eyes, blinking blearily and groaning again as he slowly moved his head into a more comfortable position. "What?" he growled when he saw Liliane standing in front of the pane of his mirror. (It was the only part not covered in the endless grayness, and it acted as Evariste's window to the outside.)

Liliane thoughtfully tapped her chin. "I'm not sure if it's disappointing or gratifying to see you, the treasured prodigy of the Veneno Conclave, brought so low so easily. Your constitution is worse than we expected."

Evariste coughed and made himself move slowly—which wasn't too difficult as every muscle in his body ached after his magic was drained. "How could it be disappointing?"

"Because if you're one of the greatest the Conclave has to

offer, it's maddening that it has taken us so long to best them." Liliane made a long-suffering sigh as she wrapped a lock of her hair around her finger.

She was deceptively beautiful—with blonde hair that hung in ringlets, sparkling eyes, and an inviting smile. And while most of the black mages favored darker shades for their clothes, Liliane was dressed in a gown of lavender velvet with silver embroidery. Fragrant white flowers were tucked into her hair and woven around her right wrist in a bracelet.

But for all of her smiles and look of innocence, there was something dark in her that played in the shadows of her eyes and the way her expressions seemed more like a mask—as if she hadn't learned how to smile as a child and had only been instructed how to feign it as an adult.

"So long?" Evariste asked, grasping the importance of Liliane's off-handed remark. "You speak as if you have been at this for centuries."

Liliane smiled and raised an eyebrow. "And to think I assumed you were intelligent." She fussed for a moment with one of the flowers in her hair. "Though perhaps you have a point. Despite the generations of planning, it wasn't until my husband passed away in a tiny skirmish in Baris that we *finally* began making progress."

Generations of planning?

"And now our strategies are finally coming to fruition. Once Acri returns, the bloodshed can truly begin."

Evariste wanted to curse at Acri's name—he was Liliane's dark and twisted son who had been sent out to kill Angelique.

He knew Angelique could best the deadly young mage...if she used her war magic. And that was something she had refused to do since the day Evariste took her on as his apprentice.

But Liliane had dispatched Acri weeks ago, and he had yet to return. That alone was highly encouraging.

Evariste boosted himself up so he stood, though he took a few tottering steps for show. "You're waiting on him? Why? He's obviously no match for Angelique. It's been weeks since he left, and yet he hasn't returned to skulk around in your shadow." (Though it wasn't part of a proper plan, Evariste made it his business to insult and ruffle the black mages as much as possible. In particular, he enjoyed upsetting Liliane—who seemed susceptible to insults about her appearance.)

Liliane chuckled. "If you seek to irritate me, I'm afraid it won't work. It *has* taken my son longer than I would like to track your little apprentice, but even the strictest mage in our company would be forced to admit it's understandable given what she rides."

What? Why would it matter what she's riding? Unless, did she manage to find Emerys, and he gave her an elf mount? But she's not an elf-friend. How could she have gotten into the Alabaster Forest? Evariste kept his expression even in the hope that he could swindle more information from the woman. "If you say so." He colored his voice with obvious doubt.

Liliane rolled her eyes. "You *are* being obtuse. For even you must admit there's not an enchanter or enchantress alive who could keep up with Pegasus."

Evariste almost lost control of his jaw. *Pegasus? She's been riding Pegasus? Why in the blazing stars would she call him down? He's less safe than keeping a wild wolf in your house!*

"Constellation or not," Liliane continued. "Acri will end your little apprentice's miserable existence. The blood of ancient mage families flows within his veins." Liliane smiled fondly at the thought of her son. "He is powerful and possesses deadly magic."

"Lucky for him," Evariste scoffed.

"Not lucky at all," Liliane countered. "It took my husband and me several attempts before we had a child with magic—and a kind that was to our liking."

"*What?*"

"You *must* know, Lord Enchanter, that just because the parents possess magic does not guarantee the offspring will, and even if they do, there is no telling what sort of core magic they'll end up with or even how much they'll have." Liliane laughed airily. "Suzu is *quite* embarrassed by her powerless daughter. I'm sure she would have happily ended the girl's life if not for the meddling of her husband."

Evariste stared at Liliane. "What happened to your other children?" he asked, fearing the answer.

Liliane shrugged her elegant shoulders. "I culled them until I had what I wanted."

Evariste's stomach rolled, and he didn't have to feign the nausea that churned in his stomach. *She's not just a black mage—that's too trite of a term to describe her darkness. How could she kill her own children over* magic?

Liliane didn't seem to notice his reaction. She was adjusting her skirts as she returned to her art easel and plucked the painted canvas from its surface, tossing it on a pile of other paintings.

"That's why your apprentice is doomed, Evariste. I *chose* Acri. He will crush Angelique with all of the might I have invested in him."

Evariste watched numbly as the black mage swept from the room.

His legs gave out from under him, and he sat down hard.

This is what the Veneno Conclave is up against—a vileness that can't be fathomed. I have to get out—I have to warn them! If that is what Liliane does to her own children...I can't imagine what kind of plans she has for the world.

The thought made him shudder, and for once he gratefully looked into the unfeeling grayness of the mirror.

Minutes passed, and Evariste's thoughts eventually turned back to his apprentice. *So Angelique has taken up riding Pegasus.* He shook his head. *It's almost brilliant—there's not an animal alive that can keep pace with his top speed, and he's powerful enough to be a legitimate threat to even a talented mage. But I've only ridden him occasionally because he owes me. He has no such deal with Angelique, and she's not one to court trouble. Why, then, does she ride him?*

Evariste stared at the shadows of the cavern, his heart squeezing painfully—not from the draining he had undergone, but from concern. *What has happened that made Angel so desperate that she'd turn to a wild card like Pegasus for help? And what has been so grim that he would willingly help her?*

CHAPTER 2

Verglas was blanketed in snow.
Everything was cold and icy, but with the night so clear, the snow seemed to glow in the moonlight.

Though it was beautiful, it failed to distract Angelique from her thoughts.

She had spent the majority of the several-day-ride trying to forget about Blanche and Rein, about Evariste's absence, and even about the last few months. But the more she tried to distract herself, the more her surroundings seemed to remind her of her frequent failings in life.

I thought my days in Luxi-Domus were trying. Wasn't that life's greatest joke? Angelique stared at the ornamental reins of Pegasus' bridle. They were shiny and smudged to her tired eyes. She wanted nothing more than to lie down and sleep—even if it was in the snow—but they were close to Stil's tent. It made more sense to push on through.

Ahead of her a little sparkle of light glittered—the tracking spell Angelique was using to find her wayward friend.

Though a great deal of the trouble I've encountered recently hasn't been anyone's doing—or rather, it's the doing of black mages. She cringed in the saddle. *I detest my magic, but I am grateful Evariste insisted I keep up with my fighting abilities and had Puss drill me endlessly. I'd probably be skewered by a goblin by now if it wasn't for all that practice. It's just one more thing I have to apologize for when I finally find him.*

Though Evariste had saved Angelique, they hadn't parted on the greatest of terms. Or, rather, they had argued and weren't even speaking to each other when their home was attacked.

One would imagine that as months passed and turned into years, Angelique's guilt over the fight would decrease, but it hadn't.

Instead, the time only seemed to give her more opportunities to realize just how much Evariste had done for her—not just as a mentor but as a friend—and how poorly she had valued it.

Angelique considered draping herself over Pegasus' neck—which would save her the trouble of trying to stay upright, even if it would be a bit bumpy. She was only vaguely aware that Pegasus trailed after the sparkle as it roamed across an open plain, taking them in the direction of a pocket of trees.

Enough. I'm just tired and feeling sorry for myself. What's important is Stil. If his message is right and something is after him, this is very serious.

Pegasus snorted, and a comet blazed across the galactic swirls in his coat.

Angelique cautiously peered through the darkness, spotting tiny flames in the distance: campfires. There were at least six or seven fires—which meant it was not Stil's camp or even the camp of a tiny band of travelers.

She dug her spyglass out of her saddlebag and fitted it to her eye. It took a moment to focus on the fires, but when she did, the flickering flames illuminated the faces and clothes of the men crowded around the flames.

Most of them wore drab gray cloaks—though a few had cloaks of a softer blue hue—but all of them had the Verglas Insignia of a reindeer in front of a silver snowflake emblazoned on the back.

"Verglas soldiers," Angelique said for Pegasus' benefit—though she was almost certain the constellation didn't care. "But why are they this far south? There are only a few villages in this area, and though the border it shares with Loire is near, the two countries have had a civil relationship for centuries. And they can't be Stil's followers—he mentioned black magic at work, not soldiers."

Angelique returned her spyglass to her saddlebag. Her eyes flickered back and forth between the fires and the tipsy light of her spell, which now lingered at the treeline.

"Stil comes first," Angelique decided. "Besides, given King Torgen's mad actions last year, there's no guarantee what the soldiers are here for."

Pegasus trotted off toward the forest, snow crunching—and melting—under his hooves.

Angelique shivered. King Torgen had always been a little mad, but last year he had stretched to new lows by nearly killing the Arcainian princes and princess who had fled to Verglas to escape the witch queen who had cursed the princes to take on the appearance and mind of swans.

Just thinking of him made Angelique's flesh prickle, for the king's mad ways had been a severe punishment to his people for some years now.

But magic users are powerless to help. We can't meddle with country politics—it's not our place, and it would set a dangerous precedence.

She blinked when Pegasus trotted at the edge of the forest, but the bobbing light wove around a few of the trees. She craned her neck to watch the light, and nearly tumbled over the constellation's shoulder for her trouble.

She corrected herself and almost laughed. *Evariste always warned me to hold on when Pegasus is galloping. He'd laugh outright at me if I told him I almost fell off when Pegasus was at a mere jog!*

She grinned, but after a moment passed, the thought stopped being funny and was just another bitter reminder.

After a few more minutes of riding, Pegasus curved into the

forest, following the sparkle of the spell until it stopped just over a terrible, ramshackle tent.

Picketed outside was an ornery donkey who opened his eyes at Pegasus' approach.

Angelique slipped off her mount—pausing to sag against his warm shoulder—then greeted the donkey. "Hello, Pricker Patch."

The donkey—which was horse-sized and had been a gift to Stil from Evariste when the craftmage graduated from Luxi-Domus—smacked its lips twice, then turned its head away from her in a clear dismissal. Angelique smiled wryly and turned back to Pegasus.

"Thanks for the ride." She stifled a yawn with her hand. "I'll stay here for the night, so you can return to the sky if you want."

Pegasus was motionless, but a star on his forehead flared.

Angelique waved him off. "I'll be fine. I'll check in with Stil and then fall face-first into bed. Enjoy."

She paused for a few moments at the tent entrance to give Stil's magic a chance to recognize her, then pushed the cloth flap open.

Instead of showing the battered inside of the tent, the flap opened up into a beautiful parlor with a cheerful fire, plush cushions, and several comfortable couches.

Pleasantly, Stil was in the parlor. Surprisingly, he was not alone. Rather, he appeared to be chasing a young lady around a settee.

The female in question had dark brown hair that ended in curls and was pushed out of her face with a blue headband. Though there was a slight air of shock to her expression, the icy gray-blue hue of her eyes spoke of a certain kind of ageless wisdom—even as she chucked a pillow at Rumpelstiltskin.

"I must say." Stil ducked the pillow and frowned a little. "I pictured many reactions when I confessed my love to you. Rage was not one of them."

Angelique gaped. *Confess his love to her?! Did I push myself so far into exhaustion that I'm experiencing auditory hallucinations?*

"How could you do this!" the young lady demanded, her voice loud and full of panic.

"Why are we shouting?" Stil asked.

"I DON'T KNOW!" his apparent lady-love shouted powerfully at his face.

Angelique briefly grabbed the wall to keep from toppling over, her thoughts blanking at the odd exchange.

I don't even know what to think anymore.

The wall creaked a little, and Angelique hastily pushed off it and made an effort to stand straight when Stil and the young lady turned to face her.

Angelique smiled at the pair—though Stil twisted his lips in a frown that told her she had bad timing, and his young lady gaped at Angelique much how Angelique wished to gawk at her.

She cleared her throat—for this new silence was almost more awkward than watching their fight. "I seem to have caught you at a bad time." Angelique paused for a moment to give the pair a chance to say something.

They didn't. *Wonderful.*

"I'll just go for now," she decided—though the thought of returning to the cold broke her a little.

"Come back in an hour," Stil said.

"Wait!" The still-unnamed lady—for apparently Stil had terrible manners—zipped across the parlor and approached Angelique. "You must be here to see Stil. I apologize for our loud discussion, but you have not interrupted anything. Please, come in. Can I get you something to drink?"

Angelique stared at the girl in surprise, more disarmed by her unexpected kindness than she had been by finding her in a shouting match with Stil.

With her exhaustion leaning heavily on her shoulders and her heart still smarting from Blanche and Rein's rejection, Angelique's eyes stung.

She tried to speak, but to her embarrassment, tears escaped her control, and she burst into sobs.

She was vaguely aware of Stil sliding a brotherly arm around her and guiding her to a settee.

He crouched in front of her and placed a hand on her knee. "Angelique, what's wrong?"

Tired and defeated, Angelique shook her head. "Everything."

Her tears kept coming as Stil exchanged a murmured conversation with his companion—who disappeared through the parlor door. He awkwardly hovered around Angelique as she desperately fought to regain control of herself.

But she was so tired and so weary of dragging herself into a new fight everywhere she went. *Why can't I just find Evariste?* she thought bleakly. *If I could just find him, I could bear the rest of this.*

Her eyes still stung from her tears, and now her face was hot and itchy. Angelique let out a huff of air. "I *hate* crying. It's so useless, and it only serves to make a person damp and weary." She angrily sniffed—aware she was madder with herself for losing control than at her actual tears.

"I'm certain that after all you've gone through, and after all you've done, you deserve a good cry." Stil's voice was soft, as was his hand when he squeezed her shoulder.

He sounds so much like Evariste when he's not being cheeky about his abilities. This thought proved to be the undoing of what little self-control she had mustered, and Angelique cried harder, feeling as though she had been torn in two.

"I can't find him, Stil," she sobbed, knowing the craftmage would guess to whom she was referring. "I have looked everywhere and combed every country, and I haven't found a hint of him! I even forced my way into Ringsted to see if he was carried down there. Nothing."

"You'll find him."

"No, I won't! I haven't any place left to look! I have tracked him with magic; I have looked for enchanted mirrors; and I have even used our bond as master and apprentice in that spell you gave me. Nothing works! He might be—"

Angelique cut herself off, unable to think it or say it. Over a year had passed since she managed to briefly make a connection with Evariste and find out he was in a mirror, and she hadn't made any progress since then.

There was a possibility he was no longer alive.

But I would feel it! I'd know! So he must still be alive.

Stil shifted from his spot next to Angelique's settee and folded his arms across his chest. "I hate to mention this, but it must be connected to the evil and darkness that has been stirring across the continent," he said. "The attacks against the countries and royalty are too well done to be coincidence. Whoever is responsible for this has been planning it for years. It is very likely they knew Enchanter Evariste needed to be removed before they could launch their first attack."

Angelique rubbed her eyes, trying to get the tears to stop flowing. *I'm not certain he's entirely right. When Evariste was captured, it was because he was hit by a spell meant for me. Unless they thought the easiest way to subdue him was to first capture me? But I'm glad Stil also sees a pattern. Before I spoke with Severin and Elle about it, I wondered if I was going mad and seeing black mages under every rock.*

"They seem to be doing a fine job of sabotaging themselves." Angelique snorted and dropped her hands when tears finally stopped leaking from her eyes. "Every blasted country I run into has someone cursed—a curse which can be broken by *true love*." She scowled at the fire crackling in the fireplace, barely noticing when Stil's female companion appeared in the parlor doorway, a tea tray in her hands.

"I'm so sick of true love, the very thought makes me ill," Angelique declared. "I know love is the most powerful, righteous emotion possible, but this is sheer folly. The number of curses that have popped up in the past few years with love as the counter-agent is mind-boggling."

The young lady approached Angelique and Stil, but Angelique couldn't find it within her to muster enough elegances for her stupid enchantress act. *What I really want to do is stab a dummy straight through...maybe scream a bit. But now isn't the time for temper tantrums.*

Stil made calf-eyes at his lady as she set the tea tray down, but he managed to say, "It does seem rather odd that such a widespread campaign to spread darkness would have such a specific, repeatable weakness. One would think they would grow aware of this detail and change their arrangement."

"Why bother? Even if we manage to break the curses, I still wouldn't say we are winning," Angelique dully said. She glanced at Stil, but his gaze was fastened on his lady-love.

Hilariously, the object of his affection studiously ignored the craftmage and gave Angelique a black tea served in a beautiful blue teacup painted with white reindeer.

Ho-ho, Stil's finally met a girl who doesn't fall over him, hmm? He always had girls chasing after him at Luxi-Domus. This ought to be good for him. Angelique slightly shook her head and quickly slapped a smile on for the sake of manners. "Thank you," she told the interesting young lady as she took the cup.

"Aye. There are plenty of predicaments that have yet to be addressed," Stil said. "The Sole Princess, the Princesses of Farset, and so on."

Stil's friend—Angelique would have to chide him soon if he didn't make introductions—turned to leave, but Stil caught her by the wrist.

The young lady tried to tug her wrist from Stil's grasp with no luck.

Though the sight was a fun one to witness, Angelique's exhaustion made her slump. "It gets worse. Ringsted is plagued by a sea witch."

"What?" Stil blinked, surprise and unease coloring his voice.

Angelique nodded. "The selkies are trying to take care of her, but the humans are proving to be more of a hindrance than a help." Angelique sipped her tea, almost purring as its warmth spread through her body. "I ran into a selkie who was forcibly landed—some terrible man stole her pelt."

"*What?*"

"She feared he would make her use her powers over water for ill and asked me to seal her voice. I didn't want to take it forever, so I gave her the only escape contract I have learned to use."

"True love?" Stil asked.

"As usual." Angelique was aware of the bitter tone to her words, but she didn't much care. It was all too...*irksome*. "I meant to stay and help her, but I needed to be in Sole for the princess's birthday, and I was forced to leave her. I hoped to return to Ringsted with Blanche and Rein, but then I received word that you were in trouble."

She smiled, hoping Stil wouldn't detect the falsehood. *If he finds out Blanche and Rein all but told me they didn't want to travel with me, he'll throw a fit the next time he returns to the Conclave. And at this point, I'd rather have people willing to help me—even if they don't want me around while they do it.*

Angelique saw the way Stil's eyes narrowed slightly in suspicion. *Distract him!* She flicked her eyes purposefully at his friend and raised an eyebrow.

"Ah, please forgive my terrible manners." A bright and sunny smile bloomed across Stil's face. "Allow me to introduce you with great pleasure to Gemma Kielland, one of the most talented seamstresses on the continent. Gemma, this is Enchantress Angelique—one of the highest-ranked magic users in the Veneno Conclave."

Gemma Kielland was a serious little thing. She curtsied dutifully and murmured respectfully, "Good afternoon." But her practicality seemed to give her a hidden fire—or perhaps a backbone of steel? For she frowned down at the hold Rumpelstiltskin had on her wrist and didn't seem at all cowed.

"I am charmed, Gemma." Angelique smiled sincerely. "Although, I fear Stil has misled you: I am only an enchantress-in-training."

Stil heaved a disgusted sigh. "Everyone knows you have the capabilities. It is merely that with Enchanter Evariste...missing, he cannot bring you to the Conclave and declare you. You're an enchantress, Angelique."

Angelique shook her head. "If I was ready to be an enchantress, I would know more ways to counter curses besides using love. And all these years of running around on my own have shown me how little experience I have. Though I will venture to say my cast time and abilities have improved." She watched Gemma try to pull her hand from Stil's grasp without success. "I received your letter. You said you were being followed?"

"Hunted, really," Stil said. "By a hellhound and a rider mounted on a nightmare."

"*What?*" Angelique yelped.

Nightmares were loosely equine in form—though they were skeletal, rotting, and frankly terrible to look upon. They moved at night and hunted like a carnivorous animal. Alone, they were a terrible threat, but matched with a *rider?*

In her shock, Angelique set her teacup down with more force than necessary. "How can this be?"

"I don't know. I don't understand why, either," he said. "But it's why I fled to Verglas."

"You were smart to do so." Angelique knit her fingers together as she considered what this meant. A *nightmare*...with a *rider*.

There's no getting around it. Some evil force is at work—though we don't rightly know what it is, yet. But securing a nightmare and a being dark enough to ride it is no easy task for a black mage.

Angelique directed her gaze to Gemma. "Is the rider chasing you as well?"

Gemma did not hesitate. "No. Absolutely not."

Stil glanced worried at her. "Gemma is fleeing the country with me. She's in a spot of trouble with King Torgen."

"Ah, him." Angelique pressed her lips together with understanding. *No wonder she's running.*

"With all respect, Craftmage Stil, you were going to take me to the border, and then we were going to part ways," Gemma said.

Stil swung his hand that held Gemma's wrist and smiled at her. "Yes, but now we don't have to. Angelique will take care of the rider for me, won't you?" He turned back to Angelique with a trusting smile.

If he was anyone else, I would consider striking him with lightning. Just about every soul I meet seems to assume I can do something for them. But this is Stil, which makes it acceptable. But that doesn't address the matter of the nightmare and its rider.

She sighed as she considered the problem. "Sometimes you overestimate my capabilities."

"No, I don't. If your learned magic fails, you will just have to rely on your core magic. The rider is no match for *that*," Stil said.

Angelique considered boxing his ears for the stupid idea, but Gemma spoke up, curiosity lining her voice. "Core magic?"

Angelique took a moment to fix a properly serene smile back in place. "Enchanters are the highest rank of magic user there is," she began.

Gemma nodded.

"This is because we are able to use two types of magic: core magic and learned magic. Core magic is something all magic users have. It is what decides their focus. Stil's core magic is craft related. Weather mages have weather core magic, and so on. All enchanters and enchantresses have core magic as well—although the kind and strength varies from enchanter to enchanter. It is our learned magic that gives us a higher rank. Learned magic—things like curse breaking, enchantments, working with elements, charms, general magic—are things only enchanters and enchantresses display the ability to learn."

Angelique paused for a moment. *I hope that wasn't too much to dump on her in one go.*

"For instance, no matter how hard I study, I can never control rain," Stil said. "But Angelique—to a certain extent—can."

Gemma's expression turned thoughtful. "I see."

"There are checks and balances of course," Angelique said. "As an enchantress, I will never be as powerful in weather magic as a weather mage. And no enchanters are capable of infusing magic into weapons like Stil is—although that is to be expected as he is a genius in his core magic." Angelique smiled proudly at the craftmage.

Stil, predictably, blushed a little. (Though he was as prideful as a rooster, it had always embarrassed him whenever Angelique or Evariste remarked on his skills. Evariste had claimed it had to do with their parental pride, and though Angelique wished he would phrase it differently, she suspected he was close to the mark.)

Angelique grinned a little as Stil cleared his throat, then glanced at Gemma.

The seamstress had an eyebrow lifted slightly as she stared at Stil, but Angelique couldn't properly label what the look meant.

"Enchanters and enchantresses generally have highly specialized types of core magic, too, and they are typically very powerful," Stil finally continued. "Angelique's master is considered to be one of the greatest magic users since the Snow Queen. He was the youngest enchanter ever approved." He glanced from Gemma back to Angelique. "But we are getting off topic. Angelique, I know you can destroy the rider with your core magic."

Boxing his ears isn't harsh enough. I should like to throttle him if I can get him away from Gemma. I may have told the Council I wasn't going to listen to any stupid rules that got in the way of helping someone, but using my war magic is a line I still have no desire to cross. "Perhaps if I was approved to *use* my core magic. The Conclave still hasn't agreed to it." For Gemma's benefit she added, "My apprenticeship was and continues to be unusual because my core magic makes most...squeamish."

"I see," Gemma politely said.

Angelique could see the questions in her eyes, but when the seamstress refrained from asking more, Angelique relaxed a little. *She's a good girl—er, young lady. I think I rather like her. It would seem Stil's interest in her is warranted.* The idea felt a little foreign to Angelique—given that she and Evariste had found Stil when he was a snot-nosed kid, it seemed strange that he was old enough to pursue a young lady.

She cleared her throat. "Regardless, I am certain I could drive the rider off for a time. Although we will have to be careful. The area is crawling with soldiers."

"Pardon?" Gemma said.

"They're King Torgen's men. At first I wondered if they were the followers you referred to in your letter, Stil. But I suppose they are searching for you, Gemma?" Angelique asked.

Gemma shifted uncomfortably. "Yes."

Angelique smiled. "Do not worry yourself over it. You are safe in Stil's home, and the border is but a short ride away."

"Is it? That's a relief," Stil said. "It feels like molasses runs faster than Pricker Patch is willing to move."

"Perhaps Pegasus can speak sense into him, although I fear he is growing to be just as ornery as your donkey," Angelique said, recalling the constellation's bad humor after speaking to Blanche and Rein. "The time away from Master Evariste has been hard on him."

"Pets." Stil shrugged. "But, it would appear we are here for the night, so we should enjoy it. Tonight we will have a feast," he promised.

"I look forward to it." Angelique smiled, hoping she didn't appear as tired as she felt.

Stil, thankfully, didn't seem to notice. He was staring across the parlor as he scratched his cheek with his free hand, most likely plotting out the night's menu. "It will take me a while to get everything ready. Do you need to see to Pegasus or anything?"

"No, but if you do not mind, I think I would like to…rest for a while." The thought of a soft bed almost made her eyes flutter shut, even as she stood up.

"Certainly. Any of the rooms are open—except mine and the frost room," Stil said, finally releasing Gemma. He hustled for the parlor door so quickly it took Angelique a moment to register what he said. "Take all the time you need," he called over his shoulder.

The door swung shut before Angelique could say anything in response. "Except for…?" she muttered bewilderedly. *The frost room…that's the nicest room in his house, and he rarely lets anyone besides me use it since he complains it takes too much time to clean.*

On a hunch, Angelique turned to Gemma—who seemed to have no desire to leave the parlor now that Stil had made his exit. "Gemma, are you in the last room in the hallway?" Angelique asked.

"Yes."

"Oh," Angelique's eyes widened. *He's not just a bit smitten—this might be something more…permanent.* She thoughtfully studied Gemma from head to toe. *But it seems he chose well.* "I'm glad you are so lovely," she absently said, her usual self-control quickly dwindling in her desire to stumble off to bed. "If you will excuse me, I will see you at our banquet."

Angelique held her posture together until she made it into the hallway, then stumbled with all the grace of a baby fawn until she reached the other guest bedroom she was familiar with, the dusk room—a bedroom decorated in hues of dark blues and reds.

Staring inside at the soft bed mounded with pillows and a plush wine-red carpet, she let her head sag and accidentally cracked herself on the doorframe. "Ouch. Yep, I just need to sleep."

Angelique closed the door behind her and shuffled across the room.

I will feel better when I wake up.

If it was a lie to herself, it was a kind one. But it didn't matter; she was asleep by the time her cheek touched her pillow.

BECAUSE STIL seemingly couldn't resist showing off to Gemma, less than two hours later, Angelique found herself seated at the massive table in the tent's dining room. A few empty plates were scattered across the table's surface, but Stil had cleared the majority of them when he left to fetch dessert.

Angelique had gotten a short nap that had taken the edge off her exhaustion, so her eyes no longer felt gritty as she tried to discreetly study Gemma across the table.

The more Stil struts around, the more he reveals exactly how much he likes her.

Angelique stifled her desire to pat her over-filled belly and checked that a friendly smile was still on her lips. *I had better make the effort to befriend her.* She cleared her throat and tried to ask casually, "How long have you known Stil?"

Gemma raised her gray eyes and clasped her hands in her lap. "A few weeks. And you, Lady Enchantress?"

Here's the fun bit—do I embarrass Rumpelstiltskin or take pity on him and give her a nudge? She was a bit inclined to have her fun...but she could still make a case for him.

Angelique worked to keep her smile casual and straight rather than going lopsided. "I've lost track of the time, but years. Would you like to know more?"

Gemma adjusted the blue hairband that held her hair back from her face and nodded.

"Master Evariste and I were traveling when we found Stil in a market in Baris. He was just a youngster and was selling magic-infused items. My master recognized him for what he was and tried to get him to leave with us, but Stil was suspicious of him."

Ahh yes, if Evariste were here, he would urge me to take pity on our son and help him. He's been gone so long, but it seems like I'm reminded of him more and more every day.

Angelique hid her grimace by taking a sip of wine.

The seamstress waited patiently, nodding at Angelique to continue.

"Eventually, my master realized Stil found me less intimidating and instructed me to talk him around. I...*managed* it." It was a temptation to tell her just how Angelique had convinced the bratty Stil, but with Gemma's gray eyes on her, Angelique felt unexpectedly guilty for wanting to embarrass him, so she rushed to continue. "We brought him to the school at the Veneno Conclave where he proved to be a veritable genius at craft magic." She tapped the stem of her glass as Gemma gravely studied her.

"I see," Gemma finally said. "It is obvious you have a bright relationship with Mage Stil."

"Friendship," Angelique corrected. "I flatter myself to say I am like an older sister to him."

"Oh, no." The seamstress shook her head. "He cares for you much more than as a sister."

Angelique barely restrained herself from shivering in revulsion. *Perhaps Evariste had the right idea. Maybe we should have just let folk think he was our child.* "I fear my crying episode earlier gave you the wrong impression. I treasure Stil's friendship, but that is all we have." Angelique took another swig of her wine—this one was a little larger than polite, but was completely necessary for mental fortification.

"Perhaps that is all you *think* you have," Gemma said.

What?! Angelique choked on her wine and coughed, placing her hand on her chest. *I must have misheard her. She couldn't have really said that.*

"Right! The tarts finally set—what happened?" Stil pranced

into the dining room like a proud peacock, carrying an arrangement of tarts on one of his best silver platters.

Your sweetheart is bad at reading story cues, that's what happened. Angelique tried to call out to Stil to get him to collaborate their sibling-like relationship, but she could only cough and gurgle.

Gemma had no such difficulty, so she spoke freely whilst inspecting Stil's fancy tarts. "I was clearing up a miscommunication."

Angelique's dismay grew, and she could no longer keep the horror from her expression as she bulged her eyes and gaped at Gemma. *No, no, no, no! How—by Pegasus' constellation—could she so willfully misinterpret what was supposed to be a touching origin story?*

Gemma blinked at Angelique's gurgling, then shrugged.

Angelique longed to yell at the girl, *THIS IS NOT A SHRUGGING MATTER!*

Stil set his fancy platter down on his polished table. "I see."

Angelique could hear the faint note of suspicion in his voice and judged it was entirely necessary to beat out a hasty retreat. *If I leave them alone, Stil will get her back on the conversation I interrupted, and he can woo Gemma himself. This is why matters of the heart are ridiculous!*

Hastily, she stood, almost knocking her chair over in her enthusiasm. "As marvelous as all this food was, I find that I am simply exhausted, and I must beg your pardon and excuse myself." She made a show of yawning and daintily patting her mouth. "Thank you, Stil. The food was outstanding."

Stil's pleased grin said he knew what she was doing and was thankful for it. "I'm glad you enjoyed it."

Gemma frowned down at her pewter plate, watching Stil slide three different tarts onto it. "Why doesn't she have to eat dessert?"

Stil attempted to wink roguishly at the seamstress—which she missed entirely and only made Angelique want to roll her eyes.

He tapped the end of Gemma's nose. "Because I don't care what she does."

Yes, time to leave. I'll grow ill over the romance he's attempting to ooze. Angelique smiled encouragingly at Gemma, hoping the lack of jealousy in her manners might get through to the girl. "I enjoyed conversing with you, Gemma. I will see both of you in the morning."

"Goodnight," Stil called after Angelique as she slipped through the doorway.

Angelique paused on the other side of the door to shake her head, but before she walked down the hall, she heard Stil speak to Gemma. "That was excellent timing."

There was the scratchy thud of furniture getting pushed across the wooden floor, and Angelique paused midstep.

Did he just move his chair to sit next to her?

"Why?" Gemma asked, her voice creeping out of the barely cracked door.

"Because now we can talk. We never did finish our earlier conversation." There was more shuffling of furniture, likely as Stil tried to draw closer to his lady love.

Angelique stared at the wall. *I don't believe it. Stil—craftmage genius—is falling prey to the same fall-in-love-whilst-running-for-my-life-disease that all the royals I've met have been inflicted with.*

It was, perhaps, a tiny bit funny because Angelique *knew* Stil, and in seeing Gemma's cool reception, it was amusing to see him and his cockiness rebuffed, but it also filled her with the desire to throw her hands up over the inert silliness of it all!

"I don't recall there being anything *to* talk about," Gemma said in her calm but practical voice. She was muffled, but not inaudible through the door. "You were obviously under a lot of pressure, but now the Lady Enchantress is here."

"Gemma, I'm not a rare animal," Stil said in an almost-strangled sounding voice. "I don't undergo metamorphosis if I'm not near other magic users. The truth is, I don't really *like* many magic users."

Angelique shook her head slightly as she took a few steps down the hallway.

"That's not true; you like the Lady Enchantress Angelique." Gemma paused, then added in a rush. "Which is to be expected. She's lovely, and I think you two would do quite well together."

Angelique held her hand to her mouth and tried not to gag at the thought.

Stil merely snorted. "I am not in love with Angelique. I'm in love with you."

There was more scratching of wood furniture being moved, as Angelique paused, grudgingly admiring his forwardness. *A straight declaration, well played. And her response…?*

"Well, that's not proper," Gemma said.

Angelique smirked. *A solid miss.*

"Why not?"

"Because I am not a magic user."

"There is no rule that mages can only love fellow mages. Even if there was, your work is beautiful enough, I think it's fairly obvious you have a faint strain of magic in your blood."

As the conversation became more serious and was likely headed back into the realm of sappy, Angelique took another step or two.

"Even so, it still wouldn't be proper," Gemma said, her muffled voice barely audible.

"Why not?" Stil asked, his voice growing quieter as Angelique tip-toed down the hallway, careful not to make the floor creak.

"Because of the age difference," Gemma casually said.

Caught off guard, Angelique paused and blinked. *What?*

Stil seemed to share her confusion, for his voice was puzzled when he asked, "Age difference?"

"Of course. Surely you can't be a day younger than fifty or sixty," Gemma said with absolute sincerity.

A moment passed.

Then, Stil's shout shattered the silence. "You think I'm an *old man?*"

A bark of laughter almost burst from Angelique's mouth. It was only her quick thinking in mashing her face into a thick velvet drape that hung from the wall that let her strangle the sound of her snorts. Her chortles were soon interrupted by sneezes when it swiftly became apparent that Stil—for all of his housekeeping skills—did not often wash his drapes.

She sneezed three times in a row before she staggered down the hallway, her eyes watering. Once she was far enough away, she let herself grin, and there was a slight bounce in her step as she felt lighter than she had in weeks.

She staggered into her bedroom and cast a look of longing at the bed. "No, I ought to clean up at least a little bit, first."

She approached the wash basin filled with warm water and splashed her face, furthering the feeling of refreshment that was sinking into her heart.

She dried her face, washed her hands, and shed her shoes before perching on the edge of the bed. She let herself flop backwards onto the bed and stared at the ceiling. "I ought to change into suitable sleepwear," she said with no conviction. "Or maybe fall asleep just like this..." She yawned and rolled onto her side, her eyes fluttering shut.

The bedroom door flung open. "Angelique!" Stil shouted.

Angelique jumped off the bed like a startled cat, her heart beating erratically as her hair spilled messily over her face. "*What?*"

"Gemma pointed out that the nightmare *does* have a reason for hunting me, and it's probably not as random or inexplicable as it seems," Stil said in a rush of words.

Angelique pushed her hand out, trying to stem the flow. "Wait, stop, stop, stop. We aren't having this discussion in a bedroom."

Stil blinked. "What do you mean?"

"I mean *get out*!" Angelique flung one of her slippers at the craftmage.

He ducked it and obediently shuffled backwards into the hallway. "Who spoiled your mood?"

Angelique put on her remaining slipper, then followed Stil into the hallway to retrieve the other. "No one. But if you're serious about this Gemma of yours, you need to be more aware of your actions."

Stil's gravity abruptly left him, and he grinned. "You like her, do you?"

Angelique pushed her hair out of her face and marched for the parlor. "I do. Though it seems you have your work cut out in wooing her."

"I wouldn't say that," Stil said.

"Oh?"

"I'm handsome, and I have magic. That already makes me a desirable partner." He preened, even as Angelique paused their forward progression long enough to turn around and study him.

"Is that so?" she flatly asked.

Stil scowled. "As if you would know! You wouldn't recognize romance if it knocked you into a troll!"

"I don't think that's quite the problem here," Angelique said dryly.

"No, you are right. It's that you lived with Evariste—who is blindingly good-looking and beloved by all," Stil grunted. "I suppose it's only natural you would be deadened to the charms of those like me."

Angelique pursed her lips. "I suppose there is a truth to that." She almost turned around to grin teasingly at where Evariste would have followed behind them...if he was there with him.

Her throat tightened, and Angelique swallowed with difficulty.

They entered the parlor, and the fire in the fireplace abruptly flared, burning hotter at their entrance.

With no one besides Stil around, Angelique let herself flop gracelessly down on one of the settees. "Are you serious about her?"

"Gemma?"

"Yes."

Stil almost buried her in an onslaught of words. "Of course I am! She's amazing! She's brave—not for her sake but the sake of others—and brilliant. She might seem quiet, but it's because she sees things as they are, and she understands people. She's also a brilliant seamstress, and beautiful—her smile is *dazzling*." He shot Angelique a reproachful look. "I'm a little hurt you felt you needed to ask."

Angelique shrugged. "She is nice—I rather like her temperament—and as far as I know you've never really been as interested in another woman as you are with her, but it seems..." She paused as she tried to find the word. "Sudden? Not that it's unbelievable, but she's wanted by King Torgen. You are being chased by a nightmare and its rider."

"And a hellhound."

Angelique rubbed her temple. "Even better."

Stil perched on the edge of an armchair, his forearms resting on his knees. "You seem to be rather critical of those who find love in trials."

"Not critical," Angelique corrected. "It's just...finding love would not be a high priority if I was also fleeing a mad king or a dark creature of terror."

Stil scratched his chin. "Do you know what love is, Angel? Romantic love I mean."

Angelique shrugged. "Isn't it supposed to be like friendship, only better?"

Stil shook his head. "It can begin as friendship, but it's a bit different. I love Gemma, but it doesn't take away from my affection for you or Evariste. I'll still be there when you need me, and I'll walk through fire to get to you. But I know we'll be close no matter where on the continent you go or if months pass before I see you. Gemma, though..." Stil stared into the fire. "I don't want to part from her. And if we must, I'd spend every hour of every day thinking of her, wondering how she is, wishing I could hear her voice. I want to hold her close, and I want to experience life with her."

Angelique raised one eyebrow and scratched her ear, but Stil stared adoringly into the fire. *Blazing stars*, she thought sourly. *If love makes you into such a poetic and introspective soul, it's probably just as well it doesn't interest me. I don't begrudge Stil his Gemma, but romance seems to be a luxury I can't afford. One distraction, and I might ruin all the work I've put into my position and lose the few allies I've gathered. And given how little action the Conclave has taken against the ruin threatening the continent, I should at least symbolize mages and magic users to the royal families I've been helping.*

When Stil made no move to continue, Angelique peeled herself off the settee and sat upright. "When you came to get me, you mentioned Gemma might have figured out something about the nightmare and rider chasing you?"

Stil shook his head and turned to face her. "Right, yes. Remember how we were discussing earlier that there has been too much pandemonium to be a coincidence? And that it's likely Evariste was taken by those who have been stirring up some of this trouble?"

Angelique nodded.

"I think this is an organized attack, and that there is a darker goal in mind," Stil said.

"And what does that have to do with the nightmare chasing you?"

"I was explaining to Gemma about some of my more, um, *advanced* abilities. Particularly, I was explaining that I can cast magic on more swords at a much faster pace than the average craftmage."

"Yes," Angelique said in confirmation when Stil paused.

Stil was considered a genius for various reasons, but mostly for the speed and power at which he could work. While most craftmages might take an hour to spell one weapon with a low-level spell, Stil could work his magic on a hundred in a single day. The same went for charms he placed on jewelry and gems, cloth goods, and all other materials.

"Gemma pointed out that with the rate I can enchant weapons, I could outfit an army," Stil continued.

"Yes," Angelique repeated.

"So if things get worse, and war were declared…"

Angelique blinked twice, then said, stunned, "You could outfit our allies. That's why you're being hunted—you'd give us a big advantage, more so than any other craftmage alive."

"I don't know about *any* other craftmage…"

Angelique's thoughts raced at the unpleasant implications. *I thought there might be an enemy planning all of this—as Stil said, it's too much to be a coincidence. But this goes beyond that. They—whoever they are—aren't just seeking to stir up trouble. They want wreckage and ruin. They want* war. "Stil," Angelique said.

Reluctantly, he met her gaze.

"If they purposely took out Evariste, and are now targeting you…"

Stil grimly nodded. "It means this is far bigger, and far more serious than we thought. So…what will we do about it?"

"I don't know," Angelique said.

"The Veneno Conclave and the Council must be informed," Stil said.

"But we have no proof," Angelique pointed out.

"Not yet, but if you can put Lord Enchanter Clovicus on the trail, I'm certain he'll be able to find something," Stil pointed out. "Or at the very least use his influence to make the Conclave take note."

Angelique rubbed her eyes. "Lovelana and the committee she's running could look into it—if we could convince them to stop looking into incidents that took place over twenty years ago."

"Yes—even if those incidents were part of the bigger plan we're seeing enacted now, ten years ago is far too long for this…enemy…to clean up after themselves. It would be faster to look deeper into the witch queen Clotilde."

"Elise killed her when she and her brothers returned to Arcainia."

"Perhaps, but didn't Clotilde live in the woods where she met King Henrik? That can't have been an accident. If mages find where she was staying in the forest, they might be able to uncover additional information."

He's right. Clotilde was obviously planted to take advantage of King Henrik. It's instances like that—and the nightmare and rider following Stil—that are the most upsetting. Our enemy is clearly cunning and has been carefully strategizing against us. Has there been a movement like this since the days of the Snow Queen?

The Snow Queen was a legendary Verglas magic user. When she lived, mages had been feared and were frequently mistreated. A band of magic users, angered over their mistreatment, had banded together and swept across Verglas, planning to enslave its people. The Snow Queen had stopped them and—with help from her people—defeated their army.

She was beloved by all in Verglas and all mages—though it was difficult to know where history ended and the myth began.

Angelique slightly shook her head and refocused. "I can tell Clovicus—though if he is unable to find anything, he'll need you to collaborate. My word will mean nothing to the Conclave."

Stil's expression darkened. "After all you've done, your word should mean *more* than Clovicus'! You were the one who faced Clotilde, altered Prince Severin's curse, and studied the storms in Ringsted."

Angelique shrugged. "It is what it is."

She had sobbed out all of the hurt—or at least most of it—

when arriving at Stil's, and she wasn't very keen on rehashing the pain given that she had *finally* laughed for the first time in a long while.

Stil muttered darkly under his breath.

"You need to be more careful," Angelique said, silencing him. "I'll scare off the nightmare and rider, but I don't want you taking any foolish chances. You'll continue being a target. You can't take unnecessary risks."

Stil mulishly jutted his chin.

"I mean it, Stil," Angelique said. "I've lost Evariste. If you get taken, too..."

The fight leaked out of his shoulders. "I know," he said. "I'll be careful."

Satisfied, and assuming that was the end of the conversation, Angelique forced herself to stand.

Stil, however, wasn't finished. "But you need to mind yourself, too."

Angelique rubbed her eyes. "What do you mean?"

"If I'm a risk to the enemy, you are an even bigger threat," Stil said.

Angelique frowned. "Why? I might be more aware of what's going on than Lovelana, but that hardly makes me dangerous."

"Yes," Stil said. "But if I can outfit an army alone, you can destroy one."

Angelique's blood cooled in her veins. "That's not going to happen," she said tightly.

"Maybe not," Stil agreed. "But the enemy isn't going to see it that way."

CHAPTER 3

Angelique squinted in the blinding sunlight that the white snow reflected. "Are you sure you do not want to ride Pegasus with me, Gemma? The border is but a short distance away. We are nearly there."

After making the offer, she glanced guiltily down at Pegasus, but he didn't seem to resent the suggestion as he forged on, the heat of his hooves making the snow hiss and ice crackle.

Gemma placed a hand on Pricker Patch. "I'm fine, thank you."

Pricker Patch ignored the touch and continued to plow through the light layer of snow that covered the plain they crossed. (Given that the donkey was more likely to bite a person than ignore them, this was shocking.)

Stil eyed Gemma and the beast of burden as he adjusted the fall of his new cape—a lovely black one with fancy silver embroidery that Gemma had made for him. (Angelique knew this because Stil had smugly informed her of it before they even set foot outside.) "Don't pet him too much, Gemma, or Pricker Patch will be too deliriously happy to eat tonight," he said.

Gemma eyed the stoic donkey with clear disbelief. "I doubt that."

"Stil is right," Angelique agreed. "I have never seen Pricker Patch so..." *Relaxed? Not violent?* "...content before," she finally said.

Stil squinted past the expansive mountains that jutted into the sky like the teeth of a giant dragon. "We will confront the rider tonight?"

"Yes. I will leave soon after," Angelique said, though the thought made her weary. "Pegasus runs even better at night, and I must tell the Conclave of Gemma's observations."

Gemma continued to rub the donkey's neck as she peered up at Angelique. "So, you think it's true?"

"Pardon?"

"You think Stil is being targeted for his unique skills?"

"Yes." Angelique sank her fingers into the warm flames of Pegasus' mane. "Normally, one would not think of Stil as being a threat. He hasn't the fire power of some other mages. But if one is looking at widespread war that will cause countries to form an alliance...Stil would have a larger impact than any single enchanter."

Stil scowled at her over Pricker Patch's back and shook his head, but Gemma didn't seem to notice. She nodded thoughtfully. "I see."

Angelique smiled winningly at the craftmage.

He gave her a warning look, but his expression softened when he dropped his gaze to Gemma. "When Angelique and I go face the rider, Gemma, I ask that you remain at camp. It's going to be a battle, and I fear the rider would attack you." He reached over Pricker Patch's neck to smooth Gemma's wavy hair.

Gemma didn't protest the gesture of affection, but as soon as he finished, she readjusted her locks. "Of course," she said.

"You agree so easily?" Angelique watched warily as Pegasus pinned his ears and shook his head. When she patted his neck, he jerked his head in Pricker Patch's direction and huffed in irritation. *Ahh, he wants to go faster.* Preoccupied with her mount, she almost missed Gemma's response.

"Naturally," Gemma said. "My survival instincts are quite strong, and I know I have few—or perhaps even no—skills of combat. It would be safer for me to remain as far away as possible. Besides, someone must see that Pricker Patch and…" She nodded at Pegasus.

"Pegasus," Angelique supplied.

Pegasus swished his tail at the sound of his name.

Gemma stared at a shooting star that skid across Pegasus' neck. "Pricker Patch and Pegasus are fed and watered."

How very wise and practical. It seems every hour I come to like her more and more—even if she made the nearly unforgiveable sin of thinking Stil fancied me. Ugh.

Stil smiled sappily at the seamstress. "Good. And thank you."

Angelique, however, laughed. "I like her, Stil. You've chosen well."

"Thank you." Stil positively glowed in triumph.

Gemma didn't seem to feel the same, for she sighed loudly.

Angelique held in a snicker. "Although the lady does not seem joyous."

Pegasus pranced a few paces, flicking snow into air, then stopping to snort at the powdery stuff.

Stil sized Gemma up. "I will wear her down."

Gemma raised her eyebrows.

Angelique grinned unrepentantly. "I think Pegasus wants to stretch his legs a bit. We'll ride ahead."

"Excellent! Go on, shoo." Stil swatted his hand at Angelique.

Gemma frowned a little but reluctantly nodded as she studied Pegasus. "He does seem a bit impatient. Ride safe."

Angelique waved and spun Pegasus so he faced south again, but not before she saw Stil reach for Gemma, and Gemma dodge his grab.

"This will provide us with bonding time, darling! We can play my guessing game."

"No on both accounts," Gemma replied dryly before Pegasus bolted, leaving the lovebirds behind.

The bright sunshine of the day lifted a little of the weight that had pulled at her since realizing that Stil and Gemma were right: a war likely was on the horizon. (Even if they didn't know whom it was that they fought.)

Magic wars were not unheard of. Besides the Snow Queen's war against the Chosen, there had been others. But the Snow Queen's war was undoubtedly the biggest...until now when there was the possibility of a war spanning not a single country, but the *entire continent*.

Angelique grimaced at the thought, but when Pegasus swerved to avoid a drift, she sank lower into the saddle.

That is something to discuss with Clovicus. First, I have to scare off this nightmare and its rider that are hunting Stil.

She didn't relish the upcoming fight—nightmares were twisted —and her stomach flopped at the thought. *But I bespelled an entire city—the capital of Sole! If I can do that, I can handle a nightmare. Or rather, I'll have to—for Stil's sake. Even so...I'd rather do this with someone instead of by myself. Stil will be there, but while he can defend himself, he doesn't have many fighting abilities. I'll have to make sure I attack the nightmare* and *protect Stil.*

The thought filled Angelique with dread. She hated involving those close to her in fights. Pegasus had gotten hurt when they were attacked by a basilisk, and she'd nearly lost Puss when she was trying to heal him and had encountered a band of goblins.

And there's the worst of all...Evariste.

Pegasus finally slowed down to a prancing canter just as he released a trumpeting shout that made the flames of his body burn higher and a few black feathers twirl around them.

Angelique waited until her vision—blurry from the equine's speed—cleared, then patted his neck. "Good boy."

Pegasus snorted in agreement, then made a wide circle as they started back to the others.

One thing is for certain, we have to start preparing. Or this enemy will end us all before we can even cobble together a counterattack.

AFTER LESS THAN an hour more of traveling—when it was barely light enough to still see—Stil called a halt. "We'll pitch the tent here." To Gemma, he added, "Even after Angelique clears the rider off, I'm not keen to sleep in a realm outside the Snow Queen's protection."

Angelique remained perched on Pegasus' back for her own comfort; the powerful constellation was a soothing presence. "Where will you go tomorrow?"

"I don't know." Stil dragged the poles and tattered cloth of his tent off Pricker Patch's back.

Angelique mashed her lips together as she thought. *Severin and Elle need to be informed of our new suspicions. I was originally planning to travel to Chanceux Chateau after speaking to Clovicus, but perhaps it would be best if Stil went? Severin and all the guards that trail after Elle would surely be able to keep Stil safe.*

She absently patted Pegasus on the neck when he swished his tail and shed bright sparks in the dim light. "I suggest you go to Loire and seek out Prince Severin and Princess Elle," she said. "Though Severin's curse is broken, I feel—out of all the royals on the continent—he has the best understanding of what we are up against."

"Perhaps I should offer my services to him," Stil said as he started piecing the tent together.

Oohhh, that's an even better idea. Then I'm not the only mage at their disposal! Angelique refrained from clapping her hands in glee. "He and Princess Elle recently hosted Crown Prince Cristoph and Princess Cinderella—although by now she is almost Queen

Cinderella—of Erlauf. I believe he meant to speak to them about their goblin infestation."

"So, he's starting to organize."

"Yes."

Stil pounded a peg into place, then glanced at Gemma. "Then as long as Gemma has no objections, I think we will call upon the prince and princess."

"Do they live in Noyers?" Gemma asked, naming the capital of Loire.

"No. They live in a chateau that is quite close, though, since the roads have been repaired," Angelique said.

Gemma nodded. "I would like to travel to Loire."

Stil finished pitching the tent and studied her with narrowed eyes. "You plan to abandon me for Noyers."

Angelique hid her smile when Gemma slightly pursed her lips. *He's certainly met his match in terms of willfulness—though to Gemma's credit, she's not so much willful as she is filled with good sense.*

Stil strode up to the seamstress. "You will be able to find work there, but you will be safer with me."

"This I doubt so long as you are sought out by darkness," Gemma said rather logically.

Angelique laughed and slid off Pegasus' back, landing with a slight bounce. "She has you there."

"But I will be going to see Prince Severin and Princess Elle. She sets all the fashions for Loire. Don't you want to see her?" Stil tempted.

Gemma tilted her head as she thought.

Stil shot Angelique a smug smile—which turned tender when he again addressed Gemma. "Think about it. In the meantime, Angelique and I must leave to get rid of my stalker. Go inside and warm up before you bother with Pricker Patch. He can wait to have his dinner." Stil slid one arm around Gemma's waist and scooped her close to his chest. He used his free hand to clasp one of Gemma's mittened hands and place it on his face, smiling down at her like a lovesick boy.

Gemma exhaled loudly and looked not the least bit impressed.

Angelique observed with the same amount of enthusiasm. "I hope you can wear her down before you both die of old age."

Stil scowled at her, sneering slightly. "Thank you for the show of support, Angelique." His handsome smile made a bright return when he looked back at Gemma. "Be careful." The dolt was so daring, he kissed Gemma on her hairband, but smart enough that he beat a hasty retreat before the seamstress could smack him for his impudence.

Angelique winked at Gemma as she yanked a white fur muff from Pegasus' single saddlebag, but the seamstress seemed not to notice as she frowned at Stil's back.

Stil paused at Angelique's side. "How on earth do you stay warm in that dress?"

"It's spelled," Angelique said. "Master Evariste got it for me." She tucked her hands in her muff as they started toward the Loire/Verglas border.

Stil made a noise in the back of his throat. "Hm. Spared no expense for his apprentice, did he?"

Angelique rolled her eyes. "Enough, Stil."

Stil chuckled and walked in stride with her. "You know," he said after a few steps of silence. "I don't mean to pressure you into using your core magic or to imply that you have to use it."

Angelique glanced curiously at the younger mage. "I'm aware."

"It's just that I know with Evariste gone, I doubt there's anyone telling you that you *can* use it, much less that you should," Stil continued. "Which is stupid, because your core magic is amazing. So it's my responsibility to do it now."

She sighed, but it was easier to hold her words in than start an argument about her core magic that would never be settled.

"I heard about the basilisk," Stil added.

"I think every mage in the Veneno Conclave heard about the basilisk," Angelique dryly said.

Stil shrugged. "I don't know of anyone alive who took a basilisk on single-handedly and won."

Angelique scoffed. "That's not the reason everyone heard about it, and you know it!"

"It doesn't matter why people know about it—because they're all wrong about you anyway," Stil said. "What matters is that you took on a basilisk and defeated it, Angelique. You are *powerful*, and you're growing more and more skilled with every season that passes. That's why I talk about your core magic. Because you need to be reminded that *you* are the real genius and prodigy. Not because I'm trying to manipulate you."

"I'm aware," Angelique repeated. She smiled fondly at him and gave him a reassuring nod. "I used to get mad at Evariste for preaching to me about my magic, and sometimes you *do* go too far, and I find that I want to strangle you—or perhaps tell your new *friend* about the time you tried to invent a new heat charm and set your clothes on fire instead—but I know you mean well."

Stil scoffed at her threat and rearranged his cape before he responded. "Well, I'm glad you've realized that."

Either she was too relaxed because it was Stil, or the sense of apprehension that plagued her made her overly casual, for she shrugged. "When Evariste was taken, I realized I was offended over things that were, in hindsight, rather stupid. So what if he thought it was important that I needed to use my core magic? Not that I have changed my view on my powers or am any more willing to use them, but fighting with him about them was just so...*stupid*."

There were a million other words Angelique could have used instead of stupid, but some of them hit perhaps a little too close to home, and she was about to face off with a nightmare, its rider, and a hellhound. *Now is not the time to grow idyllic.*

Stil cleared his throat and awkwardly swung his hands. "We need to make a plan, right?"

"I've already thought of one," Angelique said. "We find the border. You stand at the edge and tempt your hunters. I'll hide on the Loire side of the border and attack from behind. With a good enough spell, that should be all that's necessary."

Stil nodded his head. "Right, because I can attack them head on."

"Only if you're cautious," Angelique warned him. "I want you to *remain on the Verglas side* of the border, no matter what. Do you understand?"

"Why don't you shake a finger in my face and shake me by the collar of my shirt just like old times?" Stil scoffed.

Angelique only smiled.

"So what's this 'good enough' spell you're planning to use?" Stil asked, unable to leave the silence alone. "Since you are against using your own magic."

"A fire spell," Angelique said. "It will take some time to cast, and I can't very well cast it ahead of time since we don't know precisely what angle they will come from, but I think it's the best option given nightmares' antipathy to light and its destructive abilities."

"Hit 'em once and hit 'em good," Stil said. "Sounds about right. If you take too long to beat it, the nightmare and rider will slip away. Watch out for that hellhound, though."

"Yeah, yeah."

A few more minutes of walking, and they finally reached the border.

Angelique tapped into her silver magic and let it thread through her hand, allowing her to see the Snow Queen's latent magic. It sparkled and churned down the border like a trickling stream. Though it was bright and beautiful, Angelique could feel the icy end that would meet any person or creature who attempted to cross the country's border with impure magic.

"How about a little more east." Stil gestured down the border, pointing to a little thatch of trees that crouched on the Loire side of the border. "You could hide there."

Angelique tilted her head. "It might work. The breeze is from the west tonight, so I'll be downwind; the hellhound won't be able to sniff me out ahead of time."

"Come on." Stil trotted ahead, leading the way.

Angelique followed behind him, reluctantly removing her hands from her warm muff.

"*Cudere.*" Stil held out a metal bar that was roughly the length and thickness of a human forearm, then tossed it into the air.

Angelique watched the silver weapon twist in the sky, stretching out into a long, double-tipped spear. One end was a curved blade with only one sharpened edge, the flat of it covered by decorative metal work and gems. The other end boasted elaborate metal wings at the base of the spearhead.

"I find it amusing," she said, "that you are powerful enough you can use your magic to combine an elf spear and a regular spear, but you can't figure out a way to divert the heat its transformation generates so you are forever throwing it like some kind of over-dramatic prince."

"I can't divert it because both blades are so powerful," Stil complained. "And the other end isn't just a *regular* spear tip—it was forged by a legendary blacksmith!"

"Sure, sure." Angelique fanned herself with her muff—just to spite Stil—as she stepped across the border. "I'm certain that's what the merchant told you. It absolutely wasn't a waste of money."

Stil muttered angrily under his breath and stood so close to the border his toes touched the line the Snow Queen's magic drew.

"Back up a step," Angelique ordered as she slunk into the tiny thicket of trees.

"Bossy as ever, I see," Stil said.

"Not quite," Angelique flicked her fingers, sending a spell spinning. "I just wanted to save you discomfort."

"Discomfort from what—Pft," Stil made a sound of distress when Angelique's spell—a gust of wind—skated across the ground, wiping her tracks clean and throwing snow into his face.

Angelique grinned as she crouched in the trees, thankful when her dress turned from a lovely shade of purple to a muted dark gray that let her blend in better. "I told you to step back," she said.

"Sometimes I wonder if the heavens gave you war magic because they knew if they gave you any sort of elemental magic, you'd be a downright terror," Stil said sourly.

Angelique dropped her muff and rubbed her hands as she considered the potential fire spells she could use on the nightmare and rider.

I need something strong. A little fireball isn't going to do it, nor will a wall of flames. It's raw destructive power I am looking for. But I never worked on a very large scale with fire—Puss was forever harping that I should use my war magic instead of attempting to control a large amount of fire, and Evariste really only taught me how to wipe flames out on a large scale. Perhaps, then, I can scale something up?

"You'll need to hold their attention for a few minutes—but *don't* leave Verglas," Angelique warned.

"I'll only budge if you're in danger," Stil said.

"That's not what I said."

"Maybe, but it's the only deal I'm going to offer you."

She rolled her eyes. "You are aware that *I'm* the one helping you, not the reverse, right? You're not in the position to make demands."

"...Angelique."

Angelique peeled a branch back so she could meet his gaze in the shadows of the trees. "It will be fine, Stil," she said with a confidence she didn't feel.

Stil nodded, then adjusted his stance so his feet were wider apart and twirled his double tipped spear before resting one end in the snow.

Angelique released the branch and settled in for what was hopefully going to be a short wait. She started gathering her magic, skimming off her powers that oozed around her in a thick river.

I could perhaps use the basic fire-starting skill. It's a beginner spell, but that also means it has solid, safe framework. I'll just need to dump a lot of power into it—which means it will still take a little longer to cast.

She shifted slightly so a stick didn't prod her back.

Yes, the fire-starting spell it is. My familiarity with it will hopefully mean it will be easy to control at a larger level.

Her decision made, she peered at Stil through the trees.

The cheeky craftmage poked his arm across the border and waved it about.

Angelique flattened her lips at the sight, but she didn't speak.

A minute or two passed, and in less time than she would have expected, she heard the first muffled footfalls of hooves.

Twisting in the thicket, Angelique hurriedly scooped more magic into her control as she peered through the night, trying to see the incoming monsters.

The nightmare was skinny and skeletal. Its sickly black coat smelled like rot, but when it peeled back its lips to reveal sharpened, jagged teeth, the potent smell of blood clouded the air.

"*Craftmage*," the rider hissed, a hooded black figure in a tattered cloak. It raised a crossbow and shot at Stil.

The Snow Queen's magic flared to life, creating a slick wall of ice that shot up in front of Stil. The crossbow bolt hit the ice with a crack, but the wall held strong.

Stil, ever the idiot, peeked out from behind the safety of his ice covering. "Hello, ugly. Missed me, have you?"

Angelique clenched her jaw as she started twisting her magic into the fire spell, wishing she could pelt Stil with an ice chunk for his jaunty attitude.

Stil planted his spear and leaned against it as he stared up at the shadowy rider, seemingly without fear. "I'll admit, I thought you'd skulk around in the shadows a bit and hope I'd be stupid enough to cross the border so you could pounce on me."

The nightmare screamed—a high-pitched, unholy sound that made Angelique's ears throb. The animal reared and lashed out with its front legs, hitting the ice slab with a thud.

Angelique cringed but held tight to her magic. *Please*, she thought. *Please don't be an idiot. Stay in Verglas, Stil!*

Rather than crumble under the onslaught, the ice wall grew, crackling as it thickened.

Angelique licked her dry lips and kept braiding more of her magic into the spell, expanding the area it would affect.

Just engulfing him in flames won't be enough—there's so much snow, the area can't really catch fire, so it will be a short-lived effect. I need some sort of physical strike.

She eyed Stil's double-tipped spear but shook her head. *I don't want to use my war magic*, she reminded herself.

Unaware of her thoughts, Stil trotted a little farther down the border, his spear hefted above his head. He paused long enough to dig a scrap of cloth with loose threads from his cloak and fling it over his shoulder.

Animated by his magic, the cloth smacked the nightmare, hitting its left, curdled-yellow eye. The cloth's threads grew longer as they slid around the creature's head, keeping its eye covered.

The nightmare thrashed, throwing its head wildly.

Stil chuckled and waggled a foot over the border like a proper idiot.

The rider snatched the cloth from the nightmare's head, the threads disintegrating in its grasp, then shot another crossbow bolt at Stil.

Stil ducked, but it was unnecessary as a stalagmite of ice shot out of the ground, blocking the crossbow. "Temper, temper," he tisked.

The rider hissed in anger.

As Stil kept the rider distracted, Angelique grabbed her muff and crept from the thicket, keeping low to the ground and staying quiet. She pressed her lips in a tight line and added more magic to the spell—she didn't want to create a little bonfire, but rather something strong enough to rattle the nightmare and rider so they left Stil alone, but she didn't know exactly how much magic that entailed…

I'm probably close. She funneled more of her magic into the spell and was considering cutting it off when she noticed Stil's odd actions.

He was ignoring the snorting nightmare and was instead frowning as he looked up and down the border.

What is he looking for?

Eventually he caught sight of her standing at the edge of the thicket. His eyes widened, and he twirled his spear above his head. "Angelique—look out!"

CHAPTER 4

A low snarl finally reached Angelique's ears.
She spun to the side to see red eyes drawing closer to her.

The hellhound—which was bigger and more muscled than a wolf—growled deep in its throat, and red foam spattered its muzzle as it lunged at her.

Angelique smacked it in the head with her muff as she struggled to hold onto her fire spell rather than release it.

The hellhound shook its head and tried to snag her skirt with its teeth, but Angelique turned on her heels and ran.

"What are you doing?" Stil shouted.

"Getting closer to the nightmare." Angelique zig-zagged a little when the hellhound almost managed to grab the edge of her white muff.

Stil almost dropped his spear. "*What*? Forget the nightmare; just use your spell on the hellhound!"

"Absolutely not," Angelique snorted. "That would be a waste."

"You're getting chased by a *hellhound*!" Stil yelled, his voice cracking with anger and worry.

Angelique decided not to waste her air and tucked her chin as she ran for the nightmare and rider. *Almost there!*

The rider had turned the nightmare around and was now considering Angelique as it slowly loaded another bolt into its crossbow.

Between the hellhound snarling behind her and the rider raising his crossbow, she was in a tricky situation. If she could just fit in a few more strides...

She heard the crunch of snow as the hellhound crouched, then lunged at her.

Angelique twisted around, but she could already tell she was reacting too late. The hellhound was going to grab her by the arm.

"Angelique!"

Stil threw his spear with a grunt. The hellhound pulled back in time to avoid the weapon, scattering snow into the air and tripping over its own paws.

"Thanks." Angelique plucked the spear from the ground and swung around with her hand extended, just as the rider set its finger against the trigger.

She hurriedly flung the spell from her, realizing—rather belatedly—that she had neglected to stop funneling magic into it, and as a result, it had grown quite potent.

"Stil, *duck*!" Angelique shouted.

"What?"

The spell ignited, belching an incinerating fire that was the size of a small horse stable into existence, shaking the ground with the release of power.

The rider shot its crossbow at the same time Angelique's spell ignited, making the nightmare rear and the shot go wide.

The fire blazed hot and high. It melted a great deal of the ice wall Stil crouched behind and set the hellhound's tail on fire.

The nightmare shrieked in the heart of the fire—but its ear-piercing scream was covered by the hungry roar of the blaze.

Angelique brandished Stil's spear above her head as she tried to line up a clear shot while the rider writhed. Flames licked at her knees, and the hellhound spun around and ran back into the shadows of the night. *Yep. I did not mean for it to get* that *big.*

Angelique's eyes watered from the smoke of the fire, but when the flames started to subside, she ran toward the nightmare and rider, hefting the spear.

She skidded to a stop, barely avoiding the flailing nightmare as it reared again. She adjusted her feet to a firm stance and waited for the nightmare to land before she stabbed Stil's spear forward and yanked it up in an upper slice.

The winged spearhead cut through the rider's chest, making an ugly wound.

The rider dropped its crossbow and grappled at its chest, a whispering hiss squeezing from it while the nightmare shrieked. But even as a tarry black substance leaked from the ugly slice, Angelique knew she hadn't inflicted the rider with a mortal wound.

She snapped her hand, channeling her powers into ice magic. She exhaled silvery puffs as she started to clamp ice around the nightmare's hooves.

The creature crow-hopped—almost dislodging its stooping rider as it broke free of the ice—then took off at a gallop, swiftly disappearing into the shadows.

Stil—who had fallen over from the force of the fire explosion—stood and flapped his cloak, brushing snow from it. "You are mad," he said. "Stark. Raving. Mad. I know Evariste wanted you to use more magic more freely, but have you lost all sense of self-preservation?"

Angelique scowled as she squinted and tried to make out the nightmare's tracks in the moonlight—her eyes readjusting to the night after nearly blinding herself with her fire. "I didn't kill him."

"After nearly being turned into a living torch and being impaled on my spear, do you *really* think the nightmare and rider are going to stick around? No." Stil violently shook his head.

"Even evil brutes like they have a better sense of self-preservation than you do."

Angelique hefted his spear as she strolled over to him, offering the weapon out. "We could try to track it tonight, but it would be hard to follow the trail. And by the morning, they'll be long gone."

"I'd say so, yes." Still took his spear and wiped the bloodied spearhead off in the snow. "But I don't know that it matters. You've certainly bought me enough time to make it to Chanceux Chateau before they come looking for me again. Even if the hellhound almost nicked you in the process." He smiled, and his striking blue eyes seemed to glow in the light of the moon and snow. "Thank you, Angelique. I owe you."

She rubbed her temple before sliding her hands back in her white fur muff. "Not at all. I'm glad I could help."

Stil set a hand on her back and they briefly leaned together, resting their shoulders against one another.

He patted her back a few times, but then marched away, bursting with impatient enthusiasm. "Seems we can return home, then! Don't you think?"

"Yes. You and your seamstress will be safe to travel in daylight tomorrow." Angelique started to slog after him, then paused and looked back over her shoulder, peering in the direction the nightmare had fled.

She couldn't help the nagging sensation that she had messed up. Again.

If I had used my war magic instead of physically thrusting the spear, I could have killed it. But even that thought made her uneasy.

Two years ago—perhaps even a year ago—it never would have occurred to Angelique to even consider using her war magic. Was she slipping, and the lure of her magic was dragging her into darkness?

But I've lost things—important things—because of my refusal to use my magic. Can't I find a balance? Or is my magic too dark to achieve even that?

"Are you coming?" Stil called, interrupting her thoughts.

Angelique ripped her gaze from the shadows and slapped a smile on her face. "Of course. I just thought I'd give you a head start so you could try and woo Gemma with your return, and then face your rejection without the embarrassment of having me as a witness."

IT DIDN'T TAKE Angelique long to say her farewells to Gemma and Stil—who gave her his old, half-ruined cloak in passing. (Angelique appreciated the gesture, for even an item that contained only half of the spells and charms Stil had cast upon it was still quite functional, but she suspected the offer was actually for Gemma's benefit, to illustrate to the seamstress just how confident Stil was in his new cape.)

As it was, not even an hour after she had stabbed the rider, Angelique and Pegasus galloped along the Loire/Verglas border, heading east to Mullberg—and the Veneno Conclave.

As the wind tugged on her clothes and the icy temperatures made her eyes sting, Angelique allowed herself to hope.

Stil was always well liked at Luxi-Domus and the Conclave, due in part to the strength of his magic and the profits he brings in from selling his wares. Between his reputation and Lord Enchanter Clovicus—if he backs me—perhaps I really can convince a few Conclave officials that things really are grim. Hopefully I can avoid speaking to the Council, though. I don't imagine they would be all that eager to see my face.

Pegasus crested a hill and galloped at a break-neck speed down the other side, but Angelique—finally used to the terror that was her mount—ignored it and instead smirked at her own thoughts. *Perhaps it would be even better to have Sybilla explain the situation. She's more respected—or perhaps liked—than Clovicus.*

Sybilla was a cheerful fairy godmother Angelique met shortly after she became Evariste's apprentice. The older woman was one of the only mages who didn't treat her with fear, and she had a kind but frank way of speaking.

Her thoughts dwelled on the cheerful fairy godmother, so she almost missed the bonfire in the distance that glowed a rather remarkable shade of pink.

Its fuchsia flames were a bright beacon that sat just in front of a rock overhang that jutted out from the base of a hill. The odd-colored flames could only be a sign of magic, but Angelique didn't know anyone who would purposely do such a thing.

She leaned back in the saddle. Pegasus, noting her interest, slowed to a trot and turned back around so she could peer at the bright fire.

She could make out a few shadowy figures seated around the flames, but between the odd color of the fire and the stars shining in Pegasus' coat, she couldn't make out any faces.

"Angelique!"

Angelique warily nudged Pegasus closer to the pink flames. "Yes?"

"What has you flying down the border at this hour? And get that suspicious look off your face—I'm not going to require an act of help from you."

Angelique finally recognized the smooth tones of Lord Enchanter Clovicus—Evariste's old master who had helped her on multiple occasions.

"Lord Enchanter Clovicus?" She pulled Pegasus to a stop and patted his neck.

"Unfortunately." The Lord Enchanter ambled closer. The streaks of silver at his temple seemed to glow extra bright between the shining moonlight and the dark of his copper hair.

Angelique slid off Pegasus' back, more than a little surprised at the unexpected run-in. "What brings you to Verglas?"

"My companions." Clovicus' upper lip curled in a very slight sneer, but he slung a friendly arm over Angelique's shoulders and spun around so he could face the fire with her. "Students," Clovicus started.

"So we've been promoted back to students, then?" a gangly boy brightly asked. "We were centipedes not an hour ago."

"Indeed," Clovicus addressed the smiling youth. "Due to Hart's efforts in healing Nami after her bout of stupidity that resulted in pink flames, you reclaimed the title. However, since you were bold enough to note the promotion, the group has now been lowered to the rank of field mice."

"Field mouse? That doesn't sound so bad," said a tall girl.

"By calling us field mice, he means we are the bottom of the food chain and easily picked off," a girl with lovely dark hair and a dark complexion dryly said.

"Exactly so, Hart. It's a shame you cannot be graded separately from your peers, but then again, they are your friends, which is also a reflection of *your* taste, so perhaps it's not such a shame after all," Clovicus said.

The girl—Hart, apparently—merely raised an eyebrow, but the young man who had first interrupted Clovicus grumbled on her behalf.

Angelique eyed the youths—for though she was tempted to call them children, she could see they were all in their early teens—counting four males and three females. "Who entrusted you with students?" she asked, realizing too late she had blurted her thoughts out loud.

Rather than being offended, Clovicus sighed. "I know—and I agree. I should be free of such little crawfish—it was a particular life goal of mine after Evariste made enchanter. But I suspect I'm being punished for all the times I barged in on the Council's meetings with you—for Tristisim made the arrangement, though Crest tried to get me out of it. Good man, that Crest." Clovicus stared at the students. "Obviously, he failed, so I was saddled with the responsibility of bringing the children on a learning exploration to Verglas."

"I thought they wouldn't let you make me your apprentice because they were resistant to the idea of you shaping young minds?" Angelique asked.

"I tried that line of reasoning as well. Tristisim told me he didn't believe I could corrupt young minds during such a short trip." Clovicus smirked. "He underestimates me, and I intend to see him pay for it."

"It's been very educational," the tall girl said.

"For land's sake, *don't* tell your instructors that," Clovicus said. "Or they'll want me to do it again! Now, students, say your greetings to Angelique—an Enchantress-in-Training who is more useful than most senior Enchanters and certainly more useful than your instructors."

"Are you *trying* to get yourself hauled in for a lecture from the Council?" asked a small boy who had a surprisingly deep, booming voice.

"What I am trying to do is make sure I don't have to repeat this experience again. And the fastest way to do that is to show Luxi-Domus that if they trust me with the minds of the future, I'll turn you all into a bunch of mouthy deviants." Clovicus jabbed a finger at Angelique. "Greetings. *Now*."

The students all stood and bowed to Angelique, murmuring their welcomes.

The short boy with the deep voice frowned and kept his eyes on Angelique even when he bowed. "Angelique, the enchantress candidate with war magic? The one everyone says is dangerous?"

Clovicus sighed. "One moment," he said to Angelique. He pointed to the boy—who still watched Angelique with suspicion—and a bubble of water formed above him and popped, drenching the student in water.

The boy coughed and sputtered as frost started to form in his wet hair. "W-what?"

"*Bad*," Clovicus said loudly, as if correcting a miscreant puppy. "Very *bad*." He folded his arms across his chest and scowled at the boy. "You *only* mouth off to someone who deserves it, or it's no longer edgy but acting like a dunce."

"You j-just...you," the boy shivered in the cold.

"You deserved it," Clovicus said. "Huddle close to the fire, and you'll dry out in no time."

The boy gave him a dirty look but did as he was told, the pink hue of the flames making his face glow.

Angelique watched the exchange with a pained smile. "This makes me wonder how Evariste grew to have such polished manners."

Clovicus rolled his neck and groaned. "He came to me partially trained in that area—he was just a twerp regarding magic and his own abilities. I thought that was bad enough, but I was terribly, terribly wrong."

"Before we left, our instructor said to remind you if you are considering murdering one of us, that it's only temporary, and you have less than five days remaining in the trip," the boy with the bright smile said.

"Of that I am *well* aware," Clovicus said dryly. He lifted both of his eyebrows and looked down at the male student shivering by the fire. "Have you grown any good sense?"

The boy eyed Angelique but kept his mouth shut.

"I suppose I'll have to consider that progress," Clovicus sourly said. A prod with his magic, and the icy water evaporated from the student's clothes with a puff of steam.

The student looked like he wanted to renew the argument, so Angelique was quick to draw Clovicus' attention back to her. "How did you know it was me when you called out?"

Clovicus scratched his chin. "As there is only one equine constellation in any realm that I know of, and only one woman capable of riding him, it was not a mentally taxing guess."

Clovicus peered in Pegasus' direction. "You seemed to be on your way to Mullberg?"

She nodded.

"The Council hasn't called you in for anything," he stated more than asked.

"No."

"Then you're going to the Conclave of your own free will?"

"I was actually hoping to speak to you or Sybilla." Angelique paused when she felt the students' curious gazes on her.

"Practice your magic," Clovicus told the students.

"We're traveling in Verglas for a history and ethics lecture, not magic practice," the wry girl, Hart, said.

"Ask me if I care," Clovicus said.

The bright boy brandished a finger in the air. "Do you care—"

"That was a rhetorical question," Clovicus said. "Shoo. Or *I'll* practice my magic on *you*."

The students grumbled, but they set about doing as Clovicus instructed.

Once they were properly distracted, Clovicus turned his sharp gaze back to Angelique and raised his eyebrows.

"I just parted with Rumpelstiltskin," Angelique began. "He was being tracked by a nightmare and rider. We chased it off, and he means to travel to Chanceux Chateau while it recovers, but it's been after him for months."

"That long?" Clovicus' lips twisted into a slight frown. "That means its more than mere happenstance or that the rider and nightmare merely stumbled upon him."

"I think it's possible he's being targeted by the same dark mages who took Evariste," Angelique said.

Clovicus' expression turned unreadable. "Why?"

"Stil has made a new acquaintance who made the remarkable observation that, if given enough time, Stil could outfit an army with spelled and charmed weapons."

"The Veneno Conclave would never allow a country to

purchase enchanted weapons in order to war with another country," Clovicus countered.

"Yes," Angelique agreed. "However, if it was human armies facing off against goblins, trolls, or any of the other creatures that have been plaguing the continent, they will have no such objection. And suddenly his abilities become much more prized."

Clovicus leaned back on his heels. "You think we're going to war?"

Now it was Angelique's turn to frown. "Yes. I can't claim to know the scale, but after everything we've seen in just a handful of years, I don't know that anyone can doubt that there is a something or someone behind all the darkness we've seen."

"I agree," Clovicus said. "But the idea of a war against dark magic is going to have the upper echelon of the Conclave running around like a flock of headless chickens."

"Perhaps, but with the nightmare and rider chasing Stil, we can't afford to tip-toe around the idea anymore. There may be other mages that will soon be targeted. We have to protect the countries *and* ourselves before we lose more than Evariste," Angelique said. Her cheek twitched when Evariste's name fell from her lips, but otherwise she managed to keep her expression bland.

"Naturally." Clovicus sighed deeply. "I suppose you'd rather have me deliver this delightful news to the Conclave than tell them yourself?"

"I highly doubt they'd hear it if I was the one to explain it."

"Rather likely." Clovicus pulled his eyebrows together, creating a V of wrinkles on his brow. "You do realize that *you* might be among those who are targeted next? The spell that hit Evariste was originally aimed at you, after all."

"But was it?" Angelique asked. "Or had the enemy calculated that the only way they'd capture Lord Enchanter Evariste was to put his apprentice—who was much less experienced—in danger?"

He grunted. "You may have a point there, but be careful. As

I've taken up the responsibility of delivering your theory to the Conclave, where will you head to next?"

Angelique stifled the desire to rub her eyes. "I still may need to go to the Veneno Conclave—unless, do you know if Blanche and Rein made it safely to Ringsted?"

"Actually, they're back at the Conclave."

"Already? Could they not make it over the Chronos Mountains?"

"Quite the opposite. They made it to Baris and learned that the selkies, led by the selkie princess you aided last summer, captured the sea witch and have broken up the storms isolating Ringsted."

"They broke up the...storms?" Angelique blamed her slow understanding on her chronic fatigue rather than true stupidity. "Then...are Ringsted's harbors open again?"

"Open and booming with business."

The news stirred relief in Angelique's chest. *Ringsted, at least, is safe. That's one less thing to worry over—and one more way the continent has fought back. Praise the heavens.*

"So, it seems I must ask you yet again, where will you head next?" Clovicus asked.

Angelique slightly shook her head, giddy with the unexpected moment of freedom. "Home, perhaps? Between dealing with the sleeping princess in Sole and answering Stil's summons, I haven't had a chance to focus on searching for Evariste in a while. There might be reports waiting for me at Evariste's house concerning the production of magic mirrors."

Since discovering roughly two years prior that Evariste was being held captive in a magic mirror, Angelique had focused on finding artisans who could create mirrors capable of being enchanted. Unfortunately, thus far, her efforts had been in vain.

"You won't continue a physical search?" Clovicus asked.

Angelique shrugged. "I don't know where else to look."

"Have you tried Zancara?"

Both Angelique and Clovicus swiveled, facing the boy with the bright smile, who was holding out a fistful of pebbles.

"*Zancara?*" Clovicus said. "The country enshrouded in isolation, where no one has gone in or out due to the *massive wall* that surrounds the whole country. *That* Zancara?"

"Yeah, well, weren't they famous for their glasswork?" the boy asked. "My Mam has a hand mirror that's been passed down through the family for generations as an heirloom, and it was made in Zancara."

"I have to say I haven't caught up on Zancara's best exports given that they closed their borders long before I was born," Clovicus dryly said.

"But have you searched Zancara?" the boy persisted.

Angelique knitted her fingers together, trying to ignore the lightheadedness of hope. "No."

Clovicus made a noise in the back of his throat but frowned slightly at the student, who was still grasping his handful of pebbles. "What do you want?"

"Oh, um, I used my alteration magic to turn my dorm key into a pebble, but I dropped it, and now I can't tell which one it is." The boy held out his handful of small rocks.

Clovicus thoughtfully stared at the night sky. "I hate Tristism," he said, finally. "Very, very much. And I'm going to see to it that he regrets ever *fathoming* this punishment."

Seeing that Clovicus was still absorbed with muttering curses to the stars, Angelique took pity on the student. "You should be able to recognize your magical signature. The pebble that has your magic is your key."

"Ahh, yes! That's brilliant! Thank you, Apprentice Angelique!" The boy trotted off with a wave, plopping down on the ground—dusted free of snow—with a graceless drop that made him knock shoulders with one of his classmates.

Clovicus finally stopped complaining to the sky and instead

narrowed his eyes at Angelique. "You're going to go there, aren't you?"

"To Zancara?" Angelique asked.

Clovicus nodded.

Angelique bought herself some time to think by checking the fishtail braid her hair—an ashy blonde color this evening—was woven into.

Zancara is a dangerous place—for those with and without magic. Their isolation is absolute. And though there are plenty of rumors, no one knows for sure what happens behind those walls—except that outsiders are not welcome and that the government remains in power.

But with that kind of isolationism, it seems possible that dark mages could have forced their way in, and none outside would be at all wiser.

Traveling to Zancara was a fool's errand, for even if she could get in, it would be harder to find a way out.

But I never thought to look there. And I'm running out of leads...

"Yes," she said abruptly. "I think I will visit Zancara."

Clovicus merely nodded again, surprising Angelique.

"You're not going to tell me I shouldn't go?" she asked.

The Lord Enchanter shrugged. "As astounding as it is—and as much as I loathe to admit it—the boy isn't wrong. It had occurred to me before that it was a possibility."

"And you didn't think to *tell me*!" Angelique was unable to entirely mask the accusing tone of her voice.

"Because it was dangerous," Clovicus grunted. "Evariste would toss me through a portal to some desert land if he heard I let you go. But you've rapidly improved at using magic over the last few years. I think you have a better chance of surviving now. And..."

The lord enchanter hesitated. An icy wind ruffled his robes as he stared out into the darkness.

"And?" Angelique prompted when he didn't go on.

"If you're right, and someone has targeted Stil as part of a concentrated effort...we need to know that Zancara hasn't been overtaken, and more than ever we need to find Evariste."

Angelique tapped her lower lip as she thought. "Because Stil can outfit a whole army, but Evariste can move them across the continent with a single step."

"Exactly." Clovicus shoved his hands into the folds of his robe. "And that's an advantage we need if war really is coming."

RATHER THAN SPEND the night with Clovicus and his students, Angelique opted to continue on—galloping west, doubling back the direction she and Pegasus had come. (Doing so took a bit of explaining, for the constellation was grumpy at the thought of retracing their path. But he grudgingly ran on, sending snow flying like ocean spray as he plowed through drifts.)

She was starting to regret the decision to continue on as the temperature dropped in the darkest hours of the night, and the wind grew almost violent in its blowing.

She passed the spot where she had stabbed the rider—obvious due to the blackened spot from her potent fireball surrounded by snow melted into ice—and continued west.

Do I have it in me to ride through the rest of the night? Or should I think about making a camp on the border? Hurrying to Zancara will do me no good—I'll need to be rested and thinking clearly, or I'll never find a way to wriggle in.

Something hard smashed into the back of Angelique's skull with a crackle.

Angelique flopped onto Pegasus' neck and would have toppled over his shoulder if he hadn't reared slightly to throw her back into the saddle.

She blinked stars from her eyes and clung to Pegasus' flame-like mane, crouching low on his back.

There was a whistling noise, and Angelique braced herself for another blow.

But Pegasus snarled and spun around. He struck out with a

front leg, and a fireball made of blue and purplish flames collided with what looked like a large snowball rolling on the ground.

Pegasus pranced up to the half-melted snowball and would have smashed it into the ground, but Angelique recognized the magic threaded through the snowball.

"Pegasus, wait! It's from Stil!"

Pegasus snorted at the snowball and made a prancing circuit around it, but he let Angelique slide from his back. He draped his head over her shoulder and bared his teeth at the snowball.

Though it was mostly destroyed, the snowball made a feeble attempt to roll toward her.

When she crouched down and touched the snowball it disintegrated, revealing a tiny scrap of paper balled in the center.

Angelique frowned at the rusty red fingerprints that dotted outside as she unrolled it, and then her heart stopped.

They took Gemma

EVARISTE WAS STILL AT IT—FEIGNING a slow recovery from another draining while really listening to Liliane and Suzu complain about their spells—when a sorcerer prowled into the cavern.

"Suzu!" he roared in a hoarse voice. "What is the meaning of this?"

Suzu sighed in long suffering and turned away from a smiling Liliane. "What is the meaning of what?" she asked in a voice brimming with exasperation.

The sorcerer brushed snow off his shoulders, then brandished a handful of letters in her face. "These!"

He paced like a caged creature as he watched Suzu glance over the letters, his burnished-gold chestplate gleaming in the flickering torchlight.

Evariste hadn't seen many mages who weren't war mages wearing armor, and this sorcerer had gone all out.

His chestplate was decorated with spirals that made Evariste's eyes hurt and seemed to move if he caught sight of them out of the corner of his eye. He had pauldrons that were covered with neatly arranged layers of dark feathers—a pattern that carried over to his somber gold cape that was brushed with melting snowflakes. It took Evariste a few moments to realize he stomped with the volume of a war elephant due to his metal boots—the same sort knights wore.

Strange garb for a sorcerer indeed, Evariste thought.

Suzu folded up the last of the letters. "I fail to see what you do not understand, my dear husband. I meant every word I wrote."

"You are no wife of mine." The sorcerer snatched the letters from her hand. "And you would threaten the life of your own child?"

"Odile is useless," Suzu scoffed. "She has the magical talent of a stone."

"She is your *daughter*."

"I am just as astonished," Suzu said. "As it stands, her only use to me is to serve as a tool to drive you forward. If you wish for her to remain with you—blissfully and stupidly content—you'll make those wyverns for us and take care of the Kozlovkan royal family."

Liliane glanced in Evariste's direction. "You're up," she observed over the squabbling of the sorcerer and sorceress.

"I'd like to be unconscious as much as possible so I don't have to see your face, but even *I* can't sleep through such shouting." Evariste yawned and made a show of groaning.

Liliane smiled wider. "Captivity has done nothing for your charm, Lord Enchanter."

"Funny, I could say the same for you all," Evariste said. "Each week you seem just a bit uglier and more annoying."

Liliane narrowed her eyes but said nothing more.

Behind her, the sorcerer bared his teeth. "Tread carefully,

Suzu. I am not one of your minions you can order to do your bidding."

"But I think I can." Suzu smiled, self-satisfaction making her red lips form a cruel smirk. "For if you don't do as I humbly request, *our* daughter shall pay the price."

The sorcerer growled like a beast.

"You're being rude," Suzu continued. "You ought to greet Liliane and tell us who granted you entry."

Liliane smiled beautifully when Suzu gestured to her. "Hello, Rothbart."

The sorcerer, Rothbart, ignored her. "No one 'granted me entry,'" he mocked. "Your defenses are too weak to keep me out!" He turned and stalked around the cavern, eyeing Liliane's stack of completed paintings.

Liliane airily laughed. "It would seem you are right. You are immensely talented, after all. We could use someone with your strength. Are you certain you don't wish to join us?"

Rothbart slightly puffed up his chest and smoothed back his mottled brown hair. He strolled back around the room, visibly preening, and for a moment, Evariste thought Liliane's flattery might have worked.

He circled back to Suzu and Liliane and smiled wolfishly, then leaned in and whispered in a harsh voice, "I'd rather *die*."

Liliane's beautiful façade cracked for a moment, and her eyes darkened as she sneered. She smoothed it over so quickly, however, that Evariste almost didn't see it.

Rothbart must have seen it too, for he tipped his head back and laughed deeply.

There's something unhinged about him, but at least he doesn't stand with Liliane.

Suzu rolled her eyes. "Begone, Rothbart," she ordered. "If you're not going to join us, you're not allowed here. And you have work to do."

Rothbart ignored Suzu and cocked his head when he saw

Evariste's mirror. "What-ho? What's this?" He stormed across the cavern, coming to a stop. "You've got an enchanter in a mirror?" It seemed he didn't expect a response, for he added in a grumble, "Must have been a stupid one to get caught like this."

"I had someone I had to protect," Evariste said.

Rothbart raised his bushy eyebrows. "Of course you did. You're an enchanter—all of you are bleeding hearts."

Evariste stretched his arms out. "Yes, it's such a shame no one here has one of those. I would pay dearly to shove a wooden stake through Liliane's heart. If she had one."

Rothbart loudly guffawed and slapped his armored belly.

Suzu forcefully turned her back to Rothbart. "To resume our conversation, there is no reasonable explanation for the way Apprentice Angelique has been able to exploit the power of romantic love on every curse we've laid."

Liliane picked up her latest creation—a painting of a pack of goblins—and cast it aside. "I don't expect we'll find a reasonable explanation, but rather a failing of ours."

Suzu squirmed a little. "Funrus believes it's the only curse alteration she knows how to perform."

"Even if it is, we shouldn't be so careless as to allow her to so deftly add in her alterations and harness romantic love," Liliane said. "To have such a repeatable mistake implies someone has repeatedly made the same error."

"We are using magic that is not our own." Suzu's voice was becoming progressively more passive and meek, even though Liliane's expression hadn't changed. "Perhaps it is because Lord Enchanter Evariste's magic cannot be used so."

"Don't be *silly*, Suzu." Evariste couldn't see Liliane's face, but her tone—though pleasant—made Evariste shiver.

Rothbart finally pulled his attention from the mirror. "You're using *his* magic to craft these curses you're casting?"

"Of course—he's another tool," Suzu said.

"And yet an apprentice is going around breaking all of them," Rothbart said.

Suzu gave him a murderous look that said she wished he would shut up. "*Yes*," she said through gritted teeth.

Rothbart looked speculatively at Evariste. "Hmm."

"Whatever the cause of this deplorable mistake, we must fix it." Liliane fussed over her easel and inspected her paints. "We can't afford for our future plans to be similarly affected. Acri will destroy her, of course, but that isn't to say someone won't take her place and continue to ruin every curse we cast."

"Not *every* curse has—"

Liliane spun around. "She altered the curse placed on the Princess of Sole. She nearly smashed the one placed on Prince Severin. She adjusted the swan curse Clotilde put on the Arcainian Princes and aided the selkies so they pulled apart the weather magic that isolated Ringsted. The *only* curse she has not romped through is the one pinning the elves down, and I imagine it's only a matter of time before she ruins *that one,* too!" Though her voice was soft and she still wore a smile, there was something hard and angry in her eyes.

Suzu bowed slightly. "We shall endeavor to fix this."

"You had better," Liliane said with the warmth of a summer day.

Evariste took a few shuffling steps backwards in his mirror, disconcerted by the woman.

Rothbart, however, ignored her outburst. He folded his arms across his chest and drummed his fingers on his biceps. "Captured because he has someone to protect, used for his magic which has forged curses with an exploitable weakness of love." The sorcerer muttered in a barely audible voice, his eyes narrowing. "Everyone knows love is the only thing that can be harnessed to break a curse, but to be so consistently weak to one *type* of love would imply..." he trailed off, then straightened. "Oh. *Oh*!" He roared in laughter again, his eyes settling on Evariste with a knowing light. "You had someone to *protect*, did you?"

He's figured something out, Evariste realized. *And whatever it is, Liliane and Suzu would kill to learn it.*

Rothbart glanced at the two women, who were ignoring the sorcerer. He didn't seem bothered; instead, he grinned. "I see so very clearly. So *that* is the way things will go, hm?" He raised his eyebrows at Evariste and...*winked*.

Just as abruptly as he arrived, he spun on his heels and stomped away.

"Finally leaving?" Suzu wryly asked.

"Yes." Rothbart said. "I hope you choke on your dinner—and if you don't, you can expect a retaliation," he warned.

"Think of your daughter, Rothbart," Liliane warned him. "You wouldn't want her to get hurt."

Rothbart paused at the cavern entrance. "You are correct. But I love few things, and Odile is one of them. And I will not take your threats sitting down." A snarl and a snap of his cloak, and he was gone.

Evariste sat down when he left and leaned back on the palms of his hands. *How very unusual. But what, exactly, was it that he just puzzled out?*

CHAPTER 5

Though they were now doubling back for the second time that night, Pegasus didn't protest. He ran so hard, his mane burned brighter than usual, and Angelique had to squeeze her eyes shut to block out the wind.

She knew they were almost to the tent when she heard Pricker Patch's worried brays, which echoed loudly in the snow-covered plain.

Before Pegasus halted, Angelique flung herself from his back. "Thanks, Pegasus—I'll be back to update you," she called over her shoulder. She yanked the tent flap aside and barreled into Stil's parlor. "*Stil!*"

She skidded into the hallway, almost stomping on her friend—who was face-down on the ground.

Her heart leaped to her throat when she saw the black arrow protruding from his bleeding shoulder.

Stil's eyes were glassy, and he licked his cracked lips. "Angelique?"

"I'm here." Angelique crouched at his side, snapping open her magic channels. Her power flooded her with an icy cold wave, and for once Angelique was glad for its rapid flow—it made it easy to lace a slow-burn healing spell with an extra jolt of power.

She slapped it on him before she even tried to move him.

"King Torgen's soldiers found us." Stil exhaled a rattling breath. "They took her. They took Gemma."

"The Verglas army doesn't use black crossbow bolts." Angelique circled him, trying to figure out the least painful way to move him.

"There was a noise. I thought it was you." Stil grunted in pain when Angelique tried to heft his upper body up. "It was the nightmare and rider."

"*What?*" Angelique almost dropped him in her surprise.

Stil groaned at the abrupt jolt, and his eyes shut.

"Stil. *Stil?*" Angelique gently shook him, but he didn't respond.

Her insides squeezed uncomfortably, but Angelique forced herself to take a deep breath.

I can't panic. It will only make me useless, and right now I'm Stil's only help. First, I need to get him off the ground and get rid of this arrow.

Angelique stood again and turned around, shrieking when she found Pegasus standing directly behind her.

"Pegasus, what are you *doing*?" she squeaked. "How did you get inside?"

The constellation flicked his burning tail and arched his neck. He lowered his head to sniff Stil's foot, then made a noise of distaste.

Angelique rubbed her face. "It seems he was shot by the rider, and Gemma was taken by Verglas troops. But I don't know what to believe, as he seems a little feverish." Angelique crouched so she could press a hand against Stil's hot forehead, confirming her guess. She winced. "I have to move him."

Pegasus made a few noises of disgust as he sneered at a large dragon statue, shouldering his way past it so he could circle in front of Stil and lower himself to the ground.

Though Stil's home was good-sized, the larger-than-life constellation took up a great deal of space, so it took Angelique some maneuvering to pull Stil onto his shoulders.

Pegasus rocked to his feet and started down the hallway, Stil draped across his back.

"Let's put him in his workshop," Angelique said. "I think he's got some healing potions in there—I'll need them when I take the arrow out."

Pegasus acknowledged her suggestion with another swish of his tail. His footfalls were loud on the wood floor, and it only took a bump from his muzzle to throw open the door to Stil's workshop.

(Angelique didn't want to think about *how* the constellation knew where Stil's workroom was. It made her even more aware that Pegasus was probably far more powerful than she realized, something she wasn't too keen on knowing given that she seemed to be forever asking him for pony rides.)

Stil's workshop was a great deal smaller than the one Angelique and Evariste shared—both in room size and in feeling.

Every surface—whether it was a wall, mantle, or table—was covered with an assortment of items.

One table was home to an assortment of glass vials and pots positioned over lit candles, sending chortling puffs of steam into the air. His workroom was lit by starfires—glowing prisms junior craftmages produced for practice by the bucketloads when first starting their training—that dangled from the ceiling. The walls were lined with pegs from which all manners of cloth and clothes were draped. Priceless gems leaked out of a wooden barrel in one corner, and when Pegasus bumped an end table as he passed through, he sent no less than three brass spyglasses rolling off it.

Angelique winced at the sound the spyglasses made when they hit the wooden floor and scrunched her eyes shut. "Stil can't ever find out you were in here, or he'll throw a fit."

Pegasus snorted, clearly communicating he didn't care what the craftmage did, then stopped by a table that was heaped with belt pouches, satchels, and leather bags.

Angelique quickly patted down the table to look for anything especially valuable or breakable, then pushed everything off.

Between Pegasus' maneuverings and Angelique tugging on Stil, they were able to pull him onto the table without smacking him or jamming the arrow farther into his shoulder.

Angelique absently rubbed her nose as she turned away from Stil and instead studied a shelf filled with vials of brightly colored potions. Stil's workshop smelled markedly different from Evariste's—which usually held the faint scent of paper and warm wax. The craftmage's room instead held the scent of dried fruits with a whiff of wood and leather.

"Thank you, Pegasus," Angelique called over her shoulder as she swiped up several vials that held emerald green- and topaz-colored potions she recognized as healing draughts.

She hurried back to Stil's side, relaxing minutely when she could see her healing spell start to work, stabilizing the mage so his breathing was no longer quite so labored.

But it's only a temporary measure at best—I have to get that arrow out.

Pegasus pressed his velvet muzzle to her temple, then made his way out, knocking over a footstool before he made it to the door.

Angelique barely noticed. She was already threading her magic through her fingers, twisting it into a spell as fine as a spiderweb. She took a deep breath, then reached for the arrow embedded in Stil's shoulder.

IN THE LATE MORNING HOURS, Stil's eyes finally fluttered open, and Angelique breathed a sigh of relief.

"Stil? How do you feel?" She set her hand against his forehead, but though his skin was perhaps a little warm, it wasn't as hot and clammy as it had been during the late-night hours.

"Angelique?" Stil moaned, his eyebrows wriggling as he scrunched his eyes shut, then forced them open again. "You got my message?"

"Yes," Angelique said. "Though I can't say I enjoyed the delivery method."

"It was all I could manage at the time," Stil mumbled into the table—he was still face down on it as Angelique didn't want him putting weight on the injured shoulder.

She was particularly grateful it took him so long to stir. She hadn't set many serious injuries before, and as a result wasn't able to extract the arrow as cleanly as she would have liked. But between the potent potions Stil had and the powerful cloud of her own magic, Stil's injury was clean and well on its way to mending.

Or at least it was, until Stil snapped to a sitting position and tried to roll off the table, only to fall on the ground in a heap.

Angelique rushed to help him stand, steadying him by grasping his elbow. "*What* are you *doing*?"

"I have to help Gemma," Stil groaned. "King Torgen's troops caught up with us. The little fool gave herself up instead of running like I told her to. She was worried about me after the rider..."

He took a few staggering steps toward the door and would have collapsed again if not for Angelique's grasp on his elbow.

"You're not going anywhere until you explain what happened!" Angelique forcibly dragged him back to the table and leaned him against the edge.

Stil hung his head, and his eyes seemed a darker blue than usual in his anguish. "You don't understand. She sacrificed herself...for me!"

With a little more prodding, eventually the whole tale spilled from Stil's lips.

Angelique hadn't managed to scare the nightmare and rider enough, for he had lured Stil and Gemma across the border and then attacked them.

They scared the nightmare off and successfully defeated the rider, though Stil walked away from the fight with an arrow in his shoulder. (He also babbled vaguely about the hellhound transforming after Gemma shoved a starfire crystal down its throat, but Angelique wasn't sure if that was real or part of Stil's fevered recollection of the fight.)

They had staggered most of the way back to Stil's tent when King Torgen's troops found them.

Rather than drag Stil down with her—or leave him to face the troops and, thus, the mad king's wrath alone—Gemma had gone to the soldiers, who officially took her into custody and were assumedly headed north.

It was a grim situation, given that before Gemma had successfully fled King Torgen, he had declared his intention to marry her, even though he had a son older than her. And if he *didn't* marry her, it was almost certain he would have her killed out of sheer spite.

"We have to ride north, *now*." Stil leaned against Pricker Patch —while telling Angelique the finer points of the night's events, he had managed to edge his way through his tent-house and outside to check on his large donkey.

"Even if you headed out now, it's not likely you could catch up with them," Angelique bluntly said.

Stil abruptly stood straight and turned in her direction. "But you could, on Pegasus."

Oh, no. No, no, no. I'm not shouldering another burden by myself! She pressed her lips together to keep the selfish thought to herself and shook her head. *But this is Stil asking. And Gemma surely deserves aid...but must I really do this alone?*

She thought for a moment, wondering how she could phrase an objection that didn't sound so selfish or whiny.

"I could," Angelique acknowledged. "But involving myself in King Torgen's affairs is the surest way to anger the Conclave. And while I no longer care what they think of me and refuse to let them waste my time with their pointless summons for every rule I break, we *need* them to understand the severity of what's going on. Meddling like this will upset them so much, they won't listen to Clovicus when he tries to reason with them."

Stil's eyes grew stormy. "I won't abandon Gemma!"

"I'm not saying you should," Angelique calmly said. "All I meant to say is that I can and will *help* you save her, but I don't want to risk doing such a thing alone."

It was true-enough reasoning. Angelique was fairly certain the Council wouldn't send a summons for her even if she tangled with King Torgen. But she was also fairly certain it meant they would give even less thought to the grave situation than they already were likely to.

"But there's no way for me to travel to Ostfold in time!" Stil ran his hands through his silky black hair and pulled on it.

Angelique looked past the mage, her eyes settling on Pegasus, who had his rump to them and was lipping a pile of loose snow. "We shall see about that."

She strode toward the constellation, her dress sweeping through the snow. "Pegasus, I need a favor."

Pegasus lifted his head and blinked his dark eyes.

Angelique nervously mashed her hands together. *It was one thing to offer Gemma a ride when we were walking. But to ask him to bear Stil while galloping?* She took a deep breath for courage. "We need to get to Ostfold—both Stil and I. If we journey at Pricker Patch's pace, we'll arrive too late. Would you carry us both north?"

His ears flicked, and Angelique could tell he was considering the matter.

She held her breath, half-prepared to run should her admittedly cheeky request offend him.

Eventually Pegasus snapped his head—his version of a nod.

Angelique straightened in surprise. "Really?"

Pegasus trumpeted so loudly, his call rolled across the plain and dumped snow off trees in the distance.

Angelique cringed at the assault to her ears. "Sorry for doubting you, and *thank you*!" On an impulse she kissed the top of his muzzle—which was as soft as velvet and zinged with a foreign magic that felt a bit like lightning on her lips.

Without waiting to see his reaction, Angelique ran back in Stil's direction, waving her hand to get his attention. "He'll carry both of us! But we'll have to find a safe place for Pricker Patch before we leave, and I'll need to put another healing spell on you."

AFTER HURRIEDLY DROPPING Pricker Patch off at the stable of the first kind farmer they could find, Angelique and Stil—riding Pegasus—galloped north.

They were forced to stop once along the way—Angelique was operating on too little sleep to make the journey without resting, and Stil needed his wound checked and re-dressed—but even with their late start, they managed to arrive in the early morning hours the night after Gemma arrived in Ostfold—and on the day she was to marry King Torgen.

Stil was muttering under his breath as he studied the royal palace, his eyebrows bunched together as he occasionally squatted down to write something in the snow.

Angelique, using a soft brush, was carefully brushing down a preening Pegasus, unsure if she was more surprised or complimented that he was enjoying the attention. She paused her ministrations when she saw what appeared to be a large wolf-like creature. Its fur was pure white, except for the black tuft at the tip of its tail, its black ears and paws, and the remarkable black swirls that encircled its eyes.

"What is that?" she whispered.

The animal was sniffing his way around the bright aqua lake that spread out just outside the palace's west side. It appeared to be making its way closer and closer to the palace, though Angelique, Stil, and Pegasus stayed among the trees that shouldered the lake, keeping out of sight.

Pegasus peered in the direction of the creature, then impatiently pawed the ground and shifted closer in an obvious command for her to resume brushing.

"What's what?" Stil sounded distracted as he wrote in the snow some more.

"That dog...thing." Angelique pointed to the animal, but hurriedly returned to brushing Pegasus when he clacked his teeth together.

Stil finally looked up. "Oh—that's the hellhound. Or what it transformed into after Gemma slipped a starfire down its throat."

Angelique gawked at it, watching as it sniffed up and down the shore, occasionally pausing to study the palace with almost the same amount of scrutiny as Stil. *This is certainly something I'll have to tell Clovicus—and research! I didn't think Stil could be correctly recalling transforming hellhounds. I've never heard of such a thing before.*

"I have a plan," Stil announced.

Angelique carefully brushed Pegasus' glossy coat, making the stars that shone on him shimmer and blast a little more gem-like light. "Yes?"

"We have to stop King Torgen," he announced. "He's gone completely mad. He's been a danger to his country for a while, and we can't leave him on the throne anymore."

Angelique stared at Stil—for such a declaration went against *everything* mages stood for. "You mean to kill him?"

Stil grimaced. "*I* don't mean to kill him. Even I must admit the Conclave's rule for us to keep out of politics is a wise one, or people would come to fear us, and we'd lose all sense of responsibility."

"But you do mean for him to die?"

He nodded. "Yes."

"And how will you accomplish that?"

Still blew out a puff of air that turned silvery in the cold and ruffled his bangs. "I'm hoping we can incite the Snow Queen's magic to do it."

Angelique pressed the soft bristles of the horse brush into her palm until they tickled. "The Snow Queen's magic adversely affects dark mages *only*. It's a safeguard, not a built-in judicial system."

"Yes, of course," Stil agreed. "But I'm hoping that because Torgen is King, the magic will make an exception."

"What do you mean?"

"In a way, when the Snow Queen embedded her magic in Verglas, she turned the entire country into a charm, much the way a craftmage can spell a gem or cape to hold spells—but instead of specific spells, she used her raw magic." Stil wiped away his drawings in the snow and stared at the palace. "While she might have done it with the intention of protecting her people from evil mages and believed she was merely emptying her magic into the ground, at its heart, she created a defense spell. Her magic reacts only to dark mages—it doesn't go creating sudden blizzards or anything like that. All it does is keep evil outside the borders."

Angelique watched the white dog-creature trot off to the north side of the palace. "But how can you exploit that? Torgen isn't a dark mage."

"No, but he *is* a descendant of her family line—specifically her brother's," Stil said. "The Snow Queen always held herself to a high standard, so with some prompting, I *think* I can get her magic to move against the king, given that he is of her family's bloodline."

Angelique frowned. "Are you certain that's even *possible*? It's magic. It behaves in set rules. Spells have to be performed correctly because magic cannot be reasoned or pleaded with. It's a tool."

"Perhaps," Stil said carefully. "But it's been long known that magic takes on some of the properties of its owner. You use magic from your soul, after all. How could you do so, without the very core of *you* affecting magic in some way? Craftmages have long theorized about it." He glanced up at Angelique. "And it's why I've always found other magic users' fear of your magic particularly stupid. You aren't just loyal and compassionate, you're dedicated to doing what's right. Your magic will never slip because *you* would never falter."

Angelique bit her cheek. *It's because they don't believe in me as you do, and they think the allure of my magic will pull me in the opposite direction.* After experiencing the heady and powerful feeling of her war magic on occasion over the past few years, Angelique was not convinced they were wrong.

But Stil had a point.

If the Snow Queen's magic retained any sort of imprint of its wielder, it was possible it would react given that the Snow Queen would never have tolerated the kind of abuse Torgen heaped upon his people.

Angelique sighed. "Very well, I can see your line of reasoning. What, then, do you plan to do?"

"I'd like to see how potent the Snow Queen's magic is around Ostfold—specifically the palace and the cathedral," Stil said. "I assume most of the Snow Queen's magic pools around the borders. But I don't rightly know how much magic rests here in the city, and I need to confirm that it's strong enough to end the king," Stil said.

"You'll be doing reconnaissance?" Angelique tapped her

fingers against her skirt as she mentally shifted through all the spells she could use. "It will be tricky given how the soldiers are swarming."

As if on cue, a band of soldiers made the patrol around the outskirts of the castle, grim frowns on their faces and their broad shoulders stooped in defeat.

Yes...all of Verglas suffers under its mad king.

"Yes, but I was thinking it will be easier to scout the area if I have a distraction," Stil said.

Angelique finally relaxed a little, warming to Stil's plan. "That's a good-enough idea. Did you have one in mind? Because I can recommend a giant flock of chickens—it's a spell I've gotten rather good at. Or perhaps fish falling from the sky? That would be even more unusual and baffling, and thus possibly a better idea."

"I think it would be better to directly distract King Torgen himself," Stil said.

"Assumedly," Angelique snorted. "But how do you intend to do that? I don't know that he would venture outside unless you had gold coins blooming from trees."

Stil nervously licked his lips. "He would be *quite* distracted if he met with an enchantress."

She narrowed her eyes. "*What*."

"He'd never harm you," Stil said, his words coming in a rush. (Probably as he tried to speak as quickly as possible before she flat-out rejected the idea.) "But he's paranoid enough that he'd likely summon a great number of guards to be present for a meeting between you two. And it would put the whole palace in an uproar—enchanters and enchantresses don't often visit Verglas given that the country really doesn't *need* magical aid with its natural defenses."

"You want me to chat with an insane king—a *murderer*—over *tea* so you can sneak around when both of us are perfectly capable of casting invisibility spells? Are you *mad*?" she demanded.

"Invisible or not, we can't take on a castle full of guards, Angelique," Stil said. "I don't want to hurt anyone. King Torgen is the one who needs to pay for his conduct. We *might* be able to sneak through the castle, but I don't want to run the risk of being discovered too early. Besides, if you speak to Torgen, you can officially ask him to release Gemma, which means the Conclave can't accuse us of acting without first seeking peace," Stil said.

Angelique sighed and pinched her eyes shut. "Wouldn't it be easier to just steal Gemma?"

"It would be easier for us," Stil agreed. "But what about the next girl he terrorizes or the next family he persecutes? He cannot be left to rule."

Once again, his words sounded so much like something Evariste would say that for a moment, Angelique couldn't speak.

He'd approve of this plan—though he would insist on going to speak to Torgen rather than sending me in. He wasn't against letting me work in dangerous situations, but he always made sure to bear the bulk of the peril—yet another thing I hadn't properly appreciated about him until now. Everyone else seems happy to send me in first.

"Fine." She sighed deeply. "I will announce myself and demand to speak with the king." She wasn't sure if she agreed to this on Stil's behalf or because of Evariste. Regardless, she'd do what she had to.

Angelique scowled and glanced at her friend. "You better know what you're doing."

"Neither your life nor Gemma's is something I take lightly." Stil's eyes glowed as he adjusted his black cloak. "This will work."

IN THE GOLDEN glow of dawn, Angelique took a deep breath as she glided up to the palace entryway. She put on her most charming and well-practiced smile, and tugged on her magic to make sure the spell that made her eyes appear a hazel green instead of her natural shade of eerie silver was working. She had considered returning her hair to its natural shade of dark brown before opting for a sandy shade. Given who she was about to speak to, it was in her best interest to appear as unthreatening as possible.

The best approach is to attempt to charm King Torgen during this distraction—or at least pacify him. Intimidation ends badly on all ends.

Angelique made her smile even brighter as she approached the guards standing outside. "Good morning. I'd like to request a meeting with the king."

The nearest guard gave her a stiff bow. "The king is not interested in meeting anyone, as it is the day of his nuptials."

Angelique's smile went a little *too* lopsided, but she couldn't help it. "Oh, he will make an exception for me. Please inform him Angelique, Enchantress-in-Training, is here. And if he is unavailable to speak to me, my duty as a magic user will dictate I instead speak to Gemma Kielland to give her my personal congratulations for today's ceremony."

To keep the edge out of her words, she slightly dipped her head in an imitation of elven grace, but it didn't matter. The guard had turned white as soon as her title had dropped from her lips, and one of his fellow guards immediately backed away and went sprinting into the castle.

Angelique had to work to keep her satisfaction from settling into her smile.

If it's a distraction Stil wants, it's a distraction he'll get.

Within minutes, King Torgen himself stalked from the palace.

His features were hardened from years of hate and seemed to be pulled back in a perpetual sneer. The whites of his eyes were a sickly yellow, but the irises were an unsettling and dark hue that seemed devoid of expression.

Angelique had never met him before—and she was grateful. Standing close to him made the hair on the back of her neck prickle.

"Lady Enchantress," he greeted. He stood too close to her, invading her personal space.

Rather than shrink, Angelique laughed airily and tossed her long hair over her shoulder, flicking the tips into his face. "You honor me, King Torgen, for as I said in my greeting, I am only an enchantress-in-training—an apprentice."

King Torgen's eyes had a mad, feverish light to them. "Oh, I am *perfectly* aware of who you are." He gestured into the castle. "Come."

Angelique followed him inside, ignoring her sense of self-preservation that screamed she was entering enemy territory. "Though officially I am here to give you my congratulations, I was wondering if I could bother you to see the royal throne room? I have heard the lore that it possesses a decorative glass throne that was originally forged for the Snow Queen."

"Is that why you are really here?" King Torgen said, his voice a throaty growl. "I imagined it was because you intended to poke your nose into my country's business. Again."

Angelique blinked in genuine confusion. "I'm certain I don't know what you're talking about."

King Torgen led the way through the wide, spacious halls of his castle. "I am well aware it was you who sent the cursed Arcainian princes and princess here last year."

"Yes, I did." Angelique slightly furrowed her eyebrows as she tried to discern the king's body language.

He walked quickly, as if he was jerked along on strings, and whenever he smiled at her, something inside of her curdled.

"They came here to seek sanctuary from dark magic, but I don't understand how that meddles in your business," Angelique said. *Besides the fact that you almost burned the princess alive because you're a madman.*

"It affects me because I meant to find whoever sent them here and have them pay a *restitution*," King Torgen said. "But I can't very well order the capture and torture of a mage, can I? Particularly when that magic user possesses war magic."

Angelique's magic flooded her body unbidden, and for once she was grateful for the cool blast of power. The way the king paced and eyed her was starting to increasingly remind her of a rabid animal.

The king marched for a set of double doors without pausing, and two servants standing just outside them scrambled to pull them open before the king barreled straight into them.

Angelique glanced back over her shoulder, and as Stil had predicted, more and more squads of soldiers slunk into the hallway, remaining on hand to protect their mad king if necessary.

You better make this plan worth it, Stil.

Angelique smiled at the soldiers, then followed King Torgen into the throne room.

Though the Verglas Palace tended to be more beautiful in its practicality, the one exception was the throne room. It was located on one of the highest floors of the castle so it could overlook Lake Sno the glacier-fed lake that abutted the palace. One wall of the throne room was made almost entirely of glass, allowing the beautiful view of the lake, while the opposite wall contained silver-glass and gold-work crafted to resemble a Verglas winter scene.

King Torgen's throne was carved of wood and placed on a marble dais, but there was a second throne crafted of glass that had been shaped to resemble a chair made of ice. This second throne was located farther back in the room, and instead of facing the entrance of the throne room, it was positioned to take advantage of the giant window.

If she hadn't been overly aware of the king stalking back and forth behind her, Angelique might have enjoyed the moment.

"It is beautiful." Angelique broke the silence as she studied the glass throne. "And a proper monument to the Snow Queen.

Its purity reflects her unflinching desire for justice and to do what was right."

King Torgen snorted as he passed her and strolled up to his throne, plopping down in it with a general disregard.

Angelique risked another peek over her shoulder. Only a few of the guards had entered the throne room. *I want them all inside, rather than out and listening for any odd noise Stil might make. I guess it's time to poke the bear.*

She tried to adopt an air of sternness as she looked out through the window, at the beautiful Lake Sno which reflected the orange rays of the rising sun. "I know you have taken Gemma Kielland against her will and are forcing her to marry you." She turned around to stare down King Torgen, taking care to keep her expression and body language unflinching.

A cruel smile edged its way onto King Torgen's lips, and he leaned forward almost eagerly. "Oh?"

He twitched his fingers, and Angelique could hear the quiet footfalls of more soldiers filing into the throne room behind her.

Got him—well, I've got the distraction anyway.

She licked her lips and refused to drag her gaze away from the mad king, even though her spine shivered from the many eyes fastened on her back. "You should release her."

"No."

"It is an abuse of your position."

King Torgen laughed—a high-pitched, unhinged sound. "So says a mage, hmm?"

Angelique frowned in her confusion.

"No, no. Gemma Kielland is too valuable to lose. I don't know how she's spinning flax into gold, but she'll fill my coffers and get me out of debt to festering *Arcainia*." The king snarled the name of the smaller country with such ferocity, he spit.

Stil! You spun gold for her—and you didn't think to tell me? You love-addled fool!

"She is a citizen of Verglas." Angelique's voice was perhaps a little too hard for the unbothered/serene aura she was trying to give off, but his actions were unforgivable as a royal—who *should* rule with a conduct as strict as the Veneno Conclave's many regulations. "You cannot abuse her like this."

"I am king. I can do whatever I wish within the borders of my own country." King Torgen cracked another smile, his lips curling back in an unsettling grin. "Do you mean to try and stop me?"

CHAPTER 6

"Does that mean you will not listen to my words alone?" Angelique boldly asked.

"Don't cross me, *Enchantress*," the king said in a voice of ice. "Or you will learn just how unforgiving Verglas truly is." Another twitch of his fingers, and Angelique heard the scrape of swords being drawn and the rattle of spears.

He wouldn't try to kill an enchantress-in-training. He can't be that mad. But Angelique had to clench her hands to hide the way they shook. "Is that a *threat*?"

His smile grew even larger, revealing his gums. "Yes." He stood and sauntered down the stairs, his hands tucked behind his back. "All of you mages are a bunch of pacifists. You're useless. The Veneno Conclave spends most of its time mewling about its glory days in the past. You may have cowed all the other countries for centuries, but *I* will not be deceived. As such, I will do whatever I desire."

Though the last sentence was particularly concerning, Angelique didn't dare address it head-on. *I have to think my words through carefully,* she thought, *because only an unhinged man would dare to utter such insults to a mage.* "Your censure of the Conclave is both harsh and untrue," Angelique said. "Mages dedicate their lives to help those in need."

The King sneered. "If that is so then explain to me, *Enchantress-In-Training*, why it is that *you* are the only magic user involving herself with royalty?"

Angelique warily tilted her head. "What do you mean?"

"I know all about your little trail across the continent. Besides helping those ratty princes and the princess of Arcainia, you put all of Ciane under a sleep spell and got yourself involved with the cursed prince in Loire. I don't need a spy network to hear of your exploits. I thought I might be excused a visit from your...*vigilance*...given Verglas' natural defenses, but obviously I was wrong."

Again, he didn't stop his saunter until he invaded her personal space, standing so close to her that Angelique could smell the rotten stink of his breath. He narrowed his eyes as he leaned even closer. "Whatever it is you're fighting, your precious Conclave is *terrified* of it. You might try, but you haven't the power to stop the countries from doing whatever they wish—or Erlauf wouldn't have so effortlessly conquered Trieux. The age of mages is ending, little enchantress."

Something snapped in Angelique. Her magic curled around her, putting iron in her spine so it was *she* who leaned into King Torgen. "I don't care," she hissed. "I don't care about power balances. I don't care what the Conclave says or does. What I *do* care about is doing what's right. Release Gemma Kielland. Or it is *you* who will be forced to pay restitution."

The soldiers closest gulped audibly and rattled their weapons —though Angelique wasn't sure if it was for fear of her or fear of their king.

King Torgen retreated a step, his eyes skittering back and forth from Angelique to the guards who were slowly edging around the perimeter of the room. He licked his lips, and

Angelique could *see* his desire to shed her blood as it bloomed in his yellow-y eyes.

For him, I would use my war magic, she decided. *I hate it, and I hate using it even more. But evil like this cannot be allowed to run freely. If he dares to attack me...*

Angelique smiled, raised an eyebrow, then made a show of staring at the closest guard's sword.

Dim recognition twisted his face. "Leave!" King Torgen snapped. "You have delivered your baseless warning. I will not surrender Gemma Kielland, and if you try to interfere, you will pay. My guards will see you *out* of Ostfold. Do not try to return."

Angelique smoothed her face, not allowing her inner cringe to show. *I hope I didn't just mess things up for Stil.* She rolled her shoulders back and nodded to the guards who slowly approached her, allowing them to lead her from the room.

As she left, King Torgen shouted. "Your time has ended, Enchantress! You're too late now! You will lose *everything*!"

The doors to the throne room slammed shut, cutting off the rest of his tirade.

She couldn't entirely disguise the shiver that wracked her shoulders as she heard the mad king's babbling shouts through the door.

He can't be right. Mages are still powerful. We can stop whatever enemy is trying to attack the continent. We're not too late.

And yet, something inside Angelique whispered that perhaps the king was more right than she knew...

An unnecessarily large squadron of soldiers marched Angelique out of the palace and through the quiet streets of Ostfold. (The city was unnaturally still. Angelique wasn't certain if it was because the citizens were collectively holding their breath for the king's wedding or if it was *always* like this.)

The soldiers respectfully bowed to Angelique again once they escorted her outside the city gates, then stood at attention at the sides of the gates.

Clearly they are waiting for me to leave. I guess all I can do is go south and then double back around Lake Sno.

Angelique gave them a friendly smile and started to march south. She waited until she was hidden by a copse of trees before she cut west.

She found Pegasus, who gave her a cursory sniff before he went back to digging in the snow, then tried to wait patiently for Stil to return from his mission.

By the time he finally appeared, she had pulled her white fur muff from Pegasus' saddlebag and was sitting on a log, a white cloak draped across her shoulders.

"I hope you made that worthwhile," she sourly said. "Because speaking to King Torgen was even less fun than we thought it would be!"

"It was quite worth the trouble," Stil assured her with a large smile. "I now have a cohesive plan."

Angelique waited for several long moments, but he said nothing more. "Do you care to share your great brilliance, or does your plan require secrecy?" She arched an eyebrow and watched Stil enthusiastically rub his hands together.

"Yes, of course I'll explain it." He hesitated. "I actually will need your help."

Unsurprised, Angelique mashed her face in her white muff in an effort to scratch her nose without removing her hands from the warmth. "After all of this, I expected as much."

"In my search, I met two men—I believe they were Gemma's guards when she was held captive in the dungeons," Stil said. "They provided me with some greatly useful information and agreed to help me."

Angelique scratched her ear. "How did you meet them?"

"Er, I went to the dungeons to see if King Torgen was keeping Gemma there—he's not. Thankfully, however, I encountered the guards instead."

"Do they know where Gemma is being kept?"

Stil's easy-going manners left him, and he narrowed his eyes, his lips curling into a snarl. "Yes. It seems King Torgen has her locked in his wife's old quarters."

Angelique grimaced. "That seems twisted, somehow."

"Agreed," Stil said in a very dark and not at all Stil-like voice. He shook his head and continued. "By the time I met the soldiers, I had already confirmed that there isn't enough of the Snow Queen's magic residing in Ostfold for me to properly rile it. But they were able to confirm a location that had it in plentiful amounts."

"Oh?"

"Yes." Stil swiveled and pointed west, to the tall mountain that was rather distinct among the northern mountains due to its unusual rounded top. "Fresler's Helm."

Angelique turned slightly on her log so she could also look at the mythical mountain. Legend had it the Snow Queen had once lived on Fresler's Helm and had, in using her vast powers, blown the top of the mountain to smithereens.

"The soldiers said they've heard rumors from other mages that a great deal of magic still pools around Fresler's Helm."

"Understandable given its history. But how will that aid your cause?" Angelique glanced at her friend and finally stood.

Stil cracked his knuckles. "It's why I need your help. I'd like you to travel there and wait for my signal. When you see it, I want you to build the biggest snow storm you can. The bigger you can make it, the more the Snow Queen's magic will notice, and hopefully then I'll be able to draw it in."

"And the signal?"

"The soldiers and I are going to plant starfires around Ostfold.

They'll help me light them up when the time comes." He held up one of the small, prism-like crystals as a sort of prop.

Angelique glanced at the mountain speculatively. "I suppose with a spyglass I'll be able to see it."

"It puts you alone on the mountain, though." Stil frowned so deeply his forehead wrinkled.

Angelique snorted. "Fresler's Helm is far less dangerous than bearding King Torgen."

"Undoubtedly, but I don't relish the idea of sending you off alone." Stil folded his arms across his chest and stared down at his feet.

Angelique's heart warmed. *I've helped princes and selkies, kingdoms and duchesses. But I think Stil and Puss are the only two who have ever thought of my wellbeing in asking for aid. I'm so glad he has found Gemma, even if it means I am no longer most important to him.*

"I'll be fine. I'll have to ride Pegasus to make it in time for the wedding, and he's a force to be reckoned with on his own." She glanced at the constellation to see if he minded, but he was studying a tree with flattened ears and a serious look of contemplative disdain. *I hope he doesn't attack that tree just because it displeases him...*

Stil slowly nodded. "Once you set off your snow storm and rattle the Snow Queen's magic, I'll call to it and hopefully incite it to take care of King Torgen."

"Seems like it will work," Angelique said. "You're going to crash the ceremony, I assume?"

His grin was back. "Precisely."

Angelique rolled her eyes. "You always did have a flair for drama."

"You'll do it, then?" Stil rubbed his palms on the legs of his pants.

"Of course," Angelique said, surprised he seemed so concerned. "This will be hardly anything—approaching King Torgen was *far* more nerve-wracking."

Stil bobbed his head in a nod.

Curious, Angelique tilted her head. "Do you think I'm not skilled enough to start a snow storm? I'm actually fairly competent in my weather magic—"

"No, no, it's nothing like that at all." Stil held out his hands to stop her. "It's just, I realized while I was snooping around the palace that I'm just adding to your burden. You're doing so much around the continent, and I needed your help not only to fight off the nightmare and rider, but to save Gemma as well. And I haven't even aided you much in your search for Evariste."

Angelique tugged Stil into a hug. "You're important to me. I *want* to help you." She paused when she felt him rest his chin on her shoulder and decided to lighten the moment. "Though I would have rather liked to hear this appreciation before you sent me off to chat with King Torgen."

"Sorry."

"I'm *teasing*."

"Maybe, but you have a point."

Angelique stepped out of the hug, but she kept her hands on Stil's shoulders so she could squeeze him. "You'll save Gemma and sweep her off her feet. Together you'll visit Prince Severin and Princess Elise—that's where I will extract my bill. You can explain to them everything that has happened."

Stil nodded and inhaled deeply.

"You can do this," Angelique said. "Your planning is sound."

He finally cracked a smile. "Thanks...Angel."

Angelique playfully smacked him upside the head like an older sister. "Impudent welp."

"You should have raised me better."

She snorted. "Yes, I should have!"

Stil laughed outright, and Angelique waited for his chortles to subside before she set her shoulders. "Very well, let's begin. Where in the city are you planting the starfires, and approximately when should I begin watching for them?"

"I should have made him promise to fill out my paperwork for a year. *At least*." Angelique's teeth chattered, and even with her bespelled dress, a heat charm lent to her by Stil, her white cloak, and fur mittens, she was still cold.

"On the bright side, it will be child's play to start a blizzard when the weather is already so terrible." She scowled as she gripped her hood to keep the wind from yanking it off her head.

Although the noon sun was out and the sky was a bright blue, it was freezing. The wind was especially brutal as it crested around the sides of the mountain, picking up speed as it howled across the bare ridges near the mountaintop. It ripped through her normally warm dress and pelted her face with icy bits of snow. *Breathing* was even painfully icy. And she could do little to warm herself besides pace and keep her face pointed east toward Ostfold.

Pegasus would occasionally stand next to her and block her from the wind—when he fancied. But he also spent a decent portion of his time chasing off any birds that dared to fly in the icy weather and investigating whatever interested him.

Presently, he approached her—burning a trench in the snow with his flaming hooves—and curled around her like a sort of living blanket.

Angelique patted his neck. "At least it's not as bad as the time we crossed the Chronos Mountains, right? Though then we were moving; now we're stuck here like snow bears." She squinted, trying to see between the snowflakes the wind flung in the air and peer down the mountainside. The trees at the base of the mountain looked like miniatures in a child's playset, and miles of snow-covered territory stretched out before her.

"Well, the view is beautiful," She fitted her spyglass to her eyes and peered at Ostfold—a tiny, walled spot on the horizon. It took only a moment to confirm that the starfires in the snow-crusted city had not yet been activated. She then pressed the spyglass into the folds of her skirts—if she kept it out, the blasted temperatures made the thing so icy cold, it stuck to her skin (as she had discovered when she first took up her post). "Though I do think it would be a more comfortable temperature if we were at the base of the mountain, like Stil planned."

When Angelique had arrived at Fresler's Helm, she made the unfortunate discovery that Ostfold could not be seen at the base—or at any other point until one climbed high enough that they were above the mountain's tree line. Which was why Angelique and Pegasus were huddled not much below the domed top of the mountain, affording them an excellent—if not blindingly white—view.

Another glance at Ostfold—still no starfires—and Angelique gave herself permission to pace a little.

At this height, when she turned in a circle, Angelique could also see the mountains that stretched north and south, creating a natural barrier between Verglas and its western neighbor, Kozlovka. (Verglas was hedged in by mountains, with an impassable range to the north and two smaller ranges—one stretching down its eastern border, the other the western border.)

The mountain ranges made for breathtaking views. But Angelique's gaze went from admiring to puzzled when she saw a cloud of glowing light peeking out around the ridge of a more southern mountain that appeared to be close to Kozlovkan territory. "What is that?" Curious, she unearthed her spyglass and peered through it, refocusing it on the light.

As she watched, ice—thick and tall—shot out of the ground, forming a craggy wall. The wall glowed—the silvery blue light Angelique had noticed.

Even this far away, Angelique could tell it was obviously the Snow Queen's magic. She lowered the spy glass and tapped it against her thigh.

"It seems someone—or something—evil is trying to get into

Verglas." Angelique rubbed her red nose and offered Pegasus a worried smile when he, too, peered in the direction of the Snow Queen's glowing magic.

"Could it be the nightmare again? But Stil was certain they destroyed the rider." Angelique mashed her lips together until Pegasus nudged her. "You know...I've always wondered about the Snow Queen." Angelique leaned into Pegasus, taking refuge in his hulk and warmth. "Like Stil said, she kicked out the evil mages who were invading her country. But why did she push her magic into the very ground when—based on her powers that we can *still* see today—she could have easily torn the army to shreds by herself? Did she expect them to come back and try again?"

The idea was boggling to Angelique—she couldn't imagine anyone willingly facing the Snow Queen if even half of the myths about her were true.

Pegasus curled his upper lip back and sneered at the glowing smudge that was the magic-made ice wall.

Angelique pressed her fur mittens to her frozen nose. "I bet the attempted intruder is a mountain hag. They're mostly found in Kozlovka, and I don't think any dark mage would be stupid enough to try and get into Verglas, much less attempt mountain travel in early winter."

Pegasus arched his neck and pawed the ground, sending smoldering flecks of fire into the air.

Angelique fitted the spyglass to her eye again, her brow furrowing as she watched another flash of snow-blue light followed by the formation of another giant chunk of ice. But even with the spyglass, she couldn't make out the source of the magic's antagonism.

"Hmm." She turned herself back to Ostfold and had to refocus the spyglass so she could see the glittering Lake Sno and the walls of the lovely city.

Angelique thought she saw a faint shimmer at the far side of the snowy capital. She leaned forward, straining to study the city, when abruptly it blazed with light—thanks to the piles of starfires Stil and his soldier helpers had fixed to a tower in the palace and the walkway above the city gates.

Angelique collapsed her spyglass and blinked, trying to clear the stars from her eyes caused by the bright blaze. "Right, that's our cue."

She ripped her mittens off—making it easier to manipulate her magic—and started channeling her silvery powers.

Magic twined through her fingers as she twisted, transforming it from her war magic into weather magic. She started with the wind—she needed to blow the blizzard down the mountainside, for that's where Stil was expecting the storm to be. Once the howling gusts barreled down—making the pine trees groan and sway with the force of the wind—she added a shot of water and tried to adjust the temperature, warming it just a little bit. (If the air was too cold, it wouldn't snow, no matter how much power she used.)

Angelique nodded in satisfaction as she watched the storm clouds form near the bottom of the mountain, then started pushing raw magic into the spell.

The clouds swelled, growing larger and dumping big snowflakes as the wind carved out expansive drifts.

She glanced at Ostfold, where clouds were starting to form as well.

"I think I'm done." She added another shot of power to her blizzard, but it already was a smothering mass of white. "A few more minutes and I think we can—"

All of Fresler's Helm started to rumble, and rock shook beneath Angelique's feet.

She fell to her knees and felt a cool and heavy magic blaze pressing down on the mountaintop with such force it was difficult to breathe.

Raw magic briefly swirled around her—like a wolf stalking its prey. Abruptly as it powered up, it left, rushing down the mountainside.

Angelique shivered and climbed to her feet, her knees still shaking even though the pressure had disappeared with the magic. "Well." She slightly shook her head and leaned into Pegasus when he bumped her with his shoulder. "I think we can go down the mountain."

Pegasus tossed his head and neighed—or rather snorted his version of a neigh, which seemed akin to how Angelique imagined colliding comets would sound.

She peered in the direction of Ostfold, which was entirely veiled by snow-swollen clouds. "And I guess Stil's theory was correct."

ANGELIQUE WATCHED PEGASUS' constellation bob around in the sky, circling other stars and settling into the entirely *wrong* spot of the sky.

At least someone is having fun. She glanced at Stil's tent—which was illuminated by the fire Angelique had built in front of it while wasting time.

If I go inside now, what are the odds I'll walk in on them kissing? I'm thinking higher than I'd like to bet against.

Gemma Kielland had been successfully rescued, and—as Stil had hoped—the Snow Queen's magic had ended King Torgen's life.

Angelique had only seen Stil for a snatch of a moment when she had returned from Fresler's Helm and found all of Ostfold in a bit of an uproar.

He had assured her Gemma was safe, but he was able to give her little more than the barest facts besides saying their plan had worked.

No one was distraught at the King's passing. It was more... that they almost didn't know what to do now that the mantle of oppression had lifted. (Though it seemed, based on the laughter and music that radiated from the city, mostly they were celebrating.)

King Torgen's son, Toril, had already been named and crowned as the new monarch. And despite his parentage, the people of Ostfold were embracing their new king, shouting cheers and blessings in his name.

Angelique brandished a finger at the sky. "Stay up there tonight," she told the celestial horse—though she wasn't even sure he could hear her. "We'll head out tomorrow morning."

A part of her longed to begin the journey to Zancara immediately, but she was running on entirely too little sleep, and breaking into Zancara would require every scrap of intelligence she could muster, so she was better off waiting. (Even if it meant housing with the lovebirds—who *had* to have confessed their love to each other based on the soppy glances they were exchanging when Angelique saw them arrive.)

Angelique fluffed Pricker Patch's hay for him, then patted the ornery donkey. "What do you think? Is it safe?"

Pricker Patch flicked his ears and placidly chewed his hay.

Angelique scratched her cheek and considered the tent. She broke her reverie, though, when she heard the quiet crunch of snow.

"I should have known you'd be behind this."

A woman stepped into the orange light of the crackling fire. There was a pinched tilt to her brow, but her voice was beautiful and positively musical.

She had magic for certain—Angelique could feel a hint of it—but she stared at Angelique with *familiarity*.

Angelique blinked. *She looks familiar, but I don't recognize her.* She settled a calm smile on her face and rested a hand on Pricker Patch's back. "I apologize for my bluntness, but do I know you?"

The woman's expression grew even stormier. "I'm Melody—a music mage," she said, her tone stiff. "We met at the christening of Princess Rosalinda."

It took a moment before Angelique was able to place her—and it took *all* of her self-control to keep her eyes from widening.

When she met Melody, the music mage appeared to be roughly in her early twenties with flawless skin, a stick-slender body, and big eyes.

She was still beautiful and slender, but she had smile lines now, and a streak of silver complimented her light hair.

I forgot that mages age only a little bit slower than regular humans. I saw it in Stil, obviously, but besides him, I really only see other enchanters and enchantresses. There is Sybilla, of course, but now that I think of it, I don't know that she's aged at all from when I first met her...curious...

"Hello, Melody." Angelique slightly bowed her head in a gesture of respect. "It is a pleasant surprise to encounter you again."

(Not really, given that Melody had spent the majority of the time at the Christening giving Angelique dark looks, but given the warm way she watched Lord Enchanter Evariste, it was hardly surprising. It seemed like most females who admired Evariste all followed such behavioral patterns. He had seemed oblivious to their feelings, but he also had never treated any of them with the familiarity and warmth he showered on Angelique. She used to squawk whenever he hugged her, and now...)

"King Torgen is dead," Melody said, pulling Angelique from her regret-filled thoughts.

Angelique nodded. "Yes."

Melody slightly pursed her lips. "We're supposed to stay out of politics."

"Stil didn't kill him," Angelique mildly pointed out.

"No, he just incited the Snow Queen's magic to do it for him." Melody sighed—a sound so musical it almost sounded like a strum of a harp.

"What the king was doing—the way he acted—was wrong," Angelique pointed out.

"Yes," Melody admitted. "But it is not our place to mete out justice or decide who should rule." She studied Angelique with eyes that were more wary than angry.

Small blessing, I suppose. She really disliked me when we last met.

"This is why the Council thinks you're dangerous, you know."

"I beg your pardon?" Angelique barely kept the squeak of surprise out of her voice.

Melody gestured back to the palace. "You're not wrong about King Torgen, but there are things we can and cannot do as mages. You insist on working outside those boundaries—something the rest of us cannot afford to do."

"*Every* mage can afford to help those who need it," Angelique fiercely said.

"We have a duty to protect everyone from dark magic," Melody said. "But we cannot recklessly aid royalty as you have, or soon they will begin thinking of us as allies, and *we* will be pulled into a power struggle, too. And that would be our end."

"If we stop helping people, *that* will be our end."

Melody merely shook her head. "I will inform the Veneno Conclave of the events of today."

Angelique shrugged. "I wouldn't expect anything less, and I have nothing to hide, either."

"Yes, perhaps." Melody narrowed her eyes. "Where will you go next?"

I can't tell her I plan to break into Zancara—that would make even the calmest mage flip a table. But I need a reason to be there if other mages happen to find me. "I'm going to Kozlovka," Angelique vaguely said. "Perhaps I'll swing down into Farset to see if there is any news of the elves."

Melody's gaze softened minutely. "You continue to search for Lord Enchanter Evariste?"

"Er, you have heard that I am?"

"Rumor has it that you are."

I don't want to admit to it—because it will make everyone fussy given that there's an official committee that's supposed to find him—but what other believable response is there? Though I suppose it's better they think I'm obsessed with finding Evariste than cavorting with Prince Severin and Princess Elle in an effort to track this widespread enemy we're encountering.

"I do use the occasional tracking spell to search for him during my travels." Inspiration struck, and Angelique added, "I was hoping to set one off near Zancara—I'm curious to see if the wall affects the spell at all."

Melody nodded slowly, her eyes sweeping up and down Angelique. "I don't like you," she said bluntly. "And I don't believe you should be allowed to keep your magic. But I wish you luck on your search for Evariste all the same."

"...Thank you?" Angelique was more than a little confused what the expected response would be. (She had received far more scorn from other mages before, so being told to her face she was disliked was hardly anything new. But the well wishes were.)

Angelique watched Melody retreat back into the darkness. She slightly shook her head in disbelief before tottering over to the fabric tent flap. She shoved it aside and slipped into Stil's parlor.

She was immensely relieved to find that Gemma and Stil were seated on a settee together—snuggled up like sleepy kittens—but they were *not*, thankfully, in the process of kissing.

"Good evening," Angelique said.

The strange white dog was sitting at Gemma's feet, but at Angelique's entrance, it stood up, stretched, then trotted over to her, making a sniffing inspection of her skirts.

Stil didn't move from the settee and gave Angelique the cockiest and most smug smile she had ever seen. Gemma, on the other hand, blushed bright red when Angelique wriggled her eyebrows at the pair.

"I'm glad to see I haven't stumbled onto anything untoward," Angelique laughed. "It seems as though congratulations are in order?"

A slight smile transformed Gemma's usually grave expression into something warm and light. "It seems."

"It seems? It *seems*?" Stil scoffed. "We have exchanged confessions of love—the world is now perfect!"

"You overly estimate the weight of our relationship on the destiny of the world," Gemma said.

Angelique chuckled and drifted farther into the room. "I'm glad you two reached an understanding. Truly, all my well wishes and congratulations are yours."

Stil's eyes practically glowed with happiness as he and Gemma stood. "Thank you, Angelique."

Angelique hugged them both—first Stil, then Gemma.

The seamstress' face was a soft shade of pink, but she surprised Angelique by squeezing her tightly during their embrace.

Angelique patted her on the back. She suspected if she hadn't been so tired, she might have shed a tear or two on behalf of the happy couple, particularly when Stil threw his arms around both of them and shoved his head into Gemma's hair, laughing.

"So you'll both be going south to Loire?" Angelique asked when they finally broke up the three-person embrace.

Gemma's smile fell slightly. "No, not yet."

"Gemma feels like she needs to stay—to support Lady Linnea," Stil scooped Gemma close, ignoring when she tried to pry herself from his grasp. "With the state of the continent—and my promise to you—I *need* to meet with Prince Severin and Princess Elle. *But*, I'll come back in a month to sweep her south with me."

Gemma elbowed Stil. "We agreed it would be early spring."

"We did," Stil nodded. "But I can still hope that with enough pleading, you'll move the date up."

"If you insist on trying, I might not be able to leave until fall," Gemma said wryly.

"You wouldn't do that to me," Stil said.

"Try me." Gemma eyed Stil, but when she redirected her gaze to Angelique, the set of her lips softened. "I am sorry you had to come back to help Stil and were unable to ride on to the Veneno Conclave as you had planned."

"There's nothing to apologize for. I actually ran into Lord Enchanter Clovicus and told him everything," Angelique said. "He's going to bring the matter before the Veneno Conclave himself. With Clovicus as the presenter, it's likely the Conclave will take the matter more seriously. I was actually traveling back west when I received Stil's message that you had been taken."

"That explains it." Stil flicked his black bangs off his forehead. "I actually didn't have much hope that my message would catch up with Pegasus in time. He's too fast. I guess it's a good thing you were doubling back. Where will you go next?"

"Zancara," Angelique said.

"*Zancara?*" Stil yelped.

"Yes." Angelique rolled her shoulders back and tapped a little of her magic—just enough for Stil to feel so he'd remember just who he was talking to. "When I ran into Clovicus, we discussed the lack of progress in finding Evariste. It was suggested I investigate Zancara in case he's been stashed there. Evidently they used to export legendary glass items."

Stil frowned. "I can see the logic—though I don't much care for it."

"Too bad. I'm going," Angelique flatly said. "Though I was hoping, given your wanderings, you might have contacts that could help me get through—or under—Zancara's blasted wall."

Stil's frown softened as he mused over her words. "I don't know of any way past that wall. But I know a smuggler who takes goods in and out of Zancara via the ocean. She should be able to help you—or at least share some pointers."

"Given that I have no possible leads, I'll take whatever advice I can get," Angelique dryly said.

"Yeah," Stil agreed. "I think it's pretty likely she could get you in, actually. Her name is Captain Neely. She's based in the Farset city of Tylis."

"Tylis—that's an ocean and river port city, correct?" Angelique said.

"Yep! It's a fun place." He cast a sly glance at Gemma. "It's pretty populated, so it always has beautiful and luxurious cloth."

"Does it?" Gemma politely inquired.

"Some of the best I've seen," Stil said in a sing-song voice. "I don't suppose, Gemma, you'd be game to go with Angelique and me and see it right now?"

Gemma narrowed her eyes. "You have to go to Loire to speak to Prince Severin and Princess Elle—you owe it to Angelique. And I'm remaining here to help Linnea. *No.*"

Stil winked. "Can't blame a man for trying."

Angelique's smile grew fond as she watched Gemma eye Stil, and Stil arch an eyebrow and smile handsomely. She stifled a yawn and allowed herself to lean against the open settee as she changed the topic. "Pray do tell me, was it a daring rescue, Gemma?"

"You think I'm capable of anything *except* being perfectly debonair?" Stil asked.

Angelique smirked. "Given that I once saw you bested in chess by a cat, yes."

"Roland is a *magic, talking* cat. He hardly counts as a feline," Stil complained. "And I had only stayed with you and Evariste at your home for a week at the time. Roland had months of practice before I arrived."

"He goes by Puss, now," Angelique said.

"Yes, yes, that's right. But take a seat—I'll give you the full story," Stil said.

Angelique raised her eyebrows. "Are you certain? You two looked rather comfortable before I arrived."

Stil smirked, but Gemma cut him off before he was able to say anything inappropriate. "Sit," she ordered, absently resting her hand on her new pet's head when the white canine pushed against her legs. "You deserve an explanation, and I want to thank you for your part in my rescue."

CHAPTER 7

The port of Tylis—the place where Stil's recommended smuggler/captain made her base—was a city that had tried to stake a claim for itself in the wilds of Farset and had not entirely succeeded in its venture.

Tylis was perched precariously on a rocky shore, invaded by the ocean to the west and boxed in by a frothing and foaming river to the south. The city technically possessed two ports—a river one with immense wooden docks, and an ocean port with ancient stone docks that were crusted with barnacles and dried salt.

Since Captain Neely made the river port her haunt, it was there that Angelique went, dodging the impressively large trees and bushes that erupted from the ground.

(Greenery seemed to ignore mankind's attempt to build up the river port, so much so that it was not unusual to see sailors hacking back branches from trees that leaned out over the river so they could dock their vessels. Nor was it unusual to see wild animals like foxes or raccoons trot through the docks with aplomb, unbothered by humans as they went on their way.)

Angelique watched an osprey land on the mast of a small skiff and scream at a trader until the man swore at the bird and threw a fish at it to silence it. *I wonder if it's because the elves made their home in Farset that things are so wild here.*

The citizens of Tylis didn't seem to mind the vivid wildlife that surrounded them. Rather, the biggest trees that grew out of the port were used to fly colorful flags; fishing nets were conveniently hung over the strongest bushes to make mending them easier, and Angelique even saw a sailor let a wild forest cat on the ship, which emerged several minutes later with a large rat dangling from its mouth.

Yes, this certainly has to be the influence of the elves.

Angelique paced the length of the river port three times before she found the ship she was looking for: Wrecked Lyfe.

Though the boat looked questionable—with a square sail yellowed and tattered with age and what looked like holes in the wooden bow—Angelique could faintly feel the thrum of magic around the skiff. Picking at it revealed spells for water resistance, smoother sailing, and the like—and whoever had done it was *good.*

It might look like a wreck, but those spells are worth more than many of the ships here in port. It's a show.

Angelique wiped her clammy hands on her clothes—she had shed her dress in favor of loose trousers, fur-lined boots, a thick linen shirt that draped almost to her knees, and a fur-lined vest that fastened under her left arm. It was warmer here in Farset than it had been in Verglas, but the wind was raw enough to turn Angelique's skin pink, and the temperature was still icy.

Hopefully the costume was inconspicuous enough that she wouldn't garner attention in Zancara—something her enchantress dress would most assuredly accomplish.

She took a breath, then strode up to Wrecked Lyfe. "Excuse me, Captain Neely?"

A woman, who had been wrestling with rope on a bench in the skiff, warily stood and eyed Angelique. "Who wants to know?"

"My name is Angelique. I was given your name by craftmage Rumpelstiltskin," Angelique said.

Instantly, the other woman's eyes lightened. "You're the famous Angel, are you? Where's your Evariste? From the way Stil gabbed about the two of you whenever I saw him, you are rarely separated."

Her words—though said in fun—were worse than if she had stabbed Angelique with a sword. The sudden onset of her guilt and frustration swarmed her, but it was the unexpected sense of *loss* that almost threatened to drown her.

Angelique's smile tightened against the storm of her emotions. "He's missing at the moment, though I am looking for him."

The woman's broad smile turned into a grimace. "That's right; the last time I saw him, he mentioned the Lord Enchanter was taken. My apologies for my thoughtlessness."

Angelique tilted her head and studied the woman, noting the way her emotions were clearly broadcasted on her face. *I don't think that is accidental...* "You aren't sorry," Angelique finally ventured. "That was a test to see if I really am Angelique."

The woman's over-done grimace faded into a slight quirk of her eyebrow. "Perhaps." She didn't look at all sorry. Instead, she agilely leaped from her boat to the dock, landing with a grunt. She flicked her long skirts—which hit her at the shins and were layered for warmth—then crossed her arms over her chest. "How can I be of service, Lady Enchantress?"

"I need to get into Zancara."

"Oh my, but that's illegal." Captain Neely pressed a hand to her chest as though she might swoon.

"Evariste might be there," Angelique bluntly said. "I need to search it to be certain. Stil said you might be able to help me."

Captain Neely's falsified shock faded. She studied Angelique, then tipped her head toward her craft. "Why don't you step into my workshop?" She easily jumped the railing and seated herself on a wooden bench in the belly of the skiff.

Angelique hopped onto the railing and crouched there for a moment, studying the skiff.

Given Evariste's ability to transport them, Angelique had ridden on very few boats since her apprenticeship—and most of them had been since he'd gone missing.

Almost reluctantly, she lowered herself into the gently rocking boat and took a seat on another wooden bench across from Captain Neely's.

Neely crossed her legs at the knees and braced her hands on her bench. "What you're thinking of is dangerous. No one really knows what's going on past Zancara's borders."

"Even smugglers like you?"

Neely shook her head. "I've never met those I conduct business with, and they don't volunteer any information—just goods." She said, not even bothering to deny her career.

Angelique frowned. "How is that possible?"

"I didn't stumble into this business—or this relationship. I was born into it," Neely said. "My father was at this post before I was, and my grandmother before him. We have a system that's been in place for decades. It's the same way for all those who manage to smuggle Zancarian goods." Neely brandished a finger. "But I can tell you that it's dangerous."

That's hardly surprising. How else could they have maintained such strict isolation unless they had something backing up their policies?

Neely scratched her nose. "Since it has closed borders, the Veneno Conclave hasn't had any say about citizens with magic born in Zancara. I don't know precisely what role they fill, but I do know they are there and watching. As a result, no smuggler I know of uses active magic to retrieve or deliver their goods. You can use a spell or two woven into your boat or clothes, but anything more and...well... There have been rumors of one or two folk planning to attempt it to secure bigger loads, but they're never heard from again."

"I suspected as much," Angelique said. "In the past, the

Conclave has tried dispatching mages to test the wall. They never were able to breach it. Whatever goes on behind those walls, Zancara has powerful mages under government control."

Or perhaps it's the opposite, and magic users control the government? If Zancara is used as the homebase for dark mages, it's possible they've taken over the government.

"But do you understand what that means?" Neely gripped the edge of her bench and leaned forward until Angelique could see the faint dusting of sun-freckles on her nose that were almost covered by the woman's tan skin. "You have to be careful with whatever magic you use because whenever you use it, you'll give yourself away."

The smuggler had a point.

Though Angelique was cautious with using her war magic, she was less cautious with other kinds—particularly the illusions she used to color her eyes and hair. *I'll have to cut them off for the duration of my travels—hopefully I won't look too out of place. I'll need to limit myself to spells that are only necessary—like the tracking spell for Evariste.*

"Heading into Zancara is *madness*," Neely continued. "You can get in, but getting out is awfully unlikely."

"I have no other choice." Angelique gripped the railing of the skiff until a splinter pricked her palm. "We *need* to get Evariste back. I've risked my neck more times than I care to remember just trying to help countries *survive*."

She realized too late she had spoken more than Neely would likely know; not everyone was aware of the struggles of neighboring countries.

But understanding lit Neely's eyes as she leaned back. "The elves...there's something to their disappearance?"

"Most likely." Angelique squared her shoulders and forced her chin up.

Neely pressed her lips together as she gazed from Angelique

to Wrecked Lyfe's tattered sail. "If you get your Evariste back, will you be able to help the elves?"

"Definitely," Angelique said without pause. "Evariste is an elf-friend. He can enter Alabaster Forest as he wishes."

Neely sighed and rubbed her temple. "I can't take you to Zancara soil, but I can drop you off near the shoreline—past all the nasty traps and gifts they set up to keep entrepreneuring folk out."

Angelique exhaled in relief. "Thank you—"

"Don't thank me yet," Neely warned her. "Once you're in Zancara, you're on your own. I'll watch for you at my drop spot, but if you never show, I won't risk coming after you. And I'm not doing this for free, either!"

"I understand," Angelique said. "When do we leave?"

Neely grumbled about crazy mages under her breath, then stood easily despite the shifting of the boat. "My next drop is scheduled in five days. You best make peace with your life before then because chances are you won't be coming back."

ANGELIQUE NEVER THOUGHT she had any particular expectations of what to expect for a smuggling run...but she did know that this was certainly not what she had mentally prepared for.

"We have two types of mead for your selection today, a black mead with Torrens' famous black currants, and a Loire sack mead—which is more of a dessert drink." Farraige—Neely's younger sister and only crewmate of the small skiff—held out two bottles of mead, her expression pleasant even as the skiff whipped around in a tight turn and she was nearly tossed off her bench.

"Um," Angelique eloquently said.

Neely whooped from where she stood on the prow of the ship, laughing into the fierce wind. "We're about to breech the first wall of waves. Hang on!"

"I recommend the black mead, because it will better match this evening's selection of refreshments," Farraige mildly said.

Angelique clung to her bench—which was thankfully nailed to the ship—and watched Neely run down the length of the railing and hop off at the stern to adjust the rudder.

"Is that a yes to the black mead, then?" Farraige asked.

"No, no thank you, I don't need anything to drink," Angelique said.

The boat rocked violently, and up ahead, Angelique saw a large wave—taller than a rearing horse—crest with a roar.

"Are you certain?" Farraige again held the bottles out. "Given where you are about to go, a drink might do you some good."

Angelique shut her eyes and held on to her seat as Neely directed the boat so they hit the wave at an angle rather than prow-first.

The boat rocked and water sloshed over the sides, soaking Angelique and the smugglers, but the ship sailed on.

Angelique spat out a mouthful of salt water and stared at Farraige, who was still holding out the bottles of mead with ease, even though water dripped from her nose.

"Yes," Angelique said. "I'm certain."

Farraige shrugged and popped the bottles into a cubby under her seat. "As you wish."

"Far, duck!" Neely shouted as she yanked on a rope that changed the angle of the sail, swinging it around.

Farraige effortlessly ducked, and the wooden bar the sail was tied to whistled overhead. When she popped upright, she was holding a wheel of cheese and what looked like dried jerky. "This evening's rations are cheese from Erlauf and dried venison produced here in Farset in a method taught to our forefathers by the elves themselves."

"Shouldn't you be helping Neely?" Angelique asked.

"Not at all. My role for this voyage is to see to your needs," Farraige said.

Behind them, Neely grabbed hold of a rope tied to the mast and jumped, swinging out over the ocean and peering into the murky waters. "Rocks to the starboard!"

"One moment please." Farraige grabbed a wooden pole and whirled around. She jabbed it into the ocean with such force, she grunted.

Neely, meanwhile, changed the angle of the sail again, and it wasn't until they scooted away that Angelique realized Farraige had slammed her pole against an immense boulder that just barely peeked up out of the ocean.

"Any sign of the sea dragons?" Farraige asked.

"None yet." Neely patted the hilt of her saber, then returned her attention to steering the ship.

Farraige nodded and flicked a pocket knife off her belt, which she used to cut a wedge of cheese. As the boat rocked and groaned, and frothy water occasionally sloshed over the railings, she arranged the cheese slice on a piece of jerky and offered it out to Angelique. "The flavors combined like so are quite delicious."

"I really don't need anything," Angelique said.

"But you will need your strength to swim to shore," Farraige insisted.

"I'll be fine." Angelique scrunched her eyes shut when a high wave flecked water in her face.

"Far—they've scented us!" Neely unsheathed her saber and used it to point into the sea.

Farraige tossed the cheese and jerky in her cubby and pulled out a crossbow from behind her. "Very good, Captain." She slid a bolt into place and stood firmly as the boat rocked.

"Portside!" Neely shouted.

A sea dragon—which was a little like a snake in shape, although it was much larger, possessed infinitely more teeth, and had transparent fins that framed its head—exploded out of the water with an angry hiss.

Farraige calmly shot it in the head, and it fell back into the angry sea.

Two sea serpents emerged from the water at the back end of the boat—one coiling around the rudder—but Neely dispatched both with well-aimed stabs.

"Do you want me to use my magic?" Angelique asked as salt water stung her eyes. "The sea serpents, at least, I could subdue."

"Nah." Neely shook her head and leaned into the freed rudder, re-positioning the bobbing boat. "We're already deep in Zancara's waters. This close to shore, we'll risk catching their attention."

A sea serpent slithered up the prow and tried to launch itself inside the boat, but Angelique snatched up the pole Farraige had used to push off the rock and jabbed the sea serpent in the chest, knocking it overboard. "Exactly how close are we?"

"Not far now." Neely wiped water off her forehead, then yanked hard on the rudder as her sister shot another sea serpent. "Whenever we hit serpent territory, it means we're getting close. If the sea wasn't so rough, you'd be able to see the shore now."

Farraige swiped a silver spyglass from her cubby. "For your viewing pleasure," she said.

"I'd rather beat off these sea serpents first," Angelique said.

"We're heading into a big wave. Hold on!" Neely cheerfully called.

Angelique lunged to grab the ship's mast just as a massive wave crested directly above them.

Icy cold water pummeled them, and for a moment, Angelique thought the ship might sink or split in half from the way it groaned and shook.

But after a moment, the powerful spells woven deep into the skiff engaged, and the ship abruptly stabilized on the water.

Farraige pushed her wet hair out of her face and started bailing out the boat with a bucket. "We have almost reached your destination," she announced. "Do you require any beverages or sustenance before you leave?"

"No!" Angelique smashed the head of a sea serpent with her wooden pole and nudged its limp body over the side of the boat.

Farraige diligently worked at bailing out the ankle-deep water. "Do you have any possessions you would like to retrieve for your travels?"

Angelique swiped Farraige's crossbow and leaned over the side of the ship to shoot a sea serpent lurking there. "You're dropping me in open water."

"Perhaps, but one must never make assumptions about a client's travel itinerary," Farraige said.

"The sea serpents are starting to retreat. We're entering the safe zone," Neely said.

Farraige cleared her throat. "Very well, then. Thank you, Lady Enchantress Angelique, for joining us on today's voyage. We wish you luck in your ventures in Zancara and sincerely hope you are here for pick up two weeks from today."

The ocean grew calm, then eventually stilled like glass, and Farraige dropped her bucket. "Otherwise, you may choose to use an alternative method to leave Zancara, in which case we must say our farewells."

"We're here." Neely tossed an anchor over the side of the boat. She collapsed the sail, then used the pole Angelique had abandoned to drag what looked like floating parcels closer to the ship.

Farraige scrambled to loosen the parcels' ties and hoist them into the skiff with a rather heavy-sounding clank.

Neely nodded at the rocky shore. "There's your destination. According to old maps from before Zancara's isolation, there's a small village a mile or two inland. I wish you luck—I hope you find Lord Enchanter Evariste."

Angelique nodded and felt for the two waterproof pouches tied to her belt. "Thank you—and thank you for bringing me here."

Farraige stopped poking the parcels long enough to gravely bow her head. "It was our honor."

Angelique hopped onto the railing and pulled off her boots. She tied them together with a string and slung them over her shoulder. She peered down at the ocean—which though quiet was still dark and angry-looking. She grimaced, took a deep breath, then dropped into the water.

It was shockingly cold and made her gasp. Her magic swamped her, driven by the shock, and Angelique hastily shoved it back down.

I can't get caught.

She started paddling her way to shore, noting that Neely and Farraige must have exchanged the goods quickly, for they were already throwing the parcels back into the sea. She paused as her thoughts lingered on something Farraige had said, and she turned around—treading water—as Neely started pulling up the anchor.

"You said I could use another method to exit Zancara?" Angelique asked.

"Of course," Farraige blinked. "Easiest way I know is to scale the wall. A few pieces in the southern-most bit are low enough to climb over." She shook her head in pity. "Best not use magic to achieve it, though. I saw a mage once knock himself silly trying to do so."

"The wall can be *climbed?*" Angelique yelped.

"Of course it can," Neely snorted. "The trick is not getting *shot* by a crossbow on your way over. But it's time for us to cast off. Good luck!" Neely started pulling on various ropes, hoisting the sail and changing the angle of it as Farraige finished bailing out the boat.

"Good luck, Enchantress!" the younger smuggler called.

Angelique grunted in the back of her throat and went back to swimming.

The ocean's icy temperature made it a little hard to breathe, and her fingers and toes were starting to tingle.

Waves still rocked the ocean, occasionally making Angelique bob higher or pushing her closer toward shore.

Her breath came harder and harder, and Angelique almost cried with relief when her feet scraped the sandy ocean floor.

Soon, she was able to trudge rather than swim. She carefully picked her way around the enormous black rocks that cluttered the shore, making it more of an exercise of climbing.

A foaming wave only knocked her into a rock once, but she jarred nearly every bone of her body in the process and scraped her palm. A few moments later, Angelique was able to climb onto the rocky shore, hoisting herself out of the ocean's cruel reach.

Her lungs ached as though they might burst, and when she licked her lips, the taste of sea salt stung her tongue. She grimaced but focused on yanking her belt pouch open with stiff, half-numbed fingers. She had to pour the contents of the pouch onto her hand—her fingers were too numb to make out any of the items by touch alone.

After pawing through the contents, she scooped up a ruby and whispered through chattering lips. "*Heat*."

Warmth flooded her, and the ruby depths of the gem glowed as the spell activated and wrapped around her, drying her clothes and hair, and restoring feeling to her extremities.

Angelique sighed in relief and dumped the gem and other charms back into the pouch, then secured it to her belt.

She had taken Neely's advice into consideration and—rather than casting spells herself—she had chosen to bring a number of charms she either already had on hand (gifts from Stil over the years that she kept in her saddlebag) or purchased during the wait for the voyage.

She paused, then, on an impulse, yanked the other pouch open, her fingers brushing her other charms.

The most important one was a rough, wooden carving of a heart, which carried a tracking spell. She had made the spell herself, but commissioned a craftmage to transfer the magic to the wooden heart.

The carving made her tuck her chin and twist her lips into a frown. She would have preferred *any other* shape besides a heart, but it was the only piece the craftmage had on-hand that was strong enough to contain the tracking spell.

Assured the charm was still there, Angelique pulled the pouch strings tight—closing it. Next, she took inventory of her clothes, slipping on her boots after confirming the heat charm had dried them, and tugging her fur vest straight.

Her hair was the last to be fixed. She pulled it out of the ruined braid she had put it in for the voyage and let it drape around her shoulders.

She tugged on one of her locks and studied the brunette shade, almost unpleasantly surprised by how dark her natural hair color was. (She hadn't let it shine through very often, and she *never* revealed her naturally silver eyes if she could help it. But she couldn't risk keeping the illusion spell going if even half of Neely's suspicions were true.)

She longed to use the tracking spell already, but she'd rather get farther inland to give the spell a better starting point, and she didn't dare loosen it until she had a better grasp on Zancara's state —both magically and governmentally speaking.

She shoved some of her hair back with a warm, blue-colored headband Gemma had made for Angelique before they parted ways, brushed her clothes off one last time, then started the hike up the rocky hill—which wasn't quite steep enough to be called a cliff.

Unlike Verglas, Zancara wasn't covered in snow—though the temperatures were still plenty cold, and the wind was almost violent in its strength. But the exertion of the climb kept Angelique reasonably warm, so when she finally scrambled off the rocky crest, her nose was red with the cold, but she wasn't shivering.

She crossed a rolling plain—which was an unappealing shade of brown as the grass had already died. The plains butted into a small forest of beech trees and silver pines, and it was there that Angelique heard the first sounds of humanity.

Cautiously, she tip-toed through the forest, pausing when the trees opened up enough to give Angelique a view of the village Neely had described.

Thankfully, it seemed the years of isolation hadn't hurt the village. Instead, it had expanded and resembled a rather good-sized city.

The village—or city?—rested on the slope of a rather lopsided hill, which looked as if a giant had chopped it at the crest and stomped the other half, making the stomped half more of a sheer drop than a true hillside.

The entire city was built at an angle on the slope, but it practically glittered among the trees that ringed the hill because the majority of the buildings were constructed with plaster and painted a blinding white color.

The larger buildings were all built out of stone bricks, and they loomed above the cheerful white village homes and shops.

Even from this distance, Angelique heard the faint clang of bells and the happy chatter of people.

She scratched her head as she studied the city. *It doesn't look like I expected. I thought the isolation from the rest of the world—much less the Veneno Conclave—would have been detrimental to Zancara. But I suppose I'm about to find out.*

Angelique took a breath, then started making her way toward the city.

CHAPTER 8

Angelique wasn't an idiot. She didn't charge right in. Instead, she spent most of the afternoon hiding in the trees, trying to get a gauge on the city.

She spent a night in the forest—only daring to use the heat charm when she couldn't ward the chill off no matter how deeply she burrowed under dead plant-life for insulation. But by late morning—after confirming a healthy flow of trader and traveler traffic through the city—Angelique felt confident enough to enter.

She kept her mouth shut—the Zancarian people tended to speak quicker, and their vowels were shorter than in other countries. As Luxi-Domus spent years drilling their students in speaking without accents—couldn't have someone guess what country a mage had once called home, after all—Angelique knew her pronunciation would give her away, and she wasn't confident she could mimic the accent very easily.

Instead, she kept a slight smile on her lips and was quick to make it brighter and wave whenever someone looked her way.

She was thankful to see her clothes didn't look *too* out of place—there were a few men and women dressed somewhat similarly who were clearly foresters. With luck, folk would assume she was a forester as well.

And though her silver eyes were still off-putting, her dark hair didn't make her conspicuous at all. Rather, the village was swirled with hair and eye colors of all shades, making Angelique no more remarkable than anyone else.

Angelique smiled and nodded as she passed a man and a woman, each wearing a crimson red and royal blue uniform. She assumed they were soldiers. And it wasn't until Angelique was two stalls down, peering at a table of elaborately embroidered hair veils that Angelique realized she felt a spark of magic.

One of them is a mage.

She couldn't tell which one—she wasn't sensitive or skilled enough in magic detection to follow such a faint spark.

She forced herself to meander to the next stall, so terrified she couldn't even comprehend what she was looking at as she tried not to attract attention.

Angelique risked glancing back, relieved to find the uniformed duo chatting and laughing as they continued down the sloping city street.

Zancara recruits mages for its army? That's a frightening thought—though perhaps it is necessary depending on the state of the government... but the more I watch them, the more I think those two don't really feel like soldiers.

Angelique rubbed her nose in the cold, then began picking her way up the slanting street.

She ran into another pair of similarly uniformed men outside an immense brick building that sat in the heart of the city.

The building was rectangular in shape, although the front door was ornamented by two bell towers, and the massive wall it was set in was capped in a triangular shape. Both the wall and the towers were elaborately decorated with florid columns, carvings, and depictions of the Zancara symbol, a lynx.

The rest of the building was simple—except for a few sculptures at the corners—and time and weather had worn it to a muted shade of gray, but the beauty hadn't faded at all.

The uniformed men leaned against the large building, chatting with a man selling salt-preserved fish.

Angelique didn't feel magic coming off of either of them as she cautiously walked past, but she did hear pieces and bits of their conversation.

"—have to get a mage to bless the traps if they keep falling apart."

"There *is* a craftmage in the Magus Mercado right now. Or Doña Trini might be able to use some sewing magic to fix it for a cheaper price."

"Maybe. How's the wife?"

Angelique strolled out of hearing, and instead took up a post across the street, watching folk stream in and out of the ornate building for a good hour before she finally worked up the courage to venture inside.

The building housed what Angelique would have called a market...except there was a strong buzz of magic, and a good number of the stalls only had folk standing at them and no goods in sight.

Angelique watched a woman bustle up to a man and set a teapot with a cracked lip on the table.

"Can you fix it, Don Vasco?" the woman wrung her hands and bit a lip. "It is a family heirloom from my husband's grandmother."

The man smiled soothingly. "Of course—just a bit of alteration magic will fix it right up."

The woman heaved a sigh of relief. "Bless you—your regular price?"

"Yes, please." The man spoke absently as he studied the teapot.

The woman set a coin on the table, but the man didn't even look at it as his hands glowed a pale salmon color.

Angelique felt the faintest tang of alteration magic and watched the teapot mend itself.

It was then that Angelique realized she stood in a *magic market*. Here, people bought charms, goods, or even services in exchange for coin or bartered goods.

Angelique almost sat down in her shock at the foreign idea.

Most Conclave Mages weren't allowed to sell their services—all requests went through the Veneno Conclave. The only ones who got away with it were high-level mages who aided people at their discretion but still had to accept the majority of their assignments from the Conclave, or craft mages who could sell wares—but there were plenty of special rules and regulations to cover them.

I don't think Zancara is ruled by mages—black or otherwise. But I had better try to figure out how much magic is used before I loosen my tracking spell.

ANGELIQUE SPENT a week poking around Zancara before she felt secure enough to loosen her tracking spell.

She hadn't uncovered much about Zancara's methods of operation, except that the country as a whole seemed oddly intact. It was still ruled by a royal family, who seemed to keep the country well-regulated without being tyrannical.

Mages, it seemed, were considered regular citizens and were allowed to do what they pleased with their lives. Although, Angelique *had* learned that the uniformed men and women were called *escolta*—and they were not soldiers but were hired by the royal family to protect and guard the people of the city they lived in.

It was the presence of the escolta that made Angelique realize there was little chance the black mages—or whoever was trying to wreck the continent—had set up camp in Zancara. The borders were too tight for black mages to easily slip through, and the escolta would jump on a black mage in a moment if he or she used their magic, given that a fair number of the escolta themselves had magic.

In fact, it is very likely an escolta will feel what I'm about to do and track me down. Angelique nervously rubbed her hands together and checked one last time for any feeling of magic or sound of humanity in the forest in which she was hiding.

She had spent the week traveling east across southern Zancara and had made the calculated decision to release her spell in the wild, which meant traveling until she came to spot overgrown and rocky enough that it was not hemmed in by pastures and crops.

There was a smallish town to the north—it had the same magic market that most cities seemed to have, as well as a few escolta—but it was far enough away that Angelique was almost certain her pre-made spell would be able to slither past without detection.

Also, she wasn't too terribly far from one of the lower pieces of wall that Neely had described. (It was low because the frothing river that ran from Swan Lake in Kozlovka down to Farset flowed fast on the other side of the wall, but if things got ugly, a river was hardly the worst thing Angelique would face.)

"Now I'm just making myself worry," Angelique scoffed. "I need to act, or I'll be here all day."

Her hands shook as she carefully slid the wooden heart from her pouch. After all of these years, it hurt to hope again.

Which was stupid—judging by the state of the country, Angelique knew the chances of Evariste being hidden in the rocky country were slim.

But I've searched everywhere! He has to be here—where else could they have hidden him that my magic couldn't find? How much power could they have to be able to hide him—not just from me, but Lord Enchanter Clovicus, Sybilla, Lady Enchantress Lovelana—all of them!

Her fingers trembled so badly, she almost dropped the wooden heart.

Angelique took a deep breath and *tried* to clear her mind of her thoughts, but she couldn't entirely dampen the feeling of hope that made her ears ring and her stomach turn summersaults.

She extended a finger—summoning the *tiniest* bit of magic that wrapped around her fingertip in a swirl—then tapped the carving, releasing the spell.

The heart glowed a soft pink color, and the spell dripped down from the pointed bottom, almost making it resemble a bleeding heart.

The spell detached from the carving and hovered in the air for a moment—a churning, glowing orb—then it sped off through the trees.

Angelique returned the carving to her pouch...and waited.

Her magic curled around her feet—tempting her to draw upon it in case someone felt the spell and traced it back to her—but she forced herself to ignore it.

She checked to make sure her hair was secure in a loose bun—she didn't want it flopping in her face if she had to run—fixed her boots, then paced to keep warm, for it was colder this far inland.

She expected the spell to take at least an hour—if not an afternoon—to search Zancara. (She had gone for a more powerful and precise spell even though it risked drawing more attention to herself because she didn't know if she'd ever get a chance to loosen a second spell.)

But only half an hour had passed before Angelique felt the spell fizzle and drop off.

It had found nothing.

Evariste wasn't in Zancara.

Angelique nodded twice and walked a few steps before the crushing defeat caught up with her.

Despair flattened her, and she dropped to her knees.

He's not here. He's not in Zancara. Then where in the blazes is he?!

The world seemed to shift so she couldn't tell up or down, and she tried not to think of what this meant.

He's still alive—he has to be! But what do I do now? Have I missed something? Do I need to search the rest of the continent more thoroughly? Or perhaps...did they use his magic to go to a different land?

Angelique felt like a fish suffocating outside of water. She couldn't get any air, and hot tears welled up in her eyes.

Then a stick cracked.

Everything in Angelique stilled. Her thoughts fell away, and she stared down at the ground, unflinchingly, as she strained her ears and listened.

There was only silence—pure silence. No birds, no breeze, nothing.

Angelique narrowed her eyes but stayed where she was as she felt for any magic in the air.

There!

She threw herself to the ground, and something whistled overhead. It struck a tree trunk just in front of her with a thump.

Angelique craned her head, her heart beating faster as she saw the black blade embedded deep into the tree.

She rolled, flipping herself over her shoulder so she was in a crouching position and facing whoever had thrown the knife. She expected to see a uniformed escolta emerging from the forest, but instead a disheveled young man stepped out of the trees.

He had fine black clothes lined with black fur and a leanly muscled frame that most girls would sigh over, but what Angelique noticed first about him was his red eyes. They were a dark, glittering shade of blood red, and—Angelique suspected—were even more unsettling than her own strange eyes.

He has magic for certain. Perhaps he's an off-duty escolta? Angelique cautiously flexed her fingers behind her back and let some of her magic curl around her fingers as the mage glared at her.

She couldn't and wouldn't hurt a Zancarian. The country had done nothing to provoke such a response—it was she who had flagrantly ignored their laws. *But I cannot let myself be taken.* As her magic tickled her senses, she started to angle herself into a position that would best let her run.

"Finally," he growled. "I've found you."

The black fur and heavy fabrics of his clothes spoke of money, but he had a leaf in his tousled black hair and dark circles around his eyes. The closer he drew to Angelique, the more she could swear the air carried the faint scent of dried blood.

Something is off—he's not an escolta. He's not even from Zancara! He doesn't have the accent.

His breath was uneven and his smile a bit unhinged as he took another step toward Angelique. "*You*," he said. "Do you have any idea how long I've been tracking you? What an *irritant* you've been?"

For a moment, Angelique almost relaxed. *Is he from the Veneno Conclave? They're the only ones who are eternally frustrated with me like this.*

She winced when more magic than she wanted flooded her, making her feel colder than she already was. *No...he's a threat.* She glanced at the black dagger still dug into the tree trunk. It was made out of a black substance, and Angelique could feel the spark of magic within it. *More than a threat, it would seem, if he has war magic. But war mages are usually excited to see me, and he...*

"I even had to chase you here. To *Zancara*! You cost me weeks! And I had to lower myself to flatter that *music mage* to learn you were coming here." He grimaced in revulsion and glared at Angelique with anger. Abruptly, he flicked his hand out, and smoky black shadows condensed into the hardened shape of a sword. He lunged at Angelique with unnatural speed, stabbing his sword at her gut.

She ducked to the side, avoiding the strike, and darted behind a tree. *He's a black mage. He must be—but why is he following me?*

"And still you keep *running*," the young man growled. "Like a stupid little mouse." He tried to chase Angelique around the tree, but she was able to stay just ahead of him.

She threw a water and an ice spell at him—hoping to freeze him in place—but an iridescent green shield flashed into place, blocking the strike.

He has magical protection? This is bad; that means he's prepared. But for what?

"Who are you?" Angelique asked.

He unfortunately ignored her. "How does someone as weak as *you* even get a constellation to tote them around? It's unfathomable!" He flicked a finger at Angelique, spinning a black dagger at her.

Angelique threw up a shield just in time, then roughly twisted a fistful of her magic into a fireball that she flung back at him.

It glanced off his magic-forged shield, dissipating instantly.

It confirmed both of Angelique's fears—he didn't make the shield—it was attached to the gold necklace he wore. Even worse, the shield was *strong*. He had allies—skilled ones.

The war mage swung again, his shadow blade slicing straight through the tree trunk.

Angelique gaped at the falling tree. *Forget trying to wheedle answers from him. Facing a war mage in Zancarian soil isn't wise given it's unlikely I'll be able to physically overpower him since he'll have physical training. It's time to run.* She spun around and raced through the forest. *If I get close enough to the wall, I think I can risk using my magic to fight him off...but if I use it now, I'll just bring the escolta down on us.*

Pain bloomed on her forearm. She glanced down to see a slash wound just above her wrist. Blood was already welling and coloring her shirt. *How did he hit me? If he threw a blade and only grazed me like this, it should have fallen.*

Angelique's thoughts ground to a halt as a black dagger whistled past, missing her only because she had staggered from her arm wound. The dagger abruptly changed course *midair*, and went flying back the direction it came.

His magic isn't just making weapons out of shadows; he can also control them to a certain extent. Which means I can't count on running. He'll kill me before then, Angelique dimly realized.

She increased her speed and started zig-zagging through the trees. It meant she wasn't putting any distance between her and the black mage, but it made her a much more difficult target. *Change in plans,* she decided. *I need the escolta.*

Between weaving serpentines, Angelique altered her path so they ran slightly north. Close to the nearest village.

Somewhere behind her, the war mage roared his anger. Hopefully he hadn't realized what she had planned.

No longer trying to hide her presence, she slapped a healing spell on her arm. It was small—she couldn't manage anything big while running—but at least it would deaden whatever pain her adrenaline didn't overrun.

Despite the icy temperatures, sweat dripped down Angelique's back. She clamped down on the terror that threatened to overtake her and focused on surviving. All of Puss' drilling and Evariste's teaching fell into place as Angelique planned her next few moves.

She twisted some of her magic and shoved it into the ground. A beech tree sprouted from the ground full grown, the wood of its trunk groaning.

The war mage sliced through it with a roar, and it fell with a crash.

Angelique circled round a bush and used magic to peel up giant flakes of the icy ground.

The mage jumped the fallen tree trunk and landed on top of the curled crust of ground, which flaked and disintegrated underneath him.

He crouched with a chuckle. "It's almost offensive how long you managed to avoid me, given how *inept* you are at this." He sneered. He threw out his arm, and a black spear formed.

He flung it at Angelique, who threw up a much larger defensive shield than the weapon warranted.

The shield sparked, then collapsed with a ground-shaking boom that shook the trees.

The black mage stalked after Angelique with a crooked grin. "It's unbelievable that you are truly *this bad* at magic given what a pain you've been."

Angelique ignored the taunt. She confirmed that the trees were thinning out before she stopped leaking magic like a sieve and focused on running, holding her injured arm tight to her side.

The black mage growled as he barreled after her, chasing her out of the forest and into the open.

The town Angelique had been trying to avoid was within eyesight. It was surrounded by rolling plains to the north, the infamous wall made of huge boulders to the east...and a line of escolta dressed in gleaming uniforms to the south.

She almost whooped in glee at the sight. *I hoped they would feel my magic, but this is more than I expected!*

Behind her, the black mage swore, jarring Angelique from her thoughts.

She poured on the speed, mentally tracing out a path that would skirt the escolta but hopefully take her close enough that they got a chance to either scare off or swat off the war mage.

A growl, and the war mage was almost on her. "You did this on purpose!"

Angelique snorted. "You thought we could throw that much magic around without being noticed?"

"*Halt! Display your permits!*" an escolta shouted, barely audible above Angelique's heavy breathing.

The war mage's expression turned ugly, and with an animalistic roar, he flung an armload of black daggers at her.

Angelique threw up another shield, but she miscalculated, leaving a tiny sliver of herself uncovered, and a black dagger slashed the back of her right calf. She swallowed a shout and shoved her hand through her shield—which held the rest of the weapons back—channeling a gust of wind straight into the mage's chest.

He was sent skidding backwards. He created a black sword and stabbed it to the ground, halting himself and staying upright. A push off his weapon, and he was chasing after Angelique again, catching up with her faster than a regular human would.

"Display your permits—*now*!" an escolta wearing a feathered hat shouted.

Both Angelique and the mage ignored him as they ran—the war mage throwing bladed weapons at Angelique that she veered to avoid.

Pain gnawed at Angelique's calf and forearm, and she was aware she was leaving a blood trail. But even so, she noticed when the feather-hatted escolta stepped back and spoke to her men.

The escolta raised their arms, and the hair on the back of Angelique's neck prickled.

Magic churned at their palms, and Angelique threw herself to the ground.

"Got you!" The war mage smashed his booted heel onto Angelique's right heel, pinning her in place. He smiled viciously and formed a black sword as Angelique curled into a ball and prayed she survived.

Just as the war mage started to stab his sword down, a boulder the size of a large kettle smashed him between the shoulder blades, tossing him to the ground like a rag doll.

Angelique pressed herself closer to the ground. Pain radiated from her injured wrist as sweat dripped off her nose. Vines tried to wrap around her wrists, but it only took letting a little bit of her core magic flicker to slice straight through them.

The black mage struggled to his feet, only to get a fireball to the chest. His defensive shield deflected the flames, but the spell hit him with enough force to make his shield recoil and to toss him to the ground again.

Angelique waited until she heard the escolta leader shout before she leaped to her feet and started running for the wall again.

High above her, a hawk screamed and dropped into a nose dive, aimed straight for her.

Angelique twisted a bit of her magic and thrust her arms up, rebuffing the hawk with a gust of wind—though she noticed whatever good the healing spell had worked must have been undone by the tumble to the ground, for her forearm wound was now bleeding even heavier.

The hawk screamed and retreated, its voice almost covering the low growl of a wolf.

Angelique glanced back over her shoulder, her heart faltering at the sight of a giant white wolf racing toward her.

Shapeshifter mage—wolves don't get that big naturally.

Angelique kept running as she struggled to choose what spell to twist her magic into. (She *would not* harm an escolta. Not unless things were truly dire.)

The wolf howled, and Angelique tugged on her magic, hurriedly forming another blast of wind. She scooped up a handful of snow and fired off the gust of magic at the same time, flicking stinging snow into the wolf's eyes.

The beast (mage?) shook its head and leaped, slamming into Angelique's back, sending her crashing down.

The air was ruthlessly knocked from her lungs, and the wolf kept its front paws on her back, its claws ripping through the thick layers of her clothes and digging into skin and muscle.

Angelique's head yanked back in pain, but she had no air to scream.

There was a commotion off to her left, and she thought her lungs might collapse when the wolf pushed off her back and bounded toward the black mage, who was struggling against a regular army of vines.

Angelique lay still for a moment—until air finally filled her lungs again—then bolted. She heard the escolta shout, but she kept running, even as the trickle of warm blood dripping down her back made her shiver.

She almost cried in relief when she reached the wall and started forging her way up its uneven side.

The black mage roared, making her twist hazardously to peer back over her shoulder.

A veritable hoard of black weapons surrounded the black mage as he viciously sliced through the vines. He ran for the wall, but the shapeshifter mage was right on his heels.

He's terrifying. How can he keep going like this?

Angelique's nails chipped and her fingers bled as she climbed the wall, wedging her feet in crevasses between the giant stones.

She slipped, banging her knee into the wall, and more than once the rocks were slippery with her own blood.

But she reached the top. Even though her lungs burned and her eyesight briefly wavered, Angelique swung her legs over the lip of the wall.

On the other side, the river foamed. It was flowing swiftly—not at the speed of rapids, thankfully, but fast enough that if she wasn't careful, she'd half drown herself from the cold and her fading strength.

The black mage roared behind her, finally having reached the base of the wall after stabbing the shapeshifter escolta in the shoulder.

Angelique reflexively threw up a defense shield, blocking the black arrow he flicked at her.

The black mage threw himself at the wall, his words dripping with fury. "I'm going to make you *suffer* for this!"

Without hesitation, Angelique flung herself off the wall, landing in the river with a tremendous splash. The water was as cold as she feared. As she sunk deep, sharp bits of slushy ice jabbed her skin.

The shock reflexively pried her mouth open, almost choking her on icy liquid.

When her feet hit the bottom of the river, she shoved off it, breaking the surface with a sputtering cough.

She weakly swam for shore—which was dusted with snow.

The war mage breeched the top of the wall and flung another dagger at Angelique.

She dropped to her knees and threw a defense shield up, but her grasp of the spell faltered; the dagger punctured the spell, the very tip of the weapon scratching her cheek.

A bolt of angry lightning struck the wall, narrowly missing the war mage—a warning from the escolta to *leave*.

The black mage flung himself into the river as Angelique tried to move, but found she couldn't feel *anything*. She hastily twisted her magic into a heat spell, which returned feeling to her limbs and dried her clothes.

She left a magic trap behind her and ran—or jogged, really, as her strength was starting to fail her.

The war mage burst from the river and walked straight into Angelique's trap. The ground beneath his feet swirled in a magic sort of quicksand.

"Blast you!" the war mage howled.

Angelique grinned and glanced back over her shoulder. She almost stumbled over her own feet when she saw him dragging himself out by grabbing the pole of a long spear he had fashioned from shadows and wedged into solid ground.

Angelique only made it a few more paces before he pulled himself entirely free and limped after her.

He's not self-trained—he's too good at this.

Angelique's only consolation was that the black mage seemed as frustrated with her as she was with him.

"Why won't you *die*? He's been in our grasp for years—you should be an easy mark! You're so *weak*!" The black mage growled in irritation and flung half a dozen daggers at her.

Angelique skid to a stop, and for a moment time froze. Her fear fell away and her pain faded.

"He's been in our grasp."

Could it be?

She extended her hand, and the mage's tarry daggers halted a finger's width from Angelique's body.

Slowly—painfully—she turned around.

Her muscles trembled, and her breathing was ragged, but her magic lashed angrily around the black daggers, humming with power.

Angelique stared at the black mage and licked her cracked lips. "*What did you say?*" she asked, barely able to speak louder than a whisper.

The mage's face twisted with rage as he pushed his palms out in front of himself and poured more of his magic into his weapons.

Angelique let more of her magic flood her. Through her powers, she could feel the sharp, magic-formed weapons. They were a stinging, smoky sensation, but a flicker of her magic eradicated the feeling.

The mage pushed his daggers with more and more magic until his face was red with strain and a vein throbbed in his temple, but Angelique held them with ease.

"What did you say?" she demanded. Magic was the only thing keeping her up, but she wouldn't give up now.

He has to be referring to Evariste!

Angelique's stomach churned—she wasn't sure if it was the price of her magic or the emotions that rippled through her.

"Who sent you? Who are your allies?" She took a wobbly step toward him—her entire body protesting the abuse—and something in the mage changed.

There was an odd light in his eyes that hadn't been there before. Not malice, not glee...

Blood dribbled from her wound, and Angelique finally realized the ringing in her head was not from shock, but blood loss.

I...I'm going to faint. And then he's going to kill me.

Her knees started to wobble, but before she collapsed, there was a deafening thunder—a triumphant note blasted at the volume of a landslide.

Cold, black nothingness enveloped her, and it took Angelique a moment to realize she hadn't fallen unconscious, but that *something* surrounded her.

Vaguely, she heard the war mage scream, and her heart beat faster with fear.

But then there were a few pinpricks of dazzling light, warmth, and—when her legs finally did give out—a soft sensation draped around her shoulders and brushed her neck. As she finally drifted off, she frowned in puzzlement.

Is that...am I feeling feathers?

CHAPTER 9

Angelique woke to stars.

It took her several long and confused moments to confirm the stars were not, in fact, in the sky, but glowing on Pegasus' belly.

Aching, she pushed herself up on her elbows and squinted in the dying sunlight, learning that Pegasus stood directly over her, his back legs braced on either side of her.

She froze in fear.

If he steps on me, I'll die.

Pegasus sneezed and flicked his flaming tail.

He stepped over her—Angelique held her breath for *that* moment—then turned around and sniffed her.

"Hello, old friend." Angelique raised her hand to scratch her forehead. The gesture made a knife blade of pain shoot through her injured back, but she relaxed when Pegasus pressed his muzzle to her temple and lipped her hair.

She flipped over so she could boost herself up onto her knees as she groaned. "You have no idea how happy I am to see you." Angelique coughed, trying to clear the rusty sound from her voice.

She blearily peered around, but the war mage was nowhere to be seen. She rubbed her aching wrist and glanced up at Pegasus. "Did he run?"

Pegasus audibly ground his teeth.

Angelique laughed. "I'll take that as a yes." Shakily, she rose, taking inventory of her injuries before placing a few slow-burn heals on herself that would address the worst of them.

"It's good he's gone—he would have killed me while I was out of it. But I think he was with the group that held Evariste. If I could have questioned him..." She shook her head and tried to dislodge the thought from her mind.

He's long gone. However, I might be able to pick up his trail. He could lead me to Evariste...

She groaned as she rolled her shoulders back, then glanced curiously at Pegasus. "How did you know where to find me?"

Pegasus swished his tail.

"Er, okay, obviously you've always been able to find me, but why did you come? I didn't call for you...did I?" Angelique frowned in thought. *I suppose it's possible I might have called for him when I passed out, but I'm pretty sure Pegasus is what scared the mage off.*

Pegasus snorted at Angelique's injured forearm with enough force he wetted her clothes.

"You knew I was injured so you just...came?" Angelique asked.

Pegasus pressed his muzzle to her temple for several sweet moments, then he *pushed* her hard enough to make her stumble.

"Hey," Angelique protested as she staggered a few steps.

Pegasus stared at her with fathomless eyes, and Angelique could have sworn he quirked an eye at her.

"Well, I...that mage found me and...he was a war mage, you know, so I couldn't beat the snot out of him like Puss—that is, Roland—would want me to and so, um..."

I'm babbling to a constellation, trying to make an excuse for my injuries, she dimly realized. *And this is probably the least surprising part of my week.*

Pegasus pawed the ground—spawning a blue flame despite the dusting of snow, then turned in a circle.

Angelique rubbed the back of her neck and watched him, more than a little confused.

The constellation looked at her over his shoulder and stamped a hoof, then lipped a stirrup of his saddle.

"I don't want to go just yet," Angelique said. "I'd like to use a few spells and see if I can pick up the black mage's tracks. He mentioned Evariste—I think. If he's with the mages who have him captured, he's our best lead."

Angelique couldn't say exactly how Pegasus did it, but something dark brushed her mind.

ONE.

The impression was both strong and ancient, and it ran through her whole body.

Angelique's breath was shaky, and her legs trembled a little.

However he had accomplished it, Pegasus had been clear. He would allow her to cast one spell, and then they would ride to the nearest city to get her injuries seen to.

"Okay." Angelique cleared her throat and tottered back toward the river.

She shivered in the cold air—it was even cooler in Kozlovka than in inland Zancara. She tried to tug her ripped clothes closer before recalling she was officially out of the no-magic zone.

"Of course!" A few twists and turns of her magic, and a heat charm settled over Angelique, warming her from the inside out. She sighed in relief, wriggling her toes in her boots until Pegasus shifted. "I'm hurrying!"

Angelique frowned in concentration as she carefully sifted her magic through her fingers, swirling it into the most powerful spell she could muster.

Perhaps Pegasus is right to have us leave, Angelique thought as sweat beaded on her forehead. *I believe my injuries lost more blood than I thought—I feel lightheaded and just a bit...strange.*

Her magic flowed easily enough, but Angelique had to shake her head and peel her eyes open wide to keep her vision from blurring.

It was a good thing she was so skilled at tracking spells—but by the time she finished, she had to sit down. She flicked the silver orb, sending it off on its way, then staggered back to Pegasus and his prominently flattened ears.

"There. We just have to wait for it to ferret out information." Angelique slipped her foot into the saddle stirrup and tried to boost herself onto Pegasus' back, but her leg gave out and she collapsed, slamming into the ground. "*Ouch!*"

Pegasus grumbled under his breath and lowered himself to the ground.

Angelique slipped into the saddle and clung to him as he rocked to his feet. Once they were stabilized, she patted his neck. "Thank you. If you like—" She stopped talking when she felt the spark of the tracking spell fizzle. "It...died?" she said dumbly.

She reached for the spell and felt nothing.

It had been unable to find any trace of the black mage and collapsed on itself.

How is that possible? He was just here! No, that can't be right! I just did the spell wrong. It was my fault—this isn't another dead end!

Pegasus started walking, going east.

"No, Pegasus, wait," Angelique objected. "I did the spell wrong. You have to wait!"

The constellation ignored her and moved into a fast trot, jostling her so all she could do was hold on or fall off.

Angelique gritted her teeth, and angry tears prickled her eyes. *I'll find that black mage. I'll follow him all the way back to Evariste.*

EVARISTE WOKE with a crick in his neck.

Another day, another draining.

Though his body ached and his nerves felt raw, Evariste forced himself to stay in a collapsed heap. At least an hour or two passed before he heard footsteps and the soft murmur of Liliane's voice.

"The second prince of Loire continues to be a problem." Her voice was resigned, as if she were discussing a poorly made dress.

"Can't you attack him?" asked a male voice that sounded faintly familiar.

"It's been tried, but ever since his curse broke, he's been well guarded. The tenacity of his low-born wife hasn't helped. She always sniffs out the few attacks that have managed to slip past the guards," Liliane sighed.

"It seems, then, that we lost our chance when Apprentice Angelique was suspiciously on hand to alter his curse."

Liliane lightly laughed. "As if your attack hasn't gone afoul because of her?"

"Princess Rosalinda sleeps—and has already been sleeping for months." The male voice was haughty now. "Even better, Angelique put the entire capital under a sleeping spell. The Magic Knights and all of Sole are out of our way. Isn't that what my assignment was?"

Princess Rosalinda? Then he must be—

"I suppose. You have done well enough, Carabosso," Liliane unknowingly confirmed Evariste's guess. "But I wouldn't rest on your laurels just yet."

"Yes, Liliane," Carabosso said in a surprisingly meek voice.

There was some quiet shuffling, and Evariste dared to crack his eyes open just enough to peer at the pair.

Liliane was prepping a canvas and starting to mix paints as Carabosso hovered a safe distance away. "There is nothing to be done, then, about the Loire prince?" he asked.

Liliane paused long enough to smile over her shoulder at the pale rogue mage. "Of course there is," she said in a voice as sweet as honey. "We just have to change our strategy a little."

Carbosso tilted his head. "In what way?"

"We will murder his brother, the Crown Prince of Loire." Liliane mixed yellow and blue paints, adding in a swirl of red, to get the muddy shade of green she was looking for.

"Won't he be *more* difficult to assassinate?" Carabosso asked.

"Surprisingly, no. To start with, he doesn't have a wife capable of fending off murder attempts. And these days Prince Severin is forever surrounded by clouds of military men due to his endless strategizing. The Crown Prince—famous for being a well-meaning idiot—is not so occupied."

"I see. I imagine the death of the Crown Prince would shake Loire," Carabosso said.

Liliane dabbed her brush in the green paint and made the first mark on the white canvas. "Yes. But what we're really after is that it will ruin Prince Severin and stop this little resistance of his in its tracks." She offered Carabosso a warm smile. "He loves his brother with a foolish devotion. If the Crown Prince dies, the oh-so-intelligent Prince Severin will go into shock, giving us an opening to strike."

"I see." Carabosso pressed his fingertips together as he appeared to think through the matter.

"Of course," Liliane continued. "We could keep trying to fight through Prince Severin's defenses or even attack that wild wife of his. But this method will require the least effort and—if the mages handle it right—might even be able to make his murder appear politically motivated."

"I see the wisdom of the plan." Carabosso bowed his head. "As expected of you, Liliane."

Evariste clenched his jaw. *I thought Liliane was the mastermind because the others were scared of her, but perhaps I am wrong. They seem to respect her in some twisted way. She seems more strategic than Suzu and the others...maybe that's her skillset—more than the creature-conjuring.*

Liliane dabbed more paint onto the canvas. "I've already dispatched two mages to handle it. They are young and relatively new recruits, but given that they will be attacking an unprepared target, I have hopes."

"And if they fail?"

"Then we'll use what little they *do* learn for our next attack." Liliane set her brush aside with a sigh.

"What is it?"

"We're in a precarious position at the moment," she said. "Attacking Prince Lucien is the only move we can truly make right now. Acri is still chasing after Apprentice Angelique, and Rothbart claims he needs more time to properly attack Kozlovka. I don't enjoy being in a position of ignorance. I'm positive that no matter the outcome we can use it to our advantage, but *we're* not supposed to be the ones who feel blind."

Carabosso's boots scraped the ground as he turned in a circle. "Can't the mirror your pet enchanter is trapped in function like a magic mirror if you use his magic? You could check on Rothbart—or Acri."

"Rothbart's castle is guarded just as closely as our caves, I'm afraid," Liliane placed a hand on her cheek in an expression of disappointment. "That man is paranoid."

And rightly so if his accusations are even partially correct.

"However, there are other mages I would like to check on."

Evariste shut his eyes again when he saw Liliane rise, the cascade of her gold hair falling over her shoulder.

The pair's footsteps grew closer, pausing just in front of his mirror.

"Worm," Carabosso said in an imperious tone. "Stand."

Evariste didn't move.

"Funrus drained him of his magic earlier," Liliane said. "It fatigues Evariste for many hours afterwards."

"Is it our duty to worry how tired he is?" Carabosso kicked the frame of the mirror. "Wake up, enchanter."

As if that accomplishes anything. But it's probably about time to start waking up, or they'll be suspicious if I stay out longer than normal. Evariste groaned and slowly covered his face with his arm.

"He'll be practically comatose for a while longer, but we can still harvest more magic from him." When Liliane began yanking some of his magic out of him, he no longer had to play up his pain, and instead growled and clutched his aching chest.

"What will you first check on..." Carabosso trailed off and looked over his shoulder. "Was that shouting?"

"I don't believe I heard anything." Liliane's fists were surrounded by blue trails of Evariste's magic. "But would you be a darling and check on it?"

I'm not sure what hurts worse—getting my magic forcibly yanked from my soul or seeing it in Liliane's clutches. Evariste glared at her as his muscles spasmed out of his control.

Carabosso took a step toward the cavern entrance but paused when the raised voices grew louder. "What—"

Acri dragged himself into the room, shedding snowflakes from his hair and shoulders and shivering. Suzu was hot on his heels.

The war mage looked ragged. In fact, he looked downright *beaten*. He had several bleeding wounds and a nasty-looking bruise at the corner of his mouth, and he moved with a slight limp.

What most relieved Evariste, though, was that the brat wasn't smug or even content. Rather, his shoulders were slightly hunched, and his red eyes were at half-mast when he glanced in his mother's direction.

"Acri!" Liliane's voice was flushed with warmth. She dropped Evariste's magic—leaving it to float uselessly around the surface of his mirror—and approached Acri. "My dear son, you are hurt. You should see that your wounds are tended to first before you tell us of your triumph." She reached out to put a hand on his cheek, but he flinched.

Evariste only half listened as he stared at the cloud of his magic. *I'm cut off from reaching it...but if it's just sitting there, could I possibly control it?*

He glanced at Carabosso—confirming the mage's attention was on the drama playing out between his leader and her son—then pressed his hands against his mirror's surface and held his breath, too afraid to hope.

Acri took a step backwards and bowed to Liliane. "My apologies, Mother."

Evariste stared as his magic drifted closer. *Come on, hurry!*

Liliane laughed. "What do you have to be sorry for? You weren't followed, were you?"

As Evariste watched, magic stopped swirling around the mirror and instead brushed against it.

Yes!

For the first time in years, he felt the pleasant hum of his magic when it tapped the spot where his palms pressed.

"No." Acri's shoulders were so stiff, one could have balanced a sword on them. "But...I failed you."

Evariste was so surprised by the brat's admission, he temporarily dropped his connection with his magic.

The cavern was silent for several long, oppressive moments.

"What?" Lilian said.

Acri audibly swallowed. "I did not eliminate Apprentice Angelique."

"*What?*" Liliane repeated in a voice hot with fury.

"We fought, but I was forced to flee when she overpowered my magic and took control of my shadow weapons," Acri said.

She overpowered him? Does that mean—did she use her war magic? She must have—there was no other way for her to fight back against Acri. But the thought both worried and encouraged Evariste.

Because if Angelique had resorted to using her war magic... just how much pain had she suffered through for the past years?

"How could she have overpowered *you*?" Liliane demanded. "After all your years of training?"

Acri took a step backwards. "She used her war magic." His

usual smug bravado had entirely failed him. Though he spoke plainly, Evariste could see the fear in his eyes.

He's afraid of his own mother?

"She isn't *trained* in her war magic! Luxi-Domus abhorred her powers," Liliane snarled.

"She's learning now," Acri said. "I poured everything I had into my weapons, and I couldn't get them back."

"No." Liliane shook her head, a sharp expression settling in her eyes. "No. She is feeble with her powers—I made *sure* of it. It is your failing that you couldn't eliminate one bumbling *apprentice*!"

"I was forced to confront her in Zancara—she purposely flashed her magic and brought the local government down on us," Acri rushed to say. "*And* she summoned that wretched constellation!"

"You should have killed her before she had time to do either of those things!" Liliane shouted, her mint-green magic flickering in her anger.

"Please." Acri dropped to a knee. "I won't fail you again. Next time—"

"There will be *no* next time," Liliane snarled. "It seems you are not as skilled as I thought. Disposing of Angelique is a task that will have to fall upon someone more dependable and talented."

Acri's jaw shook with the strength with which he clenched it. After a moment, be bowed his head. "Yes, Mother."

Evariste thought the issue was finished, but Liliane grasped Acri's shoulder, her fingers digging into the muscle.

"You are no son of mine—not when you *fail*." Her magic swirled around her hand, spinning into a painful spell based on the veins in Acri's neck. But Liliane—her eyes glowing with fury—had no mercy on her own offspring. Instead, she clenched his shoulder tighter, making Acri wince with pain. "You will pay *dearly* for this mistake so it doesn't happen again!"

She roughly hauled him to his feet and stormed out of the cavern.

Her magic encircled Acri. He took several pained steps before the magic crackled, and he collapsed, spasming on the floor.

Carabosso, Suzu, and the other mage looked away from him as Acri hissed an exhale, his face red with pain.

"Acri!" Lilian's voice was as stinging as a whip crack.

The young war mage boosted himself to his knees and staggered after his mother, pain radiating from every muscle.

Carabosso waited until the mother's and son's footsteps faded before grumbling, "She'll be in a rotten mood for a month."

"It will only push her to come up with an even more ruthless plan." Suzu briskly set about covering Lilian's paints, then glanced in Evariste's direction. "You'll dismantle whatever spells you were playing with?" She gestured to the blue cloud of Evariste's magic that freely floated around the mirror.

"Of course," Carabosso said.

Suzu shrugged and sauntered from the cavern.

Carabosso sniffed and ambled up to Liliane's barely started painting.

Evariste watched him for a moment to confirm the rogue mage wasn't going to immediately dismantle the spell. *Now's my chance. They'll be occupied with Acri, and I doubt they'll leave my own magic unattended in front of me again in the next decade.* He leaned heavily against the mirror's surface and again placed his hands flat against the glass pane.

Tantalizingly, his magic swirled closer.

A glance at Carabosso confirmed the rogue mage was still rifling through Liliane's paintings.

"Come on," Evariste whispered. "Hurry up!" He tried to mentally reach out for his magic, but rammed into the unshakeable blocks that separated him from his abilities.

Even so, his magic brushed the mirror's surface, once again filling his senses.

Yes!

He tugged it into him, breathing faster when his magic willingly followed his direction. Working quickly, he wove it into a dispelling charm, then pushed against the pane. His limbs slipped through the surface as if it was liquid, and a moment later, he popped out on the other side, breathing fresh air for the first time in years.

Unfortunately, exiting the mirror sucked up every last drop of magic Liliane had left behind.

But he could *taste* freedom now—and smell it, too.

I'll have to subdue Carabosso—there's nothing in the room for me to hide behind besides the mirror or Liliane's paintings.

Quietly as he could, Evariste stalked toward an oblivious Carabosso. He held his breath as he grabbed the stool set in front of Liliane's easel.

Carabosso started to turn around, his eyes widening when he caught sight of Evariste. He opened his mouth—assumedly to shout—but Evariste brought he stool down on his head, and Carabosso collapsed, sprawling to the floor with splintered pieces of the now-dented stool.

Not my first choice of weapon, but it will do.

Evariste eased his shoulders back, stiffening when he heard the tap of footsteps. He darted to the cavern wall, pressing himself flat against its cold, rough surface.

The stomp of surly footsteps grew louder. "Carabosso." A somewhat familiar-looking male black mage trundled into the room. "What's taking so—" He paused when he saw Carabosso's comatose body.

Evariste darted forward and struck at the mage with the stool, but it glanced off a shield made of red magic.

The mage shrieked in surprise. "Suzu!" he shouted. "The enchanter is—" He gurgled when Evariste experimentally poked the shield.

When his finger sank through its surface, he struck, grabbing the mage by the neck.

He dragged the mage toward him and swiveled so he could ram the smaller man into the cavern wall.

The mage yipped in pain, but before Evariste could follow up the attack, hot agony bloomed on his back. He heard the crackle of fire and spun around, slamming his back into the rock wall and extinguishing the flames that had singed his clothes.

"How did you get out?" Suzu flicked another ball of fire at him.

Evariste lurched forward, dragging the black mage with him and thrusting him out in front to use as a shield.

"Don't throw spells at him," the black mage gurgled around Evariste's arm pressed into his throat. "You'll hit me!"

"That's a sacrifice I'm willing to make." Suzu eyed Evariste and summoned more of her magic to her fingertips.

Evariste stiffened, hearing more footsteps echoing down the hall. He shoved the mage at Suzu, making the two collide.

Suzu snarled as they went down, limbs askew.

Evariste sprinted past them, running up the passageway that led into the cavern.

The noise of footsteps and other mages grew louder, but Evariste ran headfirst toward it.

This is the only entrance and exit to my cavern. I've made it this far; I have to get out!

He blasted out of the passageway and skidded into a large central chamber lit with braziers made of black rock. At least six tunnels broke off from the chamber, disappearing into darkness with no differentiating marks pointing to the way out.

Unfortunately, Liliane stood at the side of the chamber, a bloodied (and very likely unconscious) Acri heaped at her feet. Already six other black mages careened into the room, their hands glowing with charged spells.

"Stop him!" Liliane shouted.

Evariste threw his stool at the nearest one, smacking her in the face with enough force to throw her off her feet.

Someone tried to chuck a ball of lightning at Evariste, but he ducked it and ran toward the biggest hallway that sprouted off the chamber, hoping it was the entrance to the cave system.

A black mage lashed out with ropes, catching Evariste's wrists.

Evariste tried to yank free, but in that time a scrawny, cloaked mage scurried forward and slapped him with a pain spell.

Agony raced through his body, eating at his muscles and knifing his head with such force he couldn't see straight.

I can't give in!

Evariste grit his teeth and made it a few more steps, just reaching the largest hallway.

"If you don't down him now—" Liliane screamed.

Something thumped the back of his head, and Evariste collapsed into the comfort of unconsciousness.

CHAPTER 10

Even after resting in a building for the first time since she set foot in Zancara, it took Angelique three days to heal her injuries and restore herself to full health.

She would have left after one day, but Pegasus refused to take her and knocked her over when she tried to walk the distance by herself. Sullen, but recognizing his wisdom, she returned to the inn and twisted her magic into more healing spells that would speed up the healing process.

On the third day she remained on her feet when the constellation tried pushing her, but it still took a lot of strenuous bargaining before he took her back to the spot where she had breached Zancara's wall. It was to no avail.

No matter what spell she used, she couldn't trace the black mage.

It had been a bit of a reach, considering she had met him briefly and knew nothing about him, but Angelique was bitterly disappointed.

After two weeks of trying and failing to cast any spell that could help, Angelique was forced to recognize that the lead was temporarily unavailable. She wasn't going to give up, though.

After all, the mage had said, *"He's been in our grasp for years."* Using that particular tense implied that if it was Evariste to whom he referred—which was most likely—Evariste was still alive.

So, Angelique wrote to Clovicus, Sybilla, and Severin of her findings with the hope that they might have additional insight.

After kicking up her heels for a day or two without any news or changes, she chose to ride Pegasus back to Farset.

(Officially, it was to inform Neely she had safely made it out, but it also gave Angelique the chance to ask the smuggler if she had heard of anyone else similarly employed who had dropped off a man in Zancara.)

Angelique sat on a barrel, her hands clasped in her lap to keep her from impatiently tapping the sides of her perch as she peered up at the dusty cobwebs stretched across the ceiling rafters.

She was back in the dress Evariste had ordered for her. At the moment, the cloth was shifting from a silvery blue to a pale red color.

Farraige was making notations in a log of some sort as she went through the sisters' "store" inventory, but every few moments, she glanced at Angelique and sighed.

"What is it?" Angelique asked, hoping to distract herself as she awaited Neely's return. (The smuggler was out speaking to the last few fellow smugglers she was on good terms with, to see if they knew who had brought the black mage over. If Neely was unable to find anything, it meant another dead end. Again.)

Farraige shook her head. "Nothing," she said innocently.

"If it's nothing, why do you keep sighing?"

Farraige slightly pursed her lips. "I was just thinking of lost revenue."

Angelique blinked. "I beg your pardon?"

"It's like this." Farraige put her logbook aside, then scooted closer to Angelique. "I'm really impressed you survived Zancara, yeah? I haven't heard of anyone who has made it out after putting even a big toe on Zancarian soil. But..." She sighed again.

Angelique finally gave into the impulse and tapped her fingertips on her barrel. "But?"

The slant of Farraige's eyebrows turned sorrowful. "I could have made so much money if you died, and I wrote a ballad about the ghost of the beautiful enchantress that now haunts the shores of Zancara."

Angelique stared at Farraige. "What."

Farraige impatiently pushed her hair out of her face. "People *love* a good drama, and Zancara's neighbors like to be told that *someone* is making the country regret—even a little—its isolation."

"You wanted me to die...for the sake of money."

"I didn't *want* you to die." Farraige made a scoffing noise at the back of her throat and rolled her eyes. "But it would have been better if you weren't so thoughtful and decided to let Neely know you made it out. She'll never let me release my song now that she knows you're alive—which is a real shame since I finished the first verse. It describes your sorrowful walk on the beach, your ghostly skin sparkling with shed tears. Would you like to hear it?"

"No, thank you," Angelique said.

"Are you sure?" Farraige started rummaging through the drawers of her rickety desk. "I should actually take this time to ask about your motivation. I decided to portray you and your Lord Enchanter as star-crossed lovers, forever separated even though your hearts are entwined."

Angelique almost fell off her barrel. "You *what?*"

Farraige paused in her search. "I'm not wrong, am I?"

"You are most *definitely* wrong!" Angelique shook her head to clear her mind of the mental disturbance it was experiencing at the suggestion. "On all counts!"

"Really? So sorry, don't know how I came to that conclusion—though it is a pity. Romance and drama, when combined, can really sell a ballad." Farraige scratched her head. "So you two weren't forcefully separated from each other?"

Angelique leaned against her barrel for support. "Er, no, we were."

"Oh. Then you haven't been searching for him for roughly four years?"

"Almost five, actually."

Farraige's eyebrows raised. "And you haven't given up yet?"

"No," Angelique said. "And I never will."

"Mmhmm. And didn't I hear you telling Neely that this Lord Enchanter of yours bought and ordered the dress you're wearing?"

"Yes," Angelique reluctantly admitted. "But I think you're getting the wrong impression."

"But am I *really?*" Farraige asked. She flicked up three fingers. "Because the way I see it you two were torn apart, you've been searching for years, and yet you wear a token of his affection. That's three for three. Are you *certain* you're not star-crossed lovers?"

Angelique was unable to speak in her horror.

She just—that is so incorrect—I am NOT...what?!

Despite her horror, Angelique was dimly aware that if Evariste could hear this conversation, he'd likely break a rib laughing.

The door to the small home banged open, and Neely strolled through. "Afternoon," she lazily called.

"Captain Neely," Angelique turned toward the smuggler, eager to abandon her conversation with the younger sister. "Did you find anything?"

"I'm afraid not. None of my fellows transported anyone—mage or otherwise—to Zancara. And there's no one else to ask, I'm afraid, as that covers everyone. Well, it covers all of the good ones, I suppose. Sorry, Lady Enchantress."

Angelique tried not to let her disappointment show. "Thank you for making the inquiries on my behalf." She sighed a little. "He got into Zancara somehow. But I suppose it's possible he got in the way we both got out—over the wall."

"That's not all the news I have." Neely glanced back over her shoulder. "I ran into a lad who was skulking 'round the docks. Said he was looking for you." Neely beckoned with her hand. "Come in, laddy!"

A familiar young lad—who would probably protest the idea that he was still a child—grinned as he strolled into the smugglers' home. He doffed his cap and bent at the waist—his scarf and snow-dusted cloak almost falling from his shoulders. "Good Day, Lady Enchantress Angelique!"

"Oliver." Angelique slid off her barrel in her surprise, recognizing the Chanceux Chateau stable boy and the loyal employee of Prince Severin and Princess Elle of Loire. "What has brought you to Farset?" *Has he grown again? But I only saw him a few months ago!*

"You have, Lady Enchantress." He smiled easily as he pulled a rolled-up scroll from his belt. "I have news from Prince Severin and Princess Elle."

"Oh?" Angelique took the scroll, surprised at its heft.

"Madame Elle meant to come herself, but His Highness forbade it," Oliver said. "He was going to send a Ranger, but Mademoiselle insisted it was unfair to keep her from coming if he meant to send a Ranger. I am their compromise."

Angelique laughed. "For that, I am grateful. It's lovely to see you again. Do you need to leave right away?"

"His Highness said he expected a reply." Oliver twitched his shoulders back, all seriousness.

"And you are to take it back?"

"Yes! It will be my honor." Oliver planted his fist over his heart and bowed.

"Very well, then. Neely, might I impose on you a bit longer and read my letter here?" Angelique asked.

The smuggler stretched her arms above her head. "Of course! Take all the time you need." She motioned for Angelique to sit in one of the creaky armchairs. "You, too, laddy. Set your feet up!"

Angelique hefted herself back onto her barrel, barely noticing when Oliver did as instructed and plopped himself down in a chair next to Farraige, who was giving him a calculated inspection.

Probably trying to judge if she can make any coin off him. A tiny smile cracked Angelique's lips as she unrolled the scroll. Her smile both broadened, then shrank as she saw what Severin had to say.

Lady Enchantress Angelique,
Elle and I have successfully organized a Summit regarding the darkness that we suspect is plaguing the continent. Most countries have agreed to attend. I would like to extend an invitation to you, as well.
Your expertise of magic and knowledge of all the events that have taken place over the past few years would be indispensable to the Summit. Please consider joining us.

The letter continued in much the same vein. The Summit—as Severin called it—was to be held in mid- to late-spring. Approximately a season away. It seemed most countries were sending at least one representative, and many were sending princes and princesses.

It was a good sign, for in sending their children—the future rulers of their countries—the royals were communicating that the problem was an important one, and that they were invested in seeing it through. Hopefully. (Though there was no telling for certain.)

There was one thing, however, that bothered Angelique about her invitation.

'Your expertise of magic and knowledge of all the events that have taken place over the past few years would be indispensable to the Summit...' Does that mean no other mage will be present? Did he try inviting the Veneno Conclave? I know from our conversation months ago that his priority is engaging the other countries, but surely he cannot mean for me to be their sole magical contact.

Angelique played with the rolled corner of the scroll. "Oliver?"
"Yes, Lady Enchantress?"

"Do you know if Severin invited anyone else from the Veneno Conclave to attend?" Angelique raised her gaze to the stable boy, who was drinking from a steaming mug.

"I apologize, Lady Enchantress, but I don't know. His Majesty expected you to have questions, however, and told me to extend to you an invitation to call upon him and Madame Elle at Chanceux Chateau whenever is convenient to you."

Ahhh, so this is merely the lure to draw me to him. There's no way we can adequately discuss this over a few mere correspondences. And with Pegasus willing to tote my carcass around, it would be faster just to speak with him.

She tilted her head while she mentally replayed Oliver's words. "Madame Elle, not Her Highness?"

Oliver grinned. "Madame Elle does not easily bear being called a royal and insists the household calls her Madame."

The thought made her smile for a moment as she let the scroll roll up. "I should have guessed. But, more importantly, I think I will forgo a reply and simply seek your master out post haste."

Oliver nodded, chugged the hot beverage in his mug—Angelique would have paid to find how he did so without scalding his mouth—and stood. "Very good, Lady Enchantress. His Highness said to tell you they will have a room ready for your arrival."

Angelique cocked her head at the wording. "And what will you do?"

"Follow behind as soon as I am able."

Angelique shook her head. "No, that's silly. Pegasus knows you, and you haven't gotten *so* big that he can't still carry us both."

Oliver's somber expression transformed into a mischievous grin. "I was hoping you might say that. It's why I volunteered to come!"

Angelique pushed her eyebrows up so high her forehead wrinkled. "You *want* to ride Pegasus?"

Some of Oliver's childishness returned in the shining of his eyes and the way he wriggled like an excited puppy. "Of course!

How many regular folk can boast a constellation has given them a ride? And his *speed*! It's a thing of beauty to behold!"

Angelique cracked a smile. "At least it seems you are in a position that suits you well. Do you have supplies or a steed of your own?"

Oliver shook his head. "His Highness rented me a horse from a stable—I returned him to the branch's local building when I first got here afore I started looking for you on the docks."

"Very well. It's late, but we can at least get some distance behind us tonight. I just have to pick up my saddlebags from my room and call Pegasus." Angelique swiveled so she faced the smuggler sisters, who sat together. "Neely, Farraige, thank you for your aid and hospitality."

"My pleasure!" Neely winked. "If you find yourself needing to go back to Zancara, I hope you remember us!"

Farraige smiled hopefully. "With all that has happened, are you still so opposed to the song that stands in remembrance of you, Lady Enchantress?"

"Yes," Angelique said vehemently. *The last thing I need is a rumor about Evariste and me being star-crossed lovers. That is something The Council would not overlook, even if I refuse to return to the Conclave to be lectured.*

"If you are so eager to make money off songs," Angelique continued, "why don't you write of the elves' absence?"

Farraige rolled her eyes. "You obviously haven't got a seller's sense, Lady Enchantress. A song about the missing elves would sell poorly. People love a good tragedy, but they don't want to be reminded of the real tragedies that haunt us in our waking hours."

Neely nodded, her expression serious. "She's right, Lady Enchantress, but fear not! I'll not let her release your song. We wouldn't be able to advertise ourselves as the first smugglers to successfully drop someone off on Zancarian soil *and* see them alive and out of the country if she had everyone singing about your death!"

Angelique stared at the pair. "I'm not sure which of you is more driven by the lure of gold."

Neely and Farraige exchanged looks.

"It's probably about equal," Farraige admitted.

Angelique shook her head. "Thank you—for everything the two of you have done," she repeated.

"It was our honor." The sisters bowed together—Neely giving Angelique a playful wink when she popped upright.

Angelique raised her hand in a last farewell, then motioned for Oliver to leave their home first.

Once outside, Oliver pulled his scarf tighter around his neck, trying to keep off the chill of the winter air. "Are we off to your inn next, Lady Enchantress?"

"Yes. I can't summon Pegasus in the city. Such close quarters would greatly displease him." Angelique glanced at her companion. "When he arrives, we'll still have to ask if he agrees to let you ride him before we set out."

"Of course!" Oliver said with a little too much enthusiasm. "And then, we'll *fly*!"

RIDING PEGASUS, Angelique and Oliver made absurdly good time, even though they stopped to spend their nights at inns.

As Pegasus galloped along, his flaming mane flickering in the winter wind, Angelique tried to calculate if it would be hours or a day until they reached Chanceux Chateau, when she saw a cloud of smoke smeared across the sky.

Smoke was not an unusual thing to witness, but the size of the cloud was troubling, and it had a dark shade to it that Angelique didn't find particularly comforting.

"Pegasus, could you pull back, please!" she shouted above the wind.

Oliver, who sat behind her, clinging to her waist, whooped. "This is a riot!"

When Angelique glanced over her shoulder, she saw the stableboy wore a smile so big it almost split his face. His face was red from the cold and the wind, and the tufts of hair that peeked out from under his wool hat were wild, but he seemed rather pleased with their pace.

Angelique spared him a smile. "I'm glad you are comfortable. But what do you make of that cloud?"

"Smoke?" Oliver suggested.

"Yes, but I'm not so convinced it's from something as benign as a kitchen fire," Angelique said. "Pegasus?"

Pegasus lifted his large head and sniffed, as if testing the air. He exhaled loudly through his nostrils, releasing hot puffs of steam, then tossed his head.

"You don't like it either?" Angelique asked.

Pegasus shook his head.

"I was thinking perhaps we ought to take a small detour and investigate it—it's not too far out of our way. Just a little more south than we need to go. Any objections?" Angelique glanced back at Oliver—who shook his head—then returned her gaze to Pegasus.

Pegasus puffed some more steam then shook his head again—making his flaming mane hiss and crackle.

He was off with a snort, kicking up snow with every stride.

Angelique felt her face might possibly freeze at the speed Pegasus galloped, making a wide curve that took them off their trajectory for Chanceux and toward the smoke.

They rounded a slight hill and a tiny copse of trees and popped out by a smoldering village.

Pegasus skidded to a stop, and Angelique felt all of the constellation's muscles tense as he pranced, turning in a tight circle that would have spilled Oliver over the side if he didn't have an iron grip around Angelique's waist.

The village was still intact, and it seemed that most of the flames were out. Two buildings were little more than charred remains—they, likely, were the major source of the smoke, particularly given that it seemed like both buildings were storage barns filled with hay and straw. Villagers ran around the rest of the burnt structures like ants, stamping out the few remaining flames. A few soldiers were aiding them, moving injured civilians to the undamaged buildings.

But that's not enough soldiers to make up a squad, so what are they doing here?

Angelique gazed past the village and saw an organized band of soldiers running from the village. They were kitted out in Loire colors and were clearly in pursuit of...*something*.

"Oliver, see if you can grab my spyglass from my saddlebags—please," Angelique said.

After a bit of rustling, Oliver passed the spyglass up. Angelique fitted it to her eyes and fussed with the lens for a moment, trying to get it to focus.

Abruptly, the far landscape focused, revealing what looked like ambling mounds of rocks and bark wearing a haybale on their heads.

Trolls.

Less humanoid appearing than their bigger cousins, ogres, trolls possessed a somewhat human-like frame and wore armor of bark or frayed animal hides. They had massive noses that poked out of the mess of their hay-like hair that erupted from their skulls and faces.

Trolls sometimes used crude weapons and occasionally fashioned headbands decorated with antlers or horns, but between their size (quite a bit taller than the average human, but not quite as large as ogres) and their dim intelligence, they were a danger more because they could flatten a village in their stomping temper-tantrums than because they could rip the arms off a man.

The Loire army was on foot, desperately chasing the pack of

five trolls. It looked like they had a few men on horseback, but it was unlikely they would catch up to the monsters—who would search out another small village and destroy it in their hunt for food.

"We've got to help them," Angelique decided. "Oliver, you need to get off."

"I'll pass, Lady Enchantress," Oliver said.

"This is *not* up for debate." Angelique said kindly but firmly.

"I won't get in the way—I promise," Oliver said.

The problem isn't you, but me. If my war magic slips from my control...

Angelique cleared her throat. "Oliver."

The stable hand sighed. "Very well. Be careful, Lady Enchantress." He slid from Pegasus' back and nimbly landed on the ground, twirling around so he could bow to them.

"We'll come pick you up after we stop the trolls." Angelique raised her hand to wave, but Pegasus was already striding off in a ground-eating trot. Another moment and he shifted into a thunderous canter.

They ripped past the village, then the Loire soldiers, creating a strong wind and sending snow swirling into the air. Pegasus passed by the trolls, then slowed down and cut to the side so they were planted directly in front of the incoming trolls.

Angelique clambered off Pegasus' side, her heart beating a little frantically as she stared down the trolls—that hadn't slowed and instead seemed to have increased the pace of their rolling, shambling run.

She started to pull her magic in as she pondered what sort of attack she could use.

Trolls are fairly susceptible to elemental magic, but considering I'm facing more than one, it would be tough to divide my attention and attack and hold them all with elemental spells. I could use an illusion of course, but there's no guarantee they'll fall for it. Perhaps it's time to get a bit creative...

Angelique took a deep breath. She hadn't faced many trolls.

The only one she could recall was the troll she had botched destroying when she was a new apprentice. And now she was about to face down *five* of them.

Her magic threaded through her fingers, and Angelique twisted it. She swallowed hard as the trolls galloped toward her, gaping grins twisted on their craggy faces as their eyes dimly lit with excitement.

Angelique's spell rested in her hand. *I have one shot to get this right*, she realized. *Or they'll trample me.*

With that cheerful reminder, Angelique spread her feet wider apart, digging her heels in.

She gritted her teeth, and the ground trembled as the trolls stomped closer and closer.

Angelique waited until she could *smell* them—they always stank of dank and stalled water. They were only a few horse lengths from her before she threw her first spell and scrunched her eyes shut.

Light exploded in the trolls' faces with a thrum so loud and so deep, it shook Angelique's bones.

The knock-back of the spell threatened to toss Angelique off her feet, but she was prepared and grimly remained upright.

The trolls, however, tripped over their feet and clawed at their eyes, the shining light having effectively blinded them.

Angelique hurriedly twisted her magic into a second spell and threw that one, as well.

It settled over the trolls in a murky cloud—a war magic spell that acted half like a sedative and half as a dazing spell. It made the trolls dumbly stay seated, blearily blinking and swaying as if they might flop over entirely.

Angelique noticed one of the trolls was only under a corner of the spell, and it seemed to be almost out from under its influence as it angrily eyed Angelique and started to inch toward her.

Angelique's war magic called to her—a tantalizing song of metallic notes. Vaguely, she was aware of every weapon the Loire soldiers carried on them, but she ground her teeth and shoved her core magic away.

The fifth troll took a swipe at Angelique, its grimy fingers almost brushing her skirt as she leaped backwards.

Angelique set her jaw as she poured more power into the spell that kept the other trolls dazed. She kept a wary eye on the fifth troll—which was trying to lumber to its feet—and ripped the ground open beneath the dazed trolls, creating a deep crack in the earth.

The trolls tumbled down, screaming as they fell. Angelique mercilessly slammed the earth back into place, crushing them all in one go.

The last troll roared, and Angelique hastily constructed an ice shield, making it large enough to provide cover for Pegasus as well.

The troll punched through the wall as if it were glass, and Angelique instantly raised another shield, thickening the original and encompassing the troll's fist so it was stuck, unable to pull its hand free.

It howled in anger and beat on Angelique's ice shield, making it crack ominously.

"Back up, back up, *back up!*" Angelique urged Pegasus as she hastily retreated.

The wall shattered with the scream of cracking crystal, sending shards of ice everywhere.

Angelique was already twisting a spell when the troll bound for her, but before she could fire it off, the creature abruptly stopped, then slumped over, dead. Several arrows and a well-placed spear protruded from its back.

Angelique raised her gaze to the incoming Loire troops. They marched intently toward the sole troll body, quickly surrounding it.

Their leader—one of the men mounted on a horse—directed

his steed in her direction, and Angelique recognized the coal black hair and stony expression.

"Prince Severin." She offered him a friendly but false smile as she tried to shrug off her leftover magic that still prickled around her. "I must say I am surprised to meet you here."

"I received word of some trolls bothering nearby villages." Severin dismounted his horse and made several discreet hand gestures to his men, who saluted and moved into a new formation. "Reports say they wandered in from Farset."

Angelique frowned. "*Farset?*"

"So my Rangers say," Severin grunted. "I am inclined to believe them, as the trolls left a clear trail of destruction in their wake." He rested his hand on the hilt of his sword and eyed the troll. "Might I add a belated welcome back, and a congratulations at being the first confirmed outsider to enter and exit Zancara in years?"

"Ahh, yes. It's a dubious achievement, but useful." She cringed. "Though given that I don't wish for the Conclave to learn I trundled through it, I would appreciate it if you would refrain from discussing it at the Summit."

He nodded. "Thank you for the detailed description of the country. I wish they hadn't chosen isolation, but I'm glad to know they haven't rotted with corruption or become the base for our enemy. Did you find any additional leads on the mage that attacked you?"

"No. The smugglers I worked with said no one admitted to dropping him off in Zancara's waters. Oliver found me at that point and delivered your message." Angelique glanced again at the soldiers surrounding the troll. "He's with me—I left him back in the village. We were on our way to Chanceux."

"Thank you for granting him passage," Severin said. "Though by your presence, I assume that means you have concerns?"

"About the Summit? Partially. I wanted to ask you a few questions."

Severin nodded and gestured north, toward the smoldering village. "Very well. Do you mind if we travel while we talk?"

"Not at all." Angelique meant to elegantly turn around, but she was unaware Pegasus was *right behind her*, and as a result slammed into his shoulder.

Pegasus snorted his version of a laugh—which was breathy and involved steam snorted from his nose.

Thankfully Severin didn't witness her embarrassment. He had turned back to his men, speaking to the soldier who possessed the most badges and braiding on his uniform. "Investigate the troll; see what you can uncover, then return to the village to aid with cleanup."

"Yes, sir." The soldier saluted him, then started shouting instructions to the rest of the unit.

Angelique climbed onto Pegasus' back, and Severin remounted his horse. The animal gave Pegasus the side eye and pranced for a few steps.

Pegasus ignored the horse the way one might brush off a fly and grumbled as he started off, his star-studded coat dazzling in the pale afternoon sunshine.

"I must beg your pardon for my poor manners," Severin began as his horse finally settled in and they rode side-by-side—Angelique markedly higher on Pegasus' tall back. "I have failed to thank you for your help with the trolls."

"I'm glad I happened to be on-hand to help," Angelique said.

Severin nodded. "We couldn't have caught up with them on foot. I would have had to go after them with a cavalry unit—and I'm not sure we could have mustered in time to catch them before they left Loire." He glanced at Angelique. "Watching you fight certainly showed what an advantage mages have over such dark creatures."

Angelique shrugged uncomfortably. "Enchanters and enchantresses certainly have an advantage, but not all mages could have stopped the trolls. It depends heavily on their core magic."

Severin's stony expression didn't shift much, except for an extra crease on his forehead. "Yes, I suppose that is true."

Angelique waited for several long moments, but it seemed he had nothing more to add. "I had a few things I wished to ask you about the Summit," she said.

"Ah, yes. How can I help you?"

"Are all countries sending a representative—besides Zancara, I assume?"

Creases formed around the corners of Severin's mouth, and his leather gloves creaked as he clenched his fingers. "Not quite. Mullberg chose not to send a representative. Queen Faina sent a letter explaining she saw no need for the Summit as Mullberg hasn't encountered any difficulties."

I would certainly hope *they wouldn't. It would be embarrassing to the highest degree if dark creatures ran amok in the Veneno Conclave's backyard.*

"Was there anything else you wished to know?"

Angelique pressed her lips together, considering her words. "I was wondering if you notified the Veneno Conclave of the meeting."

"I imagine they are aware of it, but I did not send them a specific invitation," Severin bluntly said. "I saw no point, given they have made it clear the Conclave is not in a position to help."

"It sounds like you've exchanged messages with them," Angelique observed. *Perhaps they would listen to* him*!*

"I have," the sour tone of Severin's voice was not at all encouraging. "It seems they are at least aware something is stirring, but I suspect they are afraid. Based on reports I've received from other countries, it seems like the Veneno Conclave is consolidating its forces at its base. Some high-level mages are still being sent out on assignments, but for the most part, it seems help will not be forthcoming," Severin said.

Angelique wanted to groan. She had thought if the Conclave heard how serious things were from a source other than her, they would maybe take the observations more seriously. *How can they just stand by? Perhaps Severin is wrong, and they are really that unobservant? But no...surely they must know between all the reports of curses and with master mages like Blanche and Rein going off. I would have thought they would have done* something! *Particularly after hearing how Stil was hunted down—though perhaps that only added to their fright?*

She stifled a groan. *If Evariste was here...*Angelique almost snorted at the thought. *If Evariste was here, my life would be drastically different right now. But he's not. Which means I need to talk to either Clovicus or Sybilla. A mere letter won't do this time.*

"Their reaction is why I have concluded that it is better not to include any other mages in our plans," Severin continued.

The announcement shocked Angelique from her thoughts. "I apologize—what did you say?"

"You and the few craftmages that have taken up residence in Loire as a result of Rumpelstiltskin's arrival will be the only mages present at the Summit," Severin said. "And I will not plan for mages in our strategizing."

Oh, no. No, no, no. We need to save the continent, which means I cannot be the only active magic user at their beck and call. I'll die of exhaustion! The continent is huge—even with Pegasus carrying me from one end to the other and the craftmages supplying charms, I cannot possibly help as much as he seems to think I can!

"I must beg you to reconsider," Angelique blurted out.

Severin glanced at her. "Oh?"

"Even if the Conclave seems unwilling to help, individual mages—particularly those who are more powerful or older and thus are more able to make their own schedules—might lend their aid," Angelique said.

Severin raised an eyebrow. "They would go against the Conclave?"

"Given that you are attempting a multi-country conversation, I doubt the Conclave would forbid it," Angelique said.

The edges of Severin's mouth angled down. "I do not want to build a plan and raise hopes that will be dashed." That announcement alone created a sour feeling in Angelique's stomach, but his next declaration turned her blood cold. "Combined with the Conclave's fear and the general lack of aid from mages, I fear our world is on the cusp of change."

"Oh?"

"Yes. It seems to me that the reign of magic is over."

CHAPTER 11

Angelique struggled to keep her expression placid as she listened.

Severin continued, "Previously mages were relied upon to provide support and peace, but that is no more."

His words were eerily similar to King Torgen's prediction. What was worse, Severin was a renowned tactician and was the commanding general of Loire's forces. He would not say such a thing lightly.

"Magic is not in danger of disappearing," Angelique said. "And the enemy we face—whoever it is—has magic at their disposal."

"I am not arguing the survival of magic, but rather the era it has ignited," Severin said. "Previously, the Veneno Conclave and all mages worked to fight any magical threat the continent faced. That is no longer the case. They are still respected, but as they are able to help us less and less, their political power naturally wanes."

"Perhaps it is true the Conclave has weakened in its resolve, but that is by no means a permanent thing," Angelique said.

Severin said nothing in reply, but Angelique saw something flicker in his eyes.

"You disagree?" she asked.

"The only way I see a reversal taking place is if the Conclave makes an abrupt adjustment, which would need to be almost volatile in its strength in order to stop its current trajectory. Even if Lord Enchanter Evariste returns, I do not know that he would be able to turn the Conclave from its path. I apologize, Angelique, but I fear that our hope must rest on you."

His words were a weight on her shoulders, threatening to crush her under expectations and duty.

No, I—I can't do this myself! He must be wrong—this can't be the end of magic. At least, I won't let it go without a fight. Fine, so the Conclave is a dead-end, but I know there are other mages that can help! "Severin," Angelique started. "I cannot be your sole magical support. I am already stretched past my abilities. I cannot handle much more. *I need help.*"

"And you think there are other mages who will offer their help?"

"Yes," Angelique said. "You just need to reach out to them on an individual basis."

"You say I need to reach out?" Severin asked. "You won't include yourself on the invitation?"

Angelique laughed outright. "No, I'm afraid if we did so, they would be more likely to refuse you. But I am good friends with a particularly popular and well-connected fairy godmother. I will approach her—I'm certain she will know whom we should invite, and who will be most sympathetic to the cause."

"Very well," Severin said. "If I might impose upon you, please contact her."

"It will be my pleasure!" Angelique almost bounced on the saddle in her joy. *Sybilla will know whom to ask. I can put up with their disdain and fear if it means I don't have to do this alone anymore!*

A small part of Angelique also rejoiced for magic itself. *This is one last opportunity for us to prove ourselves. To show we will not fade quietly into the pages of history, but that we will stand our watch and protect this land. This is not the end of magic—not by a long shot!*

Pegasus, picking up on her good mood, pranced a few steps. Angelique tried to cling to his back in as stately a manner as she could. "I think it would be best if I took several invitations that outline the purpose of the Summit when I call on Sybilla."

"Of course," Severin said. "I mean to return to Chanceux tomorrow. Please allow me to invite you to return with me. Elle will be pleased to see you again, and I will write out as may invitations as you desire."

"I don't wish to impose."

Severin made a noise that sounded an awful lot like a cat's short growl. "Believe me, it is not an imposition at all. Your presence might distract her for a week or so, which means I won't have to have triple the usual guard on her to make sure she doesn't get it into her foolish mind to run off on some self-assigned Ranger mission."

Angelique laughed as she recalled the last time she had come across the unusual princess—who had dressed up as a beggar woman and proceeded to beat senseless a man peddling black magic charms. "Can even a triple guard keep her from her adventures?"

Severin scowled darkly, but the light in his eyes made him seem happier than he had since the start of their conversation. "I imagine we'll find out when we return."

ANGELIQUE STAYED at Chanceux Chateau for a week—partially because she enjoyed her time with the prince and princess, partially because it took Severin longer than expected to write out all the necessary papers, *and* partially because it took Angelique some time to hear word of Sybilla's most recent location: southern Sole.

But with the fairy godmother's location confirmed, Angelique set out...because they *needed* to recruit more mages.

(And all the delicious food and beautiful flowers of Chanceux weren't enough to dispel Angelique's worry that if they didn't recruit more, she might be crushed under the weight of expectations.)

Even with her newfound competence in tracking spells, it took Angelique days to trail Sybilla, and she was more than a little bewildered when she found the fairy godmother crouched behind a massive bush that encroached on the shore of a small lake.

She appeared to be watching a clandestine meeting of a man and woman dressed in nondescript clothes. The couple was settled farther down the lakeshore and spoke in lowered, murmured tones.

Unsure of what she was walking into, Angelique cautiously settled an invisibility charm over her shoulders before she approached the older woman. "Sybilla?" she whispered.

"Hello, dearie!" Sybilla didn't turn to address Angelique or even seem surprised to hear her. (Given Sybilla was particularly gifted at sensing magic, this was expected. Probably.) She beckoned Angelique closer as she nudged a bush branch aside. "Fancy seeing you here! What's brought you to Sole?"

Angelique crouched down next to her before letting her spell drop. "You, actually."

"In that case, take a seat. You'll be here a bit." Sybilla invitingly patted the ground next to her, then peered back in the direction from which Angelique had come. "Where's that overgrown star of yours?"

"Pegasus returned to the sky for the night." Angelique glanced up at the sky—which was a swirl of blush pink and a fathomless blue. Only the brightest stars were out...and Pegasus' constellation. (Tonight he didn't bob around, but it seemed to Angelique he was not in the exact place he should be, either.)

"I see." Sybilla pushed aside a branch, going back to watching the man and woman, who were conversing with serious expressions.

"What are you doing here?" Angelique asked, more than a little curious. "Helping with a love confession?"

"Nothing nearly so romantic—but it's at least twice as fun! I'm here to uncover and punish an illegal trade route of stolen magical artifacts." Sybilla adjusted her spectacles with a cheerful smile that made the wrinkles around her eyes even deeper.

"I beg your pardon?" Angelique said after several moments of stunned silence.

"There's always been a black market for illegal or stolen magical artifacts," Sybilla said. "But it's gotten worse over the years, to the point where it has become downright troubling."

"Yes, I've heard as much."

Sybilla shook her head. "It's worse than you think. I found evidence that a Legendary Weapon from Sole was purchased through this route."

"A *Legendary Weapon?*" Angelique yelped.

"Try to keep your voice down, dearie," Sybilla said, as unconcerned as a summer day. "And yes. We'll have to tell the King of Sole—once his granddaughter wakes up, that is. But the Legendary Weapon is just the tip of what I've found, too."

She peeled back another branch of her bush and made a tisking sound. "Considering this is a transaction that was finalized on the black market and is now just waiting for the actual exchange, they undergo an *extraordinary* amount of polite niceties," Sybilla sighed. "I would have thought the illegal activity would have meant they wouldn't have to follow such bosh. But it seems they are even more determined to observe all unnecessary drabble. Yet another reason why it's despicable!"

Angelique shook her head, trying to come to terms with the fact that the illegal market had grown so powerful. *That a national treasure could be bought...how horrible.*

"Returning to your inquiry, I'm trying to poke holes in the market and, if I can, undermine it a bit," Sybilla continued. "This pair are sealing an exchange—swapping a payment of gold for a magic lamp. Once I witness the exchange, I'm free to arrest—or punish—both sides." She frowned and jabbed her finger at the woman, who was holding a small pouch. "And you can bet I'm going to lecture them for their longwinded talks. Come, now, stop hemming and hawing and *give him the lamp*!"

Angelique studied Sybilla, taking in her sky-blue robes and hair that was still salt and pepper and had not yet faded to pure silver—though Angelique had known her for years. "I was unaware fairy godmothers were charged with this kind of work."

Sybilla nodded without taking her eyes off the pair. "It's true most fairy godmothers search out magically gifted children, but some do specialize in finding ancient artifacts. Our attunement to magic has multiple uses."

"Including breaking up illegal trade rings?"

Sybilla chuckled. "Well, there are some privileges that come with age."

Angelique was not convinced. In fact, she was starting to suspect Sybilla was far stronger in her magic than most assumed. There was something to be said for her turtle-paced aging and that the Veneno Clonclave would send her out on missions like this one.

"Galloping Gargoyles—I hope the lamp curses one or both of them. Tracking this latest batch of black-market exchanges has been dead boring, but this rates near the bottom." Sybilla squinted in the dying light. "Did he just compliment her on the braid of her hair?"

"Should I leave and return once you have apprehended the pair?" Angelique asked.

"What? Goodness, no. I have time in spades until they decide they're people of action. What did you need to see me for, Angelique?" Sybilla gave her the warm and kind smile that had first brought Angelique to adore the older woman.

Angelique released the breath she had been unaware she was holding. "I need your help—or rather, your influence. Prince

Severin and Princess Elle are holding a Summit open to representatives from all the countries on the continent. The point of the Summit is to discuss the stirring of dark magic, and the trouble that's been breaking out across the land, and hopefully strategize a plan to address it."

"Bravo," Sybilla said approvingly. "And good for them."

"Prince Severin does not intend to send an invitation to the Veneno Conclave."

"I can't say I blame him," Sybilla dryly said. "Not with the astounding degree of uselessness we've been the past few years—your actions excluded, of course, dear."

"I'm not surprised either," Angelique admitted. "And even if he did extend an invitation, I doubt the Conclave would send a representative."

"Wait, wait, wait. This might be it...." Sybilla eagerly leaned forward as the man and woman shifted. "...Or not." She pushed up her spectacles and grumbled. "Perhaps they are new to this trade and are thus incredibly incompetent. Regardless...please, continue, Angelique."

Angelique slowly nodded. "But the idea of failing to invite any mages—besides myself and Rumpelstilskin and a few other craft-mages—to this Summit doesn't sit well with me."

"Oh?"

"Yes." Angelique hesitated a moment. "Severin said something that bothered me. He thinks the reign of magic is ending, that we won't be as important in the future."

"You don't like the idea of losing power?"

"No, it's more that those of us with magic are privileged, and we have a duty to help those we can. If it's not our time anymore...if we're not important...that means we aren't helping others and are wasting our gifts."

"You're not wrong," Sybilla agreed.

"I asked him if I could invite, then, individual mages who are concerned with the continent and are aware something must be done about it."

"I'd call you bold, but I've been told Prince Severin *and* Princess Elle would kill for you, so I suppose I owe you a 'well done' instead."

"You assume he said yes?"

Sybilla snorted. "You're here, aren't you? Besides, after all you have done for him, he'd be a royal donkey if he refused you something so little."

"Erm." Angelique didn't quite know what to say to that, so she chose to avoid it entirely. "He gave me a bundle of invitations. I was hoping you might help me decide whom to invite...and that *you* would be willing to send the invitations."

Sybilla peeled her gaze from the pair of degenerates. "You're afraid no one would come if you sent the invite," she said, seeing straight through Angelique as usual.

Angelique pressed her lips together and slowly nodded.

Sybilla sighed. "Some days I have half a mind to track down your instructors and give them a good thump for the anguish they have inflicted on you. But I suppose, when you do come into your own, you are going to be a force to reckon with."

Angelique blinked. "Is that a yes or a no?"

"Oh, I'll help you, indeed," Sybilla returned her gaze to the traders. "The magical community has let you carry the bulk of this burden for far too long. Yes, I know a good number of mages we can invite who *will* be interested in helping—and will act on it, too." The older woman abruptly stiffened. "I think this is it."

Angelique peered through the bush and saw the man and woman make an exchange. The woman handed over a pouch to the man. He opened it, and there was the faint twinkle of gleaming gold in the last few rays of the sun—the magic lamp.

He passed a satchel to the woman, who crouched down and twitched the flap open.

Angelique only briefly saw the coins mounded in the satchel before the woman nodded and stood.

"That was the exchange, and so here we go!" Sybilla smiled cheerfully at Angelique, but when she stood and marched around the bush, her expression turned stormy. "By order of the Veneno Conclave, you are under arrest for the illegal sale of stolen magical artifacts!"

"What?" the man yelped.

The woman threw something at them—which turned into roaring flames shaped to resemble a panther.

Angelique lunged out from behind the bush and threw her arms up, raising an iridescent shield over herself and Sybilla.

The flames slammed into the shield, pushing Angelique back a step and baking her face with the heat of the spell. But when Angelique pushed back, the flames were snuffed out, leaving a wisp of smoke behind.

"Ho-ho, good catch!" Sybilla chortled. "You really have improved over these past few years—and you were already quite talented to begin with!"

"Thank you." Angelique readied another spell as she eyed the illegal traders.

The man gaped at them—his eyes bulging like a fish out of water—but the woman turned on her heels and tried running.

"Oh no, you don't," Sybilla grumbled as she pushed up the sleeves of her robe. "Be *tortoises!*"

Puffs of oddly colored smoke obscured both traders, and a bang popped loud enough to echo across the lake.

Angelique dropped her upturned hands. "You turned them into *animals?*"

Sybilla swung around long enough to grin. "What, you think it's inhumane?"

"No." Angelique peered at the ground, spying the charred charm the woman had thrown at them. She tested it to make certain it had used all the magic it was charged with before carefully picking it up. "It's just...it takes a lot of skill and power to turn humans into animals."

Sybilla laughed loudly. "When you get to be my age, boldness gives you a power you never knew you had!"

I highly doubt that is the single reason she can manage such a transformation. It was impressive when she turned Duchess Cinderella's animals into humans for an evening, but this is an even trickier—and more dangerous process. I didn't know that anyone less than an enchanter or enchantress could even do such a thing unless they had shape-shifting magic, and I thought Sybilla was most gifted with alteration magic...

Angelique trotted after Sybilla, who was still marching ahead, her robes fluttering with her confident strides.

Angelique caught up with her by the time they reached the spot where the man had stood. Sitting in the grass was a tortoise small enough to fit on her palm. Next to him, tossed heedlessly on the ground, was the magic lamp half poking out of its sack.

The tortoise (man?) was in shock, apparently. He didn't move until Sybilla scooped him up. Then he started to wiggle, his limbs paddling the air.

"You'll face a trial, of course, once I get you back to the Veneno Conclave." Sybilla placed the tortoise in a mesh sack, then very carefully picked up the magic lamp and squinted at it.

Angelique tried to get a read on the lamp, but while she could detect the trace of magic threaded through the object, she couldn't tell much more than that. Sybilla, however, had no such problem.

"Yep, as I thought." Sybilla held out the sack so Angelique could toss the used charm inside it, then carefully knotted the mouth shut. "Cursed." She ambled over to the woman-turned-tortoise, who was still attempting a getaway—though her new body didn't seem to listen to her very well; she tilted from side to side and seemed unable to walk in a straight line.

"The lamp is?" Angelique clarified.

"Yep. Not unusual, you know, to think you're buying a magical item on the black market only to be cursed when you try to use it. Charmed artifacts are tricky. As decades pass, it seems like the magic tends to leak a bit and ends up giving the items a bit of, shall we call it…personality?"

"Like the Legendary Weapons of the Magic Knights of Sole," Angelique said. The concept of items with *"personality"* didn't bother her much, mostly because the likelihood that she would ever have to use them was quite low.

"Precisely." Sybilla scooped up the woman-tortoise and placed her in her own mesh bag. "Goodness, the two of you are heavier than you ought to be. Anyway, as a result of their quirks, magic artifacts don't much like being stolen, so it's not unusual for some of them to end up cursed."

"I'd heard of such a thing, but I haven't seen a cursed item before." Angelique watched the fairy godmother balance carrying the tortoises and the lamp. "Do you want me to drop the letters off for you at the Veneno Conclave?"

"Don't be silly—I can take them now," Sybilla said. "Or they might not make it to their intended recipients in time."

"Yes, but it looks like you have your hands full…"

Sybilla picked her way across the rocky lake shore, the tortoises making unhappy chirping noises. "I'm staying with a friend in a town not far from here. Accompany me there, stay the night, and drop your letters off."

Angelique took both of the complaining tortoises from Sybilla. "I'm afraid I cannot spend the night, but I will walk you back to your temporary residence."

"Can't stay? Are you late for a love tryst? Evariste will disapprove, you know," Sybilla said. "Actually, he'd be downright snarly about it the more I think of it."

Angelique warred between snorting at the thought of being involved in a love tryst and laughing at the thought that Evariste would *care* if she had one. She missed Evariste deeply, but she wasn't so lost to the pain of his absence to think he would be bothered—though now that she thought of it, he would probably make a few joking remarks about Stil's misfortune to have his "parents" separating.

That was something else she missed—his humor. (As inappropriate as he could be.)

"Speaking of Evariste, I'm sorry your lead from Zancara didn't pan out," Sybilla continued. "At least, I assume you weren't able to find anything more since you sent your letter?"

Angelique's good humor faded. "No, nothing." She tightened her grasp on the mesh bags.

Sybilla made a tisking noise. "You can't be upset with yourself—you were attacked in an already extremely *dangerous* land. It's impressive that you even survived the encounter."

"But maybe he could have led me to Evariste!"

"Maybe, or maybe not. The important thing is you survived to fight another day, *and* you confirmed Evariste isn't in Zancara."

Angelique pressed her lips together in an effort to keep her caustic thoughts to herself.

It seems like every possible lead I get in finding Evariste, I just mangle! Failure after failure—no matter how fast I learn to cast magic or how well I can now fight off a pack of monsters. And how is Evariste being punished for my failure?

"Every place you confirm Evariste *isn't* narrows your search," Sybilla said.

"I know most every place he *isn't*," Angelique sighed. "And it hasn't helped me much because I still cannot find him!"

Sybilla patted her shoulder, and they walked in silence for several minutes. "At any rate," the fairy godmother began. "You really ought to stay for the night."

"It would be rather rude of me to stay the night without your friend's permission," Angelique said. "And I am afraid most people wouldn't want me to stay anyway."

Sybilla scrunched up her mouth and looked like she was about to unleash a storm on Angelique.

"Regardless," Angelique was quick to say. "Whom do you think you'll invite to the Summit?"

"There're a few craftmages who will be interested—though I'd be surprised if Stil hasn't already contacted them. Those craftmages gossip worse than a bunch of noble ladies," Sybilla grunted.

"Severin confirmed a number of them have already taken up residence at Chanceux Chateau."

"I'd expect as much. Clovicus should be invited—though it's doubtful he'll be able to come—and Finnr, of course. Perhaps—"

"*Finnr?*" Angelique swung around so fast to face Sybilla, she almost knocked the tortoises/illegal traders into each other.

"Yes, he's a downright stick in the mud, but he's a good mage." Sybilla rolled her eyes. "As much fun as a bitter plum, but he's smart when the mood suits him."

Angelique licked her lips. *Finnr has always disdained me—and it seems like his distaste would only grow since I no longer toe Conclave rules at all times. His presence will make the Summit just...wonderful.*

"I see." Angelique was proud she was able to keep her voice even, but Sybilla narrowed her eyes at her.

"Don't you worry, dearie," she said. "I'll see to it that he keeps his mouth shut—no promises about his disapproving glares, though I suppose he looks at most *everybody* that way. But Finnr and I go far back. If we wish to strategize against this enemy of ours, we'll need him. I swear it," she grimly finished.

Angelique numbly nodded and resumed walking. "I see... then...whom else are you thinking of?"

"There's a mage with healing magic who might prove a proper ally—if Clovicus can't make a break for it, he'll be a good second. And then of course we should try to get a weather mage or two... are those two mages who report to you from Sole—Firra and Donaigh—are they coming?"

"Yes, I should extend an official invitation to them, though I have mentioned it in the past."

"Good, that will cover the war mages then..."

EVARISTE'S MOUTH WAS DRY—as if he had been sleeping with wads of cotton clenched between his teeth.

He was stiff, and his limbs seemed excessively heavy. Even rolling over onto his side took a great deal of effort. When he peeled his eyes open, his vision was so blurry, he couldn't make anything out besides dim light—though he did hear the crackles and pops of flames.

Where am I? The last thing I remember was running for the bigger hallway, and then...pain.

"You shouldn't have tried to escape," Liliane said.

Evariste blindly peered through the gloom, trying to make out any blob that could be her. "Pardon?"

"Or rather, it was a good thing we found out you are more capable than we believed, but your living conditions are about to get far worse as a result."

Evariste's eyes finally focused, allowing him to see Liliane standing in the shadows just outside his mirror. "What?" he said in a voice as dry as sawdust.

"We can't keep you here." Liliane perched on a chair, her skirts puffed around her. The scarlet light of the torches made her pink gown glitter red like blood. "We will *not* leave you here. While your magic has had its uses, it's become apparent to me that it—and you—are too much of a risk."

Evariste pushed off the ground so he sat up, his arms shaking from fatigue as he set his palms on the cool floor. *Just how long have I been out of it?*

"If we keep you in a magically induced sleep, you become useless to us; we cannot harvest your magic if your powers are dormant with you," Liliane said.

"So what?" Evariste said. "You're going to kill me, then?" He unflinchingly stared Liliane down, holding her gaze.

I knew this was more than a possibility. The longer they hold me captive, the grimmer the chances of survival become.

Liliane smiled, and Evariste exhaled.

I see. Death it is, then. The thought didn't frighten him—he had been through too much for that, and as a Lord Enchanter, he was always prepared to put his life on the line. But he was disappointed. *I would have liked to see Angel one last time...*

"Death would be an escape," Liliane said. "One I don't intend to allow you. Besides, if you're dead, you're just as useless to our cause as if you were sleeping. No, we shall use you in other ways."

Evariste scratched his chin. "And how do you intend to do that? Slowly dismember me?"

"Not at all." Liliane happily clapped her hands. "You'll be used to power our greatest weapon. It's practically an honor—though I expect it will be painful. You'll probably long for the familiar walls of this cave."

Evariste tried not to perk up, but he couldn't keep the surprise out of his voice. "You're taking me from this place?"

"Yes," Liliane confirmed. "But you won't be conscious for the trip. Instead, you will be punished for your actions."

He coughed. "Punished? After what you've put me through, do you *really* think you can do much more?" he scoffed.

Liliane's smile grew, but instead of brightening her complexion, it turned sinister. "Yes, in fact. Because this time it's not pain we'll be using—at least, not pain of the physical sort."

Evariste narrowed his eyes in suspicion. "Oh?"

Liliane stood and slowly approached the mirror. "I feel sorry for you, Lord Enchanter Evariste."

"Are you even *capable* of such a feeling?" Evariste asked.

"You have no idea what you're in for. You can't even *fathom* the power that waits for you once we move you. You think you're brave to make an escape attempt and brave to mock us."

"Not at all," Evariste said. "I merely don't care what you think of me, so there is no reason to hold back what I am thinking. Which reminds me, please let me take this moment to say that your fashion sense is more that of a demented fairy than aesthetically pleasing."

Liliane's smile fell from her face, and she coldly stared Evariste down. Abruptly, she thrust her hand in front of her and twisted. Her vile, mint-green magic dropped from her fingertips and rammed through the mirror, striking Evariste in the gut.

His innards cramped and spasmed, and sweat broke out on his forehead. He groaned, "What happened to a punishment that wasn't physically painful?"

Liliane's beautiful face turned cold and ugly with her sneer. "Just remember as you live through your nightmares, Angelique will *die*. Acri failed me, but I have hundreds of mages at my bidding, and hundreds of thousands of creatures at my fingertips. And after dealing with you, I'm not inclined to grant her the mercy of a swift and clean death."

Evariste laughed outright. "You are right, Liliane. I *am* sorry."

"Oh?" She shifted a step closer.

"Yes." Evariste savagely grinned at her. "Sorry I won't be here to watch when she rips you to shreds—and she will, Liliane. Every time she uses her war magic, you lot should cower in *fear*. And *when* I get out and am reunited with my apprentice, together we'll dismantle your forces until only *dust* remains."

Liliane blasted more of her magic at Evariste. It felt like something was eating away at his organs.

He grimaced and jerked in pain when Liliane yanked magic from him. It clouded around her in a blue mist. She muttered something guttural and black, and his magic surged forward. It dove through the mirror and slammed into him.

For a moment, he was enveloped in red-hot pain, and then everything was dark. Several long moments passed, and Evariste considered the blackness.

Hm. As a punishment, this isn't bad. The perpetual gray of the mirror was starting to drive me mad. This is almost...welcome.

Heavy breathing came from behind him.

Alarmed, Evariste swung around and froze in fear.

"Evariste, lad!" Clovicus staggered across the black landscape, blood dribbling from the corner of his mouth. "You have to run!" He fell to the ground with a wet cough.

"Clovicus!" Evariste threw himself to his knees and grabbed the older enchanter's arm. His skin was warm to the touch, and Evariste could *feel* the faint flutter of his heart.

"They got us." Clovicus winced and pushed his copper hair—matted with blood—off his forehead. "You have to...flee. Or else..." He grimaced, and his breath became more labored. "Or else..." He gurgled and fell silent.

"Clovicus?" Evariste's tongue stuck to the roof of his mouth as he shook his master's prone body.

"Evar."

Evariste yanked his gaze up.

Emerys, dressed in his kingly elf robes, stared sorrowfully at him. "How could you curse us?"

"It wasn't me—it was the black mages!"

"How could you lead them to us?"

"I tried to resist!" Evariste stood and took a step closer to his friend.

Emerys shook his head, his forehead wrinkling. "My people are *dying*, Evar. I'm..." He paused, then blinked as blood bloomed on the shoulder of his robes. "...dying."

The Elf King collapsed, struggling to breathe.

No...not this. Evariste stared in shock and grief at the nightmares playing out before him. He tried to close his eyes, but it was to no avail. Eyes shut or open, the visions were there.

Liliane was right. This is worse—far worse.

CHAPTER 12

Spring finally arrived, and after attending Stil and Gemma's wedding, Angelique elected to use the weeks leading up to the Summit to continue the search for the black mage that had attacked her.

She found no clues—not even a whisper of who he was or where he had come from. It matched the pattern of the black mages who had taken Evariste, which further convinced Angelique he knew where Evariste was.

She checked in with Donaigh and Firra—who had recently visited the sleeping city of Ciane—for a report on Princess Briar, submitted a report of her encounter with the black mage to the Veneno Conclave (although she carefully screened the exact location of the fight) and then chose to travel to Loire early.

Arriving before the Summit started would give her time to speak to Stil, and she had many things to discuss with Prince Severin and Princess Elle. She wanted to inform the royal pair of her arrival, which sadly meant she had to venture to Noyers first —where the toady Prince Lucien lived—before she traveled on to Chanceux Chateau.

Unfortunately, the prince and princess were rather pre-occupied, for—Angelique learned from Oliver, who was stationed in Noyers to take care of his master's and mistress' horses during their stay—there had been an assassination attempt on Prince Lucien the morning of her arrival.

It seems our enemy has given up all hints of subtlety and is now focusing on eradicating the largest threats. But I am baffled, for I don't know that Lucien is a danger to them. He's smarter and more grounded than he pretends to be—that much was obvious when I met him while Severin was still a beast in mind and body. But what kind of impact can he have that would make our enemy determined to wipe him out?

Angelique followed a butler through the winding halls of the Noyers palace, smiling awkwardly when he stopped outside an ornate door and rapped on its polished surface.

"Enter," a male growled, barely audible through the door.

In a smooth, practiced move, the butler opened the door and bowed low. "Lady Enchantress Angelique," he announced.

Angelique held in a sigh as she marched into the room—which appeared to be a salon of sorts with comfortable, well-padded furnishings and gold leaf applied everywhere. (The Loire monarchs seemed to find great comfort in gold. Perhaps there was a strain of dragon blood in their family?)

"I believe I have introduced myself to every servant in this palace—at least twice each—as an enchantress-in-training." Angelique smiled—knowing that if she didn't, the sarcasm in her voice would leak through in a most inappropriate way.

Severin bowed. "My Lady."

Elle was not nearly so taciturn in her reaction. She skipped across the salon and threw her arms around Angelique in an embrace. "Angelique, you've arrived early for the Summit!"

"I have." Angelique glanced from Severin to Lucien. "Though it seems you have already started the events without me."

Charm oozed from Lucien's smile as he strolled up to her. "Lady Enchantress Angelique." He took her hands and kissed them, his lips lingering a tad longer than was polite. "You are as stunning and beautiful as ever. Your mere presence brightens this room. For the sake of my heart I must ask, when shall you respond to my sonnets of love for you?"

He seems rather calm and blasé considering he was nearly assassinated this morning. One might think it's because he's foolish, but after seeing his franticness when Severin was hurt...could he really be this good of an actor?

Angelique hid her thoughts behind a mask of polite interest. "Prince Lucien, I'm glad to see you are in high spirits despite your dangerous experience this morning."

"Oh, it was nothing." Lucien took another step toward the enchantress. He didn't even blink when Elle openly elbowed his side. "But I am ever so pleased you have come to Noyers and the palace. As long as you are a guest here, I shall see that you are treated with every respect and courtesy."

When it looked like he was going to go in for another session of hand kisses, Angelique ripped her hands from his grasp. "Yes, thank you. However, I will not remain here long. I intend to impose on Prince Severin and Princess Elle's hospitality and stay at their chateau this evening."

Lucien's smile only grew. "How delightful! I, also, intend to stay with dear Severin and dear Elle."

His sister-in-law eyed him. "Since when?"

Lucien tugged on his waistcoat. "Since right this moment."

Severin blinked slowly, like a big cat. "I was unaware my wife had become dear to you."

Lucien chuckled. "Of course she has! After all, she's so..." He trailed off as he stared at Elle with carefully narrowed eyes. "Well, at least her bangs are finally cut evenly."

Elle magnanimously ignored the observation—probably because Lucien had shifted himself out of elbowing range. "Based on your entrance, Lady Enchantress, I assume you heard of Lucien's encounter with the rogue mages this morning?"

"Please, just Angelique. And I have." Angelique, feeling

Lucien's eyes on her, made a hasty retreat to stand by a window and hopefully look thoughtful in the process.

The corners of Severin's eyes crinkled. "Is there any sort of spell you could cast on him? Perhaps any protection charms?"

Lucien, surprisingly—or perhaps not, given his personality—rolled his eyes and seemed the most unconcerned about the attempt on his life. "Come now, you two sound like a pair of worried mothers! One assassination attempt is hardly frightening enough to begin requiring spells and charms."

"Second," Severin said.

Lucien frowned. "What?"

Severin met his gaze. "This is the second attempt."

Lucien's care-free persona dropped briefly, and his whole body tensed. "What are you talking about?"

Though the announcement surprised Angelique as well, she felt too awkward to say anything, for this seemed like a rather private discussion meant for siblings only—not outsider enchantresses.

Severin rested his hand on the back of an armchair. "Do you recall last week when we spent the morning in your study, discussing the most recent Ranger reports?"

Lucien nodded.

"Shortly after you left to have tea with Madame Belladonna, refreshments—which I found to be poisoned—were brought to the study."

Lucien's handsome and open face shifted into a scowl. "And you didn't think to tell me?"

Elle and Severin exchanged glances as Elle drifted closer to him. "We assumed Severin was the intended target and didn't want to worry you."

Ahh, that makes more sense. Severin is the one organizing the countries, after all. Given how little the Veneno Conclave has managed to do, it would not be unfounded to say he is—at this point—the greatest threat to our enemy.

Angelique stifled the desire to rub her temple and glanced at the princes and princess. Elle's gaze worriedly shifted from Severin to Lucien, while Severin watched his brother, and Lucien stared at the floor.

Better break this up before it really does become a family drama—we have too much at stake to waste time squabbling right now, and I want to get out of this city as quickly as possible.

Angelique cleared her throat. "To answer your question, Severin, I'm afraid there aren't many defensive spells available to use on humans."

Elle tapped her lower lip. "Would Craftmage Stil and his wife Gemma be able to provide a better alternative?"

Angelique tilted her head back and forth as she considered the idea. "Perhaps, if you meant for Lucien to walk around in a suit of armor at all times of the day, but even that has its limitations."

"Yes, now I absolutely need wine." Lucien stalked to the door and bellowed into the hallway. "Wine!"

Perhaps he is a tad more shaken than he lets on.

Severin ignored his brother and pushed his shoulders back, like a crouching panther. "You said there weren't many spells available to use on humans," he said. "Does that mean they can be used on animals?"

Lucien snorted. "Worried about your horse, are you? Though, now that you mention it, it wouldn't be a bad idea to have a spelled cavalry."

Angelique interlaced her fingers together as she considered Severin's question. "There are a number of very powerful strains of defensive spells that can be placed on small animals. They've existed for well over a century or two, but thus far no one has been able to adapt them for human use."

Severin folded his arms across his chest. "What kind of spells?"

Angelique strained her memory for the answer, trying to recall her long-ago lessons with Evariste that had covered the subject. "There's a certain charm that makes it impossible to shoot the creature—mostly because every time you set your eyes upon it, the spell will make your eyes water. There is another spell that will allow land animals to swim like fish, a charm that will let them survive small exposures to fires, and a particularly powerful spell that can make a creature, for all practical purposes, indestructible."

"Indestructible?" Elle asked, intrigued.

Angelique resisted the urge to scratch her nose—wouldn't be seemly as an enchantress—and recited, "They can be dropped from a third-story window and incur no harm. Though that particular spell only works on creatures that are smaller than a tea tray."

"If the spells have no use for humans, who bothered to design them?" Elle asked.

"A very powerful enchantress who owned a dozen cats and small animals," Angelique said. (She had first looked into the spell as she considered casting it on Puss, but the cat had refused—he insisted he could properly protect himself with his own magic.)

Severin rubbed his chin in a calculating manner. "I see."

Lucien's handsome smile was twisted into a scowl as he watched his half-brother. "What are you thinking?"

There was a knock at the door, and a butler entered the room with the wine Lucien had previously yowled for.

This happily distracted Lucien, who was pouring out the wine before the butler even left the room.

Severin waited until the crown prince was sipping the drink before he asked, "Is it possible to temporarily turn a human into a small animal?"

Lucien spat out his wine, spraying it all over. "No! Absolutely not!"

Angelique barely managed to hold in a cackle of glee at the prince's obvious horror.

"The situation is dire, Lucien," Severin said in a firm but coaxing voice. "We should investigate all possible methods of protection."

Lucien clutched his chalice. "I am not spending my days as a housecat."

Elle smiled winningly at her brother-in-law. "But *dear* Lucien, it would be for your safety."

Lucien jabbed a finger at her. "Not a word from you. *Severin* is at least genuinely motivated by fear and affection. You just want to laugh at me!"

Elle nodded unapologetically. "I do."

Angelique pressed her lips together as she measured out the request. *If I do enough prep-work, it will be safe enough. It's the instantaneous human-to-animal transformation spells—like the one Sybilla used—that are more dangerous. I haven't done something like this by myself, but I managed to put all of Ciane to sleep. One transformation spell can't be worse than that.*

Besides, it would do my soul good to see the flirtatious Lucien as something odious!

Angelique tried not to sound *too* happy as she spoke. "A transformation spell would take some preparation, but it could be done."

Lucien turned around to face her. "Even you have abandoned me, My Lady?"

"Would you research it, Angelique?" Severin asked.

Angelique knew her smile bordered on blinding, but she couldn't help it. (This was the first bit of fun magic she would have casted in ages!) "It would be my pleasure!"

Pouting, Lucien folded his arms across his chest. "You three cannot be serious."

"I hope it won't come to such drastic measures, but I will do whatever is necessary to protect you, brother," Severin said.

Lucien sighed and rubbed his eyes. "Bother the lot of you."

Elle laughed.

Angelique hid a smirk behind a hand and was tempted to discuss the transformation process in detail, but, unfortunately, she had questions about the Summit. "If you pardon the change of conversation, when do you expect other Summit attendees to arrive?"

"Most are scheduled to arrive over the next few days." Severin began to sift through a package of papers he had brought with him.

"Gemma and Craftmage Stil are greeting the Ringsted representatives. I estimate they will arrive in two days or so," Elle said.

"That's right," Angelique recalled. "You meant to send them to greet Prince Callan of Ringsted and Princess Dylan of the selkies once Gemma and Stil finished their wedding celebration, yes?" Angelique asked.

"Yes. I felt rotten for doing so, but Severin and I could not venture to the ocean to meet them," Elle said.

"They understood. Any news of the mages Sybilla invited?"

"We received multiple acceptance letters," Severin confirmed. "It seems we'll have a good clutch of mages present as well."

Angelique relaxed at the news. "I am gladdened to hear it is so." She glanced at Lucien, who had put away his moody frown and was now eyeing her again.

I better make my exit.

"If you will excuse me, Your Highness, I will check into the spell you inquired after," Angelique said.

That brought the scowl back to Lucien's lips, but before he could protest, Severin bowed his head. "Of course, thank you."

"I'll see you out," Elle offered with a wink. She, thankfully, waited until they quitted the salon before adding, "You can ride straight to Chanceux and do your research there, if you wish. Lucien will take ages to ride over—he'll have to agonize over his clothes for a good hour or two."

Angelique let herself laugh. "I appreciate your intuition. Thank you."

"Of course! Tell Oliver he can ride back with you as your guide, if you like. The staff have already prepared a room for you."

"Thank you for your thoughtfulness."

"Not at all—it is we who should be thanking you."

Angelique accepted the comment with a nod, then paused when she realized Elle had stopped walking. She turned back to the princess with an inquisitive look and was surprised at the seriousness that glimmered in Elle's normally laughing green eyes.

"I mean it, Lady Enchantress," she said. "I don't know that any of this would have happened without you—the Summit, certainly not Severin surviving his curse...*any* of it."

Angelique felt the tension that made her hold her shoulders back and her head up decrease slightly. "It is my duty and my honor. I only hope that mages can continue to step in as help and support—as we should have long ago."

Elle nodded. "We can hope," she hesitated, then added, "Do you have time to meet with my father-in-law before you leave for Chanceux?"

Angelique tried not to let her surprise show on her face. "By father-in-law, you mean King Rèmy—ruler of Loire?"

"Yes." Elle bit her lip and glanced at Angelique. "Both he and Severin wish to make a formal request that you place protection spells on Lucien. After that little meeting, I suspect they'll ask you to cast the indestructible spell on him."

Angelique arched an eyebrow. "Even if it means turning him into a small animal?"

Elle nodded. "Lucien doesn't have the greatest sense of self-preservation. My father-in-law thinks he's oblivious to how bad things on the continent are right now."

Angelique considered the princess' words. "You disagree?"

"I think he just doesn't care very much about his *own* life," Elle said. "If it was Severin experiencing these assassination attempts, Lucien would be foaming at the mouth. I suspect he thinks Severin's life is worth more than his."

"That's a very sad thing," Angelique said.

Elle sighed. "I agree. But will you meet with them? As soon as he can give Lucien the slip, Severin will join us."

Angelique pursed her lips. *This is another piece of political meddling that would give the Council a conniption. But if something happens to Lucien, it will have repercussions in Loire. Given that they are the strongest ally I have right now, I can't afford to let them stumble.*

But even beyond that... Angelique stared at the ground as she recalled the bone deep fear in Lucien's eyes the night Severin had been transformed. It wasn't fear for his life, but rather fear for his half-brother.

Lucien deserves to be protected. He might act like a toad, but when he truly loves, he loves deeply.

"I agree to a meeting," Angelique said.

"Thank you, Angelique." Elle laid a hand on Angelique's forearm and squeezed, shocking Angelique with the sudden affectionate contact. "It seems Loire will always be in your debt."

THE FOLLOWING AFTERNOON, a knock roused Angelique from work. She tossed a lock of her hair (a champagne/brunette color today) over her shoulder and stared down at the scrawl of spells she had made while forging the transformation spell for Lucien. (King Rèmy had indeed asked her to protect Lucien, as Elle thought he would.) "Come in."

A maid opened the door with a curtsy. "Lady Enchantress, several other magic users have arrived and wish to call upon you. May I show them to your room?"

Angelique glanced around the chamber, eyeing it to make certain she hadn't made anything too untidy during her short stay. "Yes, of course. Thank you."

The maid slipped from the room, and Angelique set about

stacking her sheets of paper, studying them one last time before she set them on her nightstand.

I'm reasonably certain I have the pre-work correct. All I need to do is cast it on Lucien.

A twitch of her fingers, and the spells—which Angelique had been carefully constructing all morning—faded. (The spellwork was set in all the parts. It would just take a nudge from her powers and a twist of her magic to bring them back. But she wasn't keen to have the other mages see exactly what she was doing. It was doubtful any of the mages attending the Summit—with the exception of Sybilla—would approve of turning a prince into a *frog!*)

Angelique glanced at the armchairs and settee placed in her room. (Elle had arranged for Angelique to stay in the family wing of the chateau rather than stay with the other guests. Angelique assumed it was because they were short on rooms.)

It's likely Sybilla. I don't believe anyone else that she wished to invite would ever think of actively seeking out my presence. Unless it's Stil and Gemma?

Her stomach sloshed with anxiety, and Angelique *hated* it.

They dislike me. I already know they dislike me. So why does it even matter who is coming and what they think of me?

Angelique's thoughts briefly returned to one of the many times she had reported in to the Council, and Lazare—the oldest Council Member who seemed half mad and frequently slept through meetings—had blurted out that the Council feared her.

The ruling body of magic users fear me—it can't get worse than that.

A gentle tap on the door signaled the maid's return.

"Come in," Angelique said.

The maid swung the door open. "Lady Enchantress—"

"Thank you, dearie!" Sybilla patted the maid on the shoulder as she edged past her and stepped into Angelique's room before the maid could announce her presence. "Angelique! I'm surprised you're housed here in the family wing—or maybe I'm not! How are you?"

Finnr lurked behind Sybilla, his stony expression clearly indicating his disapproval. With him was a portly man with thinning hair whom Angelique recognized as a healing mage, and a lean and leggy middle-aged woman Angelique *thought* was a craftmage. (The scent of leather and clay that followed her was something of a giveaway.)

"Hello, Sybilla." Angelique stooped slightly so she could embrace the older woman. "I hope you had safe travels?"

"Yes. I caught a ride with a few other mages." Sybilla patted her hair. "A frail, old thing like me can't be too careful, you know."

Finnr scoffed openly.

"Nonsense, Sybilla," the portly man chortled. "If you're frail, then I'm on my deathbed!" He smiled warmly at Angelique. "It's a pleasure to finally meet you, Apprentice Angelique. I've heard a great deal about you—but no one mentioned how lovely you are!"

Angelique had the rather rare feeling of being caught off-guard. "Thank you?"

"Where are my manners? Introductions should be made." Sybilla slapped her blue robes for emphasis. "This is, of course, Apprentice Angelique—the dear student of Lord Enchanter Evariste. She'd be an enchantress by now if not for those stodgy rules that say she can't take the examinations without him."

"She'd be *a lot* of things if not for those so-called stodgy rules," Finnr rumbled.

Sybilla ignored him and patted the rotund man on the arm. "This man—an example of decorum and charm particularly when compared to other males in the room—is Sano, a GrandMaster Healer."

His eyes crinkled merrily as he bowed. "Again, my pleasure."

"You might have heard of Craftmage Glaze from Stil." Sybilla gestured to the woman, who gave Angelique a short and snappy nod.

"And, of course, you've met Finnr." Sybilla whacked the mage in the ribs with enough force to make him crumple. "He's a GrandMaster Snow and Ice Mage. He could be a fairy godfather if he wanted, but he's so stony, children are afraid of him, which would put a real dampener on his career."

"Children do not *fear* me," Finnr growled.

"Oh, sorry." Sybilla turned back to Angelique and gave her an exaggerated wink. "It's because he hates kids."

Finnr narrowed his eyes and sneered a little, but he ignored the fairy godmother in favor of turning his stony gaze on Angelique. "It was *you* who suggested Severin invite individual mages?"

"Craftmages were already gathering here—particularly since Stil arrived," Angelique said.

"Yes, but craftmages have the freedom to peddle their wares where they wish as long as they follow payment guidelines," Finnr said. "Most of the mages Sybilla decided to invite are not usually allowed that freedom. And yet, you ask us to take a role in something the Veneno Conclave hasn't sanctioned."

"They haven't forbidden it." Sano rested his hands on his round belly. "And listening to the countries discuss the troubles that have befallen them does not go against the Conclave's code of ethics."

"Perhaps on its own, it wouldn't be troubling," the female craftmage, Glaze, said. "But given that it was Apprentice Angelique who suggested such a thing when she has already shown a general disregard for Conclave rules and regulations..." She shrugged.

Angelique started to lower her gaze and give in to the sensation of shame, then paused. *Wait, I don't care what she thinks*, she realized, half-shocked. *The Veneno Conclave has done so little, and they still haven't found Evariste. I really don't give a hoot if my so-called "disregard" upsets them.*

In her surprise, Angelique stared at Glaze, who seemed to misunderstand the look and shifted uneasily.

"Does it really matter what method was used to get you here?" Sybilla asked. "No one can deny that difficult times have befallen the continent. Similarly, it can't be argued that the Veneno Conclave is contributing in major ways—our proud organization is acting like a scared puppy with its tail between its legs. But just because our leaders are too frightened to face the darkness with raised fists doesn't mean we should follow suit. Or do you think it would not be a detriment if dark magic spilled on these lands?" Sybilla raised a silver eyebrow and looked at each mage in turn.

Sano nodded in agreement. "Very wise."

"It is." Finnr fixed his flinty eyes on Angelique. "But the presence of darkness is not an excuse to act wild—or to disregard ethics."

What have I done that disregards ethics? Yes, I have "meddled" by helping royal families survive, but I think it would be worse to stand by and watch them die! Angelique forcibly swallowed her reply—even if she didn't care if they scoffed at her anymore, she still needed their help. Releasing a tirade would hardly endear them to her cause.

"Well?" Finnr prompted.

CHAPTER 13

Another knock at the door saved Angelique from having to reply. "Yes?" she called.

Prince Lucien poked his head through the doorway. "Lady Enchantress, I am so *glad* to see you, as I missed your presence at dinner last night."

Angelique forced a laugh. "Yes, I was fatigued from my journey and thought it was best to dine in my room." *Because I was trying to avoid you.*

"I am sure," Lucien said. "I was going to ask if you would like to see the Chateau library—though perhaps this is a bad time given your company?" He curiously peered at the mages, oblivious —or perhaps uncaring—of the tension in the room.

This is my chance to end this conversation—because even Lucien's terrible flirting is better than this!

"Actually," Angelique smiled. "I believe we just finished our conversation."

Finnr did not look content, but Sybilla batted her hand through the air. "She's right, of course. Come along, everyone. Princess Elle spoke of refreshments being served in the gardens."

Sybilla sailed from the room, pausing just long enough to wink at Angelique before she was on her way, the other mages reluctantly trailing behind her.

"Then let's also make our retreat." Lucien offered out his arm, which Angelique ignored.

I should probably tell Severin that the spells are ready, so he can decide when to break the news to Lucien. Angelique shut her bedroom door and joined Lucien in the hall. "Where is the library?"

"Ah, I thought that offer might interest you. You always seem to be lurking in the palace library." Lucien furrowed his brow, perhaps puzzled by the thought the library was a desirable location.

"Though I have visited Chanceux Chateau several times, I have not yet seen the library," Angelique said carefully. "I have spent most of my time in the gardens."

"That's no surprise." A real smile temporarily flashed across Lucien's face. "Severin's flowers must be the best in the continent!"

Angelique could tell the moment Lucien's thoughts slipped from pride over his brother, for his smile was replaced with a sort of smug, smarmy grin. "We should tour the gardens together after I show you the library."

"I could not possibly monopolize your time for so long."

"Ahhh, but it's not monopolizing if I *want* to spend it with you!" Lucien actually *winked* at her and gave her a smile that said he clearly expected her to be impressed.

Instead, she had to suffocate the desire to punch his perfect nose. *I can't wait to transform him. I'm willing to cast the spell on him because I know by the affection he holds for Severin that he can't be all bad, but I will delight in his time as a transformed animal because he deserves every second of it!* "You forget your station, Your Highness," Angelique stressed the title. "You are a prince, to be shared by all."

Lucien puffed his chest up. "Perhaps you're right. But as you said, I am a prince—so who will try to correct me?"

I would like to. With a good spell—or perhaps even a fist. Ugh, he might be a good brother, but he's such a slimy little—

Unaware of her thoughts, Lucien blithely continued, "Will you not spend the afternoon with me, Lady Enchantress?"

"I'm afraid I will have to refuse," Angelique said through gritted teeth.

Lucien shook his head—assumedly because he knew it made his handsome appearance more woeful looking. "How could you be so cruel? My day shall be ruined if you do not agree to a stroll through my brother's gardens."

Angelique stopped walking. *Your day shall be ruined? Oh, I'll ruin it for you.* She turned to face the prince. "I'm afraid your day will be 'ruined' then, for you will not be going for a stroll—regardless of whether or not I accompany you."

Lucien tugged at his ridiculously puffed breeches. "Whatever do you mean?"

Change of plans. I'm not going to give Severin time to warn Lucien. I'm technically doing this spell free-of-charge, so watching Lucien's reaction, instead, will be my payment. Angelique smiled, unable to keep true joy off her lips. "Due to the recent attempts on your life, both your brother and your father officially requested that I intervene and do whatever is necessary to see that you are properly protected during this insecure time."

For a split second, alarm twisted Lucien's face. He cleared the expression and instead stood taller and laughed. "You can't mean to..." His words died as he shook his head.

Angelique's smile turned saccharine as she flexed her fingers, and the spells she had worked on previously roared to life, ready to be used. "Oh, but I do. Please allow me to assure you that I take great pleasure in this act. Prince Lucien, I curse you to take the form of what you really are, a frog."

Her magic started to churn. Lucien eyed it, then ran. He made it three steps before Angelique gave the spells a little push with her magic, and they pounced on him.

He disappeared into a cocoon of silver magic, his angry yowls assuring her that the spells were proceeding beautifully.

Angelique sauntered up to the sparkling cloud of her magic. "Until *I* break your curse, or until a girl who finds you as distasteful as I do comes to love you and gives you *true love's kiss*, you shall remain a *frog*."

She felt the spell take, settling into Lucien's bones. She allowed her grin to show, and barely refrained from clapping at the delivery of poetic justice.

There was a splat—probably Lucien in his new amphibian body falling to the ground. When her magic finally faded, having finished the transformation process, it left behind Lucien, who had taken the form of a very large frog.

Angelique smiled broadly down at the transformed prince.

Lucien—still able to talk thanks to the adjustments Angelique had made to the spells—howled in anger. "What did you do to me?!"

"Exactly as I said: I turned you into a frog."

"A *frog*?" Prince Lucien's words were nearly lost in a croak. "Why?!"

Angelique studied her nails. "You needed to be small."

"Then you should have turned me into a kitten!"

"I could have," Angelique agreed. "But I just didn't want to. Now hold still—there are a few more spells I have to place on you."

Angelique could see the glowing spellwork of the indestructible spell and transformation spell, but there were a few other protective measures she meant to add.

There was a scuttle in the hallway, and Angelique glanced up from Lucien to smile at a tidy and pretty young maid.

The maid gave Angelique and Lucien a hurried curtsey, then scurried down the hallway without meeting Angelique's gaze.

But Angelique saw the way the maid had her lips pressed together in what was obviously barely suppressed laughter.

It seems I'm not the only one who thinks Lucien deserves this temporary body.

"Change me back," Lucien demanded. (There was a slight croak to his voice that was almost certainly a result of his form.) "*Now.*"

"I could not—not after agreeing to cast these spells at your father's request." Angelique batted her eyelashes at the frog prince as her magic twined around her fingers.

"You—" Lucien growled, but he wisely cut himself off. (He didn't have to be a *talking* frog, after all.) "Take me to Severin and Elle."

Angelique quirked an eyebrow. "Was that a request or an order?" she asked, her voice deadly pleasant.

Lucien was silent for several moments, then he began hopping down the hallway. "I'm going to summon a servant," he grumbled.

Angelique pressed her lips together, then called after the angry prince. "Severin requested this because he loves you, Lucien." She hesitated, then added. "He cares for you as much as you care for him. This, I know."

Lucien paused, then nodded—or at least it appeared that he *tried* to. (There must have been some adjustment to his new froggy body, for he nearly faceplanted with the gesture.)

Angelique watched him hop off. *I hope he proves worthy of the esteem Severin holds him in. I hope he becomes the terror of whatever enemy we face. Or I'll forever regret not turning him into a giant slug.*

THE SUMMIT'S informal opening was a large and lavish dinner. It was a glittering affair with porcelain place sets, a troupe of Torrens musicians plucking away at their instruments in a corner of the room, and flowers placed on nearly every surface. Of course, the royals in attendance were turned out in their best clothes, making the hall a sea of colorful silks, polished boots, and floral fragrances.

Angelique stood at the banquet hall entrance feeling a little green around the gills as she spotted the tables set aside for the magic users. Sybilla was absent at the moment, but Finnr—most notably—was not. (Clovicus had confirmed days prior he wouldn't be able to attend, so there was no use hoping for him.)

Where are Puss and Gabrielle? If they come down, I might be able to beg off speaking with the other mages.

The talking cat and crown princess had arrived with Fürstin Elise and four of the Arcainian princes that afternoon, just in time for Angelique to have tea with them. Unfortunately, neither the black-and-white cat nor the princess were present.

"Lady Enchantress Angelique!"

All of Angelique's air left her when someone slammed into her, gifting her with a rather forceful hug.

"I thought you would be here as well! Callan, come meet the Lady Enchantress!" Dylan—the exuberant selkie princess whom Angelique had encountered the previous summer—laughed as she hugged Angelique.

When Angelique was assured her feet were securely under her, she patted the selkie princess' back. "It's good to see you again, Dylan. I'm glad you have your voice back."

"Of course! You must meet Callan—my intended. We're getting married in early summer—I tried to send you an invitation, but it does not seem like it ever caught up with you." Dylan frowned a little, but the expression transformed into a brilliant smile when her fiancé, Prince Callan, caught up with her.

The prince was perhaps a hair shorter than Dylan, but he was handsome with sand-colored hair and an easy smile. "Lady Enchantress Angelique, I must thank you for helping Dylan in her time of need."

"Please, I insist both of you call me Angelique. And it is to my sorrow that I couldn't do more for you—or for Ringsted."

Dylan shook her head. "We've got it sorted out now—all it really took was our people working together. But I couldn't have done it without you sealing my voice."

"I see. I am glad you could make the Summit."

"Naturally, my parents recommended our attendance," Callan said.

The conversation was interrupted by a rather loud and throaty growl from Dylan's stomach.

The selkie grinned unapologetically. "Shall we go in? Maybe they have put out some food even if the dinner hasn't started yet."

Callan's smile was full of sympathy. "The ham and cheese platter you had an hour ago wasn't enough, was it?"

"It could have been a little bigger," Dylan nodded.

"I'm sure we can find something inside." Callan offered out his arm, his smile turning playful.

Dylan oddly laughed at the gesture, but set her hand in the crook of his arm. "Will you come with us, Angelique?"

Angelique glanced at the mage table—which still lacked Sybilla or Stil—and felt physically ill at the idea. "I believe I shall wait another minute or two."

Dylan nodded. "We'll see you inside!" She strode in, a whirlwind of smiles and laughter, with Callan at her side.

Angelique took a breath. *It's not so much that I'm afraid of the other mages, but I have no desire to sit there and be sneered at.*

"Lady Enchantress Angelique?" asked an unfamiliar female voice.

"Yes?" Angelique turned around and tried to place the beauty standing before her.

The woman was tall and lithe, with a set to her shoulders that said she was both comfortable with herself and unafraid—obviously she had trained with weapons at some point in her life. Her terracotta skin set off the aqua blue of her gown beautifully, as did her silky black hair—half of which was pulled up into an artful braid secured into a bun at the back of her head.

The woman curtsied. "You might not remember me. I am Princess Astra of Baris, daughter of—"

"King Solon," Angelique finished. She tried not to gape at the princess, having a difficult time reckoning the tiny princess who had scolded King Solon for his loose braids with the woman standing before her now. *I saw her multiple times as a child, but it seems Evariste and I haven't visited Baris since she grew up.* "My...you..." Angelique floundered, searching for an elegant way to note the princess' aging without blurting it out like an idiot. "You look lovely."

Astra cracked a smile, and her father's good humor played in her eyes. "I thought I ought to introduce myself in case you were unable to recognize me. At the risk of being as impertinent as my father accuses me of being, you are as beautiful as ever and have not aged at all."

Angelique's smile faded slightly. "Yes, I'm starting to understand that."

Astra tilted her head as she studied Angelique. "It seems, however, that you have become one of the most respected enchantresses on the continent."

Angelique slapped a hand over her lips just in time to capture the "HAH!" that threatened to explode from her mouth. When she thought she could speak without snickering, she cleared her throat. "I'm not certain *that* is true."

"Among royalty and countryfolk alike it certainly is," Astra said. "And I don't believe it is an undeserved title."

Angelique exhaled a sharp bark of laughter. "I doubt that. If I deserved it, I would have found Evariste by now."

"The Veneno Conclave has failed to find him," Astra pointed out. "You can hardly hold yourself to standards that an entire organization cannot meet."

Angelique shrugged a little. "Perhaps. How is your father?"

"I'd like to say he's old, crotchety, and moving slower, but the only reason he is not here is because he broke his leg riding a war elephant," Astra sighed. "He sent me in his stead to deliver our report."

Angelique frowned deeply and was stabbed through by guilt. "Have things been so grim in Baris, then, that you have needed to use war elephants?"

Astra snorted. "Not at all. It was a practice drill. No, we've been bothered by harpies—and there was one bad kraken attack on the shore. But we've been watching this develop for years, so this surge of darkness has not caught us as off guard as it appears to have other countries."

"I see. Regardless, I am sorry to hear of the harpies—and kraken, of course."

"As am I." Astra shifted so she gazed into the banquet hall. "I look forward to seeing how this Summit develops."

"Severin is an excellent tactician. And..." Angelique hesitated. *This is Solon's daughter. She, more than anyone, will understand.*

"I think we've reached a crisis point," Angelique said, finally.

Astra nodded. "Too much has happened," she agreed. "If you would excuse me, Lady Enchantress."

"Only if you call me Angelique."

Astra smiled. "It will be my pleasure. I look forward to speaking more with you, Angelique."

Angelique watched the Baris princess glide off to greet the new Verglas Queen.

"Angel!"

"Lady Enchantress!"

Angelique's shoulders almost stooped in relief as she saw the next crowd of Summit attendees. "Stil, Gemma, Mage Firra, and Mage Donaigh! I cannot stress how delighted I am to see you!"

Donaigh—who was first in line—performed a low and sweeping bow. "It is my honor and pleasure, Lady Enchantress Angelique."

"Donaigh, we've known each other for how long? The formalities are unnecessary," Angelique chided. The smile faded from her lips when she saw that Donaigh's hair was messier than usual—even though he didn't wear his infamous straw hat for the dressy occasion—and Firra—who ambled behind him—seemed a little pale and tired. "How go things in Sole?"

"Could be better—could be worse, too," Firra sighed. "We haven't caught Carabosso, unfortunately."

"And the princess?"

"Sleeps on," Donaigh said grimly.

"I'm sorry," Angelique said.

Firra shrugged. "There is nothing more you can do—you've accomplished beyond what any normal mage would have—or could have."

"You can say that again." Stil veered around the pair to give Angelique a side hug. "Hello, Angel."

"Hello, and congratulations, again, on your wedding." Angelique patted Stil's back, then leaned past him to embrace Gemma.

Gemma's slight smile betrayed her deep joy. "Thank you," she said. "And thank you again for attending."

"Of course," Angelique said. "Where is Hvit?" she asked, naming the white dog Gemma had transformed from a hellhound.

"In our room," Stil said. "It didn't seem proper to bring animals to dinner. Though if Roland—that is, Puss—is here, I imagine he'll attend."

"He and Gabrielle are here," Angelique confirmed, "along with several Arcainian representatives."

"Excellent!" Stil beamed. "Shall we go, then?"

Delighted with the additional tablemates, Angelique accompanied the others. She entered last and was surprised Firra and Donaigh marched toward the mage table, but Stil and Gemma peeled off in the opposite direction.

"Aren't you two sitting with the mages?" Angelique asked.

Gemma shook her head. "Not tonight. A close friend of mine is here, so we're going to sit with her."

Almost on cue, Queen Linnea, the Queen of Verglas, stood up. "Gemma, this way! I had Princess Elle reserve your chairs!"

Gemma smiled and waved to her friend while Stil eyed Angelique. "Will you be all right over there? Do you want to sit with us?" he asked.

"It will be fine," Angelique said. "I'll enjoy the chance to catch up with Firra and Donaigh."

"I see. Seek us out if they turn out to be a bunch of bores," Stil said.

"I will."

Stil and Gemma slipped off to their table, and Angelique took the tiniest step toward the table assigned to the mages.

"Angelique!"

Angelique startled when Gabrielle gently touched her elbow. The Arcainian princess was as beautiful as ever with her honey-crème hair and amber eyes.

"What perfect timing," she started. "We wanted to ask you to sit with us!"

"Who is this *we* to whom you refer?" Puss demanded from his perch on Gabrielle's shoulder. "Goodness knows I've seen enough of the mage brat already!"

Gabrielle made a show of tapping her lip. "That's odd, considering you spent the majority of the trip planning how we could spend the most time with Angelique."

"Quiet, you impudent thing!"

Gabrielle smiled, amplifying her natural beauty tenfold, and squeezed Angelique's forearm. "Say you'll sit with us?"

Angelique was about to emphatically agree, when Prince Severin and Princess Elle joined them.

"You *see*, Severin! You shouldn't have forbid me from placing Angelique at our table," Elle complained. "I *told* you she didn't have to sit with her fellow mages." Her playful scowl turned to a grin when she glanced at Angelique. "If you want to sit with the

Arcainian representatives tonight, at least promise me you'll sit with Severin and me tomorrow?"

Severin didn't rise to his wife's bait, and instead he stared into the room with what looked like resignation. "I didn't forbid you; I merely reminded you that you could not be a glutton with the Lady Enchantress' time given her popularity among our guests." He shifted his gaze from Elle to Angelique and continued, "I believe Colonel Friedrich of Erlauf wishes to sit with you soon to deliver a verbal message from his wife, Queen Cinderella," Severin added.

"Thank you for the invitations," Angelique said when all parties had finished speaking. "I am honored by them."

Puss snorted. "With the number of countries you've helped, it would be a pretty poor showing if they weren't all clambering for your attention. Come on—tonight you are ours." Puss crouched on Gabrielle's shoulder, slightly wiggled his bottom, then leaped to Angelique's shoulder. He butted his head against hers and purred deeply.

"Excellent—that means she's ours tomorrow," Elle said. "Have a lovely evening!" A grin and a wink, and she was off again, arm-in-arm with Severin.

Gabrielle finally released Angelique's elbow so she could lead the way. "I think our table is this way, Angelique."

Angelique scooped Puss off her shoulders so she could cuddle him in her arms. She cast a quick glance at the magic users' table as Firra and Donaigh joined them with big smiles and hearty laughter, but she didn't feel at all regretful as she followed behind the princess.

Puss placed his front paws on her shoulder and latched his claws into the fabric of her gown. "You might still be a bit of an outcast among the magical crowd, but I dare say you're beloved by many of those present."

"They're very thankful," Angelique agreed.

Puss lashed his tail back and forth as he thought. "It's more than that."

"Oh?"

"Indeed. They genuinely like you—Gabrielle is terrible at toadying up to important persons, and I don't imagine Princess Elle the spitfire is much better at it," Puss said. "They consider you their friend."

Angelique paused for a moment and glanced down at the cat. "Really?"

Puss shook his head in disgust. "Only you would be emotionally oblivious enough not to notice," he grumbled.

Is that why I was given a room in the family wing? Because I'm a friend?

Puss' claws pricked her skin, bringing her back to the present. She cracked a smile at him and hurried after Gabrielle. But through the delicious dinner and the hilarious antics of the Arcainian princes, Angelique wondered.

THE SUMMIT officially began the following day, and each representative—or rather each set of representatives—took turns describing their country's grievances. It was a process that took more than one day of meetings, given the depth of the troubles.

Most problems, Angelique was aware of—the goblins in Erlauf, the various crises of all the royal families, and even the harpies Princess Astra of Baris had mentioned at the dinner. There were also, of course, the missing elves, the twelve princesses of Farset who appeared to be cursed to wear out their shoes every night, and Princess Rosalinda and the city of Ciane that still slumbered together.

But although Angelique knew of the troubles due to the role she played in them, or just firsthand knowledge from all of her travels, there were a few unpleasant surprises that bubbled to the surface several days into the Summit.

Angelique shifted in her padded chair and glanced at the other mages. Only a few of the magic users sat together; for the most part, they had been sprinkled throughout the ballroom, seated between the various royals and representatives.

Angelique was seated far apart from them, nestled in with the crowd of princes (and princesses) Arcainia had sent. Puss and Gabrielle were on one side and Princess Elise on the other. (She couldn't say she regretted this decision, even if Puss' steady side-commentary almost made her laugh at inappropriate moments on four different occasions.)

"Is that frog of a prince dangling his *feet* in a *teacup*?" Puss' voice was crusted with disdain as he peered at Prince Lucien—seated at a table just behind Severin's seat. The prince was splayed out on a velvet cushion and was attended to by a well-dressed young woman who appeared to be contemplating flattening him if her look of disgust was anything to go by.

"A frog body is too good for him," Puss continued. "You should have turned him into a *snail*, Angelique."

"Shhh," Gabrielle murmured.

Puss twitched his whiskers at the chastisement, but Angelique was glad the princess had done so, or she would have missed Emperor Yevgeniy of Kozlovka's closing remarks.

"Sorcerer Rothbart's shadow has plagued my people for *years*," he said. "We need help—of the magical sort—to dislodge him if we are to provide any sort of support."

Colonel Friedrich of Erlauf studied the emperor with his good eye—the other was covered with a black eyepatch. "You've informed the Conclave?"

"Yes," the emperor said. "No help has come."

Angelique sat dumbly in her chair—until she noticed Severin staring at her.

Great. It seems like I get to be the Conclave's representative here. That will certainly make the other mages look favorably upon me—hah!

Angelique cleared her throat. "I will admit to the Conclave's fault in this area," she said. "But I believe we were only recently informed of your situation." She glanced at Finnr, who nodded in reluctant confirmation.

Emperor Yevgeniy shook his head, and the slight downward angle of the edges of his eyes made him look tired. "I am afraid I must disagree with you, Lady Enchantress. I have been sending messages to the Conclave for years."

Years?

Surprised, Angelique glanced at Sybilla, then Finnr. Both seemed as astonished as she was, their frowns deepening.

Unexpectedly, it was Princess Astra of Baris who spoke next. "I understand your frustration." She narrowed her eyes and studied the older emperor. "But I find it disdainful that one rogue sorcerer can occupy your entire country."

Emperor Yevgeniy clasped his hands together. "Baris is only dealing with harpies, are they not?"

"Yes, but that is likely because fifty years ago we managed to fight off a wave of dark magic," the princess said. "And we had to do that *on our own*. Neither the Conclave nor any of the countries here were willing to help at the time. Back then, we all warned you that it did not bode well for the future, but our cautions were ignored. And now you say you cannot handle one measly sorcerer?"

She glanced at Angelique, giving her an apologetic look—for one of the warnings they had delivered was given to Evariste and her.

Angelique smiled and waved it off.

Prince Severin stirred from his position at the head of the room. "Baris has proven its exceptional strength and its power of foresight. But not every country can do what Baris did."

"Arcainia did." Princess Astra shifted her gaze from Angelique to Gabrielle and then Elise. "Twice. Once with the ogre, and once with a witch."

"Indeed," Puss all but chortled with glee. "But Arcainia has proven to have an exceptionally smart royal family."

"Puss," Gabrielle hissed. "You're not helping!"

Thankfully, Crown Prince Steffen—Gabrielle's husband—smiled handsomely and chose to break the growing tension. "May I assume that I am included in my family as being exceptionally smart?" the prince asked.

"On average, no," Puss said. "However, you *did* make one brilliant decision in your life which negates that."

"Marrying Gabrielle?" Crown Prince Steffen guessed.

"Naturally," Puss agreed.

Many laughed—as the prince likely meant for them to. He dramatically rolled his eyes, until Gabrielle took his hand and rested it on the table. His warm love and affection for his wife broke through the act, and he raised Gabrielle's hand to kiss it.

"Please, continue, Emperor Yevgeniy," Prince Severin said when the laughter subsided.

"I stand firm on my previous statement. If Kozlovka is to help with the efforts of this Summit, the sorcerer must be taken care of, *first*," the emperor said. "Afterwards, we can provide troops and supplies, but I am not willing to discuss how many until a plan is put into place to eliminate the sorcerer."

"Have you any other threats?" asked the bushy-haired King Godfrey of Torrens. (His presence alone was enough to make Angelique groan, for it was the King's *parents* that Angelique knew quite well. Godfrey had been a mere child when she met his parents—who were blessedly still alive but had followed the Torrens' custom of passing off rulership and abdicating before reaching their dotage.) "Any problems besides the sorcerer?"

Emperor Yevgeniy briefly bowed his head. "There has been an infestation of mountain hags for the past few winters, but they don't concentrate in Kozlovka. Rather they travel from the northern mountains and pass through, journeying south to other lands."

"This, Loire can confirm." Severin shifted through several sheaves of papers. "Previous generations rarely saw mountain hags in our lands, but we've seen a marked increase the past few years."

The debonair Colonel Friedrich rested his forearms on the table. "We've seen a few in Erlauf, as well."

"We can help combat them," Emperor Yevgeniy said. "My troops are specially trained to fight them. But the sorcerer *must* be taken care of first."

"We got *that*. You've told us at least three times now," Prince Nickolas—aka Broken Nose Twin—scoffed. He grunted slightly when his youngest brother kicked him under the table.

"I agree," Princess Astra tilted her head back to study the Emperor with glittering eyes. "Though my feelings on the matter have already been voiced."

Yevgeniy's frown became more pronounced.

However, just as Angelique feared things might turn ugly, Prince Severin intervened.

"Kozlovka does indeed need help," he said. "I acknowledge Baris's strength and bravery, but the entire central government of Sole is shut down due to a curse cast by one rogue magic user. We must proceed with caution."

Most everyone nodded, and Severin's shoulders relaxed. "Mage Firra and Mage Donaigh are present as unofficial representatives from Sole. They are tracking down the aforementioned rogue mage. Could the two of you give a report?"

"Certainly," Donaigh said. "It's going poorly, and we haven't caught him. The end."

Though it sounded like a joke, no one laughed.

"Not all of the Magic Knights of Sole were bespelled to sleep in Ciane," Firra said, starting their real report. "They are forcibly holding the lines while the royal family sleeps..."

As Firra continued, Angelique felt the prod of eyes on her. She glanced around and met Severin's cat-like stare.

The prince's eyes flicked from Angelique to Emperor Yevgeniy and back again, before he finally settled his attention on Firra.

Angelique pressed her lips together. *What are the chances that little eye flick* doesn't *mean the sorcerer is going to become a magic user's task?*

ANGELIQUE'S SUSPICIONS were confirmed that night.

She was outside, trying to find Pegasus' constellation—for she had sent him back to the sky for the duration of the summit. Her heart warmed when she found him, and she plopped down on a cold stone bench.

"That besotted with the magic beast, are you?" Puss trotted out of Chanceux Chateau, his black tail held high like a flagpole.

Angelique smiled as he jumped onto the bench to join her. "It took a constellation to replace you—doesn't that speak highly of you?"

Puss twitched his pink and black nose. "I'd be flattered if I didn't know that seething creature of stars and darkness has claimed more of you than I ever did. How are you holding up?"

"Well enough," Angelique paused, then added. "I went to Zancara."

"You *what?*"

"Obviously, that bit of news should stay quiet," Angelique blithely continued. "I told Prince Severin, of course, but I'd prefer that no mages hear of it just yet."

"You're completely mad," Puss declared. "What would drive you to attempt to visit *Zancara?*"

"I didn't attempt; I made it in," Angelique said. "It wasn't quite what I expected—there was no drudgery or rampant evil. But I was attacked by a black mage who followed me in."

"You *what?*" Puss' voice was even louder with that echo.

"He spoke of Evariste." Angelique stared at her hands, feeling lost. "I think he knew where the black mages are keeping him. And I let him go."

Once again, the sour flavor of failure filled her mouth.

Puss was silent as he stared at her.

"Or rather, I wasn't good enough with my magic to fight him properly. I passed out, and Pegasus had to defend me."

The tale of the fight spilled from Angelique's lips—how Acri had chased her across the wall and nearly killed her in their fight.

"You didn't use your core magic?" Puss asked when she finished.

"No." Angelique groaned and let her head hang. "I'm starting to think I should have. Just like I should have when the nightmare and its rider attacked Stil. Did you hear about that?"

Puss nodded. "The brat told me himself when we arrived."

"I should have killed it. I could have. But..." She flexed her fingers. "I'm afraid of what will happen if I really grow skilled at it—if I come to rely on it, or worse, if I learn to *like* it."

"Power isn't necessarily evil," Puss said. "And if you ever hope to temper it, you'll have to use it first."

Angelique made a face. "You read that in a book, didn't you?"

Puss was quiet for several long moments. "No," he finally said. "It's what Evariste told me long ago when I complained to him that you wouldn't use your war magic."

Missing Evariste was an old ache by now. But remembering how he believed in her—and the proud way he would tell others he believed in her—that was as effective as a slug to her gut.

I was so blind to the quiet shows of support he made. I took them for obliviousness. If I could go back and do it again, I'd spend less time hiding and more time showing my appreciation—or throttling past me for my stupidity.

Angelique cleared her throat and chose to change the subject.

"Will you tell Stil about the mage and Zancara, if you get a chance? I didn't think to inform him, and I don't know if Severin ever discussed it with him. When I submitted a report to the Veneno Conclave about the attack, I purposely didn't mention where I was, and for now I'd like to keep that a secret. So as long as the other mages watch me with this continued, er, diligence I don't think I could tell him without one of them overhearing. But you...?"

"No one minds a cat—even a talking one. Yes, I know; I've used it to my advantage before." Puss narrowed his bronze eyes that glowed in the faint torchlight. "And while I detest the truth of it, nothing would bring me more pleasure than to deliver such a message under their very noses."

Angelique smiled at the malicious glee in his cultured voice. "Thank you. I appreciate your help."

"I will *always* help you, Angelique."

"As will I," Gabrielle added.

Both Angelique and Puss twisted on the stone bench to watch Gabrielle step out of the shadows. She was beautiful in the evening light in a pale blue dress that set her golden eyes and hair off just so.

"I was hoping to talk to you privately, Angelique." Gabrielle glided up to their bench, a small frown edging across her lips. "To be brutally honest, you look much more tired than when we first met."

"Current events have taken a toll on us all," Angelique said.

"Maybe, but I don't see any kind of difference in your fellow mages." Gabrielle narrowed her eyes and scowled back at the castle, Puss mimicking the expression.

Their anger thawed some of the iciness that ate at Angelique, but she knew her smile was sad. "Hopefully that will change now that they see the scope of what we're facing, even if we haven't a name for the enemy, yet."

Gabrielle snorted. "They should have seen it years ago. All

this Summit does is compile the evidence in a stack so thick that if they ignore it, they'll look like flaming dolts."

"Hear, hear," Puss said.

Gabrielle folded her arms across her chest and appeared to be settling in for a good lecture when the chateau door creaked as it opened.

"Lady Enchantress Angelique?" Severin bowed slightly to Gabrielle, then turned his gaze to Angelique. "If I might have a moment of your time—alone?"

"Come on, Puss." Gabrielle held her arms out and open. "Let's see if the others are ready for dinner, shall we?"

Puss glared at Severin. "I don't feel so inclined. I am almost certain this man is going to ask Angelique for additional help when she's already done more than one could hope for."

Angelique laughed, but the humor died in her throat when Severin bowed seriously to the magic cat.

"Though I cannot refute your words, I can promise I will make every effort that I personally can to see the continent through this."

"Hmm," Puss said.

"Puss," Gabrielle said, this time her voice more coaxing. "We can help her ourselves."

I doubt that. There's only one thing Severin is likely to approach me about—that sorcerer in Kozlovka.

It seemed such a thought hadn't occurred to Puss, for he sniffed. "Very well." He jumped into Gabrielle's arms and snuggled into her, resting his furry white chin on her shoulder—which also happened to give him the perfect angle to glare at Severin as Gabrielle glided away. "I'll be watching," he warned Severin before Gabrielle disappeared inside.

CHAPTER 14

Angelique stood and brushed off her skirts. "What seems to be the problem, Severin?"

The prince was quiet for a few moments as he rubbed his eyes. "There was another attempt on Lucien's life."

Angelique stiffened. "What?"

"A snake tried to eat him when he was in the gardens. Thankfully, the maid that's been escorting him was there and kept the thing from eating him until soldiers arrived and were able to kill it." Severin sighed, and the planes of his shoulders stooped deeply. "He survived and is unharmed thanks to the spells you cast on him, but the snake was clearly of magical origin."

"I'm glad my work was able to protect him."

Severin nodded. "I'm bringing in more soldiers—I will not let my brother be killed, and there's no telling if whoever is behind this won't go for an easier target—like one of the other royals." He hesitated. "What bothers me most is that they were able to get past all our defenses."

Angelique curled her hands into fists and crumpled the fabric of her skirts. "You think there is a betrayer among us?"

Severin rested his hand on his sword's hilt. "Not among those we have here. There's no indication of it; I fear we simply have been outmaneuvered in this case." He bitterly shook his head. "They're stronger than we imagined and far more cunning."

"There is a mage with healing magic present. Do you wish for him to see Lucien?"

"No, though I must thank you for your thoughtfulness." He hesitated. "Instead, I ask that you speak to the other mages about the sorcerer in Kozlovka and request their help."

Angelique almost smiled. *I'm not particularly excited to bring the matter up, but it's better than being asked to handle the sorcerer myself.* "I can, but you might have greater luck asking them yourself."

"Unfortunately, I don't believe so. I'm hopeful the mages who are here were moved by Yevgeniy's report, but going by the comments Rumpelstiltskin has made, they may be *less* moved to help if I ask them in any official capacity, as they will then feel they are meddling in politics. Stil says most Conclave mages are...*emphatic* about staying out of such issues. You, however, can portray the request as a matter of duty." Severin furrowed his brow, making his face look severe. "We need Kozlovka's help, Angelique. This latest attempt on Lucien is more proof that we are dealing with an actual enemy, not a series of coincidences. If we are unable to organize, it might be the end of the continent." He raised his eyes—which were nearly as cat-like as Puss's. "Do you disagree?"

"No." Angelique sighed, what little good humor she had accumulated leaving her. "We've had some wins to be sure, but every time I turn around, there is a new problem that must be tackled. I don't know if they are distractions or strategic strikes, but it is clear: we have an enemy."

"Will you ask the mages?"

Angelique raised her hands—palms up—in supplication. "When would you have me address them? For I would prefer not to hold such a discussion over a meal."

"Of course—I don't know that Elle ever means to let you dine with them at dinner anyway." He folded his arms across his chest and stared out into the dim gardens. "We've heard most of the reports that summarize the difficulties and troubles plaguing the countries. Tomorrow we will begin hearing from the representatives—specifically their thoughts on our enemy," Severin said. "We need to be in agreement that something is wrong, and there is an enemy behind it. I was going to suggest you mages have a separate meeting, for I do not wish to put any pressure on you given your vows to the Veneno Conclave, though I was hoping you would discuss the matter among yourselves and perhaps even begin to add up what you might do to help."

Angelique released a bark of laughter. "That won't be a tall order," she sarcastically said. "But it is probably a wise idea. Very well, I'll bring the matter of the sorcerer forward then."

"Thank you. I can arrange a salon for you to meet in—unless you'd prefer the library?"

Angelique bit her lower lip. "The library, please."

I don't know that it will make a difference for the meeting, but I'll feel better in a library.

"Consider it done," Severin said.

Angelique studied the illegitimate prince, noting the slightly haggard look around his eyes and the corners of his mouth. *Despite Gabrielle's observations, I do think Severin carries a burden—perhaps even more vast than mine. People look to me to solve individual problems, but he is willingly trying to wrangle countries—not all of whom get along—to fight together. And that's something not even magic can accomplish.*

"How are you?" Angelique asked.

"Pleased—or as pleased as I can be given the circumstances. Everyone appears to be taking the matter seriously already—which is more than I had hoped for." He looked into the shadows of the chateau and said in a louder tone. "Wouldn't you agree, Elle?"

There was the gritty noise of sliding rock, and Elle slid down the wall of the chateau, still wearing the elaborate gown she had worn during the meetings. "How did you know I was there? I am sure I was nearly silent!"

"Your perfume gave you away," Severin said.

Elle cursed under her breath. "That's what I get for wearing a rose scent to please you." She turned to Angelique and started to wriggle her eyebrows. "How about you, Angelique? Were you shocked?" She frowned a little and added, "You don't look it."

"I don't know that after my various interesting interactions with you, you could properly surprise me anymore," Angelique placidly said.

Elle made a tisking noise. "That sounds like a challenge."

"Please do not interpret it that way," Severin sounded tired—but more of an amused sort than the weary kind he had used moments before.

Elle shook her head. "It's my honor on the line. Next thing you know, your soldiers will be able to keep up with me, and my reputation will be in *tatters*!"

Severin squinted at the sky. "Most reputations are ruined by social scandals and the like."

Elle tapped her lower lip. "In addition to defending my infamy, I could pull a noblewoman's hair or kick a duke if it would make you feel better."

"You've already kicked a duke."

"Yes, well, he deserved it." Elle primly pointed her nose into the air.

Angelique laughed. "The two of you are such fun."

Elle cackled in triumph, but Severin looked pained. "I question your definition of the word *fun*."

Elle patted Angelique's hand. "No, I think our Lady Enchantress has it right, Severin. We should re-arrange tonight's seating arrangement for dinner so Angelique can sit with me again. She was supposed to before you intervened!"

"I specifically made the seating arrangement to keep you *away* from Angelique, and Crown Princess Gabrielle, and Princess Astra of Baris, and anyone else who might—knowingly or unknowingly—encourage your antics," Severin said.

Elle frowned. "I *thought* I've been stuck with a lot of stuffy dinner mates lately."

Angelique couldn't help it; she grinned and said, "You must have sat with Finnr, then."

"A tall male mage, frowns all the time and has a face like granite?" Elle asked.

"Yep."

"Oh, yes. I've been graced with his presence *multiple* times," Elle groused. "He hasn't a sense of humor."

"What a shame," Severin dryly said.

"But I've noticed when I bring up street magic, he gets a little line right on the bridge of his nose." Elle pointed to the spot, a devious grin twitching on her lips. "Naturally, this meant we had to have an in-depth discussion about it."

Severin rolled his eyes. "Heaven, help me." He turned to Angelique. "Thank you for your willingness to talk to the mages. Now, if you will excuse us, it seems I'll need to adjust tonight's seating arrangement. Again."

Elle, grinning widely, trailed in his wake, pausing just long enough to waggle her fingers in farewell.

Angelique smiled as she watched them go, then sat back on her stone bench. "Well, then. How am I going to convince 'granite face' that we should flaunt the Veneno Conclave's inaction and take out the sorcerer?"

Unfortunately, she had no answer.

SHE STILL HAD no answer by the time the mages gathered for the private chat in the chateau library the following morning.

The dark and serious tone of the meeting was not at all relieved by the equally dark atmosphere of the library.

Though the furniture was comfortable and costly (going by the detailed carvings in even the footstools), everything was darkly colored and large, and only a few curtains were pulled back, so as to protect the shelves and shelves of richly colored, leatherbound books from sun damage. (There were so many shelves, the place was very nearly a maze.)

"Someone needs to deliver a copy of all the reports we've received to the Veneno Conclave," Finnr said—his voice as cold as his magic.

"It's not a bad idea." Sybilla folded her plump hands together and rested them on the polished table. "Then we'll have proof, so when this enemy finally unveils itself we can say, 'we told you so.'"

Finnr gave Sybilla a scathing glare—to which the woman smiled cheerily in response. "No," he said. "Because the Conclave might be swayed into moving."

"Do you really think so?" Sano—the healer—settled deeper into his chair as he propped his arms up on the bulge of his belly.

"You don't?" Glaze, the sour craftmage, asked.

Sano shrugged. "The way the Kozlovkan Emperor tells it, he's been asking for help and submitting reports for ages. If a mage wasn't already dispatched to help Kozlovka, I think it's safe to say the Conclave won't be of much assistance."

Angelique was more than a little surprised with Sano's observation, but she elected to keep her mouth shut in favor of hearing someone else get scolded and chided about rules, for once.

"But why?" Firra sat up straight in her chair with fire in her eyes. "Why won't they do more?"

Finnr's frown became more pronounced. "It's possible the Council and other top officials in the Conclave are aware of the threat and believe it cannot be beaten at this time. Perhaps they are preparing for the worst-case scenario and are working to consolidate their power."

Severin had guessed as much, but it still was a bit of a shock to hear a mage admit to it—particularly one as rule-abiding as Finnr.

"I agree with Sano," Stil said. "It's not likely the Veneno Conclave is going to change its tune. At best, some laws and regulations need to be altered so we don't get caught with our trousers down like this again." He leaned back in his chair and glanced at Gemma.

She met his gaze, but swiftly returned to working on some fancy embroidery on what appeared to be a cloak. (Though she wasn't a mage, she was still welcomed to the meeting—partially because she was Stil's wife but mostly because all the craftmages had become absurdly fond of her due to her impressive skills as a seamstress. Given that craftmages needed high-quality goods to lace a proper enchantment into an item, she had become almost a hero to the finicky mages.)

"These laws have worked for centuries," a weather mage said.

"Countries have shifted, and dynasties have fallen," Sybilla cheerfully said. "It is naïve to think that we mages need not adjust to change as well."

"We can and should try to push for changes in our laws—they do need to be updated," Firra said. "But I doubt we'll get anything changed fast enough."

Finnr narrowed his eyes. "You intend to follow in the footsteps of Apprentice Angelique and flaunt your disobedience to Conclave regulations?"

Donaigh laughed and adjusted his straw hat. "You're a bit late to the tea party, Mage Finnr," he said. "Firra and I have been flaunting rules in Sole for the last few years. You know why?" He rocked forward and braced his hands on the edges of the table, his expression dark. "Because the Veneno Conclave's obsession with rules would have allowed Sole to fall. Lady Enchantress Angelique's so-called disobedience saved a *country*. What have *you* done lately?"

Angelique tried not to smile at the war mage's loyalty. *I don't think I've heard anyone besides Clovicus and Sybilla stick up for me since Evariste was taken.* When he glanced her way, she nodded her head in thanks, making Donaigh boyishly grin.

"*Apprentice* Angelique is not a Lady Enchantress," Glaze said, her voice harsh.

Donaigh snapped his attention to her and stood. "Yeah? Well she's done more than the lot of you put together—I'd say that makes her *better* than a Lady Enchantress."

Several mages frowned, and a handful of them exchanged dark glances while Glaze visibly bristled.

And that went a bit too far. I want help—I don't want to alienate them. "Donaigh," Angelique called, her voice quiet with a mask of calm.

Donaigh plopped back down in his chair, his posture once again lax.

"Such a war mage," Glaze muttered.

Thankfully, Donaigh didn't rise to the bait. Instead, he tipped his straw hat and winked.

Angelique shoved her hands under the table, then swept her gaze across the mages crowded around the table. "A general announcement was made earlier in the Summit to be on guard for black mages, but I wish to present an official warning to those here—particularly the Master and GrandMaster Mages who possess great power."

Sano sighed deeply. "Yes, I started making a greater effort to travel with others once I heard how Stil had been attacked."

"I was also attacked recently," Angelique carefully began. "By a black mage with war magic. I was in Kozlovka, near Zancara's border wall. I wrote a report on it, but I don't know that the Conclave released it yet."

It's a bit of a fib, but unless it's unavoidable, I don't think it would be wise to admit I went to Zancara. That will get them all set off again.

The weather mage scratched his chin. "I haven't seen your

report, but I am more than a bit behind with Conclave paperwork. You got away, obviously?"

"Were you hurt?" Firra asked as she inspected Angelique with a furrowed brow.

"I was injured, but my wounds have long healed," Angelique said.

"You killed the black mage?" Finnr asked.

Angelique frowned. "He fled," she flatly said. "Pegasus arrived just as I was about to succumb to my injuries. He chased him off."

"I'm sorry to hear that," Sano said. "But I guess it proves we need to keep our guard up."

Finnr drummed his fingers on the table. "It also shows the black mages must have attained a certain level of bravado and no longer feel they need to hide to survive."

His astute observation made several mages grimace.

"They can't be that numerous and well equipped," Glaze objected. "Surely the Veneno Conclave would have learned about them far before now."

"The Conclave *did* learn about them far before now," Angelique said. "When Lord Enchanter Evariste was taken."

"Black mages don't typically work together," the weather mage pointed out. "Just because one was stupid enough to attack Apprentice Angelique doesn't mean there's a legion out there."

"Possibly," Angelique said. "Except I believe the black mage knew where Lord Enchanter Evariste is, for he mentioned him."

"And you let him go?" Glaze asked.

"It seems you are bad at listening, dear," Sybilla dryly said. "Allow me to repeat what Angelique said moments ago—*she nearly succumbed to her injuries.* Unless you like to go galivanting around while leaking blood every which way?"

Glaze lowered her eyes to the table and frowned.

Angelique ignored the exchange. "If a black mage attempts to attack a Conclave member, all efforts should be put into containing and capturing the black mage."

"So he or she can be questioned?" Stil asked.

"Exactly," Angelique said.

"Thank you for the information, Apprentice Angelique," Sybilla winked—obviously knowing the full story. "We are glad you were not gravely hurt."

The magic users nodded, and the topic was seemingly over—which came as a bit of a surprise to Angelique. *I thought they would be more upset that a black mage attacked someone. But perhaps it is a sign that they are just aware how bad things have become... Or maybe they don't care as much because it's me. Hopefully it's the former.* I pray *it's the former.*

Angelique cleared her throat. "Given that we know such threats are out there, Prince Severin has requested that we take care of the sorcerer in Kozlovka. As the sorcerer isn't interfering with the royal family and is, instead, the terror of the countryside, fighting him would not strictly be against any Veneno Conclave law."

She waited for several long moments, but no one said anything.

Oh, please, don't all rush me at once to volunteer. She fixed a delicate smile on her lips. "Who should go to investigate the sorcerer?" she prodded.

Finnr shrugged. "Out of those of us present, the obvious choice is you. You have the time and freedom to do as you like."

"You are also the only one who can cover their tracks so neatly." Sybilla sighed. "I'm sorry, dearie, but I'm afraid we'll need you to look into the matter."

Angelique wasn't exactly surprised—she had been astonished Severin hadn't just asked her to handle it. But she didn't much care for the implication she was starting to pick up on. "I am a logical choice to investigate," she agreed. "However, I cannot take a *sorcerer* down by myself."

Firra sighed. "Donaigh and I would be game if it weren't for

Carabosso—that wretch is still running free. Unless someone would like to trade?"

The other mages avoided Firra's gaze—except for Sybilla, who adjusted her spectacles, and Finnr, who looked stony.

"Carabosso isn't your assignment," Finnr said to the fire mage.

Donaigh rubbed his chin. "Yes, you ought to tattle on us to the enchanter in charge of us—oh, wait, that's Lord Enchanter Evariste, and he's *still* missing!"

"Firra and Donaigh are rightfully occupied," Angelique said. "I cannot request their help. So, it is still unresolved who will help me when I uncover enough information on the sorcerer."

Sano scratched his belly. "Do you really *need* help?"

Angelique's voice left her for a few moments as she gaped at the healer. "*Yes!*" She tried not to snap when she could speak again.

"You're nearly at enchantress level, and you have war magic," Sano said. "Is there a mage better suited to take on a sorcerer in the Conclave?"

"As Mage Finnr has noted, I am still only an apprentice," Angelique said. "And by order of the Council, I am not supposed to use my core magic. To be frank, I cannot imagine why you think it would be a good idea to send an *apprentice* against a dark sorcerer!"

"Ignore Finnr," Sybilla said. "He's just a sour puss. Everyone knows you're at an enchantress's level."

"Even so, it's hardly fair to send Angelique in alone," Stil said. "I'd go, but as a craftmage, I'm fair useless in combat. I can whip something up for you and whoever goes with you, though."

Glaze crossed her legs at the knees and scowled. "If taking care of this sorcerer is so important to you, I think you *ought* to go alone."

Angelique shook her head but was silenced when Gemma abruptly set her embroidery down and fixed her gaze on the mages. "I don't understand why you all insist on sending *only* Angelique into dangerous situations."

"It's mostly due to her core magic." Sano smiled apologetically. "You see, she has very strong war magic—"

"Please pardon my bluntness, but Stil has explained to me what Angelique's magic is." Gemma raised her chin, and her blue eyes turned icy. "But just because she can control weapons doesn't mean you should use her as the Conclave's private army. I've been told time and time again how valuable my work is to craftmages because of its quality. With her ability to control blades, Angelique should be able to carve or sew things—a beautiful and peaceful expression of her powers that you all seem intent on ignoring the possibility of."

Glaze snorted. "That's because the idea of a war mage *carving* something is ridiculous!"

"Apprentice Angelique's powers are best used in war," Finnr said. "To explain it concisely, Apprentice Angelique becoming a carver would be similar to using a war horse trained to kill and fight to give pony rides. Theoretically it might be possible, but in reality, it cannot be done. The war horse has too much power and too much fire. Apprentice Angelique is made for bloodshed and war."

Angelique felt the blood rush from her face. Her ears rang, and the world swirled around her as she stared at the tabletop.

Made for bloodshed and war...is that how they really see me? As a beast whose only use is in fighting? I can understand fearing my magic and the depth of my power, but I didn't know I had been so neatly cast into the role of barely human.

Stil, Firra, and Donaigh stood so fast, they knocked over their chairs. Their shouts were too tangled to understand, but their anger was clear in their harsh voices and stiff stances.

"Finnr," Sybilla frowned at the other mage. "That was poorly done—and too far."

Finnr shrugged. "I don't see why you insist on coddling her

and dancing around it."

Sybilla rolled her eyes. "I don't dance around it. I simply see she's capable of more than war magic and treat her accordingly. Land's sake—sometimes you're awfully stupid." She turned her sharp eyes onto Angelique. "He didn't mean it, dearie. At least not the way it sounds. Finnr is a terrible communicator—it matches his terrible personality and is the shame of his family."

"Is he that far off?" Glaze asked. "They're called *war mages* for good reason."

"Watch your mouth, Glaze," Firra warned her.

"Indeed," the weather mage drawled. "War mages hardly have the corner on disreputable behavior."

Stil snorted. "Because weather mages are known for their calm and peaceful personalities."

"At least *we* have more self-discipline than to go rambling around the continent at will!"

"It's sad," Gemma abruptly said, silencing the group again.

"What is, darling?" Stil smiled affectionately at his wife.

Gemma didn't return it, but instead she held the gazes of the mages. "Every common child is raised to respect mages. To venerate them." She slightly shook her head. "I never imagined you'd be capable of such despicable behavior and be willing to sacrifice one of your own for a stupid thing like pride."

She grabbed her embroidery and stood, leaving the silent library with her head held high.

In that moment, Angelique saw just what had made Stil fall desperately in love with the young lady.

Once Gemma left, the argument didn't renew. Instead, the mages exchanged guilty glances and avoided looking at Angelique as they stood and slowly made their way to the door.

Angelique smiled when Stil, then Firra and Donaigh turned to peer at her. She made a flicking motion with her hand. "We should leave as well," she said. "I imagine it's almost lunch."

"Technically we never resolved who should join you in Kozlovka," Donaigh pointed out.

"It's fine," Angelique insisted.

Firra groaned as she pushed her chair back from the table. "This is almost as bad as dealing with King Giuseppe."

"Don't say that." Donaigh shuddered. "It makes me remember what a wet fish he is."

Firra laughed, and soon Donaigh joined her, holding the door open for her before they slipped out.

Stil adjusted the crisp lines of his tunic and eyed Angelique. He, Angelique, and Sybilla and Sano—who were exchanging a hushed conversation at the end of the table—were the only remaining mages.

"They're idiots. You know that, right?" Stil asked.

Angelique tapped her fingers on the table. "Is it as bad as it seems?"

"What?"

"How they view me—do they *really* see me as something barely human?"

Stil sighed and rubbed the back of his neck. "Everyone is scared," he said finally. "Because of what has happened—because of what's going on. And whenever there is fear, we like to create personal boogey men. You are not meant for bloodshed, Angelique. That's their idiocy talking."

Though she didn't believe a word of it, Angelique nodded. She finally stood, idly clenching the soft fabric of her skirts in her fists. "I'm happy you found Gemma."

Stil grinned broadly. "Me, too." He ambled toward the library door, most likely to find his wife.

Angelique reluctantly followed him but was stopped when Sybilla caught her by the hand.

"We need to talk, Angelique," she said.

Angelique stared at the ground. "About what?"

"About what just took place." Sybilla sighed as the glass of her spectacles glinted. "But right now isn't the time. Promise me you'll make time for a good discussion before the Summit is over?"

"I promise."

"Good." Sybilla nodded. "Until then, ignore Finnr. He knows better, but sometimes..." She shook her head and sighed.

Angelique smiled—because that seemed better than crying. "Of course," she said. *Of course, I have to bear it. Of course, it's left to me.* Angelique pushed the thought away and squared her shoulders. "I'm still mostly concerned about the sorcerer. It is our duty to take care of him."

"Try bringing it up again in public when you tell Emperor Yevgeniy you're coming," Sybilla suggested. "Public pressure often does wonders in cases like this."

"And if that doesn't work?" Angelique asked.

Sybilla's smile turned just a bit mischievous. "Then we'll send word to Clovicus, and then everyone will *wish* they had volunteered to go!"

As the Summit progressed, the discussion shifted from a general consensus that something was wrong to a discussion of what each country could donate to the cause.

Verglas offered supplies; Arcainia vowed to send troops and some funds, and Ringsted offered the use of its vast fleet of ships —and the cooperation of the selkies who would provide safe and swift travel for the vessels.

"And what of Sole?" Prince Broken Nose of Arcainia asked.

Firra and Donaigh shook their heads. "We are only mages and cannot promise anything," Donaigh said.

Can't promise anything? From the way King Giuseppe acted when I last saw him, he'd sooner spit in someone's eye than let any knights leave Sole. Angelique kept her expression placid, offering Donaigh a smile when he glanced in her direction.

Severin flicked his eyes from his notes to the mages. "Do you believe, when they awaken, the royal family would be willing to give any sort of aid?"

Firra hesitated, then shook her head. "Unless the situation radically changes, I don't believe King Giuseppe will."

Donaigh scowled. "Briar would."

Severin paused in his note-taking. "Who?"

"Briar Rose—Princess Rosalinda," Firra said. "She is far more...open to such discussions, but she holds very little power at the moment."

"It would be best, then, if we write off Sole entirely." Colonel Friedrich ran his thumb on the lower edge of his eye patch. "If they send us anything, we may view it as a boon."

Rider Nareena—the Farset representative who was also a distant relative of the King of Farset—tapped her long fingers on the table. "It's a shame. What I wouldn't give for a squadron of the Magic Knights of Sole to take on these rogue mages—or the likes of Rothbart."

Angelique nodded and tried to ignore the way Severin's gaze turned to her.

Emperor Yevgeniy straightened. "Perhaps we could barter?"

Donaigh shook his head, nearly dislodging his straw hat. "As long as Princess Rosalinda is in danger, King Giuseppe won't be willing to send out any Magic Knights."

Firra snorted and folded her arms across her chest. "Which is beside the point, as he's not even awake to do so now."

There was a pregnant pause, and Severin's intense gaze became impossible to ignore.

Angelique sighed a little and gave into his wordless question. "Once the Summit is over, I will travel to Kozlovka with Emperor Yevgeniy to scout Rothbart," she said. "When I have an understanding of the threat he poses, perhaps other magic users will join me in facing him?"

CHAPTER 15

Angelique hadn't fully given up on the hope that *someone* might help her—particularly when facing public censure from nearly every country on the continent.

Investigating Rothbart is one thing, but facing him is an entirely different task. Come—you can't possibly expect this from me! Angelique purposely looked from mage to mage.

"Of course," Stil said. "I'll get to work on some goods while you scout it out. By the time you're back, I'll have something to help you," he offered. Again.

Angelique nodded and tried to stare down Finnr, Glaze, and a few other mages.

Donaigh narrowed his eyes for a split second, then completely transformed his face with a bright smile. "I could—"

"No, you can't," Firra cut him off. "We have to get back to Sole for Briar."

Not surprising—they said as much in the meeting. And I'm just grateful she's handling Carabosso.

Donaigh nodded and fixed his straw hat with the innocence of the summer sky. However, given that today Angelique was seated next to them, she heard the scuffle under the table as Donaigh kicked Firra.

Angelique held her smile in place and again pointedly watched the other mages.

None of them would meet her gaze.

Sybilla—seated on Angelique's other side—patted Angelique's hand. "You'll be fine, dearie."

"Sybilla is correct." Finnr's voice was creaky—from disuse, perhaps. "You, out of all of us who are gifted with magic, shouldn't have a problem offing a sorcerer."

Angelique stared at the GrandMaster Mage. *So you take great pains to remind me I'm an apprentice, but you're willing to send me off to attack a sorcerer. Your empathy is overwhelming.* She raised her chin and refused to let her eyes burn with tears. *Perhaps this is my own doing—because I spent so many years running around alone, it's assumed I can survive anything.*

"I thank you for your help, Lady Enchantress," Emperor Yevgeniy's warm gratefulness broke the icy film of Angelique's thoughts. "We will provide you with whatever resources you need to face Rothbart." His smile was so big, it made his eyes little crescents, and Angelique could not miss the slight shake in his hands.

This is why I will look into the sorcerer instead of refusing out of spite. Because Kozlovka needs and deserves the help. Because Yevgeniy wants what is best for his people. Angelique thawed enough to smile and graciously tilt her head.

However, I'm not going to let the other mages get away with this.

Angelique raised her head again, her smile a little savage this time. "Very well. Since it seems that the other mages present will be otherwise occupied, I will attempt to face this Rothbart alone—unless I go to Kozlovka and learn he is beyond my abilities. But I find myself quite *eager* to hear what the rest of the mages will be doing to aid our efforts in the meantime."

If they don't want to help me, fine. But I will not tolerate a lack of activity any longer.

Those outside the magical community must have heard the blatant challenge in her words, for Prince Broken Nose of Arcainia whistled lowly, and Princess Astra of Baris smirked.

Puss put his front paws on the table. "I would clap, if I had hands."

"I agree with the Lady Enchantress," Colonel Friedrich of Erlauf charmingly smiled. "What *are* you lot intending to do?"

The various mages shifted uncomfortably.

Angelique smiled sweetly at Finnr in particular. His stoic expression gave nothing away, but his gaze flickered from her face to the area around her. Her magic, cold and powerful, curled at her shoulders, but she didn't care. *If they're not going to help me, they have no right to criticize how I act.*

"Donaigh and I could use assistance in Sole." Firra smirked and drummed her fingers on the tabletop.

"And any craftmages are welcome to join me here in Chanceux as I work on enchanting items and equipment for use in the coming battles," Stil said.

Glaze pressed her lips together. "I have some items I need to finish and ship to their buyers, but I can return to Chanceux afterwards." She awkwardly cleared her throat and glanced at Severin, who was still taking notes. "I specialize in charming artisanal jewelry, but I can bespell sculptures, and a gem that is roughly cut."

Severin nodded as he wrote.

"I can go wherever you need me." Sano smiled. "I'd offer to stay here, but I have healing magic, so I imagine I'd be most useful with whatever troops are sniffing out goblins."

"Erlauf, I believe, is seeing the most combat." Severin shifted his gaze to the one-eyed colonel. "Would you not agree, Colonel Friedrich?"

"We'd love a healer," Friedrich said. "If the Conclave can spare you?"

Sano swatted his hand. "I'm a Master Healer—which means I can't be bossed around nearly as much as they would like. Thus, to Erlauf I shall go!"

Sybilla nodded. "Very sensible. I, unfortunately, will be unavailable for a bit longer. I took on a few specific assignments that I *hoped* would give me an excuse to ferret out dark mages, but the rogues are nowhere to be found." She slapped the table with her open palm and puffed her cheeks in her irritation. "I hope that—between all countries present—you might be able to get farther with your spies and the like."

Elle smiled widely. "That sounds doable—with some *special* help."

Severin glared at her. "*No.*"

"When I finish these assignments, I'll be free to aid you as needed," Sybilla continued. "Though I would like to put in a recommendation that something is done to search for Lord Enchanter Evariste besides the committee the Veneno Conclave has."

Startled, Angelique turned to face Sybilla so quickly her chair squeaked.

Sybilla smiled warmly and patted her hand again.

"This Lord Enchanter Evariste is one person," Queen Linnea of Verglas frowned. "I'm aware his powers are useful and would be a boon, but if we *must* assign priority—and it seems like we have no option but to do so—I think finding out what has happened to the Elves of Alabaster Forest should go first."

The bitter taste of hopes dashed once again filled Angelique's mouth, but she was so used to it by now she almost didn't have any trouble swallowing despite the rancid taste. She set her hands on the smooth, polished surface of the table, stretching her fingers wide. "Queen Linnea may be right," she reluctantly said. "Besides, King

Themerysaldi of Alabaster Forest is a personal friend of Lord Enchanter Evariste's and is incredibly powerful. If we can find him, it is likely that he'll be able to find and free Evariste with his vast magic."

"Perhaps," Sybilla cryptically said. She rubbed her hands together as her gaze turned to Finnr. "*Dear* Finnr, what will you do for this resistance?"

Finnr exhaled deeply, sounding like a displeased dragon. "You annoy me—often," he quietly growled.

"Good," Sybilla said. "You deserve a little irritation in your life."

Finnr glowered at her, then raised his gaze to address the Summit. "My magic lies in snow and ice," he said. "Like Sybilla, I have a few prior commitments, but after they are finished, I imagine I would be most useful in tracking the excess mountain hags. They will have returned to the mountains in northern Kozlovka by then, as we'll be well into summer. Unless His Highness has a better idea?" He gestured to Severin.

"If Angelique is able to take care of Rothbart, Kozlovkan troops will be able to confront the mountain hags." Severin dipped his quill into an inkwell. "For now, I will make a notation of your abilities. When you are free, I ask that you return to Chanceux Chateau, and we can decide then—for some situations may have changed by then."

"Briar Rose could be awake," Donaigh wistfully sighed.

"We can pray," Firra whispered back.

Severin shifted his gaze from Finnr to the next mage in line. "In what way will you offer your services?"

Angelique watched with great satisfaction as Severin worked his way down the line of magic users, eliciting promises of service from each of them.

A part of her was smug that she no longer carried all the responsibilities on her shoulders, but she was also more than a little glad. With each mage that spoke of what they could do—no matter if they were eager or reluctant—the representatives seemed brighter, and their posture not nearly as stiff.

They really thought we'd abandon them, Angelique realized as she watched the twin princes of Arcainia exchange rare looks of amusement when two craftmages quarreled over who would be able to enchant more weapons between the two of them.

Even if the Veneno Conclave doesn't throw its weight behind this effort, they're happy just to have us odd handful of mages help.

Angelique's gaze drifted to Finnr—who looked flinty, but not quite upset that she had forced his hand. Instead, he was also watching the various royal representatives.

I don't particularly care for him, but maybe he can convince mages who are more focused on Conclave laws to join us. Because this isn't enough. A handful of mages can't counter whatever it is that has taken down both the elves and Evariste.

ANGELIQUE PINCHED her lower lip as she studied the glowing, silver spell in front of her.

"Everything looks right..."

Gravel crunched under her feet as she circled it. When she narrowed her eyes, she could see the silver-colored spellwork and symbols that formed the enchantment. Nothing was out of place, and all loops in the spell were closed.

She surreptitiously glanced over her shoulder, but all was quiet on the front lawn of Chanceux Chateau. The windows of the magnificent manor glowed cheerfully in the dark of the night, and Angelique could hear the faint whinnies of the horses in the stable just off to the right.

She was alone.

Content with this, she squinted at the line of spell that specified the target of the tracking charm, affirming she had indeed detailed the war mage that had attacked her in Zancara.

She took a breath and sent it off on its way with a flick of her fingers. The charm trundled down the chateau drive, picking up speed as it joined the road that wove through the forest and its silver light faded from sight.

The chance that it finds something is almost zero, but I can't give up.

Angelique stretched her arms high above her head, then clasped her hands behind her back.

Although Severin had created a temporary workshop of sorts for Stil and the other craftmages, Angelique had opted to avoid close scrutiny and chose to cast her magic on the front lawn.

It was unlikely her magic had escaped the notice of the other mages, but at least she could send it off without being frowned or gawked at.

She stretched her hands wide and watched as her magic threaded through her fingers. "I suppose I ought to start thinking what spells and charms I should use on Sorcerer Rothbart," she muttered. "The Emperor did say he lived on a lake…"

Her mouth twisted with thought, Angelique began to experimentally twine a water spell together.

"Sent off another search spell, did you?"

Angelique twisted her hand, making the spell structure disappear. "Good evening, Sybilla."

"It is a good evening," Sybilla mildly agreed. "I won a bet against that roguish Mage Donaigh that Princess Dylan of the selkies could eat an entire pheasant on her own. That girl's endless appetite is going to buy me new robes!" She chortled to herself. "But why are you casting spells out here like a magical miscreant?" Sybilla peered at Angelique over the rim of her spectacles.

"I didn't want to bother anyone," Angelique fibbed.

Sybilla shook her head and looked up to the heavens. "Dearie. Your magic has the subtlety of the moon crashing into the earth. No one could possibly miss your casting when you're this close."

Angelique winced. "Then I apologize."

"No need for that! I didn't say it's an unpleasant experience. You're still searching for Evariste, then?"

Angelique shrugged. "In a way, yes. That particular spell was for the mage who attacked me. If I could just *find* him..." She trailed off and stared at the flickering flames of the braziers fastened to the sides of the chateau and stables, too broken to continue.

Sybilla nodded. "You know—once this mess is over—I reckon you could make a fortune at finding missing persons."

"I beg your pardon?"

"You have got to be more skilled at spells that search and track than any other mage in recent history." Sybilla pointed a finger to the dark sky. "Which means there is a business opportunity to be found!"

Angelique's lips twitched in a briefly-lived true smile. "Given that my success rate is woefully low, I don't know that I'd be certain about that."

"Pish-posh." Sybilla planted her hands on her hips. "You can't help it that these rogue mages are impossible to pin-point. It seems to me they must have either a mage with a particular set of skills that can block our searches, or they've been in hiding so long they've developed spells we don't know of."

Sybilla sighed and shook her head. "Once the Summit is over, I'll be the one to deliver a report of what we've learned to the Veneno Conclave."

"My deepest and most heart-felt sympathies," Angelique said.

Sybilla cackled. "You are a fun one when you're so tired your primness can't stay up!"

"I apologize."

"There is nothing to apologize for."

"May I impose upon you and request that you present a report to Lord Enchanter Clovicus as well?" Angelique asked.

Sybilla swatted her hand. "Of course, of course. I was already planning on it, for I'd never hear the end of it from him if I didn't

—and Clovicus can be a true pest when he wishes to be. But I did want to warn you...I mean to inform Lady Enchantress Lovelana of our various discussions—including the attack on you by that black mage."

"The other mages didn't seem to think the attack was important and that it is merely a sign the black mages are no longer content to hide," Angelique said.

Sybilla shook her head. "I'm not convinced. There must be more to it—given how strategic our enemy has been. But although Lovelana is all but useless as the head of the committee searching for Evariste, she has been doing her job in earnest."

"What do you mean by that?"

"She's studied every reported activity of black mages over the past few decades in great detail," Sybilla said. "She might pick up on something we've missed."

Angelique nodded.

"You don't mind?" Sybilla asked.

"No."

"Good. I know she's sometimes been a bit rude to you, but I thought she's been less of a twit since Evariste was taken."

Angelique blinked at the frank assessment and carefully chose her response. "I'm grateful that she's even tried to locate Evariste." *Even if she's been going about it in the most ineffective manner possible.*

"I suppose that's true." Sybilla pursed her lips and glanced up at Angelique. "I'm going to be blunt and say it: Angelique, Finnr was careless with his words. Well, really he was acting simultaneously pea-brained and more thoughtless than usual. It was a new low even by his stodgy standards."

Angelique gurgled what could have been a laugh if she hadn't strangled it in her throat. "I see?"

Sybilla smiled mischievously. "I can see I've shocked you. Don't worry; I'm old. It means I can say such things and people will merely think I'm turning crotchety in my dotage!" Sybilla hooted, then clapped twice in her own amusement.

"I assume you are referring to the meeting we held in the library?" Angelique asked.

"Precisely, yes. Finnr said some rather inexcusable things. I'll attempt to make a case for him and say I'm certain he didn't *mean* for them to be interpreted as they sounded."

"He called me a creature of blood and war. How else could that be construed?"

Sybilla scowled. "Yes, well, he has the sense of a cow sometimes. But whether he meant it or not, I want you to know, to be certain, that you are *more* than that. You are more than your magic—and your magic is more than a tool of death."

This sounds like an echo of the platitudes Evariste used to give me. Angelique tilted her head as she studied Sybilla. *He believed it—and I think Sybilla does as well. But neither of them has been able to present any evidence that supports their claim.*

"I can see by the stubborn angle to your chin that you doubt my words," Sybilla sighed. "But if I keep telling you long enough, maybe one day you'll believe me."

Angelique slightly bowed her head. "It is your right to speak to me as you will."

Sybilla slightly pursed her lips. "Do you know that you are feared more now than you were—say—ten years ago?"

"Because Evariste is not here to hold my leash?" Angelique couldn't entirely keep the sarcasm out of her voice. "If they're that frightened, they should put a bigger effort into finding him."

"No, no, no. It's not that. It's your principles."

Angelique frowned so deeply she felt her forehead wrinkle. "I beg your pardon?"

Sybilla's voice turned instructive as she waggled a finger at Angelique. "When it was discovered you were to be the first ever enchantress with war magic, it made them a bit uneasy. Humans—

even magic ones—are creatures of habit. Of course, something new would make them wary. When it became apparent there was no easy way to test the *depth* of your magic, they came to fear you."

"Because of what I'm capable of," Angelique said.

"Close—but not quite. Because of what you're capable of if you were turned against the Conclave." Sybilla slightly shook her head. "For all that the world applauds heroes, it does not *like* heroes that are so beyond the reach of others that they cannot be beaten."

"That's why they call me a risk," Angelique said.

"Precisely. It doesn't excuse their horrible treatment of you, but at least you can follow their thinking. But now? Now they are petrified because you have principles."

Angelique grimaced. "Petrified? It's really that bad?"

"You're focusing on the wrong word, dearie." Though Sybilla's words were kind, there was a sharpness to them that made Angelique look at her. The older woman's eyes practically glowed, and for once, her cheerful smile was gone.

Angelique got the feeling she was waiting for the right question, so she ventured a guess. "Why do they fear my principles? I took many ethics courses in Luxi-Domus, and Evariste himself pressed the importance of duty and honor."

"Some would say Evariste—and perhaps all those classes—went a tad too far," Sybilla said. "Because you are so intent on doing what is *right*, and you are so fixated on shunning what is wrong—or even questionable—that you cannot be manipulated. Personally, I don't think either are to blame; you came to us this way."

Angelique squinted as she puzzled through Sybilla's words. "I'm afraid I don't follow you."

"Think of all that has happened since Evariste's capture," Sybilla prodded. "You flagrantly broke dozens of Conclave laws and muddled in continent politics—all in the pursuit of doing what was right. When chided, you refused to stop, and when threatened, you did not fall in line."

Angelique frowned. "That makes me a rule-breaker, not a mage of principles."

"Except it *does*," Sybilla said. "Because you also continue to be extremely reluctant to use your core magic, even when it would be the easiest way out. You're not a monster, Angelique, *because* you think and weigh out your actions. Because you're willing to sacrifice if it's the right thing. Given that there is no one who can counter you, it scares folk to know you follow a code of ethics, not orders."

"But if that's so...isn't that a good thing?" Angelique spoke so softly it was barely a whisper.

Sybill sighed. "It is." She reached up to cup Angelique's cheeks with her soft hands and gazed at her with the love of a grandmother. "Unfortunately, they're still scared. But there will come a time. You will not bend, and then everyone will see the sterling core of your character. Until then, I apologize for the thoughtless idiots like Finnr."

She released Angelique, only to hug her close. "You're a good girl." She rubbed circles on Angelique's back, as if she were a child that needed soothing. "And one day, we're going to need you more than ever."

The very thought made Angelique grimace. *I don't like the sound of that. Not. At. All.*

BY THE FOURTEENTH day of the Summit, things were starting to wind down. (The exception was another assassination attempt on Prince Lucien, but the young lady who served as his handler fended off the attack until guards arrived, so the Crown Prince of Loire was uninjured. Angelique had been consulted, but it was Stil who took point in the next layer of protections, leaving Angelique free to focus on the "fun" that waited for her in Kozlovka.)

As the days passed, the representatives came up with several key strategies and plans that they would take back to their home countries. After lasting a full fortnight, there were only a few more details to work out before the Summit could be declared over.

"I believe it would be wisest to create a council of military advisors that will stay connected through messengers and magical means," Severin said. "I will be the military leader and contact for Loire, and Colonel Friedrich will serve as the military contact for Erlauf and will report to his father, Commander Lehn. I ask that once your contact is picked, you send them to Loire to be introduced to others and to receive training for advanced use of a magic mirror."

"Each party of representatives will be given a magic mirror to take to their home country," Elle said. "The mirror will give us a way to remain in contact as we make adjustments to our strategies."

"Constructed by yours truly!" Stil smiled dazzlingly at the representatives—who nodded their thanks—then turned to see if Gemma was watching. (She wasn't.)

Glaze added after several moments of silence, "We don't have the mirrors prepared yet, but by the time the representatives are chosen, they will be completed."

Princess Astra shook her head like a wild horse. "I still don't feel we are taking enough action. We should band together to declare war!"

"War against whom?" Prince Steffen of Arcainia asked. "As poor as things appear, there is no unifying factor in the trials we face. There hasn't been a pattern any of us have been able to discern." He leaned back to avoid Puss when the black and white cat deliberately climbed on the table.

"You cannot think to deny the calamity we each have been facing these past few years," Princess Astra said.

"I'm not," Steffen said. "It merely makes no sense to declare war against an enemy we cannot define." He scowled when Puss sauntered past him, flicking his tail under his nose.

"What he means," the youngest Arcainian prince who was also, apparently, the charmer of the bunch, began, "is that since there is no common thread, no proof of uniting forces, we have nothing to declare war against. It's obvious from the widespread unrest that something is happening, and the attack on royals means it is likely someone is pulling the reins. But we *cannot* declare war against an enemy we don't know."

Severin looked up from his papers. "I agree. We have no idea who our enemy is, nor what land is harboring them."

"Could something have happened to Zancara?" Rider Nareena of Farset suggested.

Angelique managed to hold her placid expression and intended to keep her mouth shut—she didn't exactly want the other mages to become aware of her escapade. But when she saw a few representatives frown thoughtfully, she knew she had to squash the idea rather than let them waste time.

I am going to hear it from Finnr—and the Conclave if Sybilla can't slip this out of the notes. But I don't want everyone wasting time on an idea I know is incorrect.

"Possibly, but not likely," Angelique said. "I stole my way into Zancara not long ago. There was no sign of black mages or dark magic."

Several of the mages—most notably Finnr—stared at her with alarm and disbelief, but the royal representatives all seemed to take refuge in her words rather than question her sanity.

It's amusing to see how things that would get me threatened with punishment in the Veneno Conclave aren't even questioned by the rest of the continent.

Princess Astra impatiently nodded. "I understand."

Finnr opened his mouth to object, but Astra ignored him and addressed Severin. "However, if we don't cut this evil off at the head, it will continue to regenerate."

"But if we cannot locate the head, how are we to cut it off?" Queen Linnea of Verglas asked.

Emperor Yevgeniy smiled in a tired but almost fatherly sort of manner. "We search and we listen. Prince Severin and Crown Prince Steffen are right. We must concentrate on preparation, sharing intelligence, and fighting the battles that come our way. All we can do is strive forward. Acting brashly will only give our enemy opportunities to strike."

Princess Astra hesitated, then nodded in agreement.

It took effort for Angelique to hold her mask in place. But she didn't want to smile sweetly, she wanted to drum her fingers on the table.

I perfectly understand Astra's point. It's safe to say dark mages are either banded with or leading whatever this is. But we don't know under whose banner or order. How is that even possible? How can they breed this kind of unity without publicly rallying behind their leader?

"We're thankful for any magical aid we can get," Colonel Friedrich of Erlauf said, tugging Angelique from her thoughts. "The mages are an advantage we didn't possess before—Lady Enchantress Angelique's efforts aside."

The room was silent for several awkward moments as several mages twiddled their thumbs or stared at the ceiling.

Sybilla delicately cleared her throat. "We shall strive to be a greater help in the future." She pointedly stared at Finnr.

"We'll see about recruiting help from others," he reluctantly said.

"Thank you," Elle said. "As Colonel Friedrich said, whatever magical aid we receive will be a true boon."

Severin picked his papers up and tapped them on the table, shifting them into an organized pile. "We all agree, then, that remaining in contact and sharing resources is the best route?" Severin asked.

There were choruses of agreement from all the representatives.

Angelique almost slumped in her chair. *I guess that's the worst of it.*

She watched, amused, as frog-Lucien flopped over the side of the table, landing on his handler's lap.

But that means the Summit is almost over, and my next task will be to investigate Rothbart. The thought made her stomach sour. *Despite Sybilla's and Finnr's belief that I can handle Rothbart, I think I will send word to Clovicus and ask for his help. It's possible Rothbart is connected to the black mages. Or this nameless enemy of ours.*

"THE STAINED-GLASS SKYLIGHTS are simply stunning in this hall, Madame Elle." Princess Astra of Baris peered up with her praise, gesturing to the beautiful flower-themed skylights.

Directly above them was a stained-glass rendition of red roses unfurling on a background of blue, with bright green thorns jutting out from their stems, and pink hearts curled around the corners.

"Indeed," Angelique added. "I believe this rose one might be my favorite."

Elle laughed. "I shall endeavor to tell Severin—it's quite new, actually. He had to replace it since I fell through the original the night he met me."

Angelique—knowing the prince and the ex-Ranger's love story—nodded in understanding.

Astra, lacking that knowledge, rapidly blinked. "I beg your pardon?"

Elle's green eyes glowed with mischievousness. "I was on the roof and—like a regular dolt—misjudged a jump and fell through the skylight. I broke my leg and was stuck here for months, but at least I got Severin for all my troubles!"

"Are roofs common locations for you to explore?" Astra asked.

Elle started to deny, but Angelique cut in. "I imagine so—if Severin doesn't catch her."

"That is perhaps, or to say, quite…perhaps even most certainly, true," Elle confessed.

Astra nodded, a genteel expression of interest. "Have you undergone special training? I must confess I never thought of becoming learned in the art of roof climbing—something I am starting to regret now."

Elle's smile grew. "It's *fun*," she said. "Chanceux has the perfect roof for climbing—I can take you up before you leave if you like."

"I would certainly appreciate a demonstration," Astra said.

Angelique took a step back, smiling when neither of the seemingly fierce women noticed, then ambled away.

The Summit had paused for a much-needed break of afternoon tea, giving all the representatives a pause from the rather grim talk.

A quick scan of the room—which Elle had informed her was called the Little Hall, even though there was nothing little about it—and Angelique espied Stil and Gemma at the other side of the room, seated at their tea table with Queen Linnea of Verglas.

Sybilla and Donaigh were two tables over, speaking with Prince Severin—who deftly stirred his porcelain teacup with a tiny silver spoon. Gabrielle and Puss were seated with the Ringsted representatives. (Gabrielle had brought Dylan, the selkie princess, a punch bowl of blueberries from her original table, forging a friendship between the two.)

Angelique's table—covered with a lace tablecloth and a vase of fresh flowers—was deserted, to her relief.

She sat down in her chair and poured more black tea from a white porcelain teapot with a flower motif into her matching cup.

I've enjoyed speaking with the royals—and seeing them when they are not *fighting for their lives in some form or another—but being able to savor silence is nice, too.*

She added a little sugar and cream to her tea before swiping a few macarons.

As soon as she did so, a maid in a perfectly pressed uniform swooped in to replace the tempting treats.

Tomorrow I leave for Kozlovka with Emperor Yevgeniy and his retinue. She sipped her tea and sat back in the padded chair, enjoying the moment of respite. *Though I don't look forward to what awaits me in Kozlovka, I am satisfied with the Summit. All of the mages who attended have committed to helping, and I have hopes they will recruit other magic users as well.*

It's frustrating that we don't know our enemy, and at this moment it seems we can only defend, not attack, but that will change as the countries continue to pull together.

Angelique ate a macaron—it was light and airy with a hint of almond flavoring. Her teacup clacked when she picked it up again, sipping delicately as she watched the three musicians—a violinist, a harpist, and a cellist—playing a sweet melody from their position in the corner of the room.

Sunlight—colored red, blue, green, and pink by the various skylights—brightened the room in jewel-toned colors. What most struck Angelique, however, was that many of the representatives were *smiling.*

Very little of the news discussed in the various meetings had been positive. But it seemed to Angelique that the event had bound the representatives together, forming a comradery that hadn't been there before.

Of course, it might also be the knowledge that they are not alone, and that they will not have to fight alone. That's good enough news to make anyone happy. Angelique sighed wistfully.

"Apprentice Angelique, might we join you for a bit?" Sano smiled and held his teacup up in an inviting gesture.

"Certainly." Angelique smiled in real pleasure at the healer mage, but the expression stiffened when she saw Finnr and Glaze lurking at his back.

Sano plopped down and helped himself to the tea, then eyed a tray of calisson candies—a confection made of ground almonds and candied fruit, topped with a thin layer of icing. "I hope you don't mind if I help myself to some treats?"

"Have as many as you like." Angelique smiled over her teacup. "A maid will replace them faster than you can consume them."

Sano raised his bushy eyebrows, then scooped three of the candies onto an unused plate as Glaze and Finnr sat down as well.

As if notified by magic, a maid appeared to replenish the supply and was gone almost before Angelique could thank her.

Sano chortled in delight, but Finnr merely frowned. "It seems this is a table for preferential treatment."

"I disagree," Angelique said. "Prince Severin and Princess Elle are perfect hosts. All the tables are frequently refreshed."

"Perhaps," Finnr said. "But not so swiftly."

Angelique exhaled. *And there goes my moment of peace.* She set her teacup down with a quiet click and then spoke without thinking. "Are you constantly searching for ways to disapprove of me, Grandmaster Mage Finnr, or is it one of your simple delights in life?"

Sano hid a smile behind his hand while Glaze stared at Angelique as if she had taken leave of her senses.

Angelique wanted to regret blurting out her thoughts, but she couldn't quite bring herself to do so. *What does it matter to me how much he disapproves? Evariste is gone, and I've been forced to tear around the countryside. What can he do to me that is worse than that?*

Finnr's expression didn't change—he didn't even blink. "I don't dislike you, Apprentice."

Now it was Angelique's turn to be shocked. "*Truly?*" She eyed him in open disbelief. "That comes as a surprise, Grandmaster Mage."

"You are intelligent and dedicated." Finnr shrugged slightly, moving his broad shoulders. "You have weaknesses—as we all do. Unfortunately for you, you also have great power, and those with great power must work harder than everyone else to contain their power and act with wisdom."

Angelique stared at the older man, not quite sure what to make of him.

He glanced at his fellow mages, then met Angelique's gaze. "Before Lord Enchanter Evariste was taken, I had no quarrel with you, for you followed Conclave law."

I still don't know that I believe him. Even before I told off the Council, he seemed to hold me in disdain.

Sano munched on a macaron. "Yes, you can't take Finnr's gruff manners at face value, Apprentice. He's far too gloomy for that." He grinned at Angelique and wiped his fingers off on a cloth napkin. "But he does raise a topic I wish to discuss with you: Lord Enchanter Evariste."

Angelique tried to distract herself by fussing with her teacup, turning it so she could admire the purple iris painted on it. "I'm afraid the black mage I mentioned previously is my only lead, at the moment."

Glaze cleared her throat. "We're not here to discuss leads."

Angelique paused. Though she kept her expression serene, she mentally raised her guard; she couldn't quite shake the feeling that she was facing down three particularly well-mannered wolves. "Then what is it you wish to speak of?" Angelique asked with a calmness she didn't feel.

Sano picked up one of his candies and tapped it on his plate. "You've spent months—"

"Years," Finnr interjected.

"Yes, years. You've spent years searching for Lord Enchanter Evariste," Sano said. "How many has it been now?"

Angelique clutched her teacup. "Five."

"In those five years, you've found very few hints of him—much less his location. Which is no reflection on you! Lady

Enchantress Lovelana has found even less, and she has a committee helping her." Sano scratched his cheek, then shook his head in open dismay. "It's a sad thing."

"...yes," Angelique slowly agreed.

"I know you have done your best, Apprentice," Sano continued. "And you've done an admirable job...but I think as part of your search, you need to prepare yourself."

Puzzled, Angelique frowned. "Prepare myself for what?"

Sano hesitated. "The possibility that Lord Enchanter Evariste is gone."

Angelique's fingers tightened convulsively on her teacup. "Evariste is alive."

"Apprentice, you can't know that," Sano gently said.

"Yes, I can," she snapped. "The black mage said they had him!"

"They didn't call him by name, did they?" Finnr asked.

Angelique glared at him—hating him more in that moment than she had over any rude or inhumane comment he had made about her or her abilities. "He couldn't have been talking about anyone *except* Evariste. No one else has been kidnapped!"

"You said yourself, Apprentice: they've had him five years." Sano said gently. "Do you really think the black mages who have done all that we've discussed at the Summit would treat him well and keep him alive?"

Angelique released her teacup so she could clutch her hands under the table. Her gaze went from Finnr—as stone-faced as ever—to Sano—whose brow was furrowed with regret and whose eyes were lit with concern—to Glaze. The craftmage stared at the tea table and wouldn't even look up to meet Angelique's eyes.

Sano rubbed his eyes. "Even if they still have him, the likelihood that he is mentally and physically sound and whole is low. They might even keep him breathing, but that doesn't mean he's aware."

Something in Angelique threatened to break.

Everything she had done on the continent was a result of searching for Evariste. She had served without resting and given endlessly because she believed that she'd find him.

Sano and his well-meaning words and kind smiles was stomping on her heart, and on the thin and wispy hope that kept her going.

"Evariste is *alive*. He has to be." She turned to Sano, a furious glare stealing over her face. "Why are you doing this? Why tell me this?"

Sano's expression remained calm and kind despite her obvious anger. "Because while there is a chance Evariste is whole and healthy, it is far more likely that he is not. I want to warn you now, so if that is what you find, despair doesn't crush you."

"Instead you'd rather let me suffocate in a world without hope. Yes, I can see how that is far gentler," Angelique said.

"You are too powerful to allow yourself to be lost in despair, Apprentice," Finnr said. "When the day comes, and you meet his kidnappers and discover his fate..." Finnr rested his hands on the white lace of the tablecloth. "The risk is too great."

Angelique shut her eyes. *I should have known somehow he'd bring this back around to my magic and how dangerous I am.*

Something in her threatened to unravel.

As painful as the reminders were of Evariste, and even as the knowledge that she had failed him continued to chip away at her will, she was at least aware this was a battle in her own thoughts.

Having Sano and Finnr—and, yes, Glaze, too, even if she hadn't said anything—essentially tell her the darkest fears she barely beat back were in fact truths...

No. No. It can't be. Evariste is alive. I'd know it if he wasn't. Somehow I would know!

Finnr sighed. "Apprentice..."

"Angelique!" Firra said in a voice as bright and warm as a fire in winter. "I was just searching for you! Did you hear that Stil apparently brought copies of some priceless history books back from

Verglas? They're about the Snow Queen. I thought you might be interested."

Angelique peeled her eyes open and stared up at the smiling fire mage.

Firra gave her a reassuring smile. Her gaze flickered to the other mages, and for a moment her eyes held the withering rage of a forest fire. But when she looked back at Angelique, her smile was in place.

She squeezed Angelique's shoulder. "Come with me, and we can look at it. Supposedly the Veneno Conclave had a copy long ago, but it must have been lost in the library fire we had a few centuries back."

"I believe Severin showed me the book you're referring to on a previous day," Angelique said.

"Perfect," Firra said. "Then you can tell me all about it!"

"I don't know that we're finished talking," Glaze said.

"That's too bad," Firra said in her sing-song voice. "You lot can go stick your heads in an outhouse and finish your conversation there, where your words belong."

"Careful, fire mage," Finnr growled.

"I always am—it's a trait we fire mages cultivate." Firra shrugged. "It's a pity; seems like it's a skill ice-and-snow mages lack."

"We should go." Sano stood, leaving his teacup behind. "I apologize if I upset you, Apprentice. I just don't want...this might not end well. And I don't want you to think you're alone in it."

Firra pointed across the room, wordlessly directing the mages.

They left without any more protests.

"What a bunch of bosh," Firra growled. "They don't want you to think you're alone, so they're just going to tell you Evariste is *dead*? Idiots." She glanced at Angelique. "Are you all right?"

Angelique nodded. "They just struck in a spot where it never occurred to me someone might try to attack," she admitted. "And it's worse because they may be right."

"They're not," Firra said flatly. "They don't know you, and they don't know Evariste. He'd never leave you. No matter how terrible it gets, he'll survive."

Angelique nodded. "Thank you, Firra."

"I'm honored I could help you, Lady Enchantress."

Angelique took a large swig of her tea, trying to ease the tightness of her throat. *I take it back. Though I don't fancy facing a sorcerer, I'm glad to leave this Summit, no matter how peaceful it might seem.*

CHAPTER 16

Two days later—after a great deal of farewells—Angelique left for Kozlovka with Emperor Yevgeniy and his forces.

Angelique had a rather joyful reunion with Pegasus, who fussed over her for the first few days of the journey and pranced more than usual, showing off to the Emperor's troops.

They kept a rather grueling pace—or rather, grueling for everyone but Pegasus—and made it to Kozlovka in good time.

"We have arrived at Tsona Palace, Lady Enchantress." Emperor Yevgeniy smiled warmly at Angelique and motioned to the castle.

The palace was a rather unique design in that it was mostly walls crowded around an abundance of towers. Each tower was topped with a bronze dome that peaked ever so slightly, so together, they resembled dollops of whipped cream in shape and texture. The rest of the palace was made of white rock, giving the place a rather glowing appearance.

Angelique forced a smile—even though it felt bone weary and thin. "It's lovely. You said Tsona Palace is your summer residence?"

"It used to be, yes. Since my sons grew up, we have not returned as often as we used to—though my oldest would prefer to make his residence here given his passion for hunting and the like." Yevgeniy squinted in the sunshine. "My wife opted to journey here after I left for the Summit, but it's just as well. As I told the other representatives, Rothbart has made his home at Swan Lake—which is not far from here."

"How fortunate," Angelique said, feeling nothing of the sort. But she made her back straight and her posture perfect.

Kozlovka needs help. I cannot fail them in this hour.

The Emperor's mount shied when he drew too close to Angelique and Pegasus.

"My apologies," Yevgeniy said as he fell back farther in the line of soldiers.

Pegasus had ignored the horse, but when it was no longer so near, he snapped in its general direction, his teeth audibly clicking.

"Steady, friend," Angelique murmured. She scratched the crest of his neck. He swatted his tail like an angry cat before letting out his breath.

Satisfied that the constellation had been soothed, Angelique leaned back in the saddle, stretching her senses.

Kozlovka was a northern country, so although summer had almost arrived, the air was cool. The pine forests were a blaze of green, and the whole country seemed to smell of damp earth.

Angelique tipped her head as she carefully felt for anything magical or off. *I can't sense anything. But magic sensitivity is an art that has continuously evaded me no matter how I work to improve.*

She stopped trying to sense the sorcerer when they were granted passage into the gleaming palace.

"Pegasus, would you rather remain here, or return to the skies?" Angelique asked when they halted in a courtyard. "I assume sometime today, I'll ride out to start my observation of

Sorcerer Rothbart, but I don't know how long it will be until I am ready."

She dismounted, cupping Pegasus' soft velvet muzzle when he pressed it against her temple.

He breathed deeply into her hair, then strode back in the direction they had come, passing back through the palace gates—to the bewilderment of the guards posted there.

Yevgeniy shielded his eyes with a hand as he watched Pegasus. "Will he be alright?"

"Yes."

Yevgeniy smoothed his well-trimmed beard. "Even with a sorcerer about?"

Angelique tried to discreetly fix one of her underskirts that made her gown puff a little. "I don't know entirely what he's capable of, but I imagine if he feels endangered, he'll simply return to the sky."

The Emperor whirled around to gape at Angelique. "Return to the *sky?*"

"Yevgeniy!" A woman with shiny blonde hair highlighted with gleaming streaks of silver glided from the castle. She was beautiful and stately with pronounced smile lines and an innate elegance that came with confidence.

It took Angelique a few moments to recognize Empress Sonya—for she and Evariste had only called on the Kozlovkan royal family a few times—and Angelique hadn't ever met either of the princes.

Empress Sonya smiled as she hurried down the steps and threw her arms around her husband.

Yevgeniy laughed, years falling from his fatigued expression as he embraced Sonya. "What a delightful welcome home!"

"Don't get too excited," Sonya said. "For it has become painfully apparent to me that our sons—while sweet—are, in fact, dunces."

Her frank words made Angelique freeze mid-step and ponder

if she had ever heard a royal mother refer to her children with such bluntness.

Empress Sonya sighed and dramatically laid a hand over her heart. "It would have been better if they were born girls. Alas!"

Unbothered by the Empress' musings, Yevgeniy caught sight of Angelique and beckoned her forward. "Sonya, you might remember Lady Enchantress Angelique—she was Lord Enchanter Evariste's apprentice."

"Actually, I still am an apprentice," Angelique repeated the mantra she had said so many times she wondered if she ought to carry copies of the statement on paper for easier distribution. "But please, call me Angelique."

Empress Sonya curtsied. "It is our pleasure to receive you here in Tsona, Angelique."

"She's here to help us with Rothbart," Yevgeniy said.

Sonya clapped her hands. "Ahh, perfect. Then she'll need to speak with both of our sons."

Yevgeniy seemed perfectly at home with the way Sonya jumped topics and calmly asked. "Why would she need to speak with Yakov and Alexsei?"

"Because they've been sneaking out ever since we arrived at Tsona and have been waltzing on the shores of Swan Lake playing hide-and-seek with Rothbart," Sonya wryly said.

Angelique was not at all surprised. Given the mischief all the royal children had gotten into over the past five years, she was more impressed that they hadn't gotten themselves cursed, transformed, or bespelled.

Yevgeniy did not seem to share her acceptance.

"T-they *what*?" He gawked at his wife.

This seems like it's going to be a longer talk than I imagined. Angelique cleared her throat. "Perhaps we could discuss this indoors?"

"Of course!" Empress Sonya smiled, magnifying her natural beauty, and set a hand on Angelique's upper back, guiding her toward Tsona. "We should retreat to my private salon—I'll call for refreshments. And my sons."

"Thank you."

"Not at all," Sonya said. "It is I who must thank you—for coming when no one else has."

SONYA HAD enough time to serve tea and snacks before a tall and brawny young man threw open the salon door. "I found Alexsei."

He and a second young man slipped into the salon, closing the door behind them.

The second lad was a little shorter and not so broad shouldered, but he had a welcoming smile and the same sharp eyes that spoke of intelligence masked with charm as Empress Sonya possessed.

Yevgeniy cleared his throat and joined his sons, resting a hand on each prince's shoulder. "Lady Enchantress, please allow me to introduce you to my sons—the Imperial Prince Yakov and Prince Alexsei," He indicated first to the taller brother and then to the one with his mother's eyes. "Yakov, Alexsei, this is the Lady Enchantress Angelique. She attended the Summit called by Prince Severin and Princess Elle, and she agreed to help us when she heard of our difficulties with Rothbart."

"I'm afraid I'm only an *Enchantress-in-Training*." Angelique said —the Emperor and Empress seemed especially inspired, though, to ignore this correction. "However, I will do my best to aid you. I had heard of Rothbart's activities before, but I thought the Veneno Conclave would send help. I apologize for the lengthy delay."

"There is no reason for you to be sorry, Lady Enchantress." Sonya took Angelique's empty teacup and set it on the cart the maid had wheeled into the salon. "The matter was out of your control, and I must confess even *we* did not know what a boil Sorcerer Rothbart has been until recently."

"Indeed," Yakov said as the younger prince, Alexsei, drew closer to his father and exchanged a whispered conversation with him. "There is a group of folk who stay at Swan Lake because Rothbart cursed them."

And there it is, Angelique internally sighed. *The obligatory curse. I hate curses. I hate dark mages who cast curses.*

Yakov continued, "They act as smugglers, but Alexsei says it's a front because they spend most of their time defying Rothbart and attempting to stop his plans."

Sonya sighed as she set her empty teacup on the cart as well. "The smugglers are perhaps the only reason there are fewer...*incidents* than one might imagine. The sorcerer obviously has power—he's set dark animals loose. Most recently, he created and *released* a wyvern. Alexsei was there when he loosened it—he and the swan smugglers were able to fight it off, but they couldn't defeat it. It's flying around our lands, now, wreaking a path of destruction."

Angelique nearly inhaled her own spit and had to clear her throat before she could speak. "A *wyvern?*"

Dragons were an unusual sight in their lands. Mages saw dragons more than the average folk, and Angelique had seen them even more often because of her apprenticeship with Evariste, who drew them in as a result of his powers.

But wyverns were rarer than dragons. Dragons had the magic to cross realms as they pleased; wyverns did not. They occasionally made it into this realm, but it wasn't often.

Which is why it was worrying that Rothbart could *create* such a beast, particularly given that they were generally blood-thirsty and destructive beasts.

The younger prince, Alexsei, turned away from his father and pushed his shoulders back. "Yes, Lady Enchantress."

What is it about this family that they don't listen to a thing I say about my title? Angelique clenched her teeth and smiled as brightly as she could manage. "Please, Angelique is enough. I was told, Alexsei, that you believe Rothbart *created* it?"

"Yes," the prince said. "He claimed as much previously, and it seems true based on its actions. When I was with the swan smugglers as they drove it off, it was almost clumsy—as if it was the first time it had been free to use its legs, wings, and other abilities. Some things it knew naturally; others it was learning through trial and error."

Empress Sonya steepled her fingers together and narrowed her eyes. "That would explain why our soldiers could not defeat it—even after Odette and her people wounded it."

Angelique's smile slid off her face. *A sorcerer who can create not just a living thing, but a wyvern? I can't recall any such thing occurring in history before! Just how powerful is he?* "It is not a good sign," she slowly said.

The eldest prince hooked his thumb on his sword belt and glanced at his father. "Would it have been better if it was a wild one he caught?"

"Yes," Angelique said, favoring bluntness over sensibilities in the ugly situation. "It is difficult to harness wild dragons and wyverns. It takes a great deal of power and many expensive spells that take a long time to produce. As a result, it also makes it impossible for every dark wizard or mage to run around with a dragon under their command. But if Rothbart found a way to *create* wyverns..."

Alexsei clasped his arms behind his back. "I think he's created just the one. Odette and her people are watching his castle. She can get in contact with Rothbart's daughter, Odile, who can verify if he's been making more."

The sorcerer has a daughter? That's just great. But they did say she's in contact with them and must be leaking information. This implies she doesn't take after her father in terms of ethics. Angelique kept her thoughts off her expression and instead zeroed in on the other question that nagged at her. "You've mentioned this Odette several times. Who is she?"

Alexsei's stance and expression softened, and a warm smile slipped across his lips, but it was the elder prince who puffed up his chest and explained, "She is the beautiful and fearless leader of the Black Swan Smugglers—the group of unfortunate folk whom Rothbart has cursed to be swans during the day and humans at night."

He directed the second half of this statement to his father, who apparently was unaware of the cursed smugglers development, for he stiffened. "Smugglers?" he said in a slightly foreboding tone that sounded angrier than Angelique had ever heard during the entirety of the Summit.

Empress Sonya leaned back into her chair with artless grace. "Peace, Yevgeniy. I've already had our intelligence network look into it."

Emperor Yevgeniy still frowned, but he said no more on the matter, even when Alexsei smiled brightly at Sonya when she winked at him.

Oh, good lord. Please don't tell me there is a budding romance in the mess and chaos of this? What am I saying? The prince is clearly part of this love-addled generation. Of course, *there is a love story.*

When Angelique finished her internal rant, the description of the smugglers caught up with her. "I beg your pardon; did you say they're cursed to be *swans*?"

"Like the Arcainian princes, yes," Alexsei said. "Rothbart invented the curse that the witch used on the princes. His wife stole a copy of the spell and sold it to the witch."

"I suppose that ties up one loose end. I always wondered where Clotilde found such a powerful spell," Enchantress Angelique mused as she recalled the black diamonds the witch-queen had fought with. It seems Puss' and her suppositions had been correct all along. Clotilde had been sent in by someone—the nameless and unidentified enemy—who had prepped her with power *and* spells.

She nodded briskly, clearing her thoughts. "Now, unfortunately, it seems Rothbart is much more powerful than I expected. Creation spells—the kind of magic used to make that wyvern—take a great deal of knowledge and power. And why has such a blatantly dark sorcerer refrained so long from doing Kozlovka a great deal of damage? I can't imagine a group of cursed smugglers could so easily stop him."

"Odette says Rothbart likens himself to a genius," Alexsei said. "He seeks knowledge for the sake of having it. Apparently, unless a display gives him the opportunity to prove his brilliance, he does not care to use his hoard of power."

If that is so, it is possible this Rothbart doesn't work with our enemy, even if he is still evil—for it seems very unlike any black mage we've encountered before.

Angelique pushed her hands into her skirts as they changed to a shimmering dark blue. "It seems this Odette is most knowledgeable of Rothbart. I believe I would like to meet her before I begin searching for the wyvern."

"You will take care of the wyvern first, and then face Rothbart?" Empress Sonya asked.

Angelique shook her head. "If Rothbart is as powerful as you say, then I will need help after all. I will send out messages to several colleagues who attended the Summit. They should still be in Loire and willing to lend me a helping hand." *Stil can forge some items for me, and with things this bad, Sybilla might delay her plans to help me. I can always send word to Clovicus, as well.*

Empress Sonya frowned slightly. "Forgive my impertinence, Lady Enchantress, but shouldn't you be enough? You are the most powerful rank of magic user there is."

Angelique tried not to bulge her eyes. *Just how powerful do you think I am if you believe I can face a sorcerer who makes wyverns when I'm still an apprentice!* She slapped her smile back on and said, pleasantly, "I tried to face Clotilde in Arcainia alone, and it went poorly. To avoid the same mistake—for I fear Rothbart is more intelligent than Clotilde and would likely build his defenses after beating me off—the wisest course would be to bring in allies."

Emperor Yevgeniy went back to smoothing his beard. "Could we aid you in any way? Troops, perhaps?" he asked. "I do not wish to place this burden on you and do nothing to aid you."

Angelique softened a little, warmed by the offer—even if she couldn't risk agreeing to it. "Though it is kind of you to offer, it is best for those without magic to stay out of such a battle. I fear the losses would not be worth it."

"I see." Emperor Yevgeniy said. "I will call for couriers so your friends can be sent for immediately. It is a shame no war mages besides the one who went to Sole attended the Summit—they would be immensely helpful in this situation."

"Perhaps," Angelique politely agreed. *As if the Conclave would ever spare them.*

Empress Sonya rested a hand on the tea cart. "How soon would you like to travel to Swan Lake to meet the smugglers?"

Angelique studied Alexsei. "You said this Odette and her people turn human every night?"

Yakov answered for him. "Yes—for the whole night."

"Then we should set out so we can reach them shortly after the sun has set."

"As you wish. Come, Yakov." Emperor Yevgeniy bowed his head and then opened the salon door—with Yakov at his side. He motioned for one of the attendants hovering in the hallway to approach them.

"In the meantime, could I interest you in more refreshments, Angelique?" Empress Sonya asked.

Angelique almost refused—before she did the math and realized she would soon be on a frenzied run through the countryside, this time chasing a wyvern. "Please—though I do not wish you to overly trouble yourself." She stood—her skirts emitting a soft hush as they fell into place.

Empress Sonya smiled serenely. "It is my pleasure." She quit the room, and Angelique started to follow her, mentally cataloging what other supplies she should request before leaving that evening.

Young prince Alexsei cleared his throat. "If I could have a moment, Lady Enchantress?"

Angelique paused at the doorframe and, slightly exasperated, raised an eyebrow. "I believe I told you to call me Angelique, Your Highness."

He bowed. "I have an additional request for you."

Additional? By the stars, I am so surprised—hah! "Yes?"

"Odette and her companions—could you examine their curse and see if you could break it?" Alexsei asked. "Odette has told me Rothbart is likely the only one who could break the spell—and that even his death would not remove it—but if you could..."

Guilt prodded Angelique, and she felt a little bad for her inner sarcasm. Inspecting a curse was easily done compared to finding a wyvern and watching a sorcerer. It wasn't just the ease of the task, but rather the reminder that she should have thought to *offer* to look at the curse that ate at her. *I can't let myself get overwhelmed now, or I won't be able to handle anything.*

"I can certainly inspect it," she said. "Though I will be the first to say I am not well-learned in countering curses. I have no knowledge of how to directly break or undo them, but I have grown better at modifying them thanks to the unusual events of the past few years. Unfortunately, I can promise nothing," she said honestly.

"I see," Alexsei's voice was heavy with disappointment.

Oh, jeez. Yes, he's certainly in love with one of the cursed smugglers. Feeling she owed him a bit of hope—for her less-than-perfect skills didn't mean it couldn't be done at all—she added, "No need to be sad, though. There is no such thing as an unbreakable curse. If I cannot modify it, I can promise someone else from the

Veneno Conclave can. Even if we are successful and slay Rothbart, Odette needn't be a swan for life."

Alexsei was all smiles again and seemed unable to stand still. "Thank you, Lady Enchantress—I beg your pardon—Angelique. It would mean so much—*thank you*!"

"It is my pleasure, my honor, and my duty."

Empress Sonya poked her head back inside the salon. "Angelique?"

Ah, yes, food!

"Coming." Angelique inclined her head to Alexsei. "If you will excuse me."

Alexsei's smile hadn't faded. "Of course. Enjoy the refreshments."

Angelique couldn't help her wry smile as she followed after Sonya. *My father always told me it was the duty of the strong to protect the weak, but it seems lately most actions I see have been done on behalf of love. Perhaps this is a note for the history books: Princes—when properly encouraged with the chance of love—are prone to all sorts of heroic acts.*

WHEN THE SKY was soaked with the colors of sunset and fluffy clouds that were turning purple with the night, Angelique—with Pegasus—joined Prince Yakov, Prince Alexsei, and their childhood friend Benno in riding to Swan Lake.

By the time they reached the lake, night had fallen, though the moon and stars played on the lake's surface, making the area brighter than the dark of the woods.

"Odette commands a rather large group of smugglers." Benno gripped her skirts in her hands as she picked her way along the rocky lakeshore. "But she has two who serve as her seconds-in-command of sorts: Nadia and Misha."

When she climbed over a fallen trunk, Benno released her

skirts, which draped around her with a silken sigh, and combed a hand through her sandy brown hair.

Alexsei cleared his throat and adjusted his stride so he was shoulder-to-shoulder with Angelique. "Nadia is the better warrior of the two, and Misha helps more with strategies and the intricacies of their operation."

"I see," Angelique said.

Yakov ignored their conversation and made a beeline up the shore, marching toward a beautiful young woman with blonde hair who was—interestingly—wearing a white shirt and black pants, unlike the rest of her female compatriots.

"Swan Queen!" Prince Yakov called in a booming voice that Angelique could hear, though she was nowhere near him.

"That's Odette, I take it?" Angelique picked her way up the shoreline with Benno.

"Yes." Benno glanced at Alexsei, who didn't run like his brother, but walked markedly faster than Angelique and Benno. "This is the Black Swan Smugglers' camp, but if you look across the lake, you should be able to see Sorcerer Rothbart's castle, even in this dim moonlight."

Angelique squinted as she tried to gaze across the large lake, making out the silhouette of the crumbling castle. "He lives there with his daughter?"

"Odile, yes," Benno confirmed. "She lives in the tower with her menagerie of animals she has saved from her father." Benno glanced at Angelique, her forehead wrinkling with worry. "She is both brave and kind. She does not take after Rothbart at all—nor does he seem to like her. Alexsei has said he is cruel to her."

"He is." Alexsei twisted awkwardly around to add his confirmation, then hurried the last few steps to the smuggler leader. "Odette?"

"Alexsei." Odette's voice was soft, but she frowned slightly. "You shouldn't have come."

"I missed you," the younger prince said in a voice that was nauseatingly smitten.

Angelique barely stopped herself from rolling her eyes. *Please, strike me dead. The emerging romance between a besotted couple is unfailingly awkward. And they have no sense of privacy!*

Odette cleared her throat. "I missed you as well—though you could have left your brother behind. Is there a reason he is irritatingly cheerful tonight?" She glanced at Angelique and Benno as they stopped just behind the princes.

Alexsei took a step to the side, allowing Angelique a better look at the cursed woman. "Odette," he started, "please allow me to introduce you to the Lady Enchantress Angelique. Angelique, this is Odette—leader of the Black Swan Smugglers."

Odette swiveled her gaze from Alexsei to Angelique. She stared for a moment, then bowed slightly. "Welcome to Swan Lake, Lady Enchantress. I hope the princes explained to you what dangers are present?"

"They did, and I must say, Odette, you are quite brave. When this incident has ended, I hope you will be honored for the great courage and persistence you have shown," Angelique said, truthfully. She tried to smile, but she was afraid it was perhaps a little worn after all the traveling.

Though the calf-eyed romance might be eye-rolling worthy, all she's done is quite impressive. It takes a certain kind of person to live in the shadow of a sorcerer and not only survive, but thrive.

Odette bowed again. "I thank you for your kind estimation, but I could not possibly hope to claim such praise."

"She's right, Odette," Alexsei insisted.

Odette raised an eyebrow at him—and he smiled in response—then shifted her focus back to Angelique. "I assume you are here for Rothbart. How can I help you?"

As Angelique looked back and forth between the couple, a tiny hint of a wry smile escaped her control. "You have guessed correctly. I am here for information about Rothbart and—first and foremost—his wyvern."

"You mean to take the wyvern out first?" Odette asked.

"Yes. Do you disagree with the plan?"

Odette plucked at a dagger attached to her belt. "No. If Rothbart has some sort of means to control the wyvern, it would be dangerous to let it live and face Rothbart when he could call it back. I don't think he *can* control it based on our observations, but it may be that he can, and it has merely not suited him to take control yet."

Angelique stifled a cringe at the rather grim thought. "Excellent, I look forward to hearing more of your insight. However, that is only part of my purpose in coming here."

Odette stared at Angelique with widening eyes.

"Prince Alexsei asked me to inspect your curse and see if I could help," Angelique continued. "Though I do not have much confidence in my curse-breaking abilities, I can tell you that there are many members of the Veneno Conclave who are gifted in such magic, and they surely will be able to aid you if I cannot."

Alexsei sidled up next to Odette and, with the subtly of a moose, curled a supportive arm around her shoulders.

Odette didn't seem to notice, as she was too busy gaping at Angelique.

"It's alright, Odette," Alexsei murmured. "You'll soon be free."

Odette willfully raised her chin and smiled shakily. "Thank you for taking the time to see if such a thing is possible."

Alexsei was watching Odette with such painfully bright eyes, Angelique—as impatient as she was with romance born during chaos—ruefully decided to aid him. *I may be jaded, but I'm not so totally unfeeling that I won't help him out even a little.*

Angelique smoothly said, "Of course, it is my duty to help those in need. But it is Prince Alexsei you must thank. It was he, as I mentioned, who told me of your plight."

Odette seemed to blush a little, and Alexsei whispered in her ear—probably something nauseatingly *romantic*.

Annnd, that's enough. We've got wyverns loose and sorcerers mucking about. They can flirt when the country is safe. Angelique clapped her hands as she took in the rest of the camp. "Now then, tell me the particulars of your curse. Were all of you smugglers cursed at once or in stages? Do you know if he used the same spell?"

Odette inhaled deeply. Angelique watched the smuggler gather herself up, and when she looked up, her gaze was steady. "There are twenty-three of us, and we were all cursed over the course of two years…"

Odette explained the intricacies of the spell—that they turned human every night, and how Rothbart had tinkered with the spellwork placed on each smuggler before giving them all the exact same curse.

However, the more she described the mad sorcerer, the more Angelique felt that he wasn't allied with the enemies the continent was organizing against.

Whoever sent Clotilde, cursed Severin, and captured Evariste had something in common: they struck hard and fast and then disappeared. Even the war mage who attacked me in Zancara followed that pattern.

But this Rothbart…he lingers. He has a daughter and a home here at Swan Lake. And while he's cursed people, until he released the wyvern, he hadn't done anything that really threatened the country. He operates differently.

Does this mean he's not working with the others?

Angelique pressed her lips together as she mulled over the possibility. She heard Odette swallow hard, and she forcibly pulled herself from her thoughts.

I can ponder it when chasing down the wyvern—besides, if I get a look at the spellwork, it might help.

She eased herself down on the rocky shore and motioned for Odette to join her. "If you would sit still for a moment, I'll inspect the curse."

Angelique slightly curled her fingers, cupping them so some of her silver magic pooled there. It prickled slightly before it settled in, a cool sensation on her palm. Holding it, she peered at Odette, tapping her powers so the magic that ensnared Odette slowly burned through, appearing around her in red chains of symbols and magic.

Angelique chose one end of the spell and started reading through it, determined to find a way to help Odette and her Black Swan Smugglers—and hopefully get some insight into the sorcerer's mind in the process.

What she found encouraged, worried, and confused her.

CHAPTER 17

Angelique raised her gaze to the sky and blinked rapidly, trying to relieve some of the strain on her eyes after squinting at glowing spellwork in the middle of the night for hours. She caught sight of some of the smugglers, who wrung their hands and fidgeted while they waited for her to speak. "Rothbart tied your spells together," she announced. "It is like a braid in a horse's mane—the braid moves down its neck as new hair is added to it."

"Do you know this for certain? Not all of the smugglers are present," Odette said.

Angelique gave in to the temptation of rubbing her tired eyes. "I don't need to see them all. I can see the spell woven among you—I can even see which directions it trails off, where I assume is the rest of your band. Rothbart intertwined the curse—and he did an unfortunately diligent job of it. If he were sloppy and there were loops that I could pick loose, I could have possibly dismantled it."

Odette brushed a thigh bandolier that held more daggers. (She seemed to have an abundance of them—something Angelique approved of, which served to make her apprehensive because she didn't quite know if that was something she *should* see as a positive or if it was the influence of her war magic.) "So, it was a poor thing to ask for?" the Swan Queen asked.

Angelique took one last glance at the curse wrapped around Odette before she released her magic—making the spell fade. "No, not at all. As it stands, I can quite easily add a modifier to the spell, giving you a way to break it."

The smugglers' camp burst with sounds of celebration.

A large man picked up a young boy and whirled him around; a few smugglers clapped and whistled, and brilliant smiles were on every face. Even Alexsei, Benno, and Yakov joined in the racket, but Odette remained quiet—and focused.

Angelique took in the rampant joy with a smile. *This is how things should be. This is what the Veneno Conclave was made for—to help people. Not to scramble to fight back. It marks out just how* wrong *the prevalent attacks by the dark mages are.*

Angelique glanced at Odette, who was still quiet, though the way her head sagged on her neck said she was just as relieved and happy as her people. She watched her smugglers carefully and occasionally conducted a visual sweep of the area—always watching.

She's a good leader. She really cares for her people.

Angelique waited for the celebratory din to quiet before continuing, "There will be a few conditions to this modifier. Unfortunately, I'm rather limited in my options."

She paused and forced a smile when she really wanted to sneer. *Limited? Hah, that's an exaggeration.*

"For your particular spell, I think it would work best to use the same modifier I used on Prince Severin of Loire for his transformation curse: to break the spell, you must fall in love with someone, and they must fall in love with you in return," Angelique waited for Odette to look at her, then clearly and loudly continued. "Let me be clear: love from *both* sides is required to break the curse. Prince Severin had a great misunderstanding about that, and it caused him much pain."

I am not making that mistake again!

She waited until she saw a few head nods before she relaxed. "Moving on! I can only cast it on one individual. The way your spells are interwoven makes it operate like one big curse, so individual modifiers are impossible."

This was actually one of the parts of the curse that greatly puzzled Angelique.

Why would Rothbart intertwine the spells? It makes it far easier to break, for if you destroy the right link of the spell, the whole thing shatters. If he truly meant to be cruel, he would have kept them individual.

"Can it be cast on anyone?" asked a male smuggler.

"Unfortunately, no," Angelique said. "As Rothbart has intertwined your curse, I need to cast it where it begins: on Odette or Zina. That's the only way I'll be able to break the curse for *everyone*. If I place it on someone who was spelled halfway through, it will only break the weave of the spell for everyone who was cursed *after* them."

No one questioned this specification of the spell—which relieved Angelique, for she didn't know how to explain to the group that Sorcerer Rothbart had very obviously crafted the spell to—in a twisted sort of way—be easily broken.

His work is complex but tidy. He clearly was creating and cleaning up these spells as he went. And they don't contain chunks of ancient magic like some of the other curses I've come across. Moreover, he's separated the part that makes them transform against their will from the actual swan bit of the spell.

Zina, the quiet but pretty young lady who had been cursed the same time as Odette—which was why Angelique had carefully combed through her spell as well—spoke up. "I believe you should place the modifier on Odette."

Odette honked like a goose. "*What?*"

Angelique glanced at Odette, then Alexsei. "That is precisely what I was going to recommend."

It'll be broken in a few weeks—or less, given what I've seen these past few years.

"No," Odette said. "It's not wise."

"It will be that much faster to break the curse if you have the modifier," Zina argued.

Odette scowled. "What are you talking about?"

Her friend frowned. "Do you really not know?"

When she stared back blankly, Zina glanced pointedly at Alexsei.

(Apparently the young prince's smitten act was obvious to everyone except Odette, if her pursed lips and stubborn expression were anything to go by.)

"I believe there might be a misunderstanding," Odette began.

Her statement was met with total rejection by her smugglers.

"I agree with Zina and the Lady Enchantress."

"It is only right that the modifier be placed on our Swan Queen."

"Hear, hear!" Yakov declared. "Worry not, fair Odette. We can break the curse together." He slung an arm over Odette's shoulders.

Odette promptly shrugged his arm off. "No, thank you."

"Then it's settled," Angelique started pulling on her magic, letting it flow through her once again. "I need a little room to work the spell, if you please."

It seemed, however, Odette was not ready to give in just yet. She spun around and called out to a female smuggler. "Nadia. Please, explain to them!"

The female smuggler, Odette, and Zina exchanged a hushed conversation—one Angelique ignored as she focused on creating a tiny, subtle strand of her magic that could safely be slipped into Rothbart's curse without making the whole thing explode.

It needs to be delicate, but strong enough to slice through the spell when the specifics of the modification are met.

Odette, her face tight with anxiety, turned to Angelique. "Is there any *other* modifier you can use?"

Angelique was unable to smooth over the cracks in her smile as Odette unknowingly poured salt in a festering wound. "Would you rather have true love's first kiss?" Her eyebrow twitched, and her voice was a tad too...*dark*. "Because that's your only other choice."

Stinking curses. I shouldn't have *to know more than that, but apparently the black mages have decided to base their* entire strategy *on curses!*

Odette cleared her throat. "No, no. Falling in love is fine." She guiltily drew back for a moment, then took a breath and squared her shoulders. "What must I do?"

Angelique forcibly released her self-irritation. "Just stand there. This won't take any effort on your part. I do apologize in advance, however; it might sting a little."

Odette stood as directed, her chin raised with confidence. She winked at her smugglers as Angelique circled her.

"Hold still." Angelique nudged her carefully crafted spell, drawing her magic's attention. It surged around her, letting her see the angry red glow of the curse's script. The curse encircled Odette, hovering a hand's width from her body.

Carefully, Angelique pinched a part of the spell and drew it back a few inches.

It didn't give.

"How charming," Angelique grumbled under her breath. She tapped her magic again, then blew on her fingers, her magic clouding her breath like stardust.

The spell flared, and Angelique could tell by the gasps and whispers around her that it was now visible to those without magic. But, goaded by Angelique's war magic, it also gave a little more now, allowing her to pull the rope-like spell farther.

Though it was a cool spring night, sweat beaded on

Angelique's forehead as she pulled the strand again, making it loosen a little more.

Thankfully nothing happened.

I didn't expect it to explode, but why did Rothbart tidy up his spell-work like this if not to plant a trap?

Angelique straightened up and caught Odette's worried expression. "Fret not," she ordered, doing her best to act like an enchantress even though she was sweating like a pig. "This is much easier than the time I added the modifier to Prince Severin's curse. He was running around—out of his mind thanks to his curse—so I couldn't weave my modifier as much as I had to forcibly apply it."

Odette nodded. "I heard an enchantress aided Prince Severin before a merchant's daughter broke his curse."

Angelique snorted as she teased the strands of the spell apart. "Elle—his wife—is many things, but 'merchant's daughter' would probably be the last title I would think to apply to her."

When Angelique had physically loosened the spell enough, she gathered up the tiny thread of the spell she had prepared before. She brushed her finger across the loop, settling the silver strand into the curse.

Angelique watched with narrowed eyes as her silver magic turned golden when submerged in the red haze of Rothbart's spell. Her thread coiled through the curse, swirling around Odette with the rest of the curse.

That was perhaps the easiest modification I've done yet. The spell didn't fight back or need to be cut or adjusted. My magic just slipped the modification in. But it is strange that the curse so easily accepted it. Usually magic won't mix—unless the spell was designed to contain a modifier. But what sorcerer would do that?

Odette exhaled through clenched teeth, though she stayed perfectly still as the magic churned.

Angelique nodded in satisfaction—thinking it was over—but to her surprise, her magic followed the spell from Odette to Zina.

The young woman yelped as the curse crackled to life—Angelique's magic effortlessly pushing along it. After a few moments, Angelique's modification to the curse wound around to the next person and on and on it continued until it spread to each smuggler.

Angelique kept her facial expression mild as she turned back to Odette. "I'm sorry, I hadn't thought—I ignorantly forgot the spell would pass through all of you as well after it was cast upon you."

"It won't cause any harm?" Odette asked as the youngest Black Swan Smuggler—a small boy, yipped when Angelique's magic passed through his curse. The red haze of the spell made the beach glow an eerie red in the dark of the night.

"No," Angelique said. "It's merely applying itself to everyone—it's why I had to cast it on you or Zina. It will apply itself to everyone—even those not here—as it is piggy-backing on Rothbart's curse and is not constrained by distance." Angelique bobbed in a slight curtsey. "I apologize—a full-fledged enchantress would have known."

This is why I don't like people calling me an enchantress when I don't have the experience!

Yakov lazily waved. "I disagree, Lady Enchantress. I have heard of the many ways you have helped the continent over the past few years. You are a very powerful magic user."

Angelique pressed her lips together and watched critically as her magic wound through the curse of the last Black Swan Smuggler, then began to fade. "Power is nothing without knowledge, and sadly, I have gaps in my education."

Benno tilted her head. "How can that be?"

"The Master I apprenticed under disappeared several years ago. I have not been able to finish my apprenticeship in his absence." Angelique tried not to droop, even though the familiar tale left a bitter taste in her mouth and twisted her heart.

It seems I am resigned to always miss Evariste...

She turned to Odette—a professional smile back on her lips. "The modification to the spell has finished. It can be broken now whenever you meet its conditions."

Odette shivered a little. "Will Rothbart know you changed it?"

"Not unless he studies it closely. I wove it in pretty well, and his spell is freestanding—which means it's not attached to his power, so he wouldn't have felt me manipulate it."

Angelique hesitated. *How do I explain the rest?*

"What is it?" Odette asked.

"The makeup of your spell is particularly confounding."

Odette shifted warily. "What does that mean?"

Angelique glanced at the shimmering moonlight that played on the lake. "It means that after you break the spell, you'll retain the spell that makes you tougher, and you'll be able to turn into swans at will."

Odette blankly stared at her. "I thought the modifier would break the spell."

"It does—it breaks the spell that makes all of this happen to you outside of your will. Though you say you bear the curse the Arcainian princes had, I must disagree with you. I saw their curse, and it was much darker and more twisted. It took away all sense of self, while it seems you keep hold of your humanity even as birds. But that is not all. This spell..." Angelique rubbed her fingers together, struggling to voice what made it so unusual. "It's done with several different strands. When I break the free-will constraint, the rest of the strands will remain intact. Of course, if you wish to have the entire thing removed, it can easily be done after the first part of the spell is broken, but you will bear no ill effects from it should you choose to let the other strands be."

A male smuggler whom Benno had introduced as Misha—one of Odette's seconds-in-command—narrowed his eyes. "Perhaps it is because it's an early version of the curse."

Angelique frowned as she considered the idea, then shook her head. "No. Rothbart has the spell laid up too nicely for that. He's done this on purpose. It's almost like an exit strategy—all he needs to do is snap the one strand. But *why* did he build it this way?"

Angelique was quiet for a moment as she contemplated the possible implications. *I might be able to figure it out if I watch Rothbart long enough, but I don't think it would be good to spy on him when a wyvern is wreaking havoc on the locals and villages.* She straightened, then said for the smugglers' benefit, "I will ponder the subject later, but for now I have a more pressing matter. What do you know of the wyvern?"

Odette turned on her heels. "Nadia?"

Nadia—Odette's other second-in-command—bowed to Odette and Angelique. "Aye."

Odette rested her hand on the other woman's shoulder. "Nadia will give you the best information. She has followed the wyvern as a swan since the morning it left our camp. She, myself, and two others faced it when Rothbart first set it loose."

Angelique smiled. "Wonderful. Please tell me everything—what are its flight patterns? Where has it struck? What common attacks does it use?"

Odette nodded to her comrade, then slipped away.

"When we first faced it, it was very awkward with its wings and limbs," Nadia said. "It was slow to fly, and it didn't have much control. Unfortunately, it has grown more skilled the longer it has been released."

"It's adept at flying now?"

"It's adequate. By the time you are able to catch up with it, I imagine it might be adept," Nadia admitted. "It will be hard to keep pace with it."

"I'm not too concerned about that part." Angelique smiled faintly as she thought of Pegasus. Keeping up with a wyvern, even a flying one, would be a breeze for the constellation. "However, I don't care for the part where it could attack me while flying," she mused. "I have good enough aim, and something as big as a wyvern will be hard to miss, but I still don't like it. But I must beg your pardon, for I interrupted you. Please, continue."

Nadia frowned thoughtfully and folded her arms across her chest as she considered Angelique's other questions. "I can point out on a map where it has hit, but it's mostly flown in a circle around Swan Lake. Sometimes it gets quite far, but it always veers back."

"Perhaps it cannot go too far away from Rothbart?"

"It's possible," Nadia said. "But I wouldn't be so sure of it. As for attacks, the most dangerous is its spit. It's highly acidic and can eat through cloth and other substances. In the air, its tail is mostly used for steering, but when landed, it's more of a hammer, and the wyvern smashes things with it. Like a bird of prey, it uses its hind legs to grasp. When landed, it's smart enough to use its wings to corral and scoop or to deflect blows."

This seems like it's going to be much more difficult of a battle than the basilisk. And that one threw me on my rear for days. Angelique's gaze stole to Odette's gleaming daggers before she realized what she was doing and forced her eyes back on to Nadia.

"You'll want to mind its talons," Nadia continued. "I saw it claw through a wooden cart once when attacking a village. Odette believes it has a keen sense of smell, so I stayed downwind from it. It's not a delightful location given how the thing reeks, but I think it's better to be safe in this case."

"What are its weaknesses?" Angelique asked.

"We wounded it when we fought it some nights ago," Nadia said. "We made some punctures to its wings and opened a nasty belly wound. Some of the soldiers it faced off against made the wound a little worse, but it doesn't seem to bother it overly much."

Nadia tipped her head back in thought. "It doesn't like its head getting hit, and we think its greatest weakness are its eyes, but no one has been able to get a good enough shot to take advantage of it." She frowned a little, then gestured at Odette. "Odette, though, hurt it when she flung a wet towel at it. The wyvern spat its acidic spit at the towel, which got plastered on the beast's face. That's mostly healed up, now, though. There's just some discoloration left."

"So I'm about to face a beast capable of flight strikes and land battles with acidic drool it can spit from a distance. Additionally, it is, based on observation, able to function even when severely injured." Angelique ticked off the wyvern's unusual abilities on her fingers, then stared expectantly at the smuggler.

Nadia nodded. "Yes."

Angelique resisted the urge to rub her eyes. *Yep. This is a lot worse than the basilisk.*

Nadia added, "I don't know if it's an encouragement, but it has to land pretty frequently—the holes in its wings mean flight takes great effort."

Angelique heaved a deep breath and forced a pleasant smile to her cheeks. "That is something," she admitted. "Next, do you mind going over the ways it attacked the demolished villages—and the soldiers?"

"Of course, Lady Enchantress."

AFTER ANOTHER HALF-HOUR of conversing with Nadia, Angelique thought it was time to depart.

As she had first considered, she decided to pursue the wyvern before returning to spy on Rothbart. She couldn't stomach the thought of leaving the creature to decimate the countryside, particularly as it stabilized its abilities, which is why she and Pegasus tore through the forest like a pair of maniacs.

But they didn't find the wyvern.

Dawn had long come and gone, and they *still* hadn't found the wyvern.

Angelique's stomach growled and, due to a general lack of sleep, the bright sunlight was a stabbing sensation at her temples.

"How can a giant wyvern be so hard to locate?" Angelique fitted her spyglass to her eye and grumbled as she searched the sky for the monster. She slowly turned in a circle so she faced south.

Off to her left, Pegasus snorted.

Angelique suspiciously pulled back from her spyglass to peer at the constellation.

Though she stood by the bank of a churning river that flowed south—to Swan Lake—Pegasus was about half of a field's length away, casting judgment on a field of pumpkin plant seedlings.

"What?" Angelique demanded.

Pegasus blew out sharply through his nostrils.

Angelique narrowed her eyes. "If you don't like pumpkins, don't stand by them."

Pegasus cocked his left back leg and flicked an ear.

"I am *not* crabby." Angelique paused, revisited her tone, then amended, "I'm not *that* crabby."

Pegasus tossed his head as Angelique once again refitted the spyglass to her eye.

There was a sour taste in her mouth that water couldn't wash away, and given that she hadn't had a chance to bathe since leaving Chanceux, she felt dirty and ratty—even if her lovely dress wasn't.

"'You can handle spying on a sorcerer,' they said. 'you're more than a match,' they claimed." Angelique uncharitably mimicked Finnr's deep voice as she ranted. "Never mind that we didn't know anything about the sorcerer, who is apparently capable of creating a *wyvern* with the hiding skills of a camouflaged moth!"

She swept the spyglass from west to east, ignoring the blue patch of earth that was Swan Lake. Southeast of where she stood, trees violently rocked, and Angelique stopped.

As she watched, the trees shook, and abruptly, a lizard-like form burst out of the forest canopy.

Measuring larger than a royal carriage, the wyvern had a leathery hide that was a sickly shade of yellow, and its throat was ornamented with a dark red frill. As Nadia had said, its bat-like wings showed multiple puncture wounds, and it lashed its long tail behind it like a rudder.

It landed on the treetop and snorted a hazy green puff of smoke.

This far away from it, Angelique couldn't hear it, but she still shivered when the creature chomped its jaws, flashing rows of pointed fangs.

It roared—which Angelique *did* hear—and extended its long serpent-like neck as it balanced on the tree and surveyed the area.

"This is it! We've got it, Pegasus!" Angelique spoke barely above a whisper—even though the creature couldn't possible hear her so far away.

Her heart stuttered when the wyvern turned in her direction. It angled its wedge-shaped head up, scenting the air.

That's right; Nadia said it might be capable of scenting prey.

Angelique froze. *Which way is the wind blowing?*

Afraid to pull her eye from the spyglass, she stiffened, trying to feel the caress of the late spring breeze.

Plants rustled and the water gushed, then Angelique felt the wind tug gently on her hair, blowing from north—where Angelique stood—to south—where the wyvern was.

Through the spyglass, the wyvern stared at Angelique. Its eyes—the angry red of molten rock—felt like they were hinged on her as it sniffed.

It leaned forward, then shifted its gaze just a tiny bit eastward. It breathed so deep its nostrils expanded once, then twice. The wyvern froze, then nearly fell off its treetop perch. It released an unholy scream as it recovered, climbing higher in the sky before it circled, flying south. Away from them.

"What the—it couldn't have been afraid of me. Why did it flee?" Angelique irately collapsed her spyglass then turned to Pegasus.

He was still standing in the pumpkin field, irritably flattening his ears at the plants that surrounded him.

Angelique strained her mind as she recalled the slight adjustment to the wyvern's head, so it hadn't been looking in her direction, but rather slightly more eastward. "*You!*" She brandished the spyglass at Pegasus, shouting to him across the field. "This is your fault!"

Pegasus stopped snorting at a plant long enough to look at her.

Angelique scrambled in his direction. "You're why it fled! It scented you and ran off! Nadia was right—we should have stayed downwind."

Pegasus, disinterested, went back to sneering at a seedling.

She stomped—carefully, for she didn't want to crush a plant—through the field. "Now we have to ride past him to get him downwind," she grumbled. "Which means more time running around."

She finally reached Pegasus and stood in front of him, planting her hands on her hips. "Well? What do you have to say?"

Pegasus sneezed in her face, spattering her with flecks of spit and snot.

He's the worst. Angelique grimaced and wiped her face clean. She glared at the constellation, who maneuvered himself so she could easily clamber into the saddle.

When he tossed his head—making his bridle jingle—Angelique sighed. "Thank you for the ride."

As she predicted, they had to chase after the wyvern and get in front of him—something they didn't accomplish until dusk that night.

As the wyvern had drawn dangerously close to Swan Lake, they let themselves be seen, scaring the creature back north.

They chased after it until Angelique nearly fell out of the saddle from exhaustion, causing Pegasus to insist on stopping for the night.

It wasn't until Angelique was curled up against his glossy back that it occurred to her that her companion had to be far stronger than she—or anyone else for that matter—knew.

For how else could his mere scent have sent the wyvern scrambling in fear?

EVARISTE SAT ON THE GROUND, his forearms pressed into his knees as the feeling of defeat ate through him.

When I was awake, at least I felt like I could get information, look for potential ways to escape, and bother the black mages for good measure. But now...

Behind him, innocents cried out in pain and death.

A cold sweat made his robes stick to him, and he rubbed his forehead.

Now, I just want it to end.

His own magic, forcefully turned against him, swirled. To his right, Lady Enchantress Lovelana cried as a lightning spell enveloped her.

"Enchanter Evariste—help, please!" she begged.

Evariste pressed his palms into his eyes. *No matter how I try, no matter what I do, it doesn't help. This really is a thousand times worse.*

Magic flared, and directly in front of him—wearing a dress of cream and purple—was the one person he had most dreaded seeing.

"Master," Angelique whispered, her eyes already glazed with pain as black magic wrapped around her neck. "Can't you save me?"

Evariste groaned from deep within his soul, and his clenched fists shook with his fury and aching pain. *I feel so useless! I can't help her. I can't help anyone! I'm a failure as a mage—I'm a failure in* all *ways! How could I let this happen?*

His magic—though separated—seemed to feel his pain, for he saw blue bits of it crawl around the floor and flicker at Angelique's feet.

"Master?" Angelique's voice shook, and her lower lip trembled.

Evariste's mind heaved and his heart felt as though someone had ripped it in two as he was forced to watch as the black noose of magic tightened around her. Sparks of his magic churned, bright in the darkness that surrounded them. His magic caressed her hand, then floated higher, disappearing from sight as Angelique started to cry and struggle against the illusionary black magic that tightened across her throat.

And then, behind her, a silvery light bloomed.

There was a sound not unlike a blade being drawn from its sheath. The light grew, a warning signal before magic slammed through the darkness, drowning the area in electrifying power. The magic was so potent and consuming, it stole Evariste's breath and made him fall to his knees. Tiny cracks appeared in the darkness, spreading rapidly.

And though he was trapped, cut off from his own powers, and suffering through torture, Evariste would have recognized the bright and shocking sensation of that magic anywhere. Only one person had the magic of an exploding star; only one person contained that kind of power.

Angelique.

Evariste's magic—trapped in the torturous spell as it was—bubbled, curling around Angelique, folding her in a soft hug.

The illusionary Angelique was frozen, and then the darkness shattered.

It was so bright, Evariste had to cover his eyes to block out the light, and then...he heard it.

"Can't even *sleep* now without having to work. I should have socked Finnr in the nose when he told me I could *handle the sorcerer*. I'm starting to think he was just hoping this would kill me," an achingly familiar voice grumbled with adorably bad humor.

Evariste slowly stood again.

He was in a forest of some sorts. It was blurry and smudged—as if whoever was picturing it couldn't quite recall the details—but sitting on a stump was a simultaneously enraged and tired Angelique.

Is this a dream? If I move closer to her, will she disappear...or is this just another memory? Evariste tried to take a step closer, but his body wouldn't move. He was almost too afraid to *breathe* and make her disappear.

Her hair was its true dark shade of brunette, and her eyes flashed silver. She wore an iridescent dress—the one Evariste had bought for her and meant to give her for her verbal test with the Council—and her hair was pushed back with bejeweled combs.

But despite her finery, she sat with her legs sprawled in front of her, dark circles under her eyes, and a crabby expression pursing her lips as her silver magic clustered at her fingertips.

Even in bad humor, she was the most beautiful thing Evariste had seen in a long time—perhaps ever.

"Angelique?" Evariste felt numb as he stared at her, afraid to hope.

"*What* do you want *now?*" She twisted to face him, and Evariste could tell the moment she saw him for she blanched. She gulped, her eyes wide, as she stared at him as if she had seen a ghost.

Would a dream Angelique react like this? I don't think so...which might mean she's a memory. But I didn't give her the dress yet, so that wouldn't be part of a recollection.

Evariste finally let himself take a step closer, which only made Angelique's eyes bigger until she was full-on bulging them at him.

"No," she said.

Evariste froze midstep. "No?" he asked.

Angelique shook her finger at him. "This is just because I'm tired, and Sano and the others put the thought in my head. *No.* It can't be true!"

Evariste drew a little closer. At this distance, he could smell the floral scent that always seemed to follow her. "What thought?" He reached out, everything in him straining as he moved to brush his fingers against her shoulder.

Angelique shot backwards, avoiding him and scurrying across the ground whilst still seated. "Oh, no. No, no, no! You're not dead. I don't care what they say—I don't even care if you're my subconscious trying to tell me that Evariste is dead. It doesn't matter. He's not!"

Evariste stared at her, stunned. Not by her outburst, but because of the way she was acting.

We've never discussed my death, so this cannot be a memory, and it's certainly not an illusion from Liliane or anyone else. They would never know to make Angelique this caustic. But that means...this really is her? How?

Normally he would have been more skeptical, but he *wanted* to believe. He so badly wanted to see her, even if it meant grasping at straws.

Angelique was seemingly unaware of his shock. She pulled her legs to her chest and was generally preoccupied with grumbling to herself. "I let them boss me around for the good of the continent, but I refuse to give them the ability to bully me in my own thoughts. I'm going to keep looking for Evariste until we find him or until I die."

She licked her lips and squinted up at the smudgy sky. "Which, given that I'm chasing a wyvern, might not be too far off?"

Evariste approached Angelique. He knelt in front of her, his hands and shoulders trembling from the force of his emotions. He shakily cupped his hands on her cheeks, making her meet his eyes. "I've missed you so much."

Angelique's eyes instantly clouded with tears. "This is unfair." A hiccup escaped her. "That you're saying that with *his* face."

Evariste lowered his hands and instead set them on her shoulders as he mentally tried to calculate how out of character it would be if he embraced her. (Frankly, he didn't care whether or not it was like him. But he got the feeling that if he came on too strongly, she'd leap out of his arms.) "It's really me, Angel."

Angelique narrowed her eyes. "But...how?"

"I don't rightly know," he truthfully said. "They were using my magic to put me in some kind of waking nightmare. When I saw you in that nightmare, my magic reacted oddly, and then I felt *your* magic." He tried to tug Angelique into a side hug, but she was an unmovable stone weighed down by suspicion. "It seems we have a connection."

"Let me guess." Sarcasm dripped from Angelique's voice as she hunched her back. "It was the power of *love?*"

Evariste held his breath. "Perhaps."

Angelique released a harsh bark of laughter. "Now I *know* I'm dreaming. It's not enough that blasted curses bother me in the daytime; they have to plague my sleep as well!"

"At least you're not the only one so bothered by it." Evariste mused on Liliane's frustration. "The black mages holding me captive are just as angry about it."

"I imagine so—it's the only reason why I'm able to disrupt their plans so often. It's pretty strange if you think about it. I would have thought by now they would have figured out a way to block that method of curse alteration." She waggled a foot in the air as Evariste sat down next to her. "It's been *years.* And they were smart enough to be able to catch you. I mean, Evariste."

"Yes. Now that you mention it, it is *very* strange," Evariste mused. *Whatever it is that causes that weakness...it can't be in the spellwork. But what, then, is it? A weakness to romantic love is oddly specific.*

"See, you're definitely made up by my mind," Angelique grumbled. "Evariste never agreed with me so much."

He grinned. "I am pleased to disagree with you, then, and insist that it really is me, Angel."

"Fine, then, where are you?" Angelique asked.

"Here, with you. Obviously."

"No—I mean where have they stashed you?"

"Oh." Evariste thoughtfully scratched his chin. "I don't actually know."

"And there we have it. Another useless delusion of mine." Angelique sounded disgusted as she pointedly shifted away from him.

"I don't know the specific location, but I can tell you we're in some sort of cave system." He discreetly tried to shift closer without her notice and covered up his actions by leaning back on his palms.

"See, but my mind could easily make up that guess." Angelique propped her arms up on her knees. "Because we haven't been able to find you anywhere above ground, that leaves only the no-man areas of the continent—mountain ranges, abandoned islands, maybe Baris' volcano and the like."

"I don't think we're located near Baris' volcano," Evariste said. "It's too cold, and I don't know if I've ever seen newly arrived black mages in anything but winter garb."

"Hmm. Okay, then how do I find you?"

Evariste sighed. "We'll think of something."

"Yeah, right. I'm now absolutely certain it's my useless delusions talking." Angelique glumly spread her fingers apart and stared at them. "I can't be thinking of useful things like the best spells to entrap a wyvern—good heavens, no. I have to moon over my teacher."

"This is what mooning looks like to you?" Rightfully intrigued —but unable to be so close and *not* touching—Evariste leaned so his shoulder was braced against hers.

"No—*no!*" Angelique scowled at him. "Not *that* sort of mooning."

"I repulse you then?"

"No. I've just developed an antipathy toward romance in the middle of a war." Angelique rolled her eyes, then poked Evariste in the ribs. (Thankfully she didn't seem to notice his wince of pain.) "It's a pattern that has popped up in my life, just like romantic love being able to bust every curse I've come across."

"Yes, that does seem odd."

"That's right! See—you *are* a figment of my imagination. How else could you know about those curses?"

"I am not your imagination," he laughed. "Though I suppose I should be grateful you think me to be a delusion rather than a torment sent by the enemy."

"I don't think that's possible." Angelique folded her arms across her chest and frowned. "At least not right now."

"And why is that? Are you in the Veneno Conclave?"

"Nope. Snuggled up with Pegasus."

"Ah. Yes, I suppose he could stop anything like that." Evariste shook his head slightly. *This entire conversation has been one surprise after another. But there's something about her point...what is causing that weakness? Rothbart seemed to figure it out when he visited, after he spoke to me and I mentioned I got captured protecting someone.*

"What else can you do to convince me that you're really Evariste?" Angelique asked.

"You are open to the idea?"

"Not really. I just don't want to sit here and think about all I have to do—or everything I should be doing."

Evariste held his breath as he slowly inched his arm around her, curling it at her waist. "Whatever you've been doing in my absence...it's been hard on you, hasn't it?"

Angelique shrugged. "It's not so bad. We've managed to scrape by and win, I guess. I'm just *tired*. And I want to find you, but I haven't been able to make much progress, and I feel like such a *failure*!"

Evariste tugged her closer, finally succeeding in half-hugging her. "You've done your best, Angel. I know you're searching for me."

"Except you *don't*. Not the real you." Despair colored her voice, and she glumly leaned forward and rested her head on her knees.

Evariste shook his head. "No, I really do know. Liliane, Acri, and the other mages who are holding me captive have complained endlessly about you. If not for you, the continent would be far worse off."

Angelique pulled back from him. "Liliane and Acri?"

"Liliane is the leader of the black mages who have me. Acri is her son—he's the one who attacked you."

I need to press my advantage—I just might be able to convince her yet. Evariste smiled at her—an expression that almost felt rusty from disuse. "Well done, by the way, in fighting him off."

"I didn't—not really." Angelique's expression was distracted as she carefully studied his face. "He almost had me, but Pegasus arrived. I think he walloped him pretty good."

"I'm sure you got your licks in," Evariste said.

Angelique leaned so close they were almost nose to nose. "...*Evariste?*" she asked in a small voice.

Evariste tilted his forehead so it rested against hers. "Yes, Angel?"

She hesitated. "I really *don't* want you to be Evariste," she finally said.

"Why not?"

"Because." Her silver eyes looked both haunted and sorrowful. "You look so...*broken*. If Evariste is in the same condition you seem to be in..." She shook her head, then abruptly shoved her shoulders back and puffed up like an angry cat. "But he's *not*! He can't be that close to death!"

"I look that bad, do I?" Evariste mildly asked. He saw Angelique tentatively raise her hand.

Sit. Still.

Her fingers trembled as she reached for his face.

SIT. STILL.

Her warm fingertips grazed his cheek, and then she flicked some of his hair off his forehead while he didn't so much as move a muscle.

If it didn't take all my effort not to yank her against me, if I had the mental capacity to spare, I'd be proud of myself.

When he could bear it no longer, he caught her hand in his and squeezed it. "I'm okay, Angel. I'll be fine until you find me."

Angelique nodded seriously. "And I *will* find you," she promised. "I'm already moving the skies with Pegasus. If I have to move the ground, as well, I will." A glassy look passed through her eyes, and she yawned.

"Sleepy?" Evariste asked.

"I'm sleepy in a dream. How stupid," Angelique muttered.

Evariste wanted to beg her to stay—he didn't know what would happen once she left, and in this moment, he could feel both sparks of his magic and the sharp but comforting edge that marked out Angelique's powers.

"Angel..." Evariste trailed off as he watched Angelique's eyes flutter shut.

Do I try to convince her it's me? Or do I try to convey as much about the enemy as I can? What's most important? He rubbed his forehead. "You should know—"

Angelique abruptly grabbed him by the shoulder and half-threw herself on him in a hug, her face pressed against his neck.

Evariste froze, except for his arms—which automatically tightened around her and clutched at the fabric of her dress.

Her soft hair rubbed against his cheek, and they were so close, her breath tickled his neck. "Evariste?" she whispered.

Evariste swallowed audibly.

She sighed a little, and Evariste could tell by the way her body relaxed, she was slipping from her waking dream. "I wish you were here," she said.

He blinked, her breathing deepened, and she was asleep. The powerful flavor of her magic faded, and Angelique disappeared from his arms as her magic retreated, breaking whatever connection their powers had forged.

Evariste sat still, trying to preserve that tiny moment of joy in his mind so he could last through whatever nightmares he was plagued with next.

Wait. He paused, revisiting his previous thoughts. *Her magic faded, breaking off the connection* our *powers forged. That means my magic—even though it's separated from me—recognized our connection and reached for her...Is that why all of these curses have romantic love as their weakness?*

Because I love Angelique?

CHAPTER 18

It wasn't until noon the following day that Pegasus and Angelique finally caught up to the wyvern.

It had landed in the scant patch of flat plains and farmland that lay between the giant forest surrounding Swan Lake and the beginning of the mountain range that separated Kozlovka from Verglas to the east.

This made it a pain to sneak up on, as there wasn't much to hide behind. Angelique was forced to use an invisibility spell, but keeping Pegasus covered was something of a struggle given his propensity to wander off when she was watching the wyvern through the spyglass.

This has all been great. *Just* great. She didn't bother to camouflage the scowl that twisted her face as she tip-toed closer to the wyvern. (She wanted to get in striking distance so she could hit it hard before it was able to flee to the sky.)

Chasing after a deadly creature is always a fun time, and I just love *dreaming of Evariste. It doesn't make me feel at all guilty or like a failure. And it's definitely not worrying that he looked like death warmed over in the privacy of my own thoughts. Yep. Just a* great *time.*

She paused when a breeze drifted through the air, bringing the wyvern's stench with it. The wyvern reeked of decay—an overpowering and sour smell that made Angelique's already upset stomach churn.

When her gag reflex subsided, Angelique resumed stalking the wyvern, tugging on her magic to confirm her invisibility spell was in place. (Pegasus' hot breath on her back confirmed he was right behind her.)

She carefully started to twist her magic, preparing for the slew of spells she planned to sling at the monster.

Her heart thudded in her eardrums, and she swallowed sharply.

The wyvern, unaware of their presence, stretched its wings out in the noon sun, growling as it twitched its tail back and forth.

This is it. I have to make my attacks count, or it will take to the sky again, and even if I engage it, I'm not certain it will stick around to fight if it catches sight or scent of Pegasus.

Angelique squared her shoulders and breathed shallowly—the wyvern's reek made her eyes water.

She pulled more of her magic, her eyebrow twitching when she felt it slide down her arms in a cool, assuring sensation. Her magic tickled her senses, luring her with a call for more.

Angelique clenched her teeth and ignored the feeling. She waited until the wyvern looked north, then moved.

Now!

Angelique's invisibility spell spilled from her shoulders as she threw the most powerful magic she had crafted—an ice spell.

Ice so thick and cold it crackled and steamed in the sunshine spread across the wyvern's leathery wings, freezing them into their stretched-out position.

The wyvern roared its irritation, tottering slightly as it swiveled back around to face her.

Angelique threw the next spell she had prepared—a sleep charm.

The wyvern's blood-red eyes shut for a moment before it shook its head free of the spell's influence. Green smog puffed from its nostrils before it spat at her.

After her fight with the basilisk, Angelique had been prepared for the sleep spell to be ineffective, so she already had a shield raised in front of her. It blocked the gooey green spit—which bubbled and frothed on her shield's iridescent surface.

Chunks of ice started to crack and fall from the wyvern's wings, so Angelique strengthened the spell, making the wings sag with the inflexible weight.

The wyvern whipped its tail at her, but Angelique grabbed the ground with her magic and ripped it up, creating a wall.

The wyvern hissed when it bashed its tail into the shield and dug its talons into the grassy turf.

I need a visual on the wound the Black Swan Smugglers gave it.

Angelique broke off a part of her earth wall and flung it at the wyvern, beaning it in the chin so its head snapped up.

For a moment, Angelique saw the injury. Though it appeared to have scabbed over, it oozed pus around the edges.

In a rush, she packed her magic into a powerful fireball—one so potent and dense it burned with the light blues and whites of a star—and threw it at the wound.

The fireball exploded with a deafening boom that shook the ground. A massive wave of heat rolled across the plain, and Angelique stumbled, her ears ringing and her eyes blurry from the white of the flames.

When she could finally see, she saw the wound was opened again—though it was an angry burnt black, and watery blood dripped from it.

In the chaos of the moment, the wyvern freed one of its wings from its ice encasing. It used the strong muscle and bone that lined the top of the wing and smashed her into the ground.

Angelique's lungs burned and she gasped, but she couldn't get enough air.

Chortling, the wyvern scrambled toward her, its acidic spit dripping from its gaping maw and hissing as it spattered on the ground.

Angelique patted the ground with her hand, flooding it with her magic.

Another earth shield sprouted in front of her. But the wyvern bit right through it.

Her body rattled and aching, Angelique twisted fine threads of her powers into alteration magic and directed it to the dirt the wyvern chewed on. It changed from rich soil to sticky spiderweb, pulling its mouth shut.

The wyvern coughed, then balanced on one foot and clawed at its webbed mouth with the talons of its other foot.

Angelique finally got enough air to roll to the side, barely avoiding the gummy mass of web the wyvern spat out.

She scrambled to prepare another attack, and somewhere nearby, Pegasus trumpeted.

The wyvern hissed at the constellation and raised its wings. It flexed, shattering the remaining ice on its left wing, which rained down on Angelique—nearly thumping her in the head.

Angelique curled in a ball until only flaky bits of ice were falling, then she sprang to her feet and yanked on her magic.

I have to keep it grounded!

She scrambled to throw another ice spell at it, but the wyvern flapped its wings, tossing her back to the ground with the force of the air. It raised grass and sediment that stung her eyes and made it impossible to see.

An angry hiss, and the wyvern was airborne.

Angelique felt the tight weave of her magic and directed it at the wyvern, but he was already too high and too far out of reach.

Angelique grasped her head and kicked the ground. "Blast it!"

Pegasus pranced up to her, maneuvering so he stood sideways in front of her, giving her easy access to the saddle on his back.

Angelique exhaled, mussing her bangs, then nodded at him. She scrambled into the saddle. "We've got to catch it!"

Pegasus tossed his head then took off at a gallop, charging across the plains, his flaming mane and tail streaming in the wind.

UNFORTUNATELY, although Pegasus kept pace with the wyvern at a slow, rolling canter, the creature soared too high for Angelique to reach him with any magic.

One hour passed, and then two, and the wyvern showed no signs of stopping.

Finally, Angelique decided to create a trap of sorts.

She and Pegasus looped wide around the wyvern—getting in front of it. Angelique then dismounted and sent Pegasus back the way they had come, so the constellation drove the wyvern toward her.

Angelique stood not far from the base of the southernmost mountain in the mountain range that separated Kozlovka and Verglas.

Sweat dripped down her spine as the hot sun beat down on her and she gathered layer upon layer of her magic.

I need to make this strong enough to stun and ground the wyvern.

Her fingertips tingled with the shocking sensation of the lightning spell that she held. Normally she didn't dare channel so much magic for a single attack spell, but she had to pin the wyvern down.

I can't trail it indefinitely!

Her magic crowded around her hands, eager for her to pull more despite the huge amount she had gathered already. She was tempted to listen to its alluring whisper—but less because the power was attractive and more because she was sweaty, dirty, and she wanted that wyvern down.

Pegasus—a smudge of black and light blue—screamed a challenge as he thundered after the wyvern, who was swiftly drawing closer to the mountains—and thus Angelique.

Angelique licked her cracked lips and hunched over her magic, trying to hide its bright light as the wyvern drew closer.

It lashed its tail through the sky, slightly adjusting its course. It must have thought Pegasus was far enough away, for it lost some altitude.

Angelique, with baited breath, felt out the distance. She had used lightning because the weather spell allowed for a greater distance...one the wyvern *just* fell in range of.

Now!

She lashed out with everything she had, pushing more power into the spell.

A massive lightning bolt cut through the sky, striking the wyvern so it lit up with electricity.

The peal of thunder that accompanied the spell was so loud it made Angelique's already abused ears ring, so she barely heard the wyvern scream as it started to fall from the sky.

Its muscles and wings twitched and spasmed.

Angelique scrambled so she wouldn't be directly under the thing as it fell, her ears still aching from the thunder.

The wyvern corrected itself at the last moment, barely curling up its legs in time to avoid scraping the ground as it climbed higher in the air.

Angelique tried to craft another spell, but the wyvern hit her in the torso with its tail, slamming her into a large boulder with a painful crunch.

She fell face-first on the ground as her hearing started to return, and she could hear the labored whoosh of the wyvern's wings.

The spot between her shoulder blades throbbed with pain—she had caught the edge of the boulder there somehow.

She peeled herself off the ground and glared at the wyvern—which was already out of reach.

"How is this *possible*? I STRUCK YOU WITH LIGHTNING!" Angrily, she sat up—then regretted it instantly when the pain in her upper back spread.

She brushed dead grass off her dress with a snarl. "How can it keep flying after being struck by lightning? This is crazy! This is *insane*! How am I supposed to beat it if it can take a fireball to the gut and a lightning bolt to the head and *keep flying*!"

She stood, and the world swirled around her, making her stagger. For a sickening moment, her stomach gurgled, and Angelique worried she might have hit her limit.

She stilled, taking inventory of her magic—which was just as pushy, cool, and tempting as usual, irritatingly enough.

Angelique peered up at the unforgiving sun, and the headache from the day before made its triumphant return.

My physical stamina is dropping fast. Even if my magic is good to keep fighting, I can't keep this sort of grueling pace without stopping. Is that what it's trying to do? Outlast me?

She wiped the sweat off her forehead and tried to straighten her throbbing back. Her eyes stung as she made out the black smudge of Pegasus, who had slowed his pace.

Good. Angelique plopped back down on the ground and leaned against the boulder the wyvern had tossed her into, intending to make the most of this unexpected break.

The pounding of her headache faded just a tiny bit as the shadow of a scrubby bush covered her. *I'm going to have to think of a trap of some sort to ground that thing. Unless I want to try slinging spells at it from Pegasus' back, but that seems needlessly dangerous and has too great of a potential that there will be innocents who are accidentally slain in the chaos.*

She patted her troubled belly. *Nadia said soldiers were sent after it. Maybe we could lure it to those areas. The scent of the soldiers might cover Pegasus' smell...*

The loud stomp of footsteps made Angelique crack her eyes open, then sit up straighter.

A man leading a horse marched not far away, heading in the direction of Swan Lake. It hurt to look at him, for he wore a burnished gold chestplate that threatened to blind Angelique in the unforgiving summer sun. His golden cape was barely any less eye-catching. Even so, there was something about him. Not cruel or dark, as the mage who attacked her in Zancara had been, but perhaps...shadowy?

It feels like he has magic, but I can't be certain. I hate my shortcomings in magic sensitivity. It's far more useful than my blasted core magic!

Despite the possibility of magic, she was certain he wasn't a mage. Given the heel-dragging the Conclave had already done, they wouldn't let any mage within reasonable distance of Swan Lake. (They couldn't risk any of their people. Although, it seemed Finnr and the others were perfectly willing to risk *her*!)

Angelique held her breath and pushed herself against the rock, hoping he wouldn't notice her. Unfortunately, he glanced once in her direction, then immediately looked at her again and stopped altogether.

She stiffened, and suspicion made her magic bubble, though she forcefully held it in check.

The maybe-magic-possibly-dangerous man raised bushy eyebrows at her. "You're an enchantress," he stated more than asked.

Angelique stood, keeping her right hand hidden behind her back as she started weaving some of her magic. (Encountering and fighting the black mage in Zancara had not done anything to make her less paranoid and more friendly with strangers.) "I'm a mage—can I help you?"

He laughed. "You're not a mage! You have far too much magic to be anything but an enchantress."

...So it has come to this. A random man I encounter in the wilds of Kozlovka is better able to sense magic than I—a trained apprentice of many years—can. She would have stared off into the distance with

grim reservation if she hadn't been still suspicious of this *talented* stranger.

"I'm an Enchantress-in-Training," Angelique corrected.

"Close enough," the stranger said. "You're here for the wyvern, I assume."

Angelique closed off the twist of her magic and held her prepared spell—lighting, again, though she was certain it would work better this time—in her hand. "Yes," she confirmed.

"Good," the man barked. "Those royal idiots should have taken care of it immediately, but they just proved their uselessness again and *missed*."

Angelique had to stiffen her back to keep from shifting. There was something about this man…he didn't feel *evil*…but she wasn't keen on letting her gaze wander from him either. "It seems to get stronger the longer it is free."

"Naturally—which is why they were supposed to take care of it quickly." He sighed and lifted a hand to his head. "You try to plan well, but it seems one can never expect enough stupidity from those around them."

Angelique frowned. "What do you mean?"

"It means I am glad to see you are here to rescue all of us…*helpless…common folk*," he said.

Angelique stared pointedly at his ornate chestplate. "You are considered one of the common folk?"

"Yes, Lady Enchantress…what is your name?" His smile was a little cloying, but Angelique didn't feel any magic stir in him.

"Angelique," she reluctantly said.

"Very good, Lady Enchantress Angelique—oh." He paused and met her gaze, studying her for several long seconds. "I would have expected someone a bit more charming."

A muscle twitched in Angelique's cheek. "*I beg your pardon?*"

"Just, he doesn't seem the type to like sarcasm. Though to survive as long as he has, I suppose he might have a salty streak as well."

"Who are you talking about?" Angelique fed more power into her lightning spell and slowly drew her hand to her side—there was something about his cagey way of speaking that set off her hackles.

"You'll figure it out eventually," the stranger said. "And if you don't, then you don't deserve an answer anyway. Besides, I don't really care about it except to confirm that you're going to slay the wyvern."

"Of course I am."

"Wonderful. Hurry up, then, and finish the job." He started to stride away, his horse following after him, but he paused after just a few steps. He looked back at her, a serious expression on his face. "I hope you give them hell," he said. "Don't hold back—and don't second-guess yourself."

Feeling bewildered, Angelique finally flicked away her crackling lightning spell.

"If anyone asks if I care, I *don't*! I'm just worried about her! And perhaps the second her," the man shouted as he resumed storming off.

Angelique narrowed her eyes as she watched him go. Again, she reached out, trying to get a sense of his magic. She still couldn't tell how much he had, but there was something *familiar* about it.

I feel like I've encountered it before...but it doesn't have that dark and oily feel black mages have. Maybe he is a Veneno Conclave mage. She raised her eyebrow as the twinkle of his burnished armor faded. *But I'd find that hard to believe.*

Fire crackled, and Angelique was almost flipped over her feet when Pegasus "affectionately" slammed his head into her.

"Ouch." She staggered a few feet. "Yes, hello, Pegasus. I'm glad to see you too."

A star twinkled on his forehead.

Angelique grimaced. "No, the lightning didn't keep the wyvern down. We'll have to try again."

He snorted and maneuvered himself so she could more easily climb into the saddle. Angelique rested a hand on the stirrup leather. "Say...that man who just left. Is he a black mage?"

Pegasus turned his head in the stranger's direction. He swished his tail, then resumed a relaxed posture.

Well, at least he's not a threat, then. Angelique struggled her way into the saddle, then closed her eyes against the consuming pain of her renewed headache. *If he was, Pegasus would have gone after him, I think. Though that doesn't mean he's a Conclave mage—just someone Pegasus has no interest in.*

It occurred to Angelique that Pegasus had no interest in anyone besides herself and Evariste if they did not pose a threat. But given Pegasus' mysterious power as a constellation, she concluded it was probably better not to think of it and turned her thoughts toward more constructive things.

"All right, Pegasus. Let's go slay a wyvern."

Pegasus blew out hard from his nostrils, producing glowing sparks. A toss of his head and he lunged into a canter, bearing down on the wyvern once again.

ANGELIQUE'S fun and games with the wyvern stretched on. Twice more, she managed to hit the monster with powerful spells, and each time it escaped her before she could successfully force it to land.

She managed to strike the belly wound again, but the wyvern got another hit in with its tail, so for her efforts, Angelique was the recipient of bruised ribs and a cut through her eyebrow that kept dribbling blood.

Night fell, and Angelique and Pegasus chased the wyvern up and down the mountain before Angelique finally came up with her new plan.

She stood alone on the mountain side, holding a flickering ball of flames to light up her location.

The light shed crawled across fractured and abandoned weapons—broken spears, snapped arrows, swords stabbed into the ground, and more—casting misshapen shadows on the ground.

Her nose twitched from the putrid smell of the dragon's spit, even though it was days old, but when hatching her plan Angelique had specifically chosen this location—one of the spots where the wyvern had fought with the Kozlovkan army and had successfully escaped.

She couldn't come up with a real reason for picking this spot. Or rather, as she gazed at the fallen weapons, she knew there was one *particular* reason why, but she couldn't—or perhaps wouldn't—admit it to herself.

Angelique cleared her throat and turned her back to the battlefield, blotting out her thoughts.

From this spot on the northern side of the mountain, she could see the glowing ring of light that traced out the boundaries of a tiny village and dimly lit its quaint buildings.

A church bell rang, and the chorus of crickets almost drowned out the faint calls of livestock. As Angelique stared at it, she smiled, then frowned.

We've chased the wyvern all around this mountain. Why hasn't it tried to go for the village? Did they fight it off before when it encountered soldiers here?

The wyvern's sputtering hiss tore through the night, pushed on by Pegasus' unique and high-pitched neigh.

Angelique let her shoulders sag and did her best to look as weary and beaten as she felt, hoping to draw the wyvern in.

She heard the rhythmic beats of the wyvern's wings, and, as agreed, Pegasus' calls fell farther behind.

Angelique held her fire higher as she squinted into the inky black sky.

There! The light of Angelique's bright flames reflected on the sicky yellow of the wyvern's leathery skin. The wyvern chortled as it circled above her, its red eyes glowing in the darkness of night.

Her heart pounded in her throat, but she played out her assigned role, gasping and staggering backwards as if frightened.

It spit at her—which Angelique ran to avoid. The green gunk hissed when it hit the ground, and each labored flap of the wyvern's wings spread the acidic scent of its spit.

Angelique fell back a few more steps, acting feeble when it really was just a feint to get out from under the wyvern because—

Pegasus—the flames of his mane and tail burning bright, and the velvet black feathers of his wings shining in the moonlight—trumpeted as he emerged in the sky. Just above the wyvern, he folded his wings and extended his front legs, smashing between the wyvern's shoulder blades in a blinding collision.

The wyvern screeched and was tossed to the ground like a rag doll, Pegasus standing on the much larger creature.

The constellation snorted as he leaped off the wyvern, disappearing over its far side.

Angelique threw her arms wide, releasing the two spells she had prepped in advance.

The ground swallowed the wyvern's feet, anchoring it to the ground while fire exploded around it.

Angelique channeled raw power through her hands, then threw it at the wyvern, hitting it directly in the wound.

The wyvern shrieked in pain but thrashed its wings, breaking through the earth's crust and pulling its clawed feet free.

It took a few fumbling steps, hobbling when it stepped on a wooden shield and the talons of its hind feet pierced straight through. It flexed its claws, shattering the shield, and its belly brushed a tree sapling as it took another staggering step.

Angelique funneled her magic into the sapling, which grew—its trunk rapidly thickening as it shot upwards. It almost impaled the wyvern, but the monster drew back just in time, so instead the tree scraped its chest and slapped its face with its new branches.

The wyvern snapped its jaws and flung itself at the tree, grasping it with its talons. It yanked on the tree trunk, ripping it from the ground roots and all, then flung it at Angelique.

She dropped to the ground and threw up a shield, yipping when the tree bounced down directly on the shield and rolled off.

While she struggled to her feet, the wyvern stretched out its wings and gave an experimental flap.

No! It's going to get away—again!

A stabbing pain ripped through her ribs as she threw more magic—this time a monsoon-level wind that yanked on the wyvern's wings, ripping painfully through the holes she and the Black Swan Smugglers had put there.

The wyvern lunged at her, spittle dripping from its teeth.

Angelique scurried backwards to avoid it, but she reopened the cut that sliced through her eyebrow. Blood dripped down her eye, blinding her on that side. She took a staggering step, barely avoiding the wyvern when it once again stretched its wings wide.

Every muscle in her body screamed with pain, and Angelique felt the edge of exhaustion loom behind her. With her good eye, Angelique glanced at the shards of shattered spears and broken arrows that littered the ground around her.

And her magic churned—powerful and without reserve.

It's war magic.

The wyvern screamed and flapped its wings, tensing its legs underneath it as it prepared to push off.

But it will flee again, and I don't have the strength to follow it any farther. It might get that village.

She felt pulled in two directions. The allure of her magic pulled on her, but it didn't quite manage to cover up the worried whisper that using it was giving in. But the weight of duty and the knowledge that if she didn't take the wyvern down now, she'd need a day to recover—which left the monster a day to kill and destroy—made her sick.

I shouldn't use my magic. The Conclave wouldn't want me to—my life isn't even in danger this time. But...

There was a long moment where the world was eerily quiet.

Then Angelique reached for her core magic.

CHAPTER 19

Her war magic ripped free with a tremendous boom that shook the very mountain.

Every sharp rock and splintered piece of wood within eyesight became a weapon in her grasp. But it didn't stop there. Her powers wrapped around the broken pieces of the shield the wyvern had stomped on and shattered, the cracked spears, abandoned swords, all the weapons the soldiers had left behind. Each jagged rock, splinter, and weapon glowed silver.

The glittering shards floated higher and higher, filling the air with a beautiful shimmer.

The wyvern lifted off, its tail dragging on the ground, but it was too late.

Angelique lifted her silver-eyed gaze to the wyvern, and the magic-infused, razor-sharp shards and weapons pierced straight through the creature's hide. Some of the pieces punched through the open wound or ripped through the frill on its neck.

The wyvern landed with a ground-shaking thump. It hissed as its eyes went glassy, then its chest stopped moving while the rest of the body sagged.

It was finally dead.

Angelique immediately broke off contact with her icy core magic and sucked in great heaves of air.

She toddled a few steps, dimly staring at the felled monster. "It only took one attack. Just a few seconds," she said, dazed.

Pegasus—his black wings disintegrating into a cloud of feathers—nickered as he trotted up to her.

She stared unseeingly at his starry shoulder. "I hit it with the fire of a star, lightning, and ice, and it didn't falter. But one blow with my magic and..."

Angelique shuddered as Pegasus curled protectively around her.

Her guts churned, but she didn't feel the tell-tale stirrings of nausea that signaled she had used too much of her power.

That's a good thing...maybe? Or maybe not, because it means I can cause so much destruction and still not run into my price.

Though her magic wasn't taxed, Angelique could feel her body shutting down. Her legs trembled, and she let herself sit down with a thump, leaning gratefully into Pegasus when he lay down beside her.

She wearily stared at the still-bleeding wyvern carcass.

More than ever before, I feel it bone-deep that my magic excels in slaughter...but what scares me most is that I don't at all regret using it.

She closed her eyes and let sleep steal her thoughts.

ANGELIQUE WAS UNSURPRISED when she opened her eyes in her dream and found a smiling Evariste sitting on a stump.

"Of course, my subconscious would make me face you after using my war magic," she muttered, "because I don't feel guilty and worried enough already."

Evariste smiled—it was the affectionate and bright one he wore whenever he was particularly happy. "Hello, my dear apprentice!"

Angelique was dismayed to see that he still looked awful.

Evariste had always been blindingly handsome, but even with his bright smile, his dream-self was only a shadow. His blonde hair—which had always been such a silky texture it made her jealous—was dull and mussed. The planes of his face were *too* sharp due to a noticeable loss of weight, and as he stood up, he moved as though it hurt.

Angelique rubbed her eyes. "Why do I torture myself like this? I don't recall being a masochist."

"I have been pondering ways I can prove to you I am not a dream," he paused, then changed his tune. "You seem upset. What happened?" He slowly drew closer, stopping just a little too near her for comfort, but his concern distracted her enough that she didn't automatically back away.

She stared up into his face. *It's his eyes that are the worst. They used to always dance—with laughter, mischief, and warmth. Now they barely glimmer.*

"You're not dead," she fiercely said.

"I'm not," he amiably agreed.

Angelique scowled. "I mean it. You're. *Not*. Dead!"

He nodded. "Quite so."

She made a noise of irritation and scratched her head. "Then why do you *look* like you're dying?"

"Angel." A playful smile that was so *familiar* it made Angelique's heart ache lingered around the corners of Dream Evariste's mouth. "When I get back, we need to revisit your lessons on bedside manners."

Her throat nearly closed, and her eyes stung.

It's so bittersweet to see him like this.

She impatiently clasped her hands together. "Yes. Well. When I do find you, we'll have much bigger problems to address." She frowned as she stared at the familiar forest. "My magic being one of them."

He touched her elbow, almost making her leap out of her skin. "Did something happen?" he asked.

She couldn't bring herself to look up. *If I see another one of his smiles, I'll start crying again, and that's probably the most useless thing a person can do inside a dream.*

"No." Her voice was unnaturally high. She cleared her throat and tried again. "No. Or rather, something happened, but I can't say it's unexpected given the events of the past five years."

"Ah."

A muscle twitched in Angelique's cheek at that oh-too-familiar sound of understanding and sympathy. *It's not him. It's just a dream.* She stared down at the hem of her skirt and wished she'd wake up, no matter how tired she was from the wyvern fight.

"If that's so, then I've a question for you. Where are we?" Dream Evariste motioned to the surrounding forest—which was cheerful and noisy with the song of birds and the occasional yip of a fox. "I haven't been everywhere on this continent, but very nearly, and I don't particularly recognize this forest."

"Of course you would want to talk about this place. If it's going to be a torturous night, we might as well go for maximum pain, right?"

"If it brings you pain, we don't have to speak of it."

Angelique scratched her nose, aware that Dream Evariste stepped even closer so their arms were always touching. *It seems I am disgustingly needy, if Dream Evariste's actions are anything to go by.*

She slightly shook her head. "No, no. If I'm going through all this effort in my own dreams, I might as well face my mountain of guilt." Angelique crossed the small clearing—hopping over the stump in the middle. She slipped past the first layer of trees and peeled back the branches of a bush to reveal an idyllic village.

It was a tiny town with only a handful of brick-and-plaster buildings that were worn gray with age. But most windows had brightly painted flower or herb boxes, and the cobblestone village square was painstakingly clean. Smoke curled from tall chimneys, and geese chuckled as a boy chased them off to graze in the green grass surrounding the village.

This close to the town, Angelique could hear the villagers call out to one another with laughter in their voices.

"What village is this?" Dream Evariste asked.

She watched a villager draw water from the well. "The village I grew up in: Joie."

"Oh," Dream Evariste said.

Angelique pursed her lips. "That was an 'oh' of judgement."

"Not at all. Rather, the size of your town explains something that had always bothered me," Dream Evariste said. "You arrived at Luxi-Domus rather late. Usually fairy godmothers and godfathers find children with magic when they are much younger. But given the size of your hometown, it is perhaps not so surprising they didn't find you until your magic emerged. But I've also always wondered what sort of place you grew up in."

Angelique couldn't peel her eyes away from her village. "It doesn't look like this anymore. When the goblins attacked, they destroyed a couple buildings."

Dream Evariste took Angelique's hand and squeezed it. "You are referring to the goblin attack in which both of your parents died and your magic manifested?"

She had no words. She could only nod.

They watched Joie in silence. Dream Evariste rubbed his thumb across the top of her hand, but she was so lost in her regrets, she hardly felt it.

"I could have saved them," she said abruptly. "If I had used my magic sooner, I could have killed the goblins *as* they attacked—not after. My parents and all the other casualties could have lived if I'd just moved a little sooner."

Dream Evariste pulled her into a hug, even though she tried to stiffen against it. "Angel, you couldn't have used it earlier, for your magic didn't manifest until after your parents had already died."

"But isn't that also my fault?" Angelique scrunched her nose and narrowed her eyes to keep the tears at bay. "Couldn't I have let my magic loose sooner? If I'd been willing, couldn't I have made it happen?"

Dream Evariste rested his chin on the top of her head. "You as a person cannot control when your magic reveals itself. You deserve no guilt for this, Angelique. You *couldn't* have done anything."

"Just like I couldn't have used my war magic and saved you when black mages took you." Her voice sounded flat and dead to her own ears.

"That also was not your fault." There was some sharpness in Dream Evariste's voice, and he shifted his hold to her shoulders and slightly pulled her back so she could look up at him. "Don't *ever* blame yourself for that."

"Why not? I could have stopped it." Angelique glumly stated. "But my magic is just so powerful and tempting it scares me stiff —and then I hesitate."

"Angel," Dream Evariste growled. "You didn't capture me and use me for dark purposes. *Black Mages* did. These black mages deserve all the blame and the consequences. You have no responsibility for their actions!"

Angelique finally met his gaze. His eyes—one blue and one green—finally had that familiar light, the kind that made him look like he could fight the world. It was the same warmth that brightened his eyes when he proclaimed they were Stil's parents and the same brightness that made black mages tremble.

All the fight in Angelique crumpled. Her voice shook as she grabbed a fistful of his robes. "Why can't I find you?" she whispered. Tears clogged her eyes so she could barely see, but she felt Evariste wrap his arms around her in a tight hug. "Why did you leave me?"

Before he could answer, she shut her eyes and fell into a less-troubled sleep.

AFTER THAT KIND OF DREAM—OR perhaps it was the most bittersweet of nightmares?—Angelique did not waken feeling particularly rested. It was the first rays of the sun that woke her at dawn—and the persistent buzz of magic.

She rubbed her face as she tried to sort through the sensations that had mounted over the night while she slept—a gnawing weariness that seeing Dream Evariste had only worsened, physical pain, and a prickling feeling. "What is going on?"

She realized she was sprawled across Pegasus—her cheek pressed into his shoulder, and carefully sat up. She blanched a little when she saw a crusted spot of drool she had left on his glossy, unfathomable coat and hurried to buff it out before Pegasus noticed.

He allowed her to take a startling amount of liberties with him, but Angelique wasn't so sure her advanced set of permissions included drooling on him.

It could have been worse, I suppose. If I had cried in my sleep as I did in my dream, I might have snotted all over him.

Pegasus waited until she scrambled to her feet before he rocked to his.

She half-expected him to shake like a horse, but instead, he turned to face the rising sun and slightly bowed to it. He jerked his head up, and all the stars and swirling galaxies that drifted across his coat flared so brightly, he was impossible to look at for a moment.

Half-blinded, Angelique tottered on her feet, blinking in confusion when Pegasus pressed his muzzle to her temple, then clip-clopped past her.

She waited until she could see again before chasing after him. From their vantage point, they could see down the mountain and had a superb look at Swan Lake.

Pegasus stretched his neck in the lake's direction then swished his tail.

"What is it?" Angelique joined him, briefly hesitating before she threw an arm over his neck.

What looked like tiny red dots clustered around one end of the lake. A miniature thread looped around an island in the lake as well. Angelique didn't need magic sensitivity to realize she was seeing Rothbart's red spellwork.

She and Pegasus tilted their heads together and watched as the red bits seemed to shatter and then dissolve.

"It seems we were not the only ones to have an eventful night." Angelique squinted and tried to feel for the magic, but all that came to her was the overwhelming cool assurance of her own powers.

No matter how I work at it, it seems true and talented magic sensitivity is beyond my abilities.

She shook her head. "I can't make heads or tails of it. Can you?"

She looked at Pegasus, who stared at her with a cocked hoof and such apathy it was a clear communication that he *didn't care* what had happened.

Angelique scratched her cheek. "Right. Well. I'll need to get back to the lake—or Tsona Palace—to find out what happened."

Pegasus maneuvered himself so he stood in front of Angelique —his saddle and her saddlebag magically back in place.

Angelique slipped a foot in the stirrup and pushed off, intending to mount up. Instead, her leg gave out, and she smacked him in the side.

Pegasus turned his neck so he could peer back at her.

She patted his shoulder. "Sorry." She tried again, and this time succeeded in boosting herself up into the saddle. "I thought the Summit would be more restful than it was. But we can't stop now —let's head to Swan Lake."

ANGELIQUE AND PEGASUS STUMBLED UPON—OR rather, almost ran over—a squadron of soldiers with carts of supplies. They were headed in the direction of Swan Lake and were led by Zina—Odette's smuggler who had undergone the swan curse at the same time as the Swan Queen.

"Zina," Angelique called.

The smuggler waved to her, beckoning for her to come to the front of the line.

As Pegasus picked his way around the soldiers, Angelique felt the dappled heat of the sunshine that managed to wriggle past the leaves.

Wait a second.

Angelique peered up at the sun, then squinted at Zina. "Your curse is broken!"

Zina laughed. "Early this morning, Alexsei finally got it through Odette's head that he loved her!"

"It seems, then, that there are many congratulations to pass around."

"More than you think!" Zina grinned widely. "Rothbart has been defeated! And three more wyverns were slain!"

Angelique almost fell off Pegasus. "*What?*"

Zina hopped once in her glee. "Last night, he let loose four wyverns—all of them were young and clumsy; they were even less sure than the first wyvern we fought." She peered back over her shoulder to confirm that the soldiers were following her. "That's right, did you kill that loose wyvern?"

"Yes," Angelique grimly said. "It took longer than I wanted, but it's done. Though apparently I should be ashamed as a mage, seeing how you smugglers killed three."

Zina shook her head. "Like I said, ours were immature. They acted a bit like gangly babies, really. Moreover, we had soldiers helping, and Odile tamed the fourth wyvern, which helped us a lot."

Angelique's mind felt rusty, and she struggled to keep up. "Odile is Rothbart's daughter, is she not?"

"Yes," Zina confirmed. "She has some magic—the power to charm animals. Rothbart always said she didn't have much power, but he must have been wrong, seeing how she's got herself a pet wyvern. Right?"

"Yes." Angelique considered sliding off Pegasus' back, but when shifting in the saddle made her bruised ribs scream, she settled back down.

I'll put a slow healing spell on myself tonight. But if there was a battle with Rothbart, I might need to use more magic today for clean up, and I don't fancy making myself ill with my price.

"How was Rothbart defeated?" she asked.

"He was wearing full plate armor and standing out on the long bridge that attached his island castle to the shore," Zina said. "He threatened Odette, and she pushed him into the lake just before dawn. That was when Alexsei told Odette he loved her, and our curse shattered."

I guess that solves the riddle of the red lights.

The smuggler grimaced. "There weren't any casualties—but loads of soldiers and a few smugglers were injured. That's why I was sent back for supplies and resources. Swan Queen was going to go poking around Rothbart's castle, but she wasn't sure what she'd find given the creatures he liked to keep."

"You think he might have made more wyverns?"

"By my tail feathers, I hope not." Zina shook her head. "But he had hellhounds and a couple of other creatures too dangerous for Odile to gentle, and he might have set a few traps as well. Swan Queen was most concerned, though, that we secure his research on the wyverns."

Angelique's blood curdled in her veins. *That's right. He made those wyverns! If his process gets leaked to our enemies, they'll be able to make an army! Though if he was allied with them after all, we may be too late.*

Angelique bit her lip as she considered the dire possibilities.

"Everything all right, Lady Enchantress?" Zina asked.

Angelique forced a smile. "Yes, I'm fine, thank you. I'm going to write a few missives. There's a Lord Enchanter I need to alert to what has happened, and I'd like to send a message to a friend of mine to request her presence. She might be able to help with those hellhounds."

"That would be wonderful," Zina said. "Odette has a hard time saying no to Odile—we all do—and it would crush her to have them put down."

"I'll have to write the letters and send them off, so I'm going to dismount and see to that, but with Pegasus, I'll catch up with you again before you reach Swan Lake," Angelique concluded.

"Thank you—for everything you have done, Lady Enchantress," Zina said.

Angelique forced a tired smile to her lips. "I am glad I can help. We'll see you shortly."

"Right!"

ANGELIQUE WROTE her letters in such haste, she wondered if they were actually legible. First, she sent off the letter to Gemma and Stil requesting their presence in Kozlovka. She folded the message in an intricate butterfly pattern after spelling the paper against water and damage. Next, she sent off a letter to Clovicus detailing all she had learned about Rothbart and the wyverns. Finally, after a few minutes of consideration, Angelique sent off one last letter to Sybilla...about Odile.

As she had promised, Angelique easily caught up with Zina and the troops and joined their march to Swan Lake.

The shore closest to Rothbart's castle was a mess. There were gouges in the ground from wyvern claws and tails, and puddles of acidic spit littered the beachy space.

But what was perhaps most surprising was the wyvern.

It was parked—sitting similar to a roosted chicken—on the shore just by the bridge that spanned the lake and connected to Rothbart's crumbling castle. It was markedly smaller than the one Angelique had just killed, but it had the same red eyes. Its leathery skin was more of a muted yellow color, and it watched the soldiers swirl around it with a cocked head.

The soldiers warily eyed it but carried on with their duties, caring for the wounded and restoring order to the lake.

Angelique stared at the creature as it used the crest of its wing to clumsily scratch its face. "That's Odile's tamed wyvern?"

"Yes," Zina confirmed.

Angelique moved—intending to slip off the saddle—when Pegasus walked forward, picking his way around a dead wyvern.

"Lady Enchantress Angelique?" A soldier trotted at Pegasus' side. "May I announce your presence to Prince Yakov, Prince Alexsei, and Odette?"

"Please do," Angelique said.

The soldier bowed, then jogged down the lengthy bridge.

"Thank you!" Angelique called after him, just as Pegasus stopped in front of the roosted wyvern.

The constellation stared down at the creature. Though he stood still, fire blazed at his hooves, and the flames of his mane hissed and popped.

"Pegasus," Angelique murmured. "What are we doing?"

Pegasus trumpeted so loudly, the pealing tone echoed off Rothbart's castle. He abruptly reared, pawing at the air, then slammed down his hooves with an impossible amount of force, making the ground vibrate.

The wyvern curled its long neck and dropped its head until its chin rested on the shore. It peered up at Pegasus and flattened its half-folded wings against its back.

Pegasus snorted and tossed his head. Then he calmly turned around and trod back to the edge of the shore—where scrubby trees met the pebble-strewn beach—and halted.

Angelique—puzzled and slow thinking—sat atop his back, until Pegasus tucked his chin to his shoulder and nibbled on her foot.

"Sorry!" She slid off the saddle but gripped the stirrup leather for support when she landed heavily. "Was that your stamp of approval?"

Pegasus flicked his ears.

She tried again. "Do you think he'll turn on us?"

Pegasus snorted, then snapped his teeth at her.

"Okay." Angelique backed away. "I guess I'll go talk with Odette. I imagine I'll be here a while—why don't you return to the sky?"

Pegasus narrowed his dark, unfathomable eyes.

"I didn't say you were crabby!" Angelique unnecessarily defended herself. "It's just, it might be a while, and you've been traveling with me. I thought you might need the rest—and never mind," she grumbled.

Pegasus had stopped listening in the middle of her babble and ambled into the forest, his coat glittering in the dark shadows.

"Such a charming and warm constellation." Angelique stalked across the shore and toward the bridge. She glanced at the wyvern as she passed it, then peered out at Rothbart's home as she marched down the bridge, closing in on it. A short wall topped with nasty-looking spikes encircled the castle, which was perched on a tiny island. The castle itself had three towers and a square-shaped keep that was several stories high.

She found the soldier waiting for her just past the castle gates.

He pointed to the castle. "This way, Lady Enchantress." He led her past a set of grimacing gargoyles—their stone faces blurred slightly by years of wind and rain—and into the rickety castle.

The place was dark and dirty and smelled faintly of sulfur. Its walls lacked any ornamentation and were instead cracked and sported an occasional broken window.

But above the ruin, Angelique heard the tones of Odette's expressive voice.

She paused at the base of the stairs, cocking her head as she listened. "It seems they are just up the stairs."

"Very likely, Lady Enchantress," the soldier said. "They were going through Rothbart's study."

"Thank you for escorting me, but you needn't take me any farther." Angelique tried to smile at the soldier, but when she inhaled deeply, pain stabbed through her ribs, making it a task not to cringe.

"Of course." The soldier bowed and left.

Angelique waited for a moment and was delighted to hear Odette's voice draw closer—which hopefully meant she wouldn't have to climb the wretched steps—which would make her breathe deeply for her troubles and stab her in the ribs some more.

Instead, she was soon able to make out the conversation.

"...Too much science for me to ponder the stupidities of Yakov's character," Odette said. It was quiet until Angelique saw her boots at the top of the stairs, and the Swan Queen continued. "We'll have to take care of those hounds soon."

"There's no need," Angelique called up to Odette.

As she watched, Prince Alexsei, and a young woman with fine black hair and liquid-black eyes joined Odette. The trio hurried down the stairs, and Alexsei and Odette bowed when they reached the last step.

"Lady Enchantress," they said. Alexsei had dirt smeared across his light armor, and it looked like a bruise was forming on his neck, while Odette's clothes stank faintly of lake water.

Angelique took in their rather disheveled appearance with sympathy—a night of fighting would make *anyone* look rough, and smiled. "I believe I said to call me Angelique."

Ever the prince, Alexsei nodded. "Angelique, please allow me to introduce you to Odile—a good friend of ours."

He held out his hand to the dark-haired young lady, who trembled slightly as she stared at Angelique.

Angelique tilted her head as she studied her. "You are Rothbart's daughter?"

Odile trembled. "Y-yes."

Fear lived in Odile's eyes—but Angelique thought she could see hints of steel to the girl as well.

She knows what it means that her father is—or rather was—a sorcerer, and she's willing to pay for it. Thawed by Odile's heart, Angelique made a greater effort to smile in an attempt to reassure her. "I am glad to meet you—I have heard much about you from Odette and Alexsei."

Much is perhaps stretching the truth, but I don't want her worrying about me—or any other mages for that matter.

"If you'll excuse my interruption, Angelique, Yakov is in Rothbart's workroom," Alexsei said. "He's searching for any trace of reference material that will tell us how Rothbart made the wyverns. He could desperately use your help."

Angelique was going to ignore the request in favor of speaking with Odile, but she didn't miss the way Odette's eyebrows furrowed in frustration at the mention of Yakov.

Let's see...Yakov. He was the brash, loud one. Yes, I can see how leaving him alone in a sorcerer's workshop is a recipe for disaster.

Angelique took the first stair the trio had descended, and curtsied slightly—not out of social politeness but because she wobbled rather ungainly and wanted to cover it up. "I see. I can't keep him waiting, then, can I? I assume the workroom is upstairs?"

"Yes," Odette confirmed. "And just down the hall."

"Lady Enchantress?" Odile called.

What must I say for people to just call me Angelique? Get it stitched into the bodice of my gown? Or perhaps have it written on the palm of my hand so I can save myself the words. Aloud, Angelique sweetly said, "Please, Angelique."

Odile blushed a sweet pink, making Angelique feel a little guilty for her irritation. "If you please, Angelique," Odile said, "why won't it be necessary to take care of the hellhounds?"

Angelique tried to discreetly fix the jeweled clips that held some of her unruly tresses pinned to her head. "I've already sent word to a good friend of mine, the Grandmaster Craftmage Rumpelstiltskin. His wife, Gemma, has some experience with transforming the dark nature of hellhounds."

Odile perked. "Transforming?"

"Yes." Angelique raised her fingers with the intension of scrubbing her eyes—they felt gritty and tired—but then remembered where she was and forcibly lowered her hands. "Gemma shoved a starfire—a crystal light—into the mouth of a hellhound that was attacking her. It transformed into a white dog and now follows her like a guard. I believe she calls it Hvit."

Odile clasped her hands together, her eyes shining with joy. "So the hellhounds don't *have* to be evil?"

"No," Angelique confirmed. *Just, please, don't ask me why. No one has figured that out.*

Odile practically sagged with relief, but her smile didn't dim even as Odette playfully bumped her.

"Why don't you check on your wyvern, then you can ask Angelique for details as she and Yakov organize your father's papers?" Odette suggested.

Odile nodded happily. "Thank you, Angelique."

"Of course." Angelique climbed a few more stairs. "Come back as soon as you're finished."

Odile waved and hurried down the hallway, leaving Angelique to finish climbing up the staircase.

That's the young lady who managed to bag herself a pet wyvern. Interesting.

When Angelique reached the next floor, she dragged her

carcass down the hall and finally let herself rub her eyes like she wanted.

When Gemma comes, she'll take care of the hellhounds, and since Pegasus didn't seem to mind the wyvern, I'm not inclined to be concerned about it. But I need to introduce Sybilla to Odile right away—before anyone from the Veneno Conclave realizes she's got a rare monster at her beck and call. Severin will need to be updated, of course. I can send missives, but I likely need to make an in-person report to both him and Clovicus after I finish here...

Angelique heard the low growls and snarls of hellhounds enclosed behind a solid door as she swept down the hallway, keeping her ear's perked for—

CRASH!

Ahh yes, the sound of destruction. That must be Yakov.

When Angelique entered the ramshackle workshop, she was startled by the disarray. Books and papers were tossed everywhere across creaking tables. A few glass vials held various colorful liquids that had obviously sat too long given the thin films that settled on the liquids and the mucus-like crud that ringed some of the mouths of the vials.

The faint scent of smoke wafted off the eldest prince and a shattered pot that looked like it had once contained a shriveled fern was at his feet, but Angelique didn't think the general upheaval of the workshop was his doing.

"What happened here?" she asked.

Yakov hopped over the broken pot. "Angelique, so glad you made it back. You destroyed the other wyvern? How'd you do it?" He rubbed his hands together, and his grin was bright. "You missed a real good fight here at the lake! Kozlovkan troops took down three wyverns and killed that sodden sorcerer!"

"So I heard," Angelique said. "What happened here?" she repeated.

"Ah." He winced. "Yes. We've been looking for Rothbart's research and papers on his process for creating wyverns and can't find them." He scratched his chin, and his fingers—black with ash—left smudgy prints on his skin. "He torched everything in the dungeon—that's where he'd been keeping the wyverns when we first found out about them. Place was still smoldering when we arrived, so he must have done it just before he came out to fight us."

Angelique frowned so deeply, her forehead furrowed. "He burned all of his work on the wyverns?"

"Yep."

But why? If he was with the enemy that we've been fighting against for years, wouldn't he have left copies for them? Unless he expected to die while enacting his plan...but he attacked Odette and the others. Why not wait for the wyverns to be in a better condition—like the one I fought?

Angelique crossed the workshop, straining with all of her senses to search for magic.

"I think Odette was hoping to find something here in his workshop, but it seems like he destroyed everything of use." Yakov wandered back over to the table that held the vials of mysterious liquids and eyed them. "It's a good thing he didn't know how powerful Odile is—else he might not have practically pushed her at the Black Swan Smugglers and would have used her to better control his wyverns."

"It takes a lot of power to control such a beast—much less change its base nature as it seems she has done." Angelique felt only faint bits of what felt like burnt-out magic in the air, and whenever she and her silver magic turned it, the tiny whiffs fled like scurrying mice. "She must at least have enough magic to make fairy godmother."

She half-heartedly paged through a leather-bound book, but she could tell from the faded ink, it was old and likely did not contain what they were looking for.

"Can't you mages sense a person's magic and their potential?" Yakov asked.

"Yes, but it's an ability and a skill. Not all mages are talented at it," Angelique said.

Yakov poked one of the vials. "Still seems a bit odd—the man could make a wyvern but couldn't judge his own daughter's potential, yeah?"

Angelique paused. "It is said that the higher level of magic you achieve, the better you should be at sensing magic. There are exceptions, of course—I am not terribly skilled at sensing magic, and it's said the Verglas Snow Queen was the most powerful mage of her time, but she could barely sense anything as well."

She tapped her fingers on the corroded table and mulled over the idea. *But Yakov is correct. Rothbart seemed to exhibit a lot of erratic behavior for someone who Emperor Yevgeniy said was the scourge of his people for years.*

He was maniacal and a mad genius—he couldn't have created the wyverns otherwise. But why would such a cunning man rush his attack, torch his work, and completely misjudge the full depth of Odile's magic? I had hoped he wasn't working with whoever has Evariste, but I didn't think it was likely. Maybe, for once, my hopes are founded? Surely he must have had a goal in mind—

A bubbling hiss filled the room followed by a heartbeat of silence, then a tiny puff of air and a loud sloshing sound.

Angelique slowly turned around to face Yakov, who was holding an empty glass vial above a glass beaker that had previously held a blue liquid. Now it contained a gloppy green mixture. There had obviously been a magical reaction, given that Yakov's face and shirt were spattered with gobs of the green mixture.

The prince nodded and set the vial down. "That was exciting."

Angelique shut her eyes and counted to ten so she could speak without shouting. "That could have been poisonous."

"Really? But it smells like vodka!" Yakov's white teeth flashed extra bright against the green of his skin.

"Please refrain from further explorations in unknown potions, Your Highness," Angelique wryly said.

"Do you think the green will come out of my shirt?"

"No."

"Ahh, such a pity!"

"I think it would be best if we switched, prince, and *I* search near the vials while you finish paging through the books." Angelique crossed the room—being careful not to trod on a shard of the fern's broken pot.

"You don't trust me?" Yakov asked.

Angelique gave him her best elegant enchantress smile. "Not even a bit."

After perhaps twenty more minutes of searching, Odile—bright eyed and slightly out of breath, veered into the room. "Have you found anything?"

"Not yet," Angelique said. "Perhaps we could search his quarters?"

"It's worth a try, but he was rather meticulous in where he kept his work," Odile said. "It's how Odette was able to sabotage his experiments so many times."

Yakov leaned against a tall workbench and propped his arm against its edge. "How is your wyvern?"

"Fine!" Odile smiled, flashing dimples in her cheeks. "Some of the soldiers have been feeding it fish from the lake, which it seems to enjoy. I mean to try feeding it some fruit or vegetables later today, for I *think* it might be an omnivore."

Angelique listened to the interaction as she poked through another pile of yellowed papers. *Yes, Sybilla was the right choice to send word to with her alteration magic. Plus, I imagine if I tried to introduce Odile to Clovicus, he would accuse me of foisting her off on him and would then train her specifically to terrorize the Council.*

"I take it you haven't uncovered anything new?" Odette leaned against the doorframe, her arrival sudden and quiet.

Angelique shook her head. "I'm afraid not."

The Swan Queen sighed. "I expected as much. Especially after..." She trailed off and glanced at Odile. Though she offered her friend a smile, her eyes seemed a little red, and her nose was slightly stuffy.

Has she been crying?

"You were fast—are you certain you're really done inspecting your camp?" Odile asked.

Odette tapped a ledger book on her shoulder. "Yes. Actually, I'll be leaving for a delivery soon. Alexsei is coming with me. But first, I need to talk to you, Odile, and you, Angelique." She glanced at Yakov. "Sorry, Yakov, but I need you to shake some tailfeathers and get lost."

He laughed deeply, not at all bothered by her blunt manner of speaking. "Of course. It seems it is to be a meeting of lovely and beautiful women. Naturally I would not be allowed. I shall check on my men and see if Lexsei needs any help!"

"Thanks, Yakov." Odette drummed her fingers on her logbook. "Odile, do you mind if the three of us speak in your tower?"

"No, not at all! This way, if it pleases you, Angelique."

Odile's tower was perhaps the most solid and beautifully decorated part of the castle.

All the windows were intact, and the floor was quite pretty with ornate tile in stylish, geometric designs. The aroma of sweet grain drifted through the tidy space, as did a wild assortment of...*magical* creatures.

Odile shooed all of the animals from the little sitting room to which they had adjourned, except for a giant moth the size of a hunting dog and a deer-like creature that vaguely resembled a unicorn, though its single horn grew out of its muzzle.

"Odile's pets can be somewhat alarming to behold, but they are harmless," Odette assured Angelique as she leaned against the wall—which was covered in white plaster.

Angelique smiled and attempted to elegantly seat herself on

an armchair covered in gold velvet. "Given that Odile tamed a wyvern, I don't imagine a moth is going to be any trouble."

Odile blushed. "You are too kind."

"Not at all," Angelique said. "I speak the truth. Now, Odette, what is it that you wished to discuss?"

Odette sighed deeply. Slowly, she opened her ledger and pulled out a small stack of papers. "There isn't an easy way to say this, but Rothbart purposely lost to us. Because he wanted to protect Odile."

Odile frowned. "After the stress of breaking your curse, have your wits become addled?" she frankly asked. "As much as it pains me to say it, my father had no regard for me."

"But he did." Odette held the papers up, took the top few and passed them to Odile, then handed the others over to Angelique. "Your mother, Sorceress Suzu, was apparently in the habit of making vaguely worded threats about you to Rothbart. In the most recent letter—I believe you have it, Angelique—she threatens to kill you if Rothbart doesn't eliminate the Kozlovkan royal family."

Angelique—in her tiredness—actually lost control of her mouth. "Huh?" She gawked at the letter she held.

Thankfully, neither of the girls noticed—Odette was watching Odile with a concerned look, and Odile almost dropped the papers. "W-what?"

"Additionally, it was not Alexsei and I who broke the curse, but rather Rothbart," Odette continued. "It seems your observations on the spell were spot-on, Angelique. The spells were tied together because then Rothbart could remove a single line and make the spells on myself, my smugglers, and the castle dismantle."

Angelique gripped the arms of the chair, her mind reeling.

Poor Odile, however, just stared blankly at her knees. "My mother wants me *dead*?"

Odette kneeled in front of her friend. "I'm sorry about Suzu

—she is obviously dark and mad beyond imagination. Her ruthless darkness bears no reflection on you, Odile—it is not your fault; there is nothing you did. Suzu is simply just a—" She cleared her throat and glanced at Angelique, then returned her gaze to Odile. "Rothbart loved you. It's why he did all of this—he wanted you to be free of him *and* your mother. Since you stood and fought with us, it removed his shadow from your future."

Odile cried. Her jaw was stubbornly sewn shut, but tears pooled from her eyes.

This is not a moment I should be intruding on.

Angelique stood. "Perhaps I should wait outside?"

Odile and Odette hugged—the shorter, dark-haired girl mashing her face into Odette's shoulder.

Angelique quietly tip-toed across the room, nodding to the large moth when it fluttered out of her way. She slipped out of the sitting room, down the hallway, and back outside into the warm sun.

Briefly, she leaned against the door. *A sorcerer lost on purpose to a hero. That has to be a first.* She squinted up at the sky. *That means he absolutely wasn't working with the black mages that captured Evariste. But...it seems it's likely his wife is.*

Angelique skimmed the top letter, taking in the sorceress' sharp words and thinly veiled threats to Odile—whom she scoffed for being incompetent at magic.

Rothbart must have known Odile's powers—how could he miss it with her menagerie in her tower? Which means he was keeping her from this...Suzu.

Angelique stared at the scribbled name, trying to fathom how *twisted* a person had to be to threaten such vile atrocities against their own child.

"Wait," Angelique rapidly blinked as her thoughts finally caught up with her heart. "This means we finally have a name! Suzu—she *has* to be linked with those who kidnapped Evariste. At the very least, she must know of them! And since we have her name, it will be easier to track her. This is a lead!"

She was so gleeful, Angelique actually hopped in a small circle. "Oh, I can't wait to tell Pegasus. And Sybilla and Clovicus! This settles it—I *have* to return to Loire to update Severin and Elle!"

Angelique was still deep in her celebration—though she had limited herself to grinning like an idiot while she leaned against the tower wall—when Odette emerged from Odile's home.

"How is she?" Angelique asked.

Odette glanced back at the tower. "Conflicted, I think. She learned that she had one parent's love all along, only to find out that her mother—whom she thought indifferent—frequently made threats on her life. But Odile has a rare and quiet strength. She'll cling to the idea that Rothbart loved her. And heaven help Suzu if Odile and her wyvern ever see her again."

The corners of her mouth turned down as she stared past Angelique. "He was a twisted, broken man. But I wished he would have sought help."

"Rothbart?"

Odette nodded. "He must have been planning this for years. When he first cursed me, he wasn't wearing that dratted gold armor that he started to wear these past few months."

Angelique wrinkled her forehead. *Gold armor…did the man I encounter while chasing the wyvern wear gold armor? Could he have been Rothbart?*

When she realized Odette was watching her, she smoothed her expression and smiled.

Odette pressed her lips together, her hazel eyes somber. "I told you all of this because I trust you with my life and the lives of my friends, Lady Enchantress. You put much on the line when you fought that wyvern, and I wish to honor that. I need you to be honest. Will Odile be safe with the Veneno Conclave?"

Angelique paused.

Any other mage would have immediately answered yes.

They would have told Odette how kind the instructors of Luxi-Domus were, how benevolent all mages were, how they strove to help each other.

But Angelique—who had been feared, scorned, and threatened—could only stare at Odette.

Odile is not Stil. Her magic is potent and powerful like his, not grim like mine...but her wyvern...and that doesn't even touch her parentage. Could she thrive as he did?

"I sent word of Odile to a dear friend of mine, the Fairy Godmother Sybilla," Angelique finally said. "She is wise, influential, and powerful. It is my suggestion that Sybilla look after Odile as a mentor. She will be able to introduce Odile to powerful mages who will make good allies."

Odette narrowed her eyes. "You're saying she'll be a good guide—so the doubters in the Conclave won't chew Odile up and spit her out?"

"It is my hope that the Conclave wouldn't *chew* anyone up," Angelique said mildly. "But Odile is in a slightly difficult position. Sybilla will give her an advantage she needs."

Odette heaved a sigh. "Thank you."

Angelique nodded. She glanced down at the letters, her gaze lingering on a line in the letter.

If you do not follow these plans, I shall take out the payment for your cheekiness on our *daughter whom you love so uselessly.*

"Don't let her leave Kozlovka," Angelique blurted out.

Odette frowned. "I'm sorry, what?"

Angelique looked up and met the Swan Queen's gaze. "Don't let her leave Kozlovka without you. Sybilla won't be able to stay with Odile all the time given her responsibilities. The Veneno Conclave will listen to Sybilla, but they do not have the greatest record at graciously accepting powers and things beyond their understanding. And Odile's control over her wyvern... add into the swirl that her mother—this Suzu—will almost certainly hear of this, and..." Angelique gestured uselessly.

Odette stood tall. Her chin rose. She slightly narrowed her eyes. And in that moment, she was every inch the Swan Queen her crew called her. "Understood," she said. "*No one* will take Odile or make her do something against her wishes."

I'm glad Odile has a friend willing to stand with her and shield her. Angelique's throat ached. *I wish I had someone like that.*

The thought was lonely enough, but almost worse was the reminder that she *did* have someone who used to act so: Evariste.

And yet she hadn't found him after all these years.

Angelique cleared her thoughts and forced a smile. "Odile is blessed to have a friend such as you."

Odette shrugged, losing her royal edge, and looked a little uncomfortable. "I'm not really anyone special." She wiped her hands on her breeches. "I can fill you in on a few of the finer details if you wish, but I'd like to keep it quick. My smugglers and I need to leave soon for our delivery."

"Of course," Angelique said. "I appreciate whatever you can share with me. Once Sybilla and the couple I mentioned earlier arrive, I hope to leave and send word to those who are investigating the darkness encroaching on our world. Suzu's name is the first lead we've had in a long while."

"Very well," Odette said. "Then let us begin."

ANGELIQUE RESTED her chin on her fist—which was propped up on the table. Spread across its surface were the dozens of letters Rothbart and Suzu had exchanged.

As she would likely be waiting for Sybilla, Stil, and Gemma for some weeks, she thought she would use the time to her advantage and see if she could glean any additional information in the letters.

If I have to read these one more time, I will shove these papers in

Yakov's mouth the next time he complains that I ought to attend an evening soiree sometime.

She groaned and rubbed her tired eyes.

I'll have to take my written copies to Severin. As a tactician, he might pick up on something that I haven't.

Odile knocked on the door. "Angelique?"

Grateful for the distraction, Angelique leaped to her feet and threw open the door to smile at the young mage—who was also her hostess, as Angelique had opted to stay with her rather than in Tsona Palace with all of its fluttery nobles and royals. "Yes?"

"A party is approaching the castle—I believe the friends you called for are among its members."

"Really?" Angelique followed Odile down the hallway and outside the tower. "Perhaps Sybilla could arrive this quickly, but I don't expect Stil and Gemma for some weeks. They would have had to ride like madmen..."

She trailed off and squinted, doubting her eyes.

For the party Odile had described were crossing the immense castle bridge, and leading them was a grim-faced Stil and a distraught Gemma with her giant white dog, Hvit, and the ever-sour Pricker Patch trailing behind her. (Gemma's feelings were betrayed only by the slight set of her lips and the wrinkle in her brow, but given that she was usually unflappable, it was a worrying development.)

"What happened?" Angelique called out to them. "Was someone attacked?"

The pair exchanged glances and inhaled deeply. "Lucien was attacked again, but he survived just fine," Gemma said in her low and soothing voice.

Angelique approached them, worried by the looks they exchanged. "Then why do you both look so...apprehensive?"

Stil hesitated. "Lucien worked out who our enemy is."

"*Lucien* did? Really?" Angelique asked, uncertain she had heard right. Her ears caught up with her doubts when she finally realized what they had said. "Wait, that's fantastic news! That's something to be celebrated!" She allowed herself a smile.

Stil avoided her gaze and peered at the ground. "Together, he and Severin were able to work out some of the tactics our enemy is using."

Angelique suppressed the desire to pinch her nose in her confusion. "But that's even better! I don't understand how such great strides forward could have you two looking like someone kicked Hvit?"

"It's the Chosen," Stil said bluntly.

It seemed to be a day of doubting her senses, for Angelique shook her head in disbelief at her obviously malfunctioning hearing. "The Chosen—the ancient enemy the Snow Queen faced in Verglas and wiped from the earth? Those Chosen?"

"Yes," Gemma said. "And they're targeting you."

CHAPTER 20

"I'm not leaving until you explain this—in *detail*!" Angelique's elegant enchantress mask wasn't merely slipping, it was all out cracking as she planted her feet and folded her arms across her chest. "You can't just tell me the Chosen are back and rush me off to Loire!"

Behind her, Pegasus tossed his head as Gemma added a few more supplies to the saddlebag attached to his tack.

After delivering the shocking development—that their nameless enemy was, in fact, the *Chosen*—Stil and Gemma had ignored her protests and forcibly packed Pegasus up, telling her she *had* to return to Loire.

It was clear they meant to drive her out if necessary, but by no means was Angelique going to be satisfied with their half-cooked explanation. She didn't care—or put much stock in—the idea that the enemy was targeting *her*. But the Chosen were an ancient enemy that was supposed to have been stomped out long ago. How, then, could they be back?

Stil must have sensed her potential mutiny as she glared at his back.

He sighed and kicked the pebbles that covered the lakeshore.

"It goes deep, Angel. Prince Lucien thinks the Chosen have been around for centuries. They've had ample opportunity to study the countries, note standard military operations, and see how they could manipulate events and our own cultures against us. The Chosen are well-informed, highly skilled—as seen by the way they took Evariste and have somehow isolated the elves—and given their use of arcane magic, they've got to have books and reading materials we thought were destroyed centuries ago. They're in the middle of leading a full-on assault on the continent in a war they've been waging against us for years."

Angelique stared at the ground, barely noticing when Hvit meandered past her so he could sit in front of Pegasus and look up at the constellation, his curled tail wiggling in joy. "But what proof do we have of this?" she asked.

"Do you really need to ask?" Gemma frowned. "You have *lived* it."

"They've been strategically targeting individual countries, trying to further weaken them." Stil waved cheerfully at Odile, who waited for them on the castle bridge where Angelique had said her farewells. "And Gemma's right—nearly every attempt they've made, you have witnessed. And stopped. It started with Princess Rosalinda."

"The Knights of Sole are the perfect troops to pit against rogue magic users." Gemma couched down and buried her hands in Hvit's snow-white fur. "With their anti-magic armor, enchanted weapons, and specific training and fighting methods, they could take out black mages with ease. Except they can't."

"Because Princess Rosalinda was cursed." Stil said. "Even before she fell asleep and you were forced to put all of the capital under a sleeping spell, King Giuseppe would never have agreed to send out Magic Knights to investigate the activity of black mages. He was too concerned with Rosalinda. As a result, the country—which normally would have been the first to investigate rogue mages—was sidelined and eventually made entirely useless."

"I can see that—and obviously Evariste's kidnapping and the disappearance of the elves," Angelique said.

Stil groaned. "Right! See the tactics behind it? The storms that would have isolated Ringsted and would have kept their fast ships from coming to the continent's aid, the beast-curse placed on Severin that would have crippled Loire's military, the attempt Clotilde made at wiping out all the Arcainian princes and princesses, which would have given the Chosen an entire kingdom—which was bad enough—but Arcainia is also the economic seat of the continent. If they managed to take it, they would have had enough money to buy legions of mercenaries."

Angelique chewed on her lip. "The increase of goblins in Erlauf kept them busy, too. If the Erlauf Prince hadn't married Cinderella and the two healed some of the rift between their countries, the goblins would have been far worse."

"Yes." Gemma stood again and approached Angelique, peering into her eyes with a sharp look that made Angelique feel like she could see into her soul.

Stil scratched his black hair and sighed. "As part of their efforts, they seem to be attacking individuals that they feel bear a strong resemblance to those who helped the Snow Queen. There was a mage who could make transportation gates—that would be Evariste's counterpart."

"A few elves helped the Snow Queen, as well," Angelique said. "It would explain why they were among the first targeted."

"Precisely, yes. And, er...the first recorded craftmage helped the Snow Queen, too. People seem to think that's why the rider targeted me." Stil briefly turned away so he could throw a pebble into the lake. The plopping noise of the water was nearly covered by the rustling leaves from the encroaching trees in the surrounding forest.

"Yes. It's fair obvious." Only now did Gemma finally look away from Angelique. She retreated back to Stil, and the two held hands before facing Angelique together.

Angelique quirked an eyebrow. "You don't need to present a united front to me. It's a lot to take in, but I understand. A little, anyway. I suspect I'll have to talk to Severin for the true gravity to sink in." She took a step backwards, then started to turn, intending to heave herself onto Pegasus' back.

"Angelique," Stil called.

"Yes?" Angelique turned back.

"There's one more person they've targeted." Stil licked his lips. "Above all, the Chosen would most fear the person—the mage—whom they believe most resembles the Snow Queen in this generation."

Angelique nodded slowly. "That would be Evariste, I'd expect?"

Gemma shook his head. "He isn't the most powerful user of magic."

Angelique frowned, her brow furrowing. "You can't mean...?"

"It's you, Angelique," Stil blurted out. "You're the Snow Queen of our time. You can save us and destroy them. At every turn, you've been the only one to resist them—the only one *able* to resist them." He spoke so fast and tightly, this was obviously what he'd been working up to saying the whole time.

Angelique shook her head. "You're wrong."

"You can't deny you're the most powerful," Gemma said.

"I can, in fact," Angelique snarled. "Because no one—not even me—knows how much magic I really have."

"Because you're so powerful, it can't be tested!" Stil burst out. "Because every gauge that has been developed, you've broken! Angelique, you're *stronger* than the Snow Queen! You could take down legions without restriction."

"I can't be her," Angelique said, her voice as hard as steel.

"There's no one else," Stil said. "And they've attacked you already—"

"*I am not her*!" Angelique shouted.

Uncomfortable silence stretched between them.

Somewhere on the lake, a fish jumped, as Gemma's and Stil's eyes bore holes into Angelique.

Stil opened his mouth to speak again, but Angelique was faster.

She threw herself on Pegasus and forced herself to nod at Stil and Gemma. "After I speak to Severin about all that has taken place here at Swan Lake, I'll send word," she said, forcing herself to sound normal.

Gemma stepped toward Pegasus. "Angelique…"

Angelique nudged Pegasus, who stretched out in a fast trot that turned into a canter once they left the lakeshore behind and entered the woods.

Angelique pressed closer to Pegasus, trying to ground her racing thoughts and frantically beating heart, which felt like it might explode from fear.

They couldn't know, Angelique consoled herself. *Gemma and Stil have no way of knowing how* frightening *it would be if I were like the Snow Queen. They have no idea how bad it would be for the world. It's one thing for the people to follow a princess with powers of ice…but for a continent to follow me, a jaded mage with magic of blood and death?*

I'm so tired. No matter how good my intensions, in my exhaustion, I might let the lure of my magic lead us all into a dark promise of power. Into death.

EVARISTE WAS SURPRISED but happy to find that even when Angelique wasn't present, he never returned to his nightmarish visions.

Her magic, it seemed, had disrupted that spell and carved him from it. He was left, instead, to wander around her smudgy forest and watch her memories of her childhood home.

It was intriguing for the first few days, but it probably would have become boring…if he wasn't so thankful to be spared the mental anguish and if he hadn't spent the majority of his time thinking through the implications of his magic's odd behavior and his loving Angelique.

He paced back and forth in the forest meadow, pausing to hop on the stump. "The strong feelings—no, there's no sense in not being honest in this instance. My *love* for Angelique has imprinted so strongly on my magic that the spells and curses Liliane and her ilk forged with it all have that weak spot—romantic love. It's likely why my magic reached for her in the middle of Liliane's wretched spell, though I'm not so deluded to think that Angelique's magic reacted out of love for me. Given how it sliced straight through, I think it's more likely her magic reacted to the threat and broke the spell. It's possible it reacted without her knowledge given that she was sleeping, and when I arrived, she was playing with her magic in her dream."

He turned in a slow circle, his heels hanging off the edge of the stump. "There is no other logical explanation for it. I suspect Rothbart thought so, as well—he did say something about me caring for another. But how, then, can we use this to our advantage?"

"I AM NOT THE SNOW QUEEN!" Angelique shouted.

Evariste carefully swiveled on the stump and watched with concern as Angelique stomped through the forest with the elegance of an angry bull.

"Severin and the others have *lost their minds* if they think I am at all like the Verglas Snow Queen." Angelique stopped short of Evariste's stump, her eyebrows slanted in an angry V. "And, obviously, this means he's not talking to any other mages besides Stil. They would have immediately laughed the idea out of existence."

She careened into motion again, circling the stump. "I mean, really. *Me?* I'm this generation's Snow Queen? HAH!" She abruptly turned to face Evariste and scowled. "What are *you* doing here?"

Evariste internally winced. "You don't want to see me?"

"No!" Angelique snapped. "Because you cannot be dead!" She glared at him for several moments, then relaxed slightly. "Well, you do finally look a bit better."

"Thank you. I feel better. Now what's this about you being the Snow Queen?"

"It's not important. I'm certainly not going to waste my time thinking about it!" She ran a hand through her hair—which was loose and a little windblown.

"Really?" Evariste calmly inquired. *I wonder if she would let me hug her, or if she's so angry, she'd stab me.*

"Yes! Why?"

It's confirmed; she'd stab me. Evariste dropped off the stump. "Because you seem rather...*incensed* about it."

"I'm not going to talk about my feelings with my personal delusion!"

"I am starting to find it a little hurtful that you keep referring to me as a delusion," Evariste mildly said.

Angelique halted and stiffly turned to peer in his direction. Her face abruptly crumpled, and she shook her head and backed up. "No. No. I don't want to talk to you."

Evariste tilted his head and took a step closer to her. "Why not?"

"Because." A little hiccup escaped Angelique, and she hunched her shoulders in misery. "When I wake up, you won't be there."

"Oh, Angel." Evariste wrapped his arms around her and pulled her tight against his chest. "I'm sorry."

"Why are you apologizing?" Angelique sniffed. "I'm the one who failed you—and I *keep* failing you! None of this is your fault—if I had just *moved* or used my core magic, you wouldn't have been taken and—"

Evariste stemmed the rush of her guilt by covering her lips with his hand. "We've already discussed this. *None* of what happened is your fault, Angel."

She blinked. "But we fought—before you were taken."

Has she been carrying this guilt all these years? Blast—and the argument wasn't even her fault. It's because I was acting childishly. My inability to deal with my feelings like an adult kept me from addressing the matter—what a mistake that was.

"And you took the spell that was meant for me." Angelique's voice was slightly muffled by his hand, and her lips brushed his palm with a feather-light touch that pulled at something in him.

Evariste lowered his head. "And I'd do it again a thousand times to save you, Angel."

He slowly let his hand drop and instead slid his arm around her waist. The way she stared at him—with *hope*—made his heart throb.

The curse that keeps my magic from me... I'm sealed until I perform my darkest desire, which is to kiss her. I wonder if I could kiss her here and if it would count—it might be the only way I confess and keep our friendship intact. She thinks I'm not real anyway. He stared at her lips.

Angelique stared up at him with rapidly widening eyes as Evariste slightly angled his head and drew closer.

When he could practically taste her breath, Angelique shot backwards like a cat with her tail on fire. "No, no, no! No. No!" She fled all the way to the edge of the woods, circled around a tree, and glared at him with suspicion when she peeked out from behind the safety of the trunk.

"I am not some soft-minded imbecile who falls in love with her teacher! This is obviously a mental failing—how could I even *dream* of such ridiculous drabble?"

Evariste let his arms fall to his side as he watched his hopes self-destruct. "Kissing me is ridiculous drabble?"

"Of course it is!" Angelique groaned and pressed her fingertips against her shut eyes. "My life is a nightmare. I can't even be sensible in the privacy of my own dreams! I'm apparently so *stupid,* I would picture something like *this*!"

Evariste clenched his jaw. "It can't possibly be that bad."

Her eyes popped open. "Yes, it is that bad!" she snapped. "It's stupid, improper, *and* disrespectful!"

Evariste fought to keep his expression mild, even though Angelique had just effectively stabbed him in the heart. *Well. There goes the dream that she'll react well when I do confess.* He forced a smile. "I see."

Angelique must have finally gotten over his actions, for she gloomily left the relative safety of the forest and trudged over to the stump, where she sat down.

Evariste let his head sag back on his neck and stared up at the sky. *Somehow, this is worse than the pain I've endured at Liliane's hands. Thinking of Angelique got me through that. And this is what she thinks of me romantically.*

Pain—a different sort of pain, an all-consuming pain that devoured his hopes—lurked at the back of his mind. Evariste inhaled deeply and forcibly pushed it back. *Even though it feels like this is the worst thing that could have happened, I need to use this opportunity to give her information. I wanted to last time, but she had been too upset initially and fell asleep before I had the chance to tell her anything.*

He cleared his throat. "Have you looked into the names Acri or Liliane?"

"No. I haven't had the time." She glanced his way, then snapped up straight again. "*And* I'm not wasting valuable resources on my personal mental ramblings."

"Tell Clovicus."

"Tell him *what*? That I dreamed Lord Enchanter Evariste tried to kiss me, as if I was some kind of lovesick fool?" Angelique indignantly snorted and tossed her head, resembling Pegasus a bit.

"If you said that, he'd be more likely to believe you really encountered me," Evariste dryly muttered.

Angelique suspiciously eyed him. "What was that?"

"Nothing." Evariste folded his arms across his chest. "But you need to tell him. Or Sybilla. I think Liliane, at least, went to Luxi-

Domus, which has frightening implications if it's true. And at least it's a name for you to search with."

"I do actually have a name—*finally*." Angelique sat up straight, seemingly cheered for the first time since she had appeared. "Suzu."

"Sorcerer Rothbart's wife—yes, she is among my captors," he hesitated. "Seeing as I said that, do you believe I am really me, now?"

"Of course not," Angelique laughed. "I already knew she was Rothbart's wife—naturally my subconscious would know, as well. I need no other proof you are my imagination besides the *asinine* display earlier."

"When I tried to kiss you?"

Angelique shivered. "Don't say it like that!"

"Would you rather I say I attempted to assault your lips with my own?"

Angelique slapped her hands over her ears. "I don't want to hear this. I don't want to know I'm even capable of *pondering* this! I thought I was better than this!"

Evariste kept up a smile even though the brightness of the forest seemed to dim, and the lingering toxic darkness seemed to grow. *It seems my worries that performing my darkest desire will end our relationship are indeed correct. Short of gagging, I don't think she could act any more disgusted. Is there something about me that she can't stomach? If I changed myself, would she still react in this way?*

Angelique stood with a sigh. "This is absolutely embarrassing. Lord Enchanter Evariste deserves better than this."

He was torn—should he save himself some pain and stop here, or risk asking and learn the truth? *I suppose, what's another stab to the heart when she's already made her stance obvious?* He lowered his hands to his hips and studied his apprentice. "Better than you imagining kissing—"

"*Yes*," Angelique loudly said, covering his words. She frowned and scratched a shoulder. "But more than just that. He deserves someone better trying to find him, better than me as his apprentice, better than..." She stared into the shadows of the forest.

Evariste slowly approached her. *How can I tell her she's being idiotic in a way she'll actually believe? I know from Suzu's and Liliane's rants that Angelique has done more than anyone else in the world would, and all of it in my name.*

Angelique didn't notice as he again closed the distance between them. She was pre-occupied staring at a mushroom. "I've used my war magic," she announced.

Evariste froze in surprise. "Really?"

"A few times." She winced. "Several times." A grimace. "A lot more than I would like."

Knowing her, that probably means she's used it twice since I was taken.

"But," Angelique continued, "I made the greatest mistake of my life when I let Evariste get taken. I don't want it to happen again, but it's still *frightening*."

"What is? Your magic?" Evariste edged across the small gap between them, his arm brushing hers. His gaze wandered to her lips, but Evariste reluctantly forced himself to switch his focus. *If Angelique uses her magic, she can devastate Liliane's forces. Much rides on her ability to use her magic. She can't be scared of it.*

Angelique stared at the ground. "Yes."

Evariste was preparing to launch into a lecture about her magic when she surprised him by continuing.

"Do you think Evariste will mind?"

Puzzled, he wrinkled his brow. "That you used your core magic? Certainly not!"

"But I don't think he realized the full extent of my magic," Angelique said. "I'm not sure anyone has. It can do things..." She shifted and looked at him with haunted eyes. "Do you think he can forgive me? For everything?"

"Angel, how many times must I say it before you believe me? I don't need to forgive you because you haven't done anything wrong," Evariste gently said. "When this is all over, and you find me, we'll sit down together, and you can tell me everything. And when your tale is told, I will tell you with absolute certainty that you did well."

Angelique pressed her lips together and slightly twisted her face. "I really miss you," she whispered.

Some of Evariste's pain thawed at her earnest expression. He gently pushed some of her thick hair from her face. "And I miss you."

"I'll find you," she vowed. "No matter what. I'll find you."

Evariste slowly eased his arms around her in a comforting hug. "I know."

He felt her breathing deepen as she pressed her face into his shoulder. Though he wished it was out of ardor, he knew it was the heavy hand of exhaustion that made her lean into him as sleep stole her away from him.

It's not her fault she doesn't see me as a romantic partner. It's not her fault I love her. This is enough. No matter how much it hurts, this is the way it has to be.

CHAPTER 21

Loire was markedly more humid and warmer than Kozlovka. Angelique had to braid her hair into a tight weave to avoid looking like a frizzy-haired goblin, and she was grateful for her dress's cooling charms as she stalked through Chanceux Chateau's gardens, searching for the master and mistress.

She had used the several-day-ride from Kozlovka and Loire to practice gently correcting Severin of the foolish idea that she was this generation's Snow Queen, so she could explain it without visibly clenching her teeth.

All I have to do is keep the front up long enough to correct him and find out what task he wants me to do next—because there is no chance they sent for me without having some godforsaken quest they want me to take up.

Angelique heard Elle's familiar laughter, so she plunged into the gardens, which were bright and bedecked with all the early summer flowers.

When she turned the corner, she was treated to a rather unexpected sight.

Severin—in a stained cotton shirt rolled up to his elbows—sat in front of a rose bush and was carefully pruning it of dead leaves and weeding around it.

Elle, however, wore a mint green gown, and though her dark hair was enviably frizz free, it looked a little mussed. As if she had recently been riding and the wind had pulled some of her locks free from the pinned style. She was addressing some of Severin's troops, her hands on her hips.

"When you travel to Erlauf," the princess said, "you will be received at what was once the Trieux royal palace. You ought to use this opportunity to see if you can uncover proof that Erlauf has dug itself out of the steep debts it had with Arcainia. Surely you'll be able to *happen* upon something that will confirm it."

One of the soldiers raised his hand.

"Yes?" Elle asked.

"Our assignment is to support the Erlauf army against goblins so they may send troops to Torrens and Sole," the soldier said. "His Highness gave us those specific instructions." The soldier glanced at Severin, who did not seem inclined to meddle in the situation and instead clipped a dead rose from his bush.

"Obviously," Elle agreed.

"Why would we be attempting to ferret out our ally's secrets?"

"Ferret out? Hardly—you're merely satisfying a tiny curiosity. And it's a *good* rumor you'd be confirming, no less!" Elle laughed falsely and covered her mouth in what was most likely a purposeful imitation of the court ladies.

I highly doubt that Elle will ever lose her intelligencer habits. But I don't know that Severin would want her to lose that extra bit of fire, either. Angelique watched the pair from the shadows. *They are a bit of an odd couple—but well paired.*

Severin finally looked up from his bush. "Elle," he said warningly.

"What? They're always so *insistent* on learning the ways of the Rangers so they can hound me endlessly—even when I'm only going on a simple social call," Elle said.

"I don't believe you've ever been on a simple social call in your life, Your Highness," the soldier said.

Elle ignored him. "It's only natural we ask them to put that training to good use!" She finished with a brilliant smile.

Severin stood and brushed dirt off the knees of his trousers. "Lady Enchantress Angelique, I am glad to see you have returned safely." He turned around and bowed to Angelique with great gravity despite the pruning shears he held.

Angelique wasn't too surprised she'd been found out. *Perhaps he still retains superior hearing from his time as a beast?*

She glided forward, offering a smile to Elle—who winked in return. "Good afternoon, Your Highnesses."

Elle swatted her hand through the air. "Yes, yes, we won't use your title if you don't use ours. Did Stil tell you what we learned?"

"He said Prince Lucien uncovered the historic patterns that pointed to the Chosen as the dark enemy we face," Angelique said.

"He did," Elle confirmed. "He *also* broke his frog spell and is in love with the most fabulous girl. She can actually bring him to heel! Can you imagine that?"

Severin ignored his wife's observations. "We've further looked into it, and it seems most likely. We put together a timeline of the catastrophic events that have taken place over the last eighteen to twenty years or so, and it seems nearly every one of them was planned or manipulated."

Elle's eyes lost their mischievous glint as she moved to stand with Severin, resting her hand on his forearm. "And nearly every last one of them, *you* put an end to," she added. "There were a few in which you were only indirectly involved—like healing Puss when Princess Gabrielle faced the ogre in Arcainia—but only a rare few happened without your presence," Elle hesitated, then added. "We've wondered if the deaths of Queen Ingrid of Arcainia and King Matvey of Mullberg were planned by the Chosen."

"Ingrid was once a powerful Lady Enchantress," Angelique said. "It seems like a plausible conclusion."

"Good. You agree, then?" Severin asked.

"I would like a more solid piece of proof," Angelique admitted, "but I might have found a way for us to secure such a thing. Rothbart has died."

"Stil and Gemma shared with us the letter you sent," Severin said. "You say he was defeated by this swan maiden, Odette?"

Angelique shook her head. "No, that is what we first believed, but Odette found some papers Sorcerer Rothbart left behind for her."

Elle frowned sharply. "I beg your pardon. Did you say he *left* papers for her?"

"It seems he was being blackmailed by his wife to attack the Kozlovkan royal family. That was why he created multiple wyverns—one of which I killed," Angelique said. "But he purposely allowed himself to be defeated—for the sake of his daughter."

"His daughter?" Severin narrowed his gold eyes. "She has magic."

"She does," Angelique confirmed. "I sent word to Sybilla—by now she has likely descended on the girl and will mentor her."

She paused for a moment. *I don't know how to phrase this next part without making Severin sound like a heartless man who is only interested in using people.* "Odile successfully tamed a wyvern," Angelique slowly said. "But she *cannot* be used in combat. She shouldn't even leave Kozlovka. If her mother finds out the true depth of her abilities, the Chosen will snatch her up."

Severin raised an eyebrow. "That is highly understandable, given what she has gone through," he said. "But you said all of this was done at the behest of Rothbart's wife. Do we know anything about her?"

Angelique grinned. "We have her name: Sorceress Suzu. It seems she traveled much based on the various stationery and inks she used to write her letters, but I left before Stil inspected them. With his craft magic, he might be able to tell something more about their origins and the writer."

Severin actually *smiled*, flashing white teeth and turning his somewhat stony facial features dazzling. "A name is far more than we hoped for."

"Yes!" Angelique enthusiastically agreed. "If I can track this Suzu, she might lead us to the mage that attacked me—or to Evariste!"

"Ah," Severin said.

Angelique paused. "Ah?"

Elle smiled. "We actually had a task we hoped you might be amenable to seeing through for us."

Angelique smiled woodenly. "Of course."

Why else would you request my presence?

"But this name is important," Elle said, "And I think you're right. Suzu may very well lead us to the Chosen—and your Lord Enchanter."

"On your behalf, we'll put our best Rangers on the matter," Severin said. "Elle and I are to attend the wedding of Princess Dylan of the Selkies and Prince Callan of Ringsted. We planned to update the other countries then. I will personally request that each country place their best agents after this Suzu. I am aware you have continuously sacrificed to help us. Please allow the royal families you have so greatly helped to aid you in this."

Angelique pushed her lips together. *I'd rather look myself, but I'm not so stupid to think that I can do a better job than true intelligence agents—particularly if even half as many are put on the task as Severin is implying.*

But I have failed Evariste deeply by taking so long to find him. I owe it to him to search.

Angelique looked away from the prince and princess.

The gold of the late afternoon sun faintly reminded Angelique of Evariste's hair, and as she thought of the man, she could almost feel the warmth of his easy smile.

Feel the warmth of his easy smile? I sound like a regular idiot. I'm losing my edge. Angelique sighed. *But he would want me to help the countries rather than search for him—he'd surely give me some long-winded lecture on duty until I gave in because I couldn't bear to listen any longer.*

But...this is the first real lead I have since discovering he's in a mirror... and I miss him so terribly.

Angelique cleared her throat. "I would appreciate that. Thank you."

Elle curtsied, and Severin bowed. "It would be our honor," Severin said.

Angelique nodded awkwardly. "What, then, is this task you wish me to see through?"

Severin set his pruning shears down. "You know the legend of the Snow Queen?"

"All mages are thoroughly schooled in it—though we lost many of our records of her when the Veneno Conclave Library burned down long ago," Angelique said.

Elle waved to the soldiers—who bowed in return—and led the way to a delicate glass door. "Lucien read that journal Stil brought back from Verglas. It describes the Chosen and how they were united under a magic user named Tenebris Malus—although then they called themselves the Allegiance of the Chosen. Those with magic were badly persecuted back then, so he promised his followers safety—and that they would conquer a country to call their own, which would be a place where no one could hurt them."

Severin held the door open, allowing Elle and Angelique inside first. "In reality, he was using them to target and attack Verglas," he said. "An evil and powerful mirror was hidden in the mountains of northern Verglas for centuries before Tenebris walked the earth. He meant to find it and use it to take over the continent and destroy those who had no magic."

Angelique glanced at their new location—a salon bedecked in gold. There was gold molding on the windows, gold-gilded frames containing paintings of horses, gold damask wallpaper, an ornate harpsichord, and a giant gold harp that was almost as tall as Elle. (Strung behind the large harp were a number of small lap harps—equally as golden, beautiful, and expensive. Angelique would bet Elle had a hand in arranging the harps, for the way they were spaced made them look rather like a mother goose with her goslings trailing behind her.)

"This room is..." Angelique hesitated, trying to find a nice way to phrase it.

"Lucien's work." Elle rolled her eyes and plopped down in a chaise lounge, draping her legs and skirts over the elongated lounge chair.

"I see." Angelique took a seat in a padded armchair (gold cushions, of course) that was so wide, it could have seated two people. "But to continue our conversation, the mirror is mentioned in academic research," she confirmed. "Particularly that the Snow Queen practically dropped a mountain on it, forever sealing it from the clutches of evil."

"The book confirms those details," Severin said. "But given that the Chosen are still alive—and actively seeking destruction—we've decided to make it a priority to confirm that the mirror is still in northern Verglas."

Angelique shifted, trying to find a spot in the cushion of the armchair so she didn't sag on one side. "It would have to be," she said. "The Snow Queen's magic covers the mountains. There's no possible way for the Chosen to reach it. The magic would stop them—or possibly kill them."

"I would have said it wasn't possible for them to kidnap a Lord Enchanter widely heralded as a genius," Severin grimly said, "but they have done exactly that."

Angelique stiffened, her posture turning unnaturally straight.

Elle frowned and shook her head at her husband, then turned her attention back to Angelique. "Queen Linnea is preparing a search party to enter the mountains. She has requested aid of the magical sort—specifically yours."

"Because she knows I'm a pushover?" Angelique flatly asked, her brow arched.

"Because she *trusts* you," Severin said. "You helped Stil save Gemma—whom the queen considers her dearest friend. Moreover, she said she admired that you were the only mage to volunteer to go to Kozlovka."

Angelique leaned back in her chair and inhaled deeply. "I can't keep going at this pace," she said finally. "I know you are asking for the good of the continent, but I *cannot* keep this up much longer."

"I know we have asked much of you, Angelique," Severin said. "I dearly wish it was not so. But the Chosen is our enemy. We cannot afford to let news of our suspicions leak, and you are the mage whom we trust most."

Angelique closed her eyes. *My whole life, I've wanted to be found trustworthy despite my magic. I've worked toward this since I was an apprentice, and I've gotten here because of all that Evariste taught me. And if I don't agree to it...who will help? Odile needs Sybilla. Clovicus might be able to help, but he hasn't spoken with Severin, much less Queen Linnea.* She let her shoulders droop minutely. *This is what I wanted. Though I do wish I knew in advance how tiring it would be. I would have made it a point to sleep more as a student.*

She sighed. "Queen Linnea's request is a logical one. I don't know that they would be able to get far into the northern mountains without a weather mage or an enchantress or enchanter."

"Then you'll go?" Elle asked.

"I'll go," Angelique confirmed.

"You don't have to go alone," Severin said. "If there is

someone you want to accompany you, we trust whomever you deem worthy of it."

Angelique nodded. "In that case, I'd like to inform Enchanter Clovicus, given that Sybilla will be unavailable and must remain in Kozlovka with Odile. I'll request that he send several trustworthy weather mages to Verglas for the occasion." *Maybe Blanche and Rein would be willing to help again. They're Master Weather Mages, and certainly capable.* She paused, thinking. *But perhaps I could save myself some time...* "Though there is a team of...*people*...I would like to request support from. I'll need funds to pay them, though."

"Of course," Elle said. "We'll provide whatever you need. It is the least we can do."

Severin scratched his chin. "We should have been providing funds to you before this, given all you have done on our behalf."

"Thank you." Angelique kept her expression open and innocent. (There was no way she was going to tell Severin she was planning to hire smugglers. She wasn't sure *anyone* would support the idea, but with their swan forms, the Black Swan Smugglers would easily be able to scout ahead and perform flyovers, giving them another set of eyes on what practically amounted to a goose chase.)

"I wish I could go as well." Severin frowned deeply. "But we *must* attend the wedding in Ringsted so we can keep our allies informed."

Elle nodded. "We were supposed to have left already, but we needed to prioritize speaking with you."

"The expedition likely won't be ready to enter the mountains until closer to mid-summer," Severin continued. "But after the wedding, I am sailing to Erlauf to organize the troops I'm sending there to support Colonel Friedrich, and to witness some of the goblin activity to help me construct a new strategy."

"King Toril and Queen Linnea won't be attending the wedding so they may oversee the preparations for the expedition," Elle said. "But we're trying to move as carefully as possible. We don't want to tip off the Chosen that we're onto them, and if they're as enmeshed in society as they seem to be, we need to give every possible appearance of normalcy."

"If they don't intend to enter the mountains for some weeks, I assume that would mean my presence is not immediately required?" Angelique asked.

"Correct," Severin said. "Is there a matter you must see to that we could help you with?"

Angelique shook her head. "It is merely that it is high time I return to Evariste's home in Torrens—to see to the building and make certain nothing has changed. From there, I will return to Kozlovka—to check with Sybilla and ask my *friends* for help."

"Sounds reasonable," Elle said.

"Is there anything besides funds that we can provide you with?" Severin asked. "The craftmages staying here at Chanceux Chateau have been producing heat charms for the excursion."

Angelique tilted her head. "I have proper clothing for the mountains, and Pegasus will make my journeys swift and short in length. But I might take some of the charms for my friends, thank you."

"Absolutely! You can take whatever you think they might need." Elle stood. "But I'm afraid we must be rude hosts and leave for Ringsted—though you may remain in Chanceux as long as you wish. I imagine you must be fatigued after your trip."

Depending which craftmages are here, I might be able to ask them for help to create string or ribbon that could hold a heat charm so the Black Swan Smugglers could wear them in their swan forms. Angelique tapped her lower lip. "I will spend the night so I can gather the heat charms. But tomorrow, it would be better if I continue on for Torrens. However, I thank you for the generous offer."

Severin strode across the room and opened a massive wooden door carved with music notes. He gestured to the dim hallway outside the door. "In that case, then, please allow me to supply you with the necessary funds. This way."

Angelique rose and started after the prince but was stopped when Elle grabbed her hands.

"We can't say thank you enough, Angelique." Elle's smile was tight, and the crinkle around her eyes betrayed her worry. "We have come this far because of you."

"Nonsense." Angelique shook her head. "This movement is a result of the efforts of the continent—as seen in the way you and Severin have united the other countries."

Elle cocked her head. "Are you really certain there is nothing more we can do to thank you?"

Angelique hesitated. *It was just a dream. A stupid, foolish dream. But...* "Could you also have the Rangers look into the names Liliane and Acri? I believe they are black mages."

"You believe?" Elle asked.

"It's a long story, but if I can confirm their names, it might be something," Angelique said.

"Very well. We'll have them look into it." Elle squeezed Angelique's hands and released them. "Safe journeys."

Angelique bowed her head. "To you as well."

"And they truly think the mirror is *real?*" Odette looked quizzical—and perhaps a little doubtful—as she picked her way through the grassy field.

Pegasus snorted, and Angelique placed what she hoped was a calming hand on his shoulder. (She particularly hoped it was calming given she wasn't riding him, but walking next to him. If he chose to prance or spook, he was going to slam into her first.) "The book was written by King Steinar—the Snow Queen's brother. It is unlikely he included such a falsehood in his record for the fun of it."

"I know," Odette was quick to agree. "It makes sense...but I always thought that part of legend was a bit like a nursery rhyme."

She turned around and peered back at the eight Black Swan Smugglers who trudged behind them—interestingly in a V shape.

I wonder if that is intentional or a habit? Angelique pondered as she admired a blooming foxglove—its purple petals a brilliant spot of color in the shade of the woods.

"It seems we will soon find out if the mirror is indeed fact or fiction," Angelique said as they left the coolness of the forest and carefully crossed what looked like planted fields. "But given the discovery that The Chosen are still alive and well, I'm inclined to believe it exists—though I wish it did not."

"I'm not afraid to admit I hope it's *not* real, because if it is, the future just got a lot darker." Odette frowned. "I wish the elves could break their curse and finally leave their woods. It would make this a lot easier."

"Yes," Angelique automatically agreed. It took her a few moments to realize what Odette had just said. "Wait, *what?*"

Odette raised an eyebrow and repeated herself. "If the elves were no longer cursed, they could leave."

"Are you referring to the Elves of Alabaster Forest?"

"I didn't know there were any other elves on the continent."

"Odette!" Angelique's voice was a little loud—and perhaps desperate. "Have you been in contact with the Elves of Alabaster Forest?"

"I have," Odette confirmed. "They're one of our clients. We deliver ètonse philtre to them. It's a draught that freezes the hearts of those who drink it and fills them with a love of dancing."

Angelique's thoughts came so fast, she struggled to comprehend Odette's explanation. "Why would they need to be filled with a love of dancing?"

"They're cursed to remain in Alabaster Forest," Odette said. "They cannot leave its boundaries. Additionally, all of their best warriors and officers—including the generals—have been cursed to wander the continent, never able to stay more than one night in any location. We also collect letters from the warriors—we call them Wanderers—and deliver them to those who remain in Alabaster Forest."

Angelique squeezed her eyes shut, stunned by the sudden epiphany. *Could I leave the Black Swan Smugglers here and run down to Farset to see the elves? Pegasus is fast, but we'd still likely delay the expedition, which may be dangerous given that we have to enter the northern mountains in the summer, or we'll surely die.* The idea ate at her, but she tried to focus on the information Odette had given her. "Who could have cursed the elves?"

"I don't know, but they did a thorough job of it," Odette grimly said. "There are particulars to their curse, but I only know a bit of it. I do know it's been hard on them. For years they've been stuck in their woods, and because they can't leave its boundaries, they haven't been able to ask for help. They were in a pretty bad spot before we Black Swan Smugglers started delivering the philtre to them, but since we were cursed ourselves, we couldn't do much more than that." Odette grimaced. "We should try to do more, but between picking up after Rothbart and keeping an eye on Odile..."

"And here I've added to your work by requesting your help," Angelique said.

"Not at all. It is we who owe you; we are glad we can aid you."

"Thank you. This matter—confirming the presence of the mirror—does need to take precedence. But once we are through this, I will prioritize the elves," Angelique said. "The King of the Elves is a good friend of Lord Enchanter Evariste."

"Ah," Odette said in a worried tone.

"Ah?"

"We are only given clearance to enter the forest for our deliveries, and sadly we *just* dropped off the most recent shipment. They won't need more until at least mid-fall. Sorry."

Angelique leaned back in the saddle. *Why is it every time I think I find a lead to Evariste—or help for him—things are complicated or delayed.*

Odette awkwardly cleared her throat. "I apologize. I forgot you wouldn't know any of this. I took Alexsei with me, so he found out when we made our last drop off. We told Gemma and Stil when we got back, but obviously the news wouldn't have reached you yet since you were off in Loire at the time."

Angelique slapped on a smile. "There is nothing to apologize for. I am glad to hear we finally have word of the elves, for no one knew what had happened. It might take us some time to reach them, but at least now I know they *can* be reached. But first, we must find this mirror."

Odette nodded and briefly turned around to signal to her people as they passed through the field and into official Ostfold territory.

Ostfold—the capital of Verglas—sat at the other end of the fields, the loud calls of goats and the hum of human chatter and laughing faintly emitting from behind its wooden walls.

Angelique lowered her gaze as she thought about what Odette had just told her. *If Stil knows, he'll send word to Severin about the elves, and he'll reach out. Ugh, but he might not find out until after he returns from Ringsted, and he's supposed to go to Erlauf, so it might take some time for the news to catch up with him.*

She pressed her lips together as she stared up at the crest of Pegasus' neck. *Yet, this is a good thing. We knew something had to be wrong with them, so it's not exactly a surprise it's a curse. In fact, it's a good thing. Curses can be broken. And once Emerys is free, I don't know if there's a power in the land that could keep him from finding Evariste.*

Still...she didn't like it. Having to choose from such high-stakes priorities wasn't a good sign.

Odette was scowling—judging by the thin wrinkles on her forehead, she was probably upset with herself. (It was an expression Angelique knew well, for she had worn it herself more times than she cared to admit over the past few years.)

Given that she liked the Swan Queen—and that if they both were moping, it didn't bode well for their trip—Angelique made a weak attempt at changing the conversation. "Have you visited Ostfold before?"

Odette shifted her watchful gaze to the city. "We've picked up goods from Ostfold before, particularly when the mad King Torgen ruled and folk were trying to escape him. Though I will say this is the first time we'll be truly rubbing elbows with royalty here."

Misha—Odette's bookish, male second-in-command—grinned widely. "Oh really? I thought you and Prince Alexsei have done far more than rub elbows..."

Odette turned around and glared at her companion. "I said it's the first time we're rubbing elbows with royalty *here*!" She muttered under her breath, then put on a smile for Angelique's benefit. "Thank you for agreeing to meet us outside the city. It was fastest for us to fly here from Kozlovka, but we don't like transforming in cities. It can be an...awkward experience."

"Thank you for agreeing to come," Angelique said. "Your wings and eyes will be an excellent boon as we try to make a trail and narrow down the possible mountains the mirror is under."

Odette shrugged. "As I said before, we owe you—for the wyvern, our curse, and helping Odile."

They were almost in the shadow of the city by now and were able to join the dirt road that led through the gates and into the city proper.

"I did not aid you with the intention of keeping you obligated," Angelique said. "Though...I must thank you the same. You are the first people to personally help me."

Odette abruptly turned toward Angelique, her mouth in a surprised 'O' shape, but Angelique was already greeting the city guards.

Though it had barely been half a year since King Torgen had died and Toril ascended the throne, there was a marked difference in the city.

The market square was crowded with wooden stalls and stands

selling everything from cheeses to wild strawberries. There was more color, too. Folk wore bright clothes and big smiles instead of nervously scuttling about as they had during Angelique's previous trip to the city.

But the biggest difference by far was the palace.

It was an unusual structure given that it was made of wood. Every part of the castle jutted up in triangular cut-outs that were intricately decorated with snowflakes and the country crest—a reindeer. It had always been beautiful, but it seemed cleaner now that the air of desperation and doom had been swept out.

Ostfold flags hung from the walls, and out front, an army officer was reviewing sword stances with recruits who—Angelique was surprised to see—were all females.

Odette eyed the recruits with interest. "I didn't know the Verglas army accepted females among its ranks."

"Historically, they haven't," Angelique said. "I imagine this is the work of the new Verglas queen."

"Remarkable." Odette pulled one of her daggers from her bandolier and balanced the blade on the tip of her finger.

When they were nearly at the palace entrance, Angelique patted Pegasus' shoulder, garnering his attention. "Do you want to leave? I don't think it will be too many days before the expedition sets out, but I don't know how forgiving you're feeling."

Pegasus set his chin on her shoulder, but before he gave any gesture to reveal his decision, someone shouted from the palace entrance.

"Angelique!"

Angelique pulled back from Pegasus, her jaw dropping when she saw a familiar head of bright copper hair marching toward her. "Lord Enchanter *Clovicus*? What are you doing here?"

Clovicus laughed as he casually ambled up to her, his arms swinging at his sides. "Don't *you* sound excited to see me? Be careful; you'll hurt my feelings."

The enchanter had traded his long, draping robes for a brilliant green tunic with embroidery that seemed to *move* in the fabric. With the glittery get-up, he looked a little more like a roguish noble than an ageless enchanter.

"I didn't know you were planning to come to Verglas," Angelique said.

Clovicus smirked. "What you mean to say is you didn't invite *me*; rather, you asked me to send weather mages. Am I wrong?"

"No," Angelique agreed. "You arrived with them, I take it?"

"Not quite," he said. "There are no weather mages here. I decided to come myself, and I suspect two enchanters on this little expedition will be more than enough to get us through the mountains."

Angelique blinked. "No weather mages?" she parroted.

"None at all."

She blinked some more. "...*why?*"

He sighed and gazed off sorrowfully into the distance. "I just get so lonely. It's only me in the Veneno Conclave—no cute little apprentice to brighten my day. Instead, I have to look at Tristisim's gloomy face far more often than I want." He winked. "When I received your letter that contained the newest findings about the Chosen and your request for weather mages, I thought this would be the perfect opportunity to rejoin common society and use my magic for something constructive."

Angelique pressed her hands together and rested her fingers—in a praying position—on her chin and lower lip. "The Council had an assignment for you that you didn't want to take?"

Clovicus laughed hollowly. "Worse," he said. "They gave me an *assistant*."

Angelique felt like his echo. "An *assistant?*"

"Yeah, some minion of Crest's named Wallace. The Council said it was to make me more efficient in my role, but I'm pretty sure he's just there to spy on me since I'm the only tie they really have to you, now, given that Sybilla has always flouted her independence." Clovicus sighed.

Angelique frowned. "What about Stil?"

Clovicus snorted. "He mailed the Assignment and Appointments Department a sketch of his donkey's rear end when they sent him a summons for a new assignment right after he got married. It nearly gave poor Alfonso a heart attack, but Sinèad thought it was great fun. Regardless, Stil has made it perfectly clear where his allegiance lies."

Warmth invaded Angelique's heart, and she knew she had to be grinning like an idiot. *I was stupid to even wonder if Stil would forget about me after falling in love with Gemma.*

Odette shifted, shaking Angelique back to the present.

"Ah, forgive my poor manners. Lord Enchanter Clovicus, may I introduce you to Odette—the leader of the smugglers that Rothbart cursed and the beloved of Prince Alexsei of Kozlovka."

Clovicus turned on his charm and smiled ruggedly. "So, you are the famed Swan Queen. Thank you for joining us on this little excursion."

Both Misha and Nadia snorted and looked away.

Odette briefly turned bright red. "I'm not a Swan Queen," she muttered.

"On behalf of Verglas, I welcome you and your compatriots. Queen Linnea will be thrilled to hear of your arrival," Clovicus said dryly. "She was less than elated when I showed up, sans weather mages."

"You've been light on the details that explain why your assistant sent you running to Verglas," Angelique said.

Clovicus rolled his eyes. "How much time do you have to hear my complaints?" He shook his head, then smiled charmingly at Odette and her smugglers. "I can escort you all to the dear queen and her sensible husband. This way."

He led the way to the Verglas palace—pausing to exchange a joke and a laugh with the guards while Angelique bid farewell to Pegasus, who picked his way west, toward Lake Sno.

Angelique watched with narrowed eyes as Clovicus greeted a

maid by name, slapped the back of a passing noble, and moved through the palace with a familiarity and general comfort that belied the fact that he was an incredibly powerful Lord Enchanter.

"Exactly how long have you been here?" Angelique asked.

"Not too long," Clovicus said. "If I dawdle too much in one location, there's a good chance my dratted assistant will find me."

Odette turned around to make a hand motion at her smugglers—who casually shifted the pattern in which they marched—then walked side-by-side with Angelique. "And what exactly does this Wallace do that you find so disturbing?" she asked with an arched eyebrow.

Clovicus sharply frowned. "He believes he is a very effective herding dog, and unfortunately, he thinks I am a sheep." He shook his head. "I'll flatter myself in saying that I am one of the most skilled Lord Enchanters alive today, but I got so because I take on missions and complete them quickly. I fill out the minimal required paperwork, which seems to offend my assistant's sensibilities."

"What does he do?" Angelique asked.

"He has absolutely no sense of personal boundaries. The Council has a yearly discussion for all high-level mages," Clovicus said. "Traditionally, it is a meeting I avoid given how excruciatingly *boring* it is."

"This year you were forced to attend?" Angelique guessed.

"My oh-so-efficient assistant confirmed on my behalf, then showed up outside my door at four in the morning to escort me to the meeting, all so he could ensure I really went." Clovicus scowled. "If I skip out on answering even a single correspondence, Wallace will track me down during my mealtime, interrupt me at a social gathering—he once followed me across the Arkane Mountains when I snuck from Baris to Erlauf in an effort to avoid him so he couldn't make me fill out the wretchedly stupid annual survey the Veneno Conclave sends to all enchanters and enchantresses." He sighed but brightened long enough to wave to a kitchen girl running down a side hallway.

"If he's not The Council's spy tasked with keeping them apprised of you, he's likely the Council's punishment against me for turning the grubby students they sent me off to Verglas to '*mentor*' into a mouthy bunch of rebels," he finished.

"I can see how he would hinder you, as you are such a...*free* spirit," Angelique said.

"I'd be less bothered if he was just a punishment," Clovicus said as they approached the doors to the throne room. His frown turned less theatrical and more worried. "But despite his diligence on my so-called behalf, I suspect he might be a plant after all—knowingly or unknowingly."

Angelique shrugged. "It's not unexpected."

He tilted his head. "It doesn't bother you?"

"I don't believe the Veneno Conclave will ever *not* be wary of me," she dryly said. "I'm more pleased that they have followed my wishes and stopped with the endless summons."

Clovicus slightly bowed his head. "May it continue to be so." He nodded to the guards standing at the door.

"Lord Enchanter Clovicus," they greeted before they set about opening the doors.

"Have you *really* only been here a short while?" Angelique asked in a whisper.

"I left as soon as I got your letter," he admitted. "But I took a ship south to Ringsted first in the hope of throwing Wallace off. We can only pray that it worked."

He held out his arm, indicating that Angelique should enter first.

Like the rest of Ostfold, the feel of the throne room had changed drastically since Angelique had last stepped foot inside it.

The glass throne was still positioned in front of the massive window, but more sunlight seemed to play across the land—

making the entire room glow a warm gold color. The air was fresher and held the faint hint of pine to it, but the most marked difference were the soldiers' expressions. Their shoulders were set but not stiff, and their expressions were stoic but free of tension lines and wrinkles.

A young man and young woman stood at the massive window.

Angelique recognized the young Queen Linnea—beautiful with her blonde hair and quick smile—though she was in an interesting wardrobe choice for the day given that she wore trousers and a violet shirt tucked into the waistline of her pants.

Logically, I think this means the pleasant man with her is King Toril. Angelique studied him as the couple turned to face them, watching the young man for any shadow of his father. *He looks kind—which is perhaps the last thing I expected.*

"Lady Enchantress Angelique, I am so glad you agreed to come," Linnea greeted her.

She and her husband strolled arm-in-arm. "Thank you for answering our request," Toril said. He bowed—deeper than he should have—to Angelique. "Please allow me to introduce myself. I am Toril. For months, I have wanted to thank you for the part you played in aiding Craftmage Stil to save Gemma and stop my father."

"It was an unfortunate situation," Angelique delicately said. "But I am glad to see that you wear the kingship well."

Toril smiled, making him look a little boyish. "Thank you. Might we enquire who your many companions are?"

"Of course." Angelique stepped aside so she could gesture to Odette and her people. "King Toril and Queen Linnea, it is my honor to introduce you to Odette of the Black Swan Smugglers and her talented companions. Odette is particular friends with the royal family of Kozlovka, and it was she and her smugglers who contained the evil Sorcerer Rothbart."

"We've heard of Odette." King Toril's smile didn't budge even when he met Odette's gaze, raising his character even further in

Angelique's eyes. "And we've heard a great deal of all the good the Black Swan Smugglers have done. Thank you for coming."

"Yes, thank you." Linnea shot Angelique a curious glance. "Though I will admit I'm a little confused why you chose to request their help, Angelique."

"Getting through the mountains will be a slow and tedious process," Angelique started.

Particularly since neither Clovicus nor I have weather magic as our core powers. I do wish he had brought someone with him, but at least we have the necessary power to make it happen.

"Odette and her smugglers will be a great boon to us as they will be able to fly ahead—unhindered by the snow, ice, avalanches, and old rockslides as we are. They might be able to narrow down the list of potential mountains to visit, greatly saving us time," she concluded.

"That's a sound plan." Linnea made a face and glanced at her husband. "It seems I have a long way to go before I can claim to be a true strategist. Scouting ahead hadn't even occurred to me."

"Be fair to yourself, Your Majesty," Clovicus winked. "You're used to solid things like weapons and men, not the twisty and whimsical ways of magic, as we are."

"You are too kind, Lord Enchanter," Queen Linnea said.

Angelique tilted her head as she observed the interaction. *Even though they all use his proper title, Clovicus has most everyone eating out of the palm of his hand. They treat him like a debonair uncle. But even though I think I have managed to convince almost everyone to use my name instead of my title, only a few—like Gabrielle, Elle, and Odette—speak plainly to me. Most continue to speak with formality, even if I've interacted with them for years.*

The thought rankled Angelique, though she couldn't exactly put a finger on *why* it bothered her. They viewed her as the elegant and kind enchantress she pretended to be. Her front was *working*—that was hardly something to be upset about.

"This does change things a bit." Linnea tapped her fingers on her side. "For the better, of course. Toril narrowed the mirror's possible location to three different mountains."

"Our findings revealed that the Snow Queen did indeed collapse part of a mountain on top of the mirror, and we already knew the general region in which the mirror was hidden," Toril said. "This narrowed the possibilities down to the three peaks Linnea mentioned. I feel quite certain we'll find it under one of those mountains, given that we had many of our scholars pore over historic texts and maps and consult local lore."

"We still have a few days of preparations, but we can begin discussing these locations immediately," Linnea said.

"Actually," Odette began, "my people and I are ready to fly."

"Really?" Toril asked. "You don't need to pick gear?"

Odette glanced over her shoulder at her smugglers. Misha and Nadia nodded.

Odette put on a professional smile. "It's not necessary. Angelique gave us what little equipment we will need." She tugged a ribbon free from the neckline of her shirt. A ruby cut in the shape of a flame—a heat charm—hung from the ribbon.

"A few craftmages are staying at Prince Severin and Princess Elle's Chanceux Chateau," Angelique said. "I asked them to create ribbons that would stretch and shrink so the Black Swan Smugglers could be comfortable—and safe—while traveling in the cold."

"Oh," Linnea blinked.

"In that case, we ought to adjourn to my study." Toril hurried toward the door. "We have better maps there, so we can point out the specific peaks."

Odette and the Black Swan Smugglers strode after the king, leaving Angelique to bring up the rear.

She smiled as she watched the smugglers murmur to one another, taking in their confident strides and the unworried way one or two of them stretched their arms above their heads.

They're used to making runs like this. I don't think it will bother them overly much, but for us it might make a heap of a difference. If they can even eliminate one mountain from the list of three, it will make our odds better and save us a great deal of time.

Angelique paused at the door. "Clovicus? Are you coming?"

"If I must," he said. "I've already heard this lecture. Twice." He reluctantly sauntered after her, one hand tucked into a pocket of his tunic.

"I imagine hearing it a third time is still better than going back to Wallace," Angelique dryly said. She waited until Clovicus laughed before adding, "And it wouldn't be a bad thing for you and I to start discussing what sorts of spells you think we'll need."

"Yes, of course. We probably ought to go inspect the start of the mountain range to get a feel for what we're dealing with before we make any concrete plans," he said.

"We can go with the Black Swan Smugglers and see them off at Fresler's Helm," Angelique suggested. "Isn't the easiest entrance to the range near it?"

"I believe so—though we can ask King Toril for confirmation. I like the way you think, Apprentice."

Angelique's smile faded a little. "I had an excellent teacher."

CHAPTER 22

"Three kinds of magic," Clovicus announced. "Rock—or earth, perhaps—snow, and fire."

Angelique glanced up at the lord enchanter. "Fire to melt the snow? Won't that make the valleys muddy messes?"

"If we used it to the extent you're thinking, we'd probably bring a flash flood down on us," Clovicus said wryly. "I intended to use it to help us with the temperature. Having floating globes of fire is an easier spell to hold onto than a weather spell to control the temperature around us. It's more passive and doesn't need to scale up and down."

A cool breeze ruffled Angelique's hair. "You think the weather will be that frigid?"

"The northern mountains are unnaturally cold," Clovicus shrugged. "Legend says it's because there is a land north of our continent, but no one knows because these mountains are impossible to pass."

"Yes, but as you said, that's a legend," Angelique pointed out.

"Don't be so sure," Clovicus said. "There is something in these mountains—something besides the Snow Queen's magic."

The wind whistled as it tore through the narrow valley between Fresler's Helm and its neighboring peaks.

Though it was summer, the wind brought a blast of cold air with it, tugging on Angelique's trousers.

"We'll have to move things bit by bit, then?" Angelique asked.

Clovicus sighed and flicked a lock of his copper hair. "Unless you want to go around blasting off power, yep."

"That probably wouldn't make Severin happy," Angelique said. "He already gave me a lecture about being discreet."

Clovicus grunted and peered up at the sky.

The setting sun was blocked by the mountains, so the sky had a halo-like glow where the mountain peaks pierced the heavens.

"I'm heading back to the camp," Clovicus announced. "They were preparing dinner when we left, and I don't mean to miss it. Are you coming?"

"I'll be along shortly," Angelique said. "Odette said they'd avoid spending the night in the mountains if they could, so they should return soon."

Clovicus shrugged. "Do what you will." He patted her shoulder then began to make his way back to the camp, where a mixture of guards and mountain guides had pitched elaborate tents lined with animal skins to block out the cold nip of the mountain air.

Angelique waited until she no longer heard his footsteps before she sat, reveling in wearing her plain but sturdy trousers.

Given that they would soon be mountain climbing—provided all went well—Angelique had opted to set aside her dress from Evariste and instead wear more practical clothing: trousers and a cotton shirt, with warmer clothes packed for the cooler temperatures.

I love my dress, but there is something very freeing about pants. They're a lot easier to scramble around in.

She hugged her knees to her chest and stared at the golden

sky. Birds chirped cheerfully in the trees, but it was too cool for bugs this close to the cold radiating off the mountains.

Angelique heard the approach of footsteps and considered getting up. *It must be Clovicus, and I don't think he'd care if he found me rolling in the dirt as long as I didn't try to make him do more paperwork.*

"Forget something?" Angelique peeled her gaze from the beautiful sky and peered over her shoulder, blanching when she saw it was not Clovicus picking his way toward her, but Lady Enchantress Lovelana.

Aw, blast it.

Angelique scrambled to her feet and brushed off dust and grass.

Lady Enchantress Lovelana was a beautiful woman who possessed healing magic as her core powers and had been charged by the Council to lead the committee tasked with finding Evariste.

She and Lovelana did not have a sour relationship, per se... But it was an acquaintanceship based on tolerance from Lovelana's end—for the beautiful enchantress had quite obviously carried the torch for Evariste when he was around—and indifference from Angelique as she had surmised that the enchantress was going to mindlessly follow protocol, which severely impeded the committee's efforts in searching for Evariste. (Namely, it meant Lovelana was looking into reports of black mages that were decades old rather than investigating the very present and active efforts of modern black mages.)

"Lady Enchantress Lovelana," Angelique said. "What an... unexpected surprise," she struggled to fill in the awkward gap.

Lovelana smiled. "I imagine so." She stopped a few lengths short of Angelique and wrung her hands for a long moment before limply dropping her arms at her side.

Angelique studied the enchantress from head to toe.

Her smile was sincere, but considering the gorgeous ensembles Lovelana usually wore, her current dress—an elegant but simple gown of rose pink—was rather understated. Most tellingly, however, was the faint crease that sliced across her forehead and the way she pressed her lips together.

"Is something wrong?" Angelique asked. "Do you have news of Evariste?"

"What? I mean, no—I'm sorry to say I don't." Lovelana went back to wringing her hands. "I heard you were here in Verglas—with business on behalf of Prince Severin and Princess Elle of Loire."

"In a way," Angelique agreed. "He has a theory about all the latest occurrences," she lamely summarized.

I understand that Severin wants us to keep this information contained and close so the Chosen don't find out about it, but how am I supposed to keep her in the dark when she's here *and can see us skulking around the mountains with her own eyes?*

Thankfully, Lovelana did not seem overly concerned with the camp—or those in it. She nodded and kept her eyes on Angelique. "I see. I went to Ostfold in hopes of catching you, but they told me you and Lord Enchanter Clovicus had traveled to Fresler's Helm."

"Yeeesss," Angelique reluctantly and unavoidably confirmed.

"I followed you here because I need to speak with you."

Oh, great. What are the chances she needs me to do something? I'd say near 100 percent. Probably needs me to retrieve something from home to help find Evariste—even though her little committee insists on looking for him in the most inefficient manner possible.

"I am honored," Angelique said with *just* enough humility she didn't think Lovelana would pick up on the sarcasm of it. "What can I do to help you?"

Lovelana knit her hands together and nodded as if she had decided something. "I believe there is a mole in the Veneno Conclave."

Still feeling snarky, Angelique deliberately misinterpreted her.

"You came out here to tell me the Veneno Conclave fortress is experiencing a rodent infestation?"

"No—a *mole*. An informant, a spy, call it what you will." Lovelana threw her hands in the air and started pacing. "Someone in the Conclave is feeding the black mages information. Of this, I am certain."

Angelique stiffened. "What?"

"I've been tracing over all the reports of black mages, trying to find a pattern to them—a way that might tell me where they are based so we could trace them to Evariste." Lovelana switched from pacing to walking in a circle around Angelique—who was so surprised she couldn't even summon an opinion to voice. "Several times, now, I've been able to uncover dens of black mages. I report my findings, of course, but by the time I travel to the location to capture the mages, they're always gone!"

Lovelana huffed in aggravation. "It makes no sense—these workshops have no reason to believe that anyone is onto them. As far as I can tell, not even the local government is aware of their existence. And yet they are always a step ahead of me! Once I thought to outsmart them, and I set up a trap—they avoided it entirely!"

"If they are as skilled as the black mages who took Evariste, it would not be surprising that they could avoid you," Angelique said. *Particularly if they're in the ranks of the Chosen, but I won't mention that just yet.*

"That's just it—they're not." Lovelana stopped her nervous pacing. "By what materials they leave behind and what I've found out about them, they are little more than petty criminals. But they are either unnaturally devious, or informed on the inner workings of the Conclave."

Angelique struggled with the idea of a spy in the conclave. Though it was a possibility that had been mentioned by Prince Severin before, it was entirely different to hear similar words from

Lovelana, the darling of the Veneno Conclave. She wrinkled her brow. "Do you think there is an informant among the staff, or...?"

"No, it's a mage. It *must* be a mage," Lovelana said. "A regular staff member wouldn't have the opportunity to see this kind of classified information." She narrowed her eyes. "You believe me, don't you?"

"Yes," Angelique said before she even realized it was true.

We figured there had to be something like this—though if Lovelana has noticed such clear proof, it might be worse than we first thought. Angelique cleared her voice, then continued. "The past few years have been turbulent. I didn't think it was possible that nearly every country suffered some sort of attack, and yet the Veneno Conclave skated through."

Lovelana's shoulders curled with relief. "Good. Thank you."

"Of course." Angelique watched Lovelana resume pacing back and forth, then cautiously said, "But...why are you telling me this?"

Lovelana met her gaze. "Because you're the only one I trust."

Angelique squinted and wondered if Lovelana was experiencing mental fatigue. *I am always the* last person *any normal mage would trust!*

"You've continued to look for Lord Enchanter Evariste, no matter how the Council has attempted to dissuade you and despite the threatened punishments from the Veneno Conclave," Lovelana said. "You want to find him. Which means you obviously aren't mixed up with those who took him." Lovelana paused. "I don't know what to do," she confessed.

Angelique shook her head and cleared her throat. "Do you think it's a single renegade informant, or more?"

"I don't know." Lovelana's face was only half visible as the lengthening shadows of the evening started blending with the dimness of night, but Angelique could still see her fright in the way her hands trembled. "I'd like to say it's only one. However, given what I've seen, it might be as many as three or five."

"It's troubling," Angelique said. "But in an organization like the Veneno Conclave, they can't hide for long—particularly now that you are watching for them."

To Angelique's shock, Lovelana sat down on the ground and shut her eyes. "I don't know what to do about it," she confessed.

"I don't know either," Angelique said. "I think the best course would be to tell those who are trustworthy."

"You have someone in mind?"

Angelique tapped her lower lip. "Clovicus and Sybilla for certain. Stil is safe, but I don't know that he could do much to help."

"Finnr is certainly trustworthy," Lovelana said.

"I suppose so." Angelique was quite proud that she managed to keep a grimace off her face. *After spending "quality" time with him at the Summit, I don't particularly care for Finnr—but she's right. He can't be the leak—not unless he is this world's greatest actor. His obsession with following rules would never let him do such a thing.*

"I will send word to Finnr. Will you tell Clovicus and Sybilla?" Lovelana asked.

"Clovicus is here—right now. We could tell him together."

Lovelana shook her head. "I don't want to linger too long. Given our...history, it will raise some suspicions if it's widely known that I sought you out. Also," Loveland slightly wrinkled her nose. "I don't know that Lord Enchanter Clovicus thinks much of me."

"Clovicus doesn't think much of anyone except himself," Angelique grumbled under her breath.

"Thank you, Angelique." Lovelana glanced at Angelique, sadness darkening her expression. "I appreciate that you listened —and believed."

"Of course." Angelique hesitated and pressed her lips together. *Do I risk sending her to Severin? We're trying to contain our actions to keep the Chosen unaware, but given that Lovelana is concerned about a possible spy, she already is extra cautious.*

"There is one last person who should know," Angelique finally said. "Prince Severin of Loire."

Lovelana staggered backwards a step, as if Angelique had assaulted her. "You want to tell a *royal* about Veneno Conclave matters? We can't show weakness to the continent, nor is it any of their business."

"I'm sorry to say it's too late for that," Angelique grimly said. "And that 'royal' has a better grasp on current events than anyone in the Conclave. For the sake of the continent, he needs to know."

Lovelana nervously patted her hair—which was pinned to the top of her head with jewel-topped pins. "Very well. Because of all you have done for the continent, I will trust you in this—though I will voice my reluctance."

"Thank you, Lady Enchantress. That is all I can ask for."

Lovelana nodded and took a few more steps away before she paused mid-step. "What are you seeking here, anyway?"

Angelique exhaled so heavily her cheeks puffed out. "I'll tell you when Severin's suspicions are either confirmed or allayed."

Lovelana nodded. "Farewell, Angelique."

"Goodbye, Lady Enchantress Lovelana."

Angelique watched Lovelana until the enchantress disappeared into the dim light of dusk. She peered up at the sky—which was a deep shade of ebony blue, studded with the glitter of stars. She turned, intending to finally go back to the camp, when she heard a faint sort of chortling-grunt.

What sort of creature makes that noise?

She swung around and spotted smudges of white flying across the sky. It took her a few moments to recognize Odette and the Black Swan Smugglers in their swan bodies.

They flew in a tight circle just above Angelique's head before one of the swans abruptly dipped.

Bells clanged, and light, wind, and dust wrapped around the swan as it dove toward the ground.

Angelique jumped back a bit when it looked like the transforming bird might careen into her, but Odette landed on the ground with a painful-sounding thud, barefoot and back in her human body as the light of her transformation magic faded.

Angelique opened her mouth to ask the Swan Queen if she was hurt, but Odette blurted out, "It's gone!"

Angelique frowned. "What's gone?"

Odette's eyes were wide with fear. "The mirror."

CHAPTER 23

Although it was nearly mid-summer, the ground of the valley was covered in frost, which crunched under Angelique's boots as she peered up the narrow channel.

Behind her, Odette and Clovicus spoke, following Angelique as she picked her way past slabs of rock and massive boulders.

"Explain it, one more time," Clovicus said.

"I've explained it *all night long*! Telling you again isn't going to change the outcome of what my people and I saw!" Odette snarled. The waves of her blonde hair looked a little flat, and her good manners hadn't made a re-appearance since she had returned with her dire news.

"Please."

When Angelique glanced back over her shoulder, Clovicus was rubbing the circles under his eyes.

"Just once more," he said.

Odette heaved a sigh. "My crew and I were investigating one of the mountains King Toril and Queen Linnea had decided upon. Half of the mountain was gone, and most of the valley was filled with stone and ice—it's a glacier, practically."

Angelique listened as she scanned the valley—one of the

entrances to the northern mountains, and the official mess she and Clovicus would have to clear if they ever had a hope of examining what Odette and her people had found. It wasn't too bad. Since everything was frozen, at least it wasn't muddy and impassable—but there was lots of rubble and ice.

Behind her, Odette continued. "In the bright sunlight, we saw the shadow of a hole. We landed and transformed so we could investigate on foot. We found a room of sorts that was cleared out of ice and rubble. There was a ruined pick axe, and the walls were dimpled from the dig, but there were also signs of someone with magic—either ice or fire—as on the ground you could see where ice had melted and then re-frozen."

Angelique jumped a little when Pegasus appeared at her side. He sniffed a chunk of ice and made his way past her, the little stars in the murky black of his coat glowing brighter than usual.

Angelique stared at a band of stars on his hipbone and heard the crunch of grit as Clovicus strode after her.

"There was a clear groove in the ground where something—like the frame of a mirror—had once been pressed into the ice," Odette continued.

Angelique winced, though she had heard the tale over a dozen times by now. *It was dire when we realized the Chosen were our real enemy, but if they took the mirror...I don't know that there's even a way to describe just how bad that would be. Could we even beat them if they have it?*

Clovicus' deep voice drew her back into the conversation. "But there was no other proof of the mirror itself?"

"Do the King and Queen of Verglas frequently bury treasure in the middle of mountains?"

"Of course not!"

"Then what else could it be? What other treasure could *possibly* be buried in an ice field in the northern mountains like that?" Odette asked.

Clovicus growled.

"Lord Enchanter," Angelique called—half reminding him to be civil and half wanting his attention. "Could we build an ice bridge that crosses above all of this?"

"Not unless you have secret skills I don't know of." Clovicus sighed and joined her in watching Pegasus pick his way across the treacherous footing. "A simple ice slab won't do the trick. You'd need an understanding of architecture basics—something I know nothing about."

Angelique nodded. "I guessed as much," she said. "Do you have a limit on your magic, or a price?"

Clovicus raised an eyebrow. "Price."

"What is it?"

He stared resolutely at the valley, where the mountains ebbed and flowed into one another like a pair of squabbling siblings. "If I use too much of my magic at once, it starts to throw fits."

"Fits?"

"It gets out of control," Clovius bluntly said. "When I was an apprentice, I used too much of my power, and my magic flattened an entire foothill in Mullberg. Thankfully, there were no casualties and only a few injuries. But it's an experience I don't fancy reliving."

The cool temperature of the air started to turn Angelique's nose red. "Does that mean, however, you could contribute a steady amount of power indefinitely, if it is a slow pull, so to speak?"

Clovicus narrowed his eyes. "Yes...what are you planning?"

"Just thinking through our options." She nodded at the valley. "How important is it that we get there fast?"

"Incredibly so."

"Enough to sacrifice secrecy?"

"*Everything* hinges on that mirror, Angelique," he said grimly. "If the Chosen have it already, then we need to prepare for the worst."

Angelique nodded. "That's what I thought, too. If Lovelana is right, and the Chosen have an informant in the Veneno Conclave, and they *also* have the mirror..." She trailed off rather than say it out loud.

It will make defeating them nearly impossible. She stared at the valley as desperation clawed at her heart. She had been scared before. She had known fear since the day the depth of her powers was discovered.

But this was different.

This was the unhinged fear that came with knowing *everything* might end. This was the hysteria of knowing that Stil, Gemma, Puss, Elle, Gabrielle—all the friends she had made might die in the coming war.

If there ever was a time I needed to exert a lot of power, this is it. We can't hesitate here—I cannot allow myself to hesitate here.

"Odette?" she asked.

"Yeah?"

"How far is the mountain from this point?"

Odette tilted her head and peered at the peaks of the mountains. "As the crow flies? Not far. Walking, though, is going to take you a while with this terrain. And it only gets worse the deeper in you go. If you don't believe me and my crew, it would probably be faster to get a mage with shapeshifting powers to run there and check into it."

"That won't be necessary." Angelique stared at the big star on Pegasus' forehead as he picked his way back up the gorge. She patted him as he passed by and circled around behind her. "I'm going to try something, Clovicus. Please steady the sides of the mountains."

Clovicus snorted. "What is that supposed to mean?"

Angelique turned around and led the way out of the valley, her hands clammy despite the cool air. "We have to get through."

"Did you just miss the entire conversation we just had?" Clovicus said—short on patience.

Not that Angelique blamed him. In the span of a season, they had gone from being proactive against their enemy to learning they were horribly late, and finally may have been out maneuvered.

Angelique grimaced as she reached the mouth of the valley. *This is going to take a lot of power. I guess it's just as well I've been pulling daring adventures the past few months, or I wouldn't have the courage to do this.*

She swallowed with difficulty as she swiveled so she again looked north into the mountain range. *It might make me miserable, and the King and Queen of Verglas might not love the scorched trail we're going to leave in our wake, but we don't have a choice.*

Clovicus frowned at Angelique and stopped at her side. "Could you stop speaking in riddles and just *tell* me what you're planning?"

Odette, seemingly knowing Angelique better—or perhaps just possessing better sense—sucked her head into her neck and crept behind Angelique.

"You might try to stop me," Angelique said.

"*What?*"

"And I'm not entirely certain it's going to work," she offhandedly added. "It's better to test it, first."

Clovicus rested his hands on his hips. "And what is it that you're going to test?"

I've fought a basilisk, a wyvern, and put an entire city to sleep. I've countered curses, had a shouting match with The Council, and I ride a constellation. I can do this. I have to. She took a deep breath. "This."

Angelique extended her hand. Her fingers shook as her silver magic threaded around her palms, twisting under her direction as she thought of Evariste…and Pegasus.

She took a deep breath, then loosened the spell.

Fire and raw power roared to life, creating a globe of fire bigger than a war elephant. The globe emitted such pure light it hummed, flames of fire wrapped around a center of solid power.

The ground shook as the globe—which Angelique had

modeled after a miniature star—lowered so it touched the valley floor, then slowly rolled forward, carving a path through the mountains like a heated blade slicing butter.

Odette started swearing and didn't stop as she braced herself against the raw power of Angelique's star.

Clovicus laughed in glee, though Angelique felt his magic flare to life as he stabilized the shaking mountainsides, holding back loosened rubble and snow. "And you say you aren't the Snow Queen?" He was barely audible above the howl of Angelique's magic.

Angelique gritted her teeth as she forced more and more power into her magical construction, fueling it as it rolled forward, consuming ice and rock alike in its inescapable blast.

The heat was strong enough, it felt like her eyebrows were getting burnt off, and the steady thrum of power the modeled star radiated rattled Angelique's bones.

Her stomach prickled slightly—the first sign of nausea—but she grimly pushed on.

She plowed a clear path through the mountains, leaving an evenly cut blackened trail carved in stone.

Clovicus misted water over it, making the rock hiss and cool.

Angelique started down the newly cut path, nudging her magic star ahead.

She eradicated the entire length of the valley before the nausea became too much. She cut off her magic and threw herself to the side, clinging to a stone boulder as she heaved.

Clovicus was by her in a moment, his cool hand resting on her temple as he pushed a healing spell into her. "So this is why you wanted to know if I could keep going," he mused.

Given that her nausea was due to her price, not an actual physical condition, Angelique doubted his magic would help her, but the sickening sensation cleared more quickly than she expected.

When her stomach stopped its violent rejection, Angelique

shut her eyes and tried not to shudder at the sour taste that filled her mouth. "My price is wretched, but in a bit, I can get up and go another round."

"Here." Odette offered her a waterskin. "Rinse your mouth out."

Angelique did as she was advised while Odette turned to Clovicus. "If she can keep this up, it won't take long at all to reach the area—you'll be able to ride horses in like it's a road to Ostfold."

"Tell the others to pack up the camp," Clovicus advised.

"Yeah." Odette hesitated at Angelique's side. "I'll see if anyone in the camp has anything to ease stomachs."

Angelique boosted herself up so she could sit on her rock. "Just put me on Pegasus. I can lean far enough over his side I won't get anything on him, and he'll make sure I don't fall off."

"Angelique…" Clovicus' eyebrows slanted down in worry.

Angelique forced herself to meet his gaze. "We have to get there. We have to know for certain just how bad it is."

"If you push yourself too far, I'll stop you," Clovicus warned her. "Don't think that just because you're powerful doesn't mean I won't knock you out like a wayward student."

Angelique laughed, then reached out to Pegasus—whom Odette had leaped away from so he could take her spot.

The constellation breathed into her hand, then looked at the slightly smoldering gutter she had carved and maneuvered so his side faced her, ready for her to slip on.

Odette was already running down the cleared part of the path they had walked across, heading back to the camp.

With Clovicus' help, Angelique scrambled on to Pegasus' back. She felt a little lightheaded, and her stomach still grumbled, but she clung to Pegasus' neck and grimly faced down the mountains.

I can make the sacrifice this time, again. I can do this, again. Once we tell Severin, it will be in his hands, and I can follow whatever progress his

Rangers have made in tracking Suzu, or I can attempt to make contact with the elves. When the war comes, everyone will work together, and even now Clovicus is with me. I won't have to forge on alone much longer. This is almost over.

With that flickering hope, Angelique licked her lips as Pegasus trotted over the cleared road with ease. Her teeth chattered in the cold, but she ignored it and instead reached out, gathering her magic again.

With a roar loud enough to split mountains, her star ignited, and the party continued forward, carving a path through the impassable northern mountains, forever changing the terrain and filling the area with the uncomfortably sharp intensity of her magic.

WHEN THEY REACHED the valley where the Black Swan Smugglers had landed, and to avoid collapsing the room Odette had found, Angelique and Clovicus created a bridge of ice after all. (They over-engineered the thing, of course, to avoid any accidents, making the ice work of the bridge thicker than stone.)

Angelique was a miserable huddle—even with her burning the way, it had taken more than a day to reach the mountain. She felt so sick, it was difficult to focus on her magic, but thankfully it didn't take much thought or power to keep fire spells active; so, as Clovicus kept the ice bridge in one piece, all Angelique had to do was feed the fire spells to keep the party from freezing to death.

She crouched on her heels and peered over the side of the ice bridge, shivering and wishing Pegasus could have come. (They left all the mounts with three of the swan smugglers and a giant fire at the foot of the bridge, not wanting to risk dragging the mountain ponies across the glacier.)

"Would you like more mint leaves to chew, Lady Enchantress?"

Angelique peered up and recognized Misha. "Thank you." She

took the offered mint leaves and popped them into her mouth, the minty flavor clearing away some of the bitter aftertaste that she hadn't been able to rinse from her mouth as she heaved her way to the mountain.

The sky was a cloudless, bright blue backdrop that almost made her eyes hurt as she shifted her gaze to the mountains. She studied the half-collapsed peak and marveled at the show of power. *Carving through stone like I did is a task of sheer stubbornness. But dropping a mountain? If this is the spot, the Snow Queen was...incredible.*

"You can see our tracks down by the hole," Misha said, interrupting her thoughts.

Angelique shifted so she could peer where he pointed, easily spotting the shadow of the entrance and the imprint of human footprints around it. "Yes," she agreed.

"We didn't see any tracks or proof of recent disturbance, though," he continued. "It makes one wonder just how long ago was the mirror retrieved: months, years, decades?"

It was an unpleasant thought; one Angelique had been trying to avoid.

"Lord Enchanter Clovicus has built us a staircase down to the glacier's surface," the mountain scout—sent by King Toril and Queen Linnea to serve as their guide—announced. "We are ready to descend."

Angelique slowly stood, momentarily closing her eyes when the world seemed to shift at a skewed angle.

A shadow fell over her as someone stepped up behind her. "Are you steady enough to go down there?" Odette asked.

Angelique opened her eyes and smiled at her. "I'll have to be."

Odette chewed on her lip, then slowly offered out her hand. "We smugglers still have all those extra spells Rothbart dosed us with—including strength. I can steady you as you climb down, if you don't mind, that is."

It so deeply amused Angelique that Odette would be

concerned *Angelique* wouldn't want to touch her she almost laughed, but a part of her realized that wouldn't assure the Swan Queen at all, so she kept her small smile in place. "I would appreciate that. Thank you."

Odette led Angelique to the edge of the bridge. The mountain guide was hopping down the stairs with the spryness of a goat, while a few of the smugglers opted to transform into swans and glide down. A number of Verglas soldiers were right on the guide's heels, but Clovicus waited for Angelique.

"You'll be fine?" he asked.

Angelique raised her hand that Odette held. "Odette has been kind enough to support me on my way down."

Clovicus nodded, his usual smile and mercurial features as still as stone as he glanced down at the hole-like entrance. "You have my thanks, Odette. Be careful," he warned the pair before he started his descent.

Odette and Angelique went next. It wasn't as treacherous as the others acted like it was. Angelique's boots never slipped on the ice steps, and the stairs were as steady as rock. But she was glad for Odette's support. Given how she had pushed herself past her price for hours, it seemed her stomach was feeling rather vindictive, and even when she stared straight ahead, she couldn't shake the feeling that the world was spinning around her.

The sensation only worsened when she set foot on the ground and felt something cold and dark ease across the snow-dusted glacier.

"Here, Angelique. You'll have to crouch down to get in." Odette sat on her heels and waddled forward. She tapped her hand—shoved in a warm mitten—on the floor of the hole. "You can tell it used to be bigger, but it filled with snow that kept freezing."

Angelique, struggling to stand straight, opted to drop to her knees and crawl forward. She nodded to the three soldiers who stood guard outside with one of Odette's smugglers, then scurried through the slanted tunnel entrance.

The deeper she went down the passageway, the stronger the feeling of darkness became.

It wasn't a tactile sensation, but rather the impression of something terrifying that made her heart beat faster and heightened her breathing.

When she finally dragged herself into the chamber, the impression spawned into an overwhelming sensation of darkness, to the point where Angelique could barely see, and she knew there was no way she could stand.

She dragged herself to the side so she didn't block the hole as a cold sweat broke out on her forehead.

The room seemed innocuous enough. Only a fine layer of snow dusted the area by the entrance. The rest of the floor was the kind of ice that had obviously been melted and refrozen, as it was shiny and had curved-over layers—like the cresting of a wave.

The walls were pockmarked, and as Odette had promised, there was a snapped-off pick-axe.

None of it seemed off, but the clawing sensation at Angelique's throat intensified the longer she was in the room.

Even worse, she felt the slow creep of her own magic as it grew in intensity. Usually it just...*oozed* around her, prickling when she was in a battle. But now...she could feel more of it prowling around her like a dragon uncoiling.

Please, please *don't let this be a sign that my magic is drawn to darkness!*

"You feel it, too?"

Angelique glanced up at Clovicus. He was standing, but his skin was ashen, and he leaned against the icy wall of the room, his gloved hands shaking.

It took her a moment to realize he meant the foul darkness, not the rebellious twinges of her magic. "Yes," she managed to spit past her numb lips.

Clovicus stared into the chamber. "I've never felt such strong and powerful darkness before."

Angelique managed to maneuver herself into a crouch. "I've never felt such a strong sensation of something *magical* before." She staggered to her feet but leaned heavily against the wall like the Lord Enchanter. "I'm not at all sensitive to magic, and I'm terrible at trying to pinpoint it despite all my practice. But this..."

"The mirror was here," Clovicus said.

"You're certain?"

"There is no other artifact made of dark magic that is this strong," he grimly said. "*Only* the mirror is capable of leaving such an impression."

Angelique tried to hide the way she arched her back when a particularly powerful ripple of her magic started to drift away before she managed to yank it back. "Trapped in here as long as it was—for centuries, even well before the Snow Queen found it—its magic must have seeped out and polluted the place. How long ago do you think it was taken?"

Clovicus pressed a palm to the icy wall. "It's hard to say. Years, I think, based on the ice. Probably decades."

"And the imprint the mirror left here is still so strong?"

"It would probably be a thousand times worse if it hadn't been on Verglas lands with the Snow Queen's magic keeping it contained."

"Which raises the point, how did the Chosen even get here?" Angelique closed her eyes and leaned her head back against the icy cold wall. It chilled her, but she welcomed the new sensation; it was able to pierce the fear the mirror's echo managed to inspire and the uncomfortable hoard of her magic. "These mountains can't be entered from Kozlovka to the west or Mullberg to the east. To enter them, you *have* to travel through Verglas, and the Snow Queen's magic protection hasn't shuddered even once."

"That is quite the puzzle." Clovicus' voice was soft, but lined with the unmistakable rasp of anger.

Her magic threatened to roll through the room like the clouds of an incoming rainstorm. *Why is it doing this?* She savagely yanked it back and glanced at Clovicus, wondering if he sensed the unusual activity of her magic.

He didn't glance her way.

I'm going to assume that means I'm clear—unless I decide to confess to someone that apparently my war magic is drawn to darkness. That's sure to win me some friends. But I've been around black mages before, and it hasn't reacted like this. Angelique mashed her palms into her eyes and refocused her thoughts. "Someone will have to tell Severin."

"As I imagine Wallace will soon catch up with me, it's probably best to have you do so." Clovicus sighed. "Though I am sorry you are stuck delivering more bad news."

"Bad news is all we seem to get these days." Angelique's voice was devoid of feeling as she stared at the ground. "Every time I turn around, it seems we uncover darker and darker secrets."

Odette, who had made a circle around the room, stopped at their huddled section of the wall. "You're that certain the mirror really was here, even though you haven't seen the impression of where the frame was in the ground?"

Clovicus took a deep breath as a sweat droplet worked its way down his temple. "The *magic* impression it left behind is quite distinctive. Further proof is unnecessary."

Angelique rocked so she stood straight, her stomach still sloshing uncomfortably. "But I would like to see the spot anyway. Evariste would never let me quit a task like this unless we made a thorough inspection."

Clovicus raised an eyebrow. "Even when the outcome is obvious, like this?"

"*Especially* then," Angelique said.

She followed Odette up the length of the narrow chamber, pausing when the Swan Queen pointed out boot prints frozen into the ice.

"Not that it was ever a question, but clearly humans took the mirror and not—I don't know...unicorns or dragons or something." Odette cringed.

Angelique set her boot next to the print, measuring it.

She was tall for a woman, and the boot print was about the same length, but a bit wider.

"There are a few different sets—another is over here." Odette set her boot by this second print. Though Odette was shorter than Angelique, this boot print was even smaller than hers. She pointed out a third set of giant prints. "Those were the three clear sets we were able to pick out—one of my smugglers was able to find several more unique prints, but they aren't as clear."

"So we know a party of people came here to retrieve the mirror," Angelique said.

"Assumedly, yes."

When a soldier knelt by the largest boot print and unrolled a piece of cloth upon which he traced out with chalk the outline of the track's imprint, Angelique and Odette moved on, stopping when they reached the far side of the room.

"This is where we think the mirror was placed." Odette crouched down and pointed to a long indentation that cracked deeper into the ice than the top layer upon which they walked. "Nadia is good at tracking. She said if you look in the layers, you can see signs of snow and ice melting and pooling with this indentation at the center."

Angelique knelt next to her—*slowly*. Not just because the nausea made her innards slosh, but also because her magic had increased its intensity. It stayed concentrated around her, but it was so thick and overwhelming, it made her head ache.

Afraid of what it might do, Angelique reverted to shoving her magic deep in her soul—more than a little worried by the way it resisted. *This is not good.*

When she was certain her magic wasn't going to break out, she peered at the crack. "A mage must have done this. A simple torch wouldn't do it."

"It wouldn't," Odette agreed. "The mirror must be quite big, given the length of the crack. Do you know its dimensions?"

"We know it was big, but not its exact size," Angelique said. "It is recorded that it has a giant red ruby at the top of the mirror, and its frame is ornate, but besides being large, those are its only distinctive properties. But you have a good point." She paused to take a steadying breath so she could at least attempt a smile, then called out to the nearest soldier. "Excuse me, could the length of this crack be measured and recorded? Thank you."

She stepped aside so the soldier could get to work, then glanced at Odette. "Did you notice anything else?"

"You might want to look at the pick-axe." Odette backed up a few steps, then pointed to the axe. The axe head was rusted, and both of the pointed tips were broken off. Its wooden handle, however, was still preserved. "Best we can tell, they used pick-axes to clear the room. I imagine they left this one behind as it would only be dead weight on the return trip."

Angelique nodded and shivered in her layers of warm clothes. "Thank you, Odette, for all your help in this. You've gone above and beyond what I asked for."

Odette pulled her scarf a little tighter around her throat. "You helped us; I'm glad we can return the favor—and it helps that you pay well." She turned in a circle and watched the soldiers meticulously record the details of the room. "You'll go back and tell Prince Severin all of this?"

"Yes. He'll have to take the mirror into account in the battle plans."

"I see. If you have any need of our services again, we will gladly help."

"Thank you." Angelique glanced at the cracked ice where the mirror had likely been positioned.

Yet again we have discovered some new way the Chosen have maimed us without our knowledge. We're nearly crippled, and we didn't even know. Clovicus should finally be able to get the Veneno Conclave stirred up with this news, but is it too late?

Her spine shuddered in the ever-present whisper of darkness as her own magic rubbed her nerves raw. *Perhaps we'll be able to recover King Themerysaldi; then things won't be quite so dire.*

"You said you won't see the elves again for months?" Angelique asked.

Odette rested her thumbs on her dagger belt. "Unfortunately. I can send word to you when we schedule our next delivery."

"Thank you." Angelique felt her stomach roil again, and her magic throbbed within her chest. She stiffly walked across the chamber and nodded to Clovicus before scrambling out of the hole.

She breathed easier once outside, separated from the leftover dark magic and granted relief from her magic's painful assault as it slowly faded.

She stared up at the cloudless blue sky, a little bewildered that it could look so cheerful when things were so dire.

Well, at least one thing is for certain. Things can't possibly get any worse.

"You surprise me at the oddest of times, Lord Enchanter."

"Hm?" Evariste was pressed against the pane of his mirror, trying to get his bearings.

He had hoped he'd be able to see Angelique again, but apparently Liliane thought the time for punishment was over—or, more likely, they had arrived at their destination—and had yanked him from the restful forest.

He had spent the few minutes he was awake trying to recover from the rather brutal yank of magic that had forcibly cut him from Angelique's smudgy forest.

He was finally strong enough to peer out of his mirror. But it was so dark outside, he couldn't make out much in the blackness of the night besides confirming they appeared to be in a bedchamber of sorts.

How charming. He rested his forehead against his mirror, a foul mood snapping at his heels. *Three times. I saw Angelique three times, and I got very little useful information to her—unless I want to count the revelation that she finds the idea of kissing me repulsive, which I don't. And now I'm back in Liliane's clutches.*

"You should have woken up haunted. Perhaps even broken. But you seem as if you've been slumbering peacefully." Liliane spoke in a normal tone as three mages he didn't recognize tiptoed around her.

Evariste owlishly glared at her. "Maybe it is that you overestimate your power."

Not only did I fail to use my chance to speak to Angelique to its fullest extent, I also failed to come up with a way to ruin Liliane's carefully laid plans. That would have been at least a little more fruitful than wondering if there were anything I could have done to make Angelique feel differently about me.

"Unlikely," Liliane flatly said. "But I suppose whatever secret hold-out you have, your next host will ferret it out."

"Oh?" Evariste planted his feet as one of the mages moved the mirror, making everything swirl. "You really think after all these years, you black mages will be able to get more out of me?"

"We won't." Liliane held up a flickering torch that cast an eerie light on her smile. "But the mirror will."

Evariste raised an eyebrow. "I'm already in a mirror," he said in a tone that suggested she was an idiot.

"You'll see." Liliane turned around and strode across the room, her torch dimly lighting the chamber.

Evariste saw a canopy bed with a slumbering woman splayed on the mattress. Her face looked vaguely familiar, and going by her lavish furniture and room, she was a royal or at least a member of nobility.

What are we doing inside the bedroom of a monarch? Are they this powerful that they can strut about with abandon?

The mirror tilted again as someone picked it up, and Evariste craned his neck to look back at the slumbering royal. He briefly saw a mist of gray magic settle over her head—a sleeping charm, if he had to hazard a guess.

Evariste frowned thoughtfully and backed up into the depths of his mirror, then charged forward and kicked out with his leg, creating a crash loud enough to rouse the deepest of sleepers.

The woman slept on.

Hmm, yes, definitely a sleeping charm.

The mage carrying the mirror gave Evariste a glare. "Stop that," he hissed.

"*Oh*," Evariste shouted. "*I apologize! Did you want me to be quiet?*"

Liliane's minions winced, but Liliane herself merely shrugged. "You can be as loud as you wish—I warded the room from sound before we entered it, and *she* won't rouse until I want her to. Though at the rate she's degrading, it won't be long before her country will *wish* she wouldn't wake." She looked meaningfully at the slumbering woman.

"Your thinly veiled attempt at baiting me isn't going to draw my interest," Evariste drawled. "Or distract me from the fact that you—whose ultimate goal is assumedly continent-wide control—find a man stuck in a mirror so burdensome you're foisting him off on something else."

"Mentioning her state was not an attempt to tempt your curiosity, Lord Enchanter." Liliane walked past Evariste's mirror, briefly leaving his sight before the minion mages swiveled his mirror. "Rather, it was a warning. For she is in that poor of a condition, and she's only been externally exposed to the mirror. You'll be living *in* it."

Evariste was only half-listening. He was still mostly occupied trying to figure out where he was—and who the sleeping noblewoman was. (He needed to be ready with his location the next time Angelique reached him.)

Lilian paused in front of another mirror set up in the chamber. It was intimidating, as it stretched quite a bit taller than the black mage, though it had a gold frame ornamented with tiny flowers and elaborate swirls that didn't match the dark feeling the mirror radiated. An egg-sized ruby was fixed to the top of the mirror, and even in the dimness of night, the stone looked like it was wet with freshly spilled blood.

Somehow, it's faintly familiar...

"You should feel honored." Liliane caressed the other mirror's gold frame with a smile more affectionate than anything she had ever pointed toward her own son. "This mirror is the most powerful weapon we have. It's a testament to your strength that I've decided to give you to it."

Ahhh, that's how I know it. Liliane was purring over it the night I arrived—she said they were planning to send it to someone. Evariste raised an eyebrow. "I'd think you have lost your mind to refer to a mirror as if it is a sentient being, but I've known you were insane since I was first captured."

His mirror rocked when two of Liliane's minions set it into place, supporting it as the third mage shuffled around the room with fistfuls of red powder.

"The mirror *is* sentient," Liliane said. "Or rather, it's as sentient as a thing can be. It's an ancient artifact that every good mage and magic user should know. Do you have any guesses?"

Evariste faked a yawn. "Basing my guess entirely off your level of joy, I'd say it must be something that makes ugly people beautiful."

"Your humor does you no good here, Lord Enchanter. Once you learn what this mirror is, you will understand just how lost you are." Liliane's smirk turned cruel. "For I do not think even *you* could withstand the mirror that the Snow Queen herself couldn't destroy."

Evariste whipped his gaze back to Liliane. "...what?"

"Don't you know the lore? It was monstrously large with a ruby as red as blood and—" she cut herself off and stooped over to flick a bit of illusion magic away from the lower right corner, revealing a crack and a missing shard. "A missing piece stolen by the Robber Maiden herself."

"That's not possible." Evariste wildly shook his head. "That mirror is stored in the mountains north of Verglas. *You*—nor your minions—have no way to retrieve it. The Snow Queen's magic wouldn't let you in!"

"And yet, here it is." Liliane leaned against the mirror with a smile. "And once we take you from your benign location and put you inside this powerful artifact, it will constantly drain you of your magic and feed on it. You will provide the power it needs as it further corrupts our target, bringing her under our sway."

The mirror's surface seemed to shift. Evariste couldn't say how—nothing in its reflection moved. But the parts of darkness it reflected seemed to grow, and the image of Evariste in his mirror warped ever so slightly.

Unsettled, Evariste drew his shoulders back. "I don't believe you."

Liliane shrugged. "It doesn't matter if you do or not. You'll know better, soon enough. If you stopped trying to annoy my mages, you might have already realized it by now."

"What do you mean?"

"Don't you hear anything?"

Evariste glared at her, but he was silent as he strained his ears. It was faint at first, but slowly grew in volume, as if the mirror had invisible fingers that were reaching for him.

Use me...

The voice was barely more than a whisper but enticing all the same. It echoed oddly—like ripples on water—and there was something about it that pulled him in.

You have such power. You should be free to do whatever you want.

Evariste swallowed hard and stared at the mirror.

Lend me your power, and we can destroy your foes and bathe the world in the blood of your enemies, with the blood of these insects who have kept you captive.

Evariste's spine tingled as he stared at the mirror with horror.

How. Did. It. Know.

The thought rang in Evariste's mind, rising above the grim realization that he was facing down a dark entity that was an entirely different level of vile evil than even Liliane.

For the mirror to *know* his circumstances and to understand how to appeal to him...Liliane was right. It was sentient, in the most awful of ways.

Liliane affectionately patted its frame. "Now do you understand?"

"Destroy it," Evariste hissed.

She blinked. "What?"

"You have no idea what darkness you're playing with." Evariste backed up, trying to put more distance between him and the ancient evil, but all he could do was back into the familiar gray haze. "It's not a tool you can bend to your will!"

"Don't be silly," Liliane said. "It's under our complete control. With it, our power will be amplified."

Show your power, the mirror whispered. *Give it to me, and the world will bow to you.*

"It's not something that can be controlled," Evariste said. "It will *kill* you."

Liliane shook her head in bemusement. "You're not going to frighten us, Lord Enchanter. And no matter what, I'm not about to let our most powerful weapon go. No, instead I will have *you* strengthen it." She shifted her gaze to the smallest of her minions—the one who had spent the past few minutes shuffling around. "Are the preparations complete?"

"Yes." The mage dropped a handful of red powder, then said a word in the language of magic and flicked a spark of her magic at the powder.

The powder ignited with a purple-hued flame that jumped from the scant mound to the intricate patterns the mage had traced out with additional powder on the ground.

Purple and red magic arose from the wisps of smoke the burning powder created. The magic rolled across the ground like tiny waves, closing in on Evariste's mirror.

Evariste ran as far back into the mirror as he could reach and mentally grabbed at his magic.

The wall was still there, cutting him off, but Evariste mentally threw himself at it again and again.

Come on—react! My magic was able to reach Angelique, can't it do something now?

The foreign magic wafted through the glass pane of the mirror and crawled toward Evariste.

He wrestled more for his magic, but the wall between it and himself was immovable and unfeeling.

Evariste growled as the red-purple magic latched around his ankles and yanked him off his feet, dragging him toward the mirror's surface. He tried to dig his fingers into the hazy gray ground, but the smooth surface offered no resistance.

"Prepare the mirrors!" Liliane shouted. "He must go straight from one to the next—we *cannot* give him the opportunity to flee!"

Inside the mirror, gray spun as the mages picked up Evariste's mirror and placed it pane-to-pane against the vile artifact.

The purple-red magic tried to drag him through the two layers of glass, but Evariste managed to grab the frame of his mirror. His fingers turned white with strain as he desperately clung to the mirror, resisting the pull of the spell.

Come, the mirror called.

"Not a chance." Evariste wedged his feet behind the frame and growled in pain when his torso started to ache as the purple-red magic wrapped around his chest and pulled harder.

"Why hasn't he made the transfer?" Liliane asked.

"It seems he's resisting."

"Well *stop* him! Shake the mirror! Smack it! Do whatever is necessary!"

The pain dug into Evariste's chest, knifing through his heart. His head fell back with agony, but he stubbornly held on until the magic of the spell almost completely enveloped him and savagely wrenched him out.

Passing through the glass layers was discombobulating, but he felt it the second his feet touched the inside of the ancient mirror.

It was colder, and instead of being surrounded by a gray mist, things were more of a rust brown—the color of long-dried blood.

"No!" Evariste threw himself at the mirror's surface, slamming into it with a painful thump. Before he could back up and try again, he was unwillingly dragged back, deeper into the shadowy brown-red depths of the mirror.

A cloudy black haze separated him from the mirror's surface. He couldn't see much beyond distant shapes and forms, and no matter how he struggled, he couldn't move.

Liliane's voice pierced the mist. "Good luck, Lord Enchanter," she called to him. "I doubt you'll last the season, but despite the *pain* you've been, I hope your death isn't too terrible!"

"You won't win whatever war you have planned, Liliane!" Evariste shouted.

She laughed. "Your apprentice is presently the greatest threat. Do you really think she alone could stop us—when we have the mirror with us?"

"No," Evariste said. "I think you'll be crushed by your own ambition and greed."

Liliane didn't answer, but he heard the quiet—but quick—clicks her shoes made on the stone floor as she marched away.

Evariste cursed and tried to pace, but found he was unable to move more than a single pace. He rubbed the back of his neck and surveyed the mirror, unease settling into his bones.

The inside of his previous mirror had smelled slightly stale. This artifact was colder, which froze Evariste's nose, but he could still smell the faint tang of blood and the suffocating scent of smoke.

He reached for his magic and grimaced when he felt nothing.

It was then that he felt something stir, and the mirror whispered.

Enchanter...

Evariste whirled around, but he couldn't see anything through the haze. "Whatever you are, get lost. I want nothing to do with you."

The whispery voice exhaled deeply.

Evariste felt something latch on to him. It wasn't a physical feeling. No matter how he turned around, he saw nothing but haze. Still, something gripped his heart like a snake burying its fangs in his flesh.

You are now MINE!

Evariste clenched his jaw. "Never!"

Your magic is.

Evariste shouted when pain ripped through him, sending him to his knees. It was worse than a draining from Liliane. This was a stabbing sensation as the mirror actively carved out and devoured his magic, which felt almost as if it was snacking on his innards.

He saw stars for a moment, then struggled against the pain and mutinously glared into the mirror's smoky depths. "Maybe," he snarled. "But I'll fight you every moment of every day!"

The mirror laughed.

Good.

CHAPTER 24

When they returned to Verglas, Angelique spent a week fully recovering from the brutal trial she had put herself through. (This, thankfully, meant it was Lord Enchanter Clovicus who was stuck telling King Toril and Queen Linnea all they had learned.)

By the time she had recovered, coded messages of their findings were sent out to the various countries, Odette and her crew had returned to Kozlovka, and Clovicus slipped back to the Veneno Conclave.

As much as she wanted to ride off to Farset and storm the Alabaster Forest to find the elves, Angelique knew the best course of action would be to find Severin. He likely had additional questions to ask and hopefully had news of Suzu. (Or Liliane and Acri, but she wasn't putting much hope or stock in her obviously delirious dreams.)

Pegasus carried her off to Chanceux Chateau in Loire, where she learned that Prince Severin hadn't yet returned and was staying with Queen Cinderella and Colonel Friedrich in the part of Erlauf that formerly was the small country of Trieux. (And that Princess Elle had taken advantage of Severin's absence and was currently missing—likely off on a self-assigned intelligence-gathering mission.)

Angelique rode on to Erlauf and expected to find the royals fighting off goblins or holding joint drills and training sessions with their warriors.

Instead, she tracked them down when they were *shopping*.

She was directed by a pair of royal footmen to seek the trio out at Luxe Mercantile, a large store that boasted some of the best luxury goods the continent had to offer—harpsichords from Torrens, priceless gems from Mullberg, beautiful grandfather clocks from Verglas, the best Kozlovkan vodka, and more.

Angelique tucked her arms close as she edged her way through the store, paranoid that she would knock something precious from a shelf.

When she passed through the tiny section of flower perfumes made in Erlauf, Angelique heard voices. She followed her ears to the part of the store dedicated to glasswork—in particular, mirrors.

Prince Severin, Queen Cinderella, Colonel Friedrich, and two others were there.

Severin and Friedrich stood together, their voices lowered in barely audible tones.

Cinderella, however, chatted animatedly to a tall man dressed in the height of Loire fashion with a brocade waistcoat and a maroon jacket. (He was likely the owner of the store.) With them was Glaze—the craftmage Angelique had met at the Summit.

Glaze narrowed her eyes, inspecting a finely crafted handmirror that had roses carved into its wooden back.

Angelique slowly drew close enough that she could hear the exchange, but paused just before joining them.

"Your Majesty," the merchant grinned playfully. "You're the queen. Do you really mean to say you cannot afford a few silver pieces more?"

"I may be queen, but why would you assume they are for me?"

Cinderella scoffed. "What would I do with twelve mirrors? What a massive waste of tax money *that* would be. In fact, now I'm terribly upset that you think I'm purchasing them for myself!" She slapped her fingers to her mouth and batted her eyes in a look of hurt.

"I misspoke, Your Majesty. All of Erlauf knows Queen Cinderella is diligent with money. I would never think so poorly of you." Though the merchant's voice was soothing and placating, Angelique could see the humor in his eyes.

Cinderella smiled brightly. "Then you won't mind giving me the market price instead of attempting to increase the price as you have admirably attempted to do, will you?"

The merchant laughed outright. "I admit defeat, Your Majesty. I cannot possibly refuse you. Very well!"

Cinderella truly is a monarch of her people. I don't think Elle or Queen Linnea could talk to their citizens like this—though Gabrielle might.

Colonel Friedrich continued to speak in hushed tones to Severin as he surveyed the area, turning in a watchful circle. When he caught sight of Angelique with his single eye—the other being covered by his black eyepatch—he paused, then smiled.

"Lady Enchantress Angelique—what a pleasant surprise." He turned back so he could shout at his wife, "Pet! Come see who just arrived."

Cinderella—gleeful over her thrifty shopping—waltzed over to him. "I managed to get us a significant discount from the budget you gave me to work with, Prince Severin—oh!" She came to a stop when she saw Angelique, and her pretty face became downright lovely when she smiled. "Lady Enchantress Angelique! How glad I am to finally see you again."

"It's been too long," Angelique agreed.

Cinderella's red hair spilled over her shoulders as she reached out to clasp Angelique's hands and squeeze them. "I insist you stay with us for the duration of your visit—how long will you remain in Erlauf?"

"Not long, I hope." Angelique looked past Cinderella and nodded to Glaze, who slowly ambled over to join them. "Hello, Craftmage Glaze."

Glaze returned the nod. "Lady Enchantress."

Angelique stared at her in surprise. *I got the opinion that Glaze didn't care for me at all, much less would bother to spare me any social politeness. Is she playing nice because of the royals?*

Glaze swiveled the mirror in her hands and stared down at it. "I have heard of the...exploits you and Lord Enchanter Clovicus accomplished." She hesitated, then said, "Thank you for your sacrifice."

Angelique arched a brow. "Clovicus wrote that I was sick, did he?"

Prince Severin bowed his head. "He mentioned something of the sort in his communication to me, yes. I am glad to see you are looking better than what he described."

"Yes, well, I won't say it wasn't worthwhile, but our findings weren't exactly encouraging," Angelique vaguely said.

Cinderella tipped her head back as she took in the purposely vague language. She finally released Angelique's hands and twirled with the grace of a dancer to address the merchant. "Monsieur, could you draw up the order papers? Glaze will pick the exact mirrors she wants, and we can finish our business when you return."

The merchant bent at the waist. "Of course, Your Majesty. Allow me to thank you for your patronage. I won't be long." He strode out of the aisle, his footsteps gradually fading.

Severin stared up at the glass chandeliers that hung from the ceiling. "He went in a back room."

Yep. He definitely retained that feline hearing.

"So that's bloody bad luck about the Snow Queen's mirror," Colonel Friedrich bluntly said. "Sorry, Pet, but it's just about the worst news of the decade," he added when he caught Cinderella eyeing him.

The queen sighed and rested her hands on the skirts of her dress—which were a beautiful shade of blue that complemented the queen's red hair, but possessed only a bit of embroidery around the neckline for embellishment. "You're not wrong. But then again, Angelique is already aware of all this, and I don't imagine she came all this way just to listen to our secondhand account of something she witnessed."

"You are here to purchase mirrors?" Angelique asked in the awkward lull of conversation.

"Yes," Cinderella smiled. "Arcainia sent us some funds, and Friedrich and Severin decided the most important things to secure first were the last few mirrors for Glaze and the other craftmages to enchant so we can all communicate easier."

Glaze nodded in confirmation. "We've begun enchanting them, but it's become apparent each country will need several mirrors, so we requested a dozen more." She glanced over her shoulder at the beautifully arranged glasswork. "If you'll excuse me, I'd like to pick the last few mirrors. It is not a decision to be made lightly, given that the better the craftmanship, the higher-quality spells we'll be able to use."

"Yes of course, go ahead, Glaze," Friedrich urged her.

Glaze nodded again to Angelique, then went back to lovingly inspecting the mirrors arranged on cherry wood shelves.

Funny how making myself sick trying to retrieve the mirror is what thawed her, Angelique mused. *I've done more dire things—like kill the wyvern or save Severin from his curse—so I wonder what it is about searching for the mirror that softened her.*

"What did you need, Angelique?" Severin asked, interrupting her thoughts with his rumbling voice.

"Did Stil's report on the elves catch up to you?" Angelique asked.

"It did," Severin said. "I have some Rangers looking into it, but my forces are split as we try to communicate the absence of the mirror to all our allies. I'll be thankful when the mirrors are enchanted and distributed."

Angelique shifted. "But you *will* do something about it?"

He nodded. "I plan to call on the Farset King by winter—he requested that something be done for his daughters, who seem to have an odd curse placed on them."

I wonder what lucky mage will be asked to look into that. Angelique barely managed to keep her sour thoughts off her face and instead nodded thoughtfully. *But winter isn't too far off. Since Clovicus and I spent midsummer playing in the mountains, and then I needed time to recover, it's almost fall now.*

"While there, I'll look into the elves—this Odette should have another delivery to make by then," Severin finished.

Relief made Angelique sag a little, so she wasn't so stiff. *They are going to do something about it, and it won't be entirely up to me—even if he does try to hoist those cursed princesses off on me. I can live with that.* She cleared her throat. "I am very glad to hear that. Thank you."

Severin bowed slightly. "Of course. If the elves can be restored, they will be a great boon to our fight."

"Yes. Speaking of which, I was hoping you had information on Suzu," Angelique said.

"I do." Severin folded his hands behind his back. "I don't have any of the written reports with me at the moment, but I can give you a summary until we return to the palace."

Angelique tried to smile serenely and not give any indication that her heart had leaped at his words. "Of course."

"She is a talented sorceress—though not nearly as notably skilled as her husband, Rothbart," Severin said. "According to reports, she's said to favor fire magic—though she is capable of a wide variety—and she doesn't seem to have a particular base location; she has been sighted in several of our allies' lands."

"We might have had her pass through Erlauf." Friedrich's dark eye grew a hardened edge.

"When Friedrich and I first met, some mercenaries attacked Friedrich," Cinderella said. "They were dressed like Erlauf soldiers but carried Trieux weapons. They admitted to being hired by a woman who was said to represent a larger group. There's a good chance it was Suzu based on the matching description—though we don't know for certain, as the mercenaries never got her name."

Friedrich scowled. "I'm betting she was likely behind the black mage that tried to kill Cinderella that same summer. He died before we could thoroughly question him, or we'd know for certain."

It took everything Angelique had to keep her hands calmly folded. "You have a physical description?" she asked in a voice that was admirably mild.

"*Elle* took it upon herself to track down a physical description." Severin scowled. "She's reported to have black hair, pale skin, dark eyes, and has a tendency to wear dark colors."

"Sounds like a ray of sunshine," Friedrich muttered.

"Anything more distinctive about her?" Angelique asked.

"Besides her power?" Severin dryly asked. "Most of the populace who have seen her are wowed first and foremost by her magic."

That's understandable. As a mage myself, I tend to forget how rare we are.

"Lately," Severin continued, "her name has been linked with Carabosso."

Angelique stiffened. "Carabosso is still acting up in Sole?" she said more than asked.

"Yes," Severin said. "It's not confirmed that Suzu is with him, but several of my Rangers and a few intelligence agents from Farset have confirmed that she is working with him."

Angelique briefly closed her eyes. *This is it. I finally have a trail I can follow—I have something I can actually* do *to search for Evariste!* She forced her eyes open and kept her expression mellow.

"We were unable to uncover anything related to a Liliane or an Acri," Severin added, "but we will continue the search."

See? My dreams are exactly that—dreams. I should have known better—Evariste would never try to kiss me!

Angelique slightly shook her head then met Severin's gaze. "I cannot thank you enough, Your Highness, for this information."

"Not at all," Severin said. "I am only sorry it took us this long to aid you." He fell silent, but Angelique could tell by the furrow of his brow and the wrinkles on his forehead that he wanted to say something.

"Yes?" She asked.

The prince stood straighter, making the muscles of his broad shoulders bigger. "You will travel to Sole, I assume?"

I'm starting to think maybe I shouldn't have pushed him to speak. "Yes," she cautiously said.

"Then I have a request."

I knew it! Angelique mentally howled. *I knew it! Am I the continent's nanny? Or just the village idiot who is incapable of refusing anyone?*

Friedrich must have sensed her great displeasure, for he gave her a slight smile that had an edge of desperation to it. "Severin was here in Erlauf when he received the communication from Lord Enchanter Clovicus about the mirror. We've been wracking our brains ever since, trying to figure out something that would give *us* an edge over the Chosen, given that they've so greatly stacked the deck in their favor."

"It is greatly troubling that they have the mirror," Cinderella agreed.

"What's in Sole?" Angelique gloomily asked.

"Information," Severin said. "My brother and I have been communicating by courier. After Clovicus confirmed the mirror was missing, Lucien pointed out there is one artifact that is just as ancient as the mirror and is mentioned in Verglas' records of the Snow Queen—though in truth, we don't know how powerful it is."

"And what artifact might that be?" Angelique pressed her lips together.

"A dagger," Severin said, "called Foedus."

"The Snow Queen's best friend—Phile, the Robber Maiden—owned it," Friedrich said. "She went on to found a thieves' guild that disappeared over time, and with it all records of the dagger, though it's said she bragged greatly of its abilities."

"Did anyone ever *witness* its powers?" Angelique asked.

"Not at the time of the Snow Queen," Severin said, "but the dagger appears in multiple historic records and was always said to possess great power. If the scant records I've found are correct, it's just as old as the mirror, if not older."

And the older the artifact, the greater the power—or so it's assumed. We lost the ability to forge such powerful artifacts before even the time of the Snow Queen. Angelique pressed her lips together as she thought. "And you think information on this dagger is in Sole?"

"Yes," Severin said.

Silence prevailed for a moment, then Cinderella rolled her eyes. "Men," she muttered. "You can't give her a bare-bones explanation like that and expect her to understand or be satisfied!" She turned to Angelique and smiled. "The Queen of Hearts was the historic Sole Queen who commissioned the elves to make the legendary weapons for her Magic Knights of Sole."

"I am well aware of Sole's history." Angelique smiled slightly to soften the dryness of her words, but Cinderella didn't seem to mind.

"Of course, but before she decided to ask the elves to forge the weapons, she gathered up historic records about weapons that had been charmed and enchanted. Ciane actually has the largest record of magical armaments in the world as a result."

"I assume that means Foedus was one of the weapons she had researched?" Angelique asked.

Friedrich nodded. "She never found Foedus, but she gathered a great deal of information on it."

"You want me to find that information?" Angelique guessed. Severin nodded.

"And you can't send one of your *Rangers* to retrieve it?"

"Not with all of Ciane under a sleep spell and protected by your magic," Severin said. "One of my Rangers almost got through, but the Magic Knight who remained behind to protect the still-sleeping Princess Rosalinda nearly killed him. And with the entire royal family sleeping, all our connections with Sole are officially cut off, so there's no way we can ask him to stand down."

"He would know you, however." Friedrich smiled winningly. "And given your role in the princess' survival, I imagine he'd let you past."

Angelique slightly tilted her head back so she could stare at the ceiling. *Yes, of* course *I'm your only option.* A slightly rebellious part of Angelique wondered if she stopped showing up so often, if Severin and the others would miraculously find a way to solve all of these supposedly-unsolvable problems if not for her.

Stop it, she told herself. *I'm just being bitter now.*

She sucked in a deep breath of air. "Are you hoping to recreate Foedus, then?"

"Not at all," Friedrich said. "We're hoping to *find* it."

"Or find more material that proves it may be useful against the mirror," Severin said. "Regardless, it seems prudent to pursue it given the attention the Chosen seem to place on the actions of the past."

Angelique sighed. "I see. Very well, then. I'd likely have to go back to Ciane, anyway, to find Firra and Donaigh; I'm hoping they'll help me if Suzu truly has joined forces with Carabosso. While I'm there, I'll see if I can find that archive."

Friedrich smiled. "Thank you, Angelique. We are very much obliged."

"Yes, thank you, Angelique." Cinderella inclined her head.

"Also," Severin started.

"*Also?*" Angelique couldn't keep the full storm out of her voice.

"I ask that you travel to Baris."

Is he joking? I do hope it's a jest.

Severin's stony expression didn't change as she gawked at him. He was serious.

The endless missions, the weeks of sleepless nights, the months without stopping all wrapped around Angelique in a blanket of anger.

"*Prince Severin*," Angelique said. "While I am glad to help, I think we need to have a discussion about my role. I am *not* your magical errand boy you can send about the world as you please. I invited other mages to the Summit. *Use them!*"

The store was as still as death.

No one stirred.

In fact, the three royals gaped at Angelique, seemingly surprised by the venom in her voice, but Angelique couldn't find it in herself to regret it.

She did, however, clear her throat and add, "I, too, am concerned with the state of the continent and how we might best counter the Chosen. But I have my own matters I must attend to."

"I understand." Prince Severin bowed so deeply she couldn't even see his face. "I must apologize, Lady Enchantress. I took liberties and did not take into account your concerns in these matters. It was my oversight and my grave mistake. I will see to it that I do not unduly burden you so in the future. Please ignore our request—we will find a different way to learn about Foedus."

Ah. Now I don't regret it as much as I feel like a selfish prat for complaining about all the effort it takes to save the world. How delightful. Though in his defense, I don't think he meant to make me feel guilty.

Angelique sighed loudly. "No—it's fine. I accept your apology, but I did not mean to say you cannot count on me for help. It's just..." she trailed off lamely. "Why did you want me to go to Baris?"

Friedrich and Severin exchanged looks. Friedrich arched his eyebrow, but Severin scowled and shook his head.

Friedrich looked like he might argue, but he glanced at Angelique, then frowned. He was silent for a few moments as he studied her. "Sorry, Angelique," he said seriously. "It's no excuse, but we're military men. We're used to moving squads and companies. You are so skilled and competent, sometimes it's difficult to remember you're a single person and not a general in charge of her own army."

"I don't think it's just that." Cinderella stepped closer, her eyes tracing Angelique's face with an uncomfortable amount of observance in them. "We forget—you did so much for us all before Prince Severin even told Friedrich and me he was thinking of holding the Summit. You've been running from country to country since this mess began, and we've only been dealing with local threats."

Cinderella hesitated, then took Angelique's hands again. "We apologize, Lady Enchantress Angelique, for forgetting how you have saved us and held the continent together when no one else would."

Hot tears stung Angelique's eyes. She blinked rapidly to hold them back. "Yes. Well. It was—it *is* my duty."

"I disagree," Severin said. "The entire continent is not your responsibility, but we thank you for what you have done to save it—and us. And we will make certain not to ask you to stand alone again."

Angelique nodded and felt something in her soften.

That's all I ever wanted. Though I'm cynical enough to know I'll just have to wait and see if their promises match their actions.

"So," she said, "what's in Baris?"

Severin shook his head. "We're not—"

"Why don't you tell me the mission, and I'll decide if it's something that truly requires my presence," Angelique suggested.

Severin narrowed his eyes, but Friedrich nodded. "Very well," he said. "A number of our intelligence agents have found magical artifacts of worth in Baris markets. We'd like a mage to travel there and confirm if they are of use or not."

Angelique relaxed marginally. "In this case, I'm afraid I cannot be much help. I'm not terribly skilled at sensing magic."

"Truly?" Friedrich asked, seemingly surprised. "Glaze said nearly every mage can sense magic."

"Indeed," Angelique sighed. "And I can, to a point. It is, however, a skill whose mastery continues to elude me no matter how I try."

"Maybe it's your great power," Cinderella suggested.

Severin tilted his head back as he thought. "Stil once described your magic as a star exploding. With that kind of power following you around, I imagine it would be difficult to sense anything past it."

"Perhaps," Angelique agreed—more to get them to stop talking about her failure than out of any real agreement. "As a result, though, I do feel it would be wisest to send someone else."

Severin nodded. "We shall make it so."

"I do have one more question about the information in Sole you want," Angelique said.

"Yes?" Friedrich perked up.

"Do you want a written *copy* of what we find?" she asked. "Not the originals, of course, but a copy of the source material—or at least annotated notes?"

"We would be delighted with whatever you can send us," Friedrich said.

"Anything will be useful," Severin added.

Angelique slowly nodded.

How, though, do I achieve that? As soon as I enter Sole, Firra will be campaigning for me to face Carabosso, and given how I am involved in Princess Rosalinda's curse, it's not an unexpected or impolite request, especially if Suzu is with him. But how, then, do I get this information back to them discreetly?

"Queen Cinderella, you said you saved some coins that were meant to be used to purchase mirrors?" Angelique asked.

"Yes."

"How much is left?" Angelique smiled slightly.

"I'll have to check the math when we get back to the palace to give you an exact number," Cinderella said. "But if there's something you feel we need to purchase, we will gladly do so."

"I'm not looking to purchase something, but I'd like to hire a trio of...*companions*...to run the notes on Foedus back to you, given that I'll likely be facing Carabosso with Firra and Donaigh," Angelique said.

"Are these the same companions who helped you scout the mirror?" Severin asked. "The Black Swan Smugglers?"

Angelique met his gaze. "Yes."

Severin nodded. "Hire them. If there aren't enough funds left over from the mirrors, I'll supplement the cost myself."

"Thank you," Angelique said.

Severin shook his head. "Not at all. Given what they've done already, their price is a true bargain."

"Let me get this straight." Odette tapped her bare foot in the yellowed Sole grass as a cool breeze tugged at her thick blonde hair. "You want us to travel with you to Ciane and stand by as you research this...Foedus."

"Yes." Angelique rested her hand on Pegasus' shoulder. He pawed at the ground, igniting a few dead leaves. (The cold of fall had already turned the forests into brilliant splashes of color, but only a few trees had already shed their foliage.) "Prince Severin is confident the Royal Library will have a record of it, even though it is a centuries-old weapon."

"So you said." Odette slightly bowed her head. "Once you have the information you want, we're to run it back to Prince Severin.

And that's it?" She rubbed her chin and squinted at Angelique. "Excuse my blunt language, but I fail to see why you need us, Angelique."

"Because I don't know how long I'll be forced to tarry in Sole," Angelique explained. "A rogue mage has been terrorizing the countryside, and given the patterns of my life, I expect *someone* will ask me to handle him. Prince Severin needs the information on Foedus as soon as possible to begin strategizing. It can't wait." She waited until Odette met her gaze. "I trust you—and Misha and Nadia—to get the notes to Severin. Speed—and keeping the notes safe from prying eyes—is crucial."

"You don't trust the Veneno Conclave, do you?" Misha adjusted his spectacles as he studied Angelique.

She paused, Lovelana's concerns floating through her mind. "I trust the organization—their mission and genuine desire to help. But I'm well aware that our enemy has had centuries to sink their claws into the continent without our knowledge. The Chosen already have the mirror. We can't take the chance that they'll intercept the message and start hunting out Foedus as well."

Odette nodded. "Right, then. Let's head out. Your...*mount* can pick up a faster pace, if you like. As swans, we can fly faster and farther than regular horses, and it seems that we have a tailwind. It's why I said we'd fly from the border of Sole to Ciane when you sent word you wanted to hire us for another job."

"Excellent, I appreciate the speed. Between sending you word and staying in Erlauf to clarify some details of our mountain expedition, I've already lost a couple weeks." Angelique bit at the inside of her cheek. "I cannot tell you how thankful I am for your help in this."

The Swan Queen awkwardly shrugged and scuffed her bare foot on the ground again. "You're doing a good thing. Besides, we *are* getting paid for it."

Her companions said nothing, but Misha raised an eyebrow at his leader, and Nadia smiled faintly.

She's not fooling anyone. She has a heart as pure as gold behind that bluster of hers. Angelique dimly realized she was smiling as well. "It is as you say."

"We can help you with your research, too." Odette picked up a leaf and tossed it into the air, her eyes narrowed as she watched which direction it blew. "Misha used to be a traveling scholar. He taught all of our band to read, write, and keep balance for our business. Skimming a few books for a mythical dagger will be a cinch."

She made a few gestures to Misha and Nadia. The pair nodded and shuffled around, prepping a small satchel with a few items in it.

Must be flight preparations.

Angelique mounted Pegasus and leaned farther back in the saddle as she stretched. "That would be greatly appreciated," she admitted. "I'm not sure exactly what we're going to encounter in Ciane—or rather what will demand my attention besides the research."

Odette handed a few daggers off to Nadia, who slipped them into their satchel. "It seems to me you're always being asked to do something—of course, I say that having requested your help first with our curse and then with the wyvern."

Angelique shrugged. "I'm an Enchantress-in-Training. It is my duty."

"If it's your duty, it stands to reason there's a number of Lord Enchanters and Lady Enchantresses—not to mention mages— they could approach and expect to receive aid from," Odette said.

"It's getting better," Angelique said. *Sort of.*

Odette shrugged again. "As you say." She glanced at Misha and Nadia, who were making some curling loops out of rope and securing it to the bag. "We're ready to leave whenever you are."

"Are you certain you don't need a longer break? You just came from Kozlovka," Angelique said.

Odette shook her head. "Our strength spell keeps us going

longer than a normal swan. We'll have to stop a few times so we can change our formation, but we can still go fairly far today. Though I'd like to stop in a town for the night."

"There are several towns between our location and Ciane," Angelique said. "It will simply be a matter of picking the one we want."

"We're flying in a southwest direction, correct?" Misha asked.

"Yes," Angelique confirmed.

"Right, then. We'll get transformed, pick up our satchel, and we can be on our way." Odette bowed again to Angelique, then trotted over to her companions.

The three of them accessed the spell that transformed them into swans, spawning bright lights and a wind that stirred up the dying grass and all the fallen leaves in the area.

Bells tolled, and Angelique raised a hand to block her eyes from the bright light of the transformation spell. When the wind dropped, she lowered her hand.

Three large swans rested where Odette, Nadia, and Misha had stood a moment ago. They stood in a triangle formation—the one at the front had to be Odette, for she grunted and grumbled under her breath as the other two worked to slip the looped rope over their heads.

Pegasus snorted and impatiently turned toward Ciane. Angelique patted his neck and called back to the smugglers. "Stop whenever you need to—I'll keep an eye on the sky."

One of the swans nodded, which Angelique took as acquiescence. Pegasus started walking, the blue flames of his mane burning higher than usual.

"It's okay, Pegasus." Angelique patted his shoulder in commiseration. "This will *hopefully* be a fast trip. We're just looking for information on Foedus—and we should look into Carabosso and Suzu as well. That's it."

Angelique should have known better than to hope that's all it would be.

As requested, the group stopped for the evening at an inn and set out at dawn the following morning, a pattern they intended to repeat for the rest of their travels.

Several days into the trip, they rode (flew?) through the rise of the sun—though as Angelique cast a glance at the sky, she could still see the hint of brilliant orange on the blue horizon.

Odette, Misha, and Nadia were blobs of white against the sky. The few clouds that dotted the sky were higher than the swans, and thin and wispy.

At least, most were.

Angelique frowned as she saw the gray haze they were closing in on. She had initially assumed it was clouds that would clear with the morning sun. But the haze was darker and much lower than the other clouds, and it drifted with the wind.

Suspicious, Angelique sniffed the air. *Is that the faintest smell of smoke? Or am I mistaking the scent in my paranoia?*

"Pegasus." She had to raise her voice to be heard above the swift cantering pace the constellation had set. "Do you smell smoke?"

CHAPTER 25

Pegasus slowed to a walk, then lifted his head high, snorting as he inhaled and exhaled loudly through flared nostrils. He pranced as he adjusted his body so he was looking directly at the smoke and braced his legs wide.

When the flames of his mane grew, Angelique peered up at the sky and whistled. It took a few notes before she got the Black Swan Smugglers' attention.

They circled low above her, and she pointed to the cloud of smoke. "We're going to check that out."

Odette, Misha, and Nadia must have understood, for they regained their lost altitude and course-corrected for the smoke.

Angelique stroked Pegasus' neck. "Let's look into it."

Pegasus threw himself back into the canter with more enthusiasm than necessary, jostling Angelique in the saddle.

She crouched low and allowed herself a moment of delusion. *Maybe it's just a farmer burning his fields or clearing underbrush.*

But as they drew closer, Angelique could see it was a large fire that belched smoke into the sky. The fire roared through what looked like a small village, consuming the timber frames of the brick houses.

The smoke stung Angelique's eyes as Pegasus halted.

The constellation screamed a challenge and reared back on his hind legs, the stars in his coat burning.

"Pegasus! Careful, please." Angelique clung to the saddle as she tried to extend her senses and feel for any magic in the area.

He bolted a few steps when a man riding a lathered horse emerged from the smoke. He wore a soldier's uniform and was barely in control of his mount as the animal shied and whinnied.

The soldier saw Angelique and managed to slow his horse, though he had to turn it in a tight circle. "He's right behind me!"

"Who?"

"The mage who did this!" The soldier gestured to the village consumed by flames.

It must be Carabosso. Angelique yanked on her magic, already spinning it into a spell. "Is there anyone left in the town?"

The soldier shook his head. "No one alive. The villagers already fled."

Her silvery magic circled around Pegasus before sweeping up the constellation's side and rubbing against her arm. Angelique grit her teeth against it, but gathered it into her spell, making it more powerful. "Go after them. I'll see what I can do to stop the mage. But send word to the nearest Magic Knight of Sole. Hurry!"

The soldier saluted her, then loosened his reins. His horse was off like loosened lightning, the whites of its eyes showing as it fled.

Angelique closed off her prepared spell and started weaving another as she glanced down at Pegasus. "Company is coming, my friend."

Pegasus struck the ground with his front left leg, shedding a wave of sparks.

"I'm not thrilled, either," Angelique agreed. "But I can't let Carabosso run unchecked."

A quick peek at the sky confirmed Odette and the others were circling overhead. *Good—I don't want them caught up in the crossfire.*

She peered over Pegasus' shoulder to glance at the ground, considered sliding from the saddle, then looked back at the village just in time to see Carabosso emerge from the smoke.

His skin was still as pale as it was the day Angelique saw him curse baby Princess Rosalinda, though the perfection of his complexion was no longer ruined solely by the puckered red brand of exile burned into his skin, but also by faint wrinkles around his mouth. Time had also made its stamp in the threads of silver that glinted in his shiny black hair.

"Carabosso!" Angelique shouted. "Stand down!"

He curled his upper lip back and sneered. "You again, Apprentice Angelique? You have the tenacity of a cockroach."

"*Stand down!*" Angelique repeated.

Carabosso rolled his eyes, then whipped a hand in front of him and made a grasping motion.

Smoke from the fire churned and separated from the blackened ruins, slowly taking on the shape of a skull. It dropped ash as it raced toward Angelique, its lower jaw gaping open.

Pegasus snorted, and Angelique felt his shoulder blades move oddly beneath her. "Steady," she murmured as she hurriedly wove a new spell.

I can handle this—particularly while riding Pegasus. I just might be able to beat him!

A horse-length before the smoke skull was on them, Angelique loosened her newest bit of magic, summoning a gust of wind so strong it made her eyes tear up.

The wind screamed as it ripped the smoke apart, dispersing it harmlessly into the air.

Angelique flicked her wrist, calling up the spell she had prepared earlier. She was just about to throw it at the rogue mage when two more figures emerged from the smoke.

The first was a woman with dark hair, thin lips, and purple

robes. She held a ball of flames, which brought to mind the description Prince Severin had given Angelique of Sorceress Suzu.

Is that her?

"Apprentice Angelique." The sorceress gave Angelique a snake-like smile. "What a pleasure it will be to end you."

"Indeed—we can put that sniveling brat in his place," the other male mage chuckled. "Unless, you choose to forsake your vows to help those in need and instead run?" He raised a black eyebrow.

The sorceress chucked the fireball at Angelique.

Pegasus screamed and leaped forward, his teeth bared, but Angelique whisked a defensive shield into place.

Carabosso smiled. "Needless to say, I will *not* be standing down. Rather, you are too late. I've already destroyed five other villages besides this one. And you're not nearly enough to stop me."

Angelique's mind raced. *I want to throw every spell I have at the sorceress, because if she really* is *Suzu that means—no. I can't dwell on this, now is hardly the ideal time to catch her when I'm so severely outnumbered like this.*

"If you peacefully surrender to us, we won't make your capture *too* painful—though I can't say anything about your *horse*," Carabosso continued.

Angelique ignored him.

Carabosso—who is confirmed to be talented and somehow sly enough to un-seal his magic—possibly Suzu—a powerful sorceress—and a third black mage. These are terrible odds.

"New plan, Pegasus." Angelique kept her voice to a low murmur as she hastily started twisting additional copies of her prepared spell. "We have to run."

Pegasus shook his head.

"I don't like it either. We—no—*I* don't stand a chance against three black mages without back up." She was vaguely aware Carabosso was still droning on during her hushed, one-sided conversation. "I can stun them, and then we'll need to find Magic Knights to serve as reinforcement. We have to capture the female *alive*!"

Pegasus swished his tail and flattened his ears.

"*However*," Angelique leaned low over his neck. "We're not giving up entirely. Let's give 'em the scare of their life and see if we can goad them into chasing after us, okay?"

Pegasus slowly exhaled—which she chose to interpret as an agreement.

Yanking on her magic, Angelique finished the extra copies of her spell—with which she had become *intimately* acquainted while chasing the wyvern through Kozlovka.

Carabosso was still monologuing as Angelique lightly squeezed Pegasus' sides.

"Let's go!" she said.

Pegasus threw himself into a canter, swiftly closing the space between them and the black mages.

Angelique clenched her teeth as she skillfully loosened her spells, sending the original and copies to strike different targets at the same moment.

"And so," Carabosso concluded, "you shall lose."

Before he could open his mouth again, lightning crackled in the sky and struck three times, hitting each mage with perfect, pin-point precision.

I guess chasing after and trying to hit the wyvern as a moving target did pay off after all!

The mages fell over, electricity crackling up and down their spasming bodies.

Angelique bit her lip and threw a hastily created ball of water at Carabosso, but Suzu snapped upright and raised a shield, blocking the move. (Already, her male compatriot was climbing to his feet.)

"Yep, we don't stand a chance. Let's fly, Pegasus!"

As Pegasus charged past the mages, skirting the burnt husk of the village, his shoulders again moved oddly.

"I didn't mean that literally!" she squeaked.

Pegasus released a throaty snort that was his version of a laugh and continued galloping.

Angelique clung to her saddle and peered up at the sky, grateful to see the Black Swan Smugglers hadn't fallen too far behind. "Let's slow down a touch so they can keep up," Angelique shouted above the whoosh of the wind. "When we get far enough away, we'll stop to decide how to proceed."

Pegasus tucked his head, making the arch of his neck overpronounced, but he slowed his pace.

Angelique leaned back in the saddle and tried to calm her frantic heart. *We made it. Though it kills me to leave Suzu, Carabosso must be stopped. If I don't mount a defense quickly enough or were to spend my time attempting to capture Suzu, how many villages would he destroy in the meantime?*

"THAT WAS SUZU." Odette gnawed on a red apple Angelique had retrieved for her from her charmed satchel. "At least, I'm pretty sure it was. I didn't see her too often at Swan Lake, but she has a pretty distinctive style. What do you think, Misha?"

"The sorceress was indeed Suzu," Misha confirmed. "Though I did not recognize her companions."

"Carabosso was the one with the mark on his forehead," Angelique said. "I didn't recognize the other black mage, either."

Misha tapped a dried chunk of jerky—again from Angelique's satchel, apparently the smugglers needed to eat frequently to keep going, an understandable limit—on his thigh. "I heard rumors Carabosso was wreaking havoc in Sole. I didn't think he was destroying towns."

"I suspect it's a new pastime for him," Angelique said.

Odette took another bite of her apple. "What makes you think that?"

Angelique studied her own half-eaten apple. "Call it instinct."

Instinct? Yeah, right! More like if he had been doing this for any prolonged period of time, I'm sure either Firra or Severin would not-so-subtly be asking me to finish him off.

She cleared her throat. "This does raise the question of where should we go next. It's important to get the information on Foedus, but it's in Ciane, which is still under my sleeping spell. If I am to face Carabosso and his 'friends,' I'll need reinforcements from the Magic Knights of Sole. It will kill two birds with one stone, so to speak, for the knights should be able to help me capture Suzu so I can question her about Evariste's whereabouts. Though I suspect Carabosso might know as well."

"We can travel to Ciane alone," Odette offered. "We've been there before."

"I feel confident I can familiarize myself with the library in a well enough manner that I can find the materials about this Foedus dagger you desire," Misha said. "I imagine by the time you return, we will have compiled all the information, and you can review it."

"That would be ideal, except Ciane is guarded by a single Magic Knight who—I'm told—takes his position very seriously." Angelique nibbled on her apple—which was the perfect balance of ripe and crisp—but she had lost her appetite in her frustration with the situation. "He isn't likely to let you inside. But maybe if I send something as a sign that you're representing me…"

Pegasus bumped her shoulder with his velveteen muzzle. Angelique offered out her apple, which he took with a contented crunch.

"Two riders are approaching." Nadia kept her left eye closed and her right eye pressed against the spyglass Angelique had lent the taciturn woman. "From the south—looks like a male and female."

Ciane is south…could it be? Angelique held out her hand—the one free of Pegasus' slobber. "Might I see?"

Nadia passed the spyglass over. "Of course, Lady Enchantress."

"Thanks for taking the watch, Nadia," Odette said. "Have an apple—and some of the cheese. It's great." Though her words were casual and she sat with her legs stretched in front of her, Angelique didn't miss the way her hands strayed to the daggers lying at her side.

"I suspect they aren't a foe." Angelique fitted the lens to her eye and carefully adjusted it to the right focal point.

The blobby figures sharpened. Angelique instantly recognized the male—she would have known that straw hat anywhere—and it only took a glance at the female with her dark hair pulled back in a ponytail and her flame-colored clothing to confirm Angelique's guess.

"That's fire mage Firra and war mage Donaigh," Angelique said. "They're personal friends of mine who have worked on behalf of Evariste and me here in Sole."

"Do you want to signal to them?" Misha asked.

"No need. It seems they're coming straight for us." Angelique collapsed her spyglass and set it in her bag as Pegasus lipped her shoulder. "Do any of you require further refreshments? I believe I have salted nuts of some assortment." She dug out another apple and presented it to the constellation, who dripped juice over her palm when he took it and crunched it in his teeth.

Odette shook her head. "I think we're fine—unless you have another piece of jerky?"

Angelique passed her two.

The Swan Queen bit down on one like a pipe and passed the other off to Nadia.

Nadia pushed her long bangs out of her eyes and took the jerky. "They seemed to be in a hurry. Do you think there is trouble at the capital?"

"Can't be." Angelique shielded her eyes and watched the mages approach. "Not with everyone sleeping."

When the duo was close enough that they were forced to slow their horses so as to not run them down, Angelique waved to the pair. "Firra, Donaigh, what a pleasant surprise it is to see you!"

"You can't imagine how relieved we are to have found you so close," Firra said.

Donaigh whipped off his straw hat and bowed to Angelique. "Though I imagine after you hear our news, you won't be nearly so glad to see us."

"I'm already aware of Carabosso's rampages through the countryside," Angelique said.

"Oh, yes." Donaigh put his hat back on. "He's been doing that for a while."

Angelique paused in her surprise. "He's been *destroying villages?* With help from other mages?"

"What? *No!*" Firra's brows furrowed with horror, and she threw herself off her horse. "Where did you hear that?"

"We saw it," Angelique said. "Carabosso and a sorceress we believe is named Suzu, as well as another male mage burned an entire village to the ground."

Firra groaned and leaned against Donaigh. "Of course he would up the ante once *she* woke up."

Angelique suspiciously peered back and forth between the two mages. "What are you talking about?"

Donaigh's shoulders dropped, and he wouldn't meet her gaze, while Firra's face crumpled with dread.

Oh no. No, no, no. They want my help with something.

Angelique didn't know if it was her long held-in-check cynicism or her magic, but something deep in her howled like a wild animal. On impulse, she extended her hand to her companions. "Before we begin, please allow me to introduce you to Odette, Nadia, and Misha. They are members of the Black Swan Smugglers—though I suppose they aren't so much members as they run it. Odette is the leader, and Nadia and Misha are her seconds-in-command so to speak."

"Hello." Odette waved to the mages, who each nodded, though they stared at Angelique.

Angelique avoided meeting their gaze, desperate to avoid as long as possible hearing whatever new task they were going to foist off on her.

Asking me to face Carabosso would be understandable. I wouldn't like it, but it's still understandable. But given Firra's entirely inappropriate loyalty to Sole, she has a history of asking me to cast spells in situations expressly forbidden by Conclave Law. I already have enough I'm responsible for; I don't need taboo work as well!

Angelique risked glancing in their direction.

"Briar Rose woke up," Firra blurted out.

Angelique paused. "*Who?*"

"Princess Rosalinda," Donaigh supplied.

"Oh." Angelique furrowed her brow, thoroughly confused. "I don't understand—how is that poor tidings? Isn't it a reason to celebrate?"

"Not quite," Firra groaned. "It's become a royal mess."

"As you probably remember, Rosalinda was spelled to sleep until she received a kiss from her true love. Well, her true love happened to be Sir Isaia—the Magic Knight who chose to guard her while she slept," Donaigh explained.

"I still fail to see the problem," Angelique said. "Magic Knights are highly respected in Sole."

"*Yes*," he said reluctantly, dragging the word out. He leaned back on his heels and folded his hand behind his head.

"Isaia is a problem on his own—he's being a stubborn mule about accepting Briar's feelings for him. But the bigger issue is King Giuseppe."

Angelique tiredly rubbed her eyes. "Why am I not surprised?"

She had...*complicated* feelings for the Sole King. She was aware he was considered a competent ruler, but in her sparse meetings with him, he had always been demanding, accusatory, and dangerously stubborn.

King Giuseppe was why Angelique had cast the sleeping spell not only on Princess Rosalinda, but all of Ciane as well. In his worry for Rosalinda, he was going to strangle the country. His daughter and only child, Princess Alessia, had personally asked Angelique to cast the spell so as to save the nation.

It seems the nap hadn't tempered King Giuseppe's bad mood.

"What's his problem now?" Angelique demanded. "If she's awake, Princess Rosalinda's curse is broken. Carabosso's spell can no longer do her any harm."

"For some asinine reason, King Giuseppe is convinced Briar Rose—that is, Rosalinda—needs a noble who can rule the country for her," Firra said.

Angelique mashed her eyes some more. "I thought that despite being raised as a peasant, your reports said she received a complete and thorough education."

"She did." Donaigh bared his teeth in a rather savage smile. "Really, I think she's better educated than the Sole nobles would *like* her to be."

"Regardless, Giuseppe has either entered his dotage or completely lost his mind, for he's decided he will pick out Rosalinda's husband for her," Firra supplied.

Odette scowled. "Why does she *need* to be married?"

"The whole country knows the condition of her curse was true love's kiss to wake her from a deep sleep," Donaigh explained. "So everyone will *also* be wondering who woke her up."

Odette glanced at Angelique when Donaigh outlined the rules, but she mercifully pressed her lips together in a line and said nothing more on the topic of Angelique's limited curse-alteration abilities.

Angelique put her hands on her hips. "What do you expect me to do? I'm not a romance facilitator—and if either of you are so dense as to suggest I make a love potion, I will blow up the gates of Ciane out of *spite*."

"No—nothing of the sort," Donaigh soothed her.

"Rather, we were hoping you might be able to talk some sense into King Giuseppe," Firra said.

"We suspect Rosalinda has loved Isaia for years," Donaigh said. "She won't take to anyone else. And though Isaia is fighting it, he loves her as well."

Angelique ground her teeth. "The Chosen have the mirror, and Carabosso is destroying villages. I do *not* have time to try my hand at matchmaking!"

"You don't need to matchmake," Firra said. "Just convince the king to think! If he blunders into this, Rosalinda will come to despise both him and her parents. Factions will form in the courts and the countryside, and things will only grow worse from there."

"Firra," Angelique barked. "I understand you love your home country, but you must understand that it is *not* our duty to meddle in politics! Rosalinda's curse is broken. I have no further ties to the country, and above all, it is not my business what the Sole royal family does!" Angelique said the last sentence in what could only be construed as a shout. It wasn't at all the sort of character she usually wanted to portray, but she was so tired—and Firra was asking her to directly interfere!

As if to highlight her anger, Pegasus pawed at the ground, and the black of his coat almost seemed to *expand*.

Angelique released the tension she was holding in her shoulders and marched past the constellation—though she patted him on the back.

She was relieved to see Odette was nodding slowly in understanding, and Nadia and Misha didn't look shocked by her refusal either.

(The refusal *was* warranted—right? As an Apprentice, it would have been overstepping her boundaries!)

Firra, however, looked crestfallen and crumpled in on herself a little.

"What about Carabosso?" Donaigh asked.

Angelique shifted her gaze to him and warningly raised her eyebrows. "What about him?"

"Carabosso is sacking towns, and all of Ciane is awake again," Donaigh said. "King Giuseppe can send Magic Knights out to fight him."

Angelique hesitated. *He has me, and he knows it.* She took a deep breath. "Yes...Carabosso must be dealt with. I was planning to mount some sort of attack against him, but if Ciane is restored, that does change things."

Firra's smile returned, and she clapped her hands, her fingers briefly crackling with flickers of fire. "You're coming to Ciane?"

"We were going to Ciane anyway." Angelique nodded to the smugglers, including them in the directive. "Prince Severin of Loire has asked us to research a legend: Foedus, the magical dagger used by the Robber Maiden during the Snow Queen's rule."

Donaigh squinted. "I thought it was a myth."

"Apparently not." Angelique started to scratch her elbow, then quickly corrected herself. "The prince has found references to it multiple times in the continent's history."

"I am reluctant to say this, lest you decide not to come to Ciane after all, but why does the prince have you chasing magical artifacts if the Chosen are on the move?" Firra asked.

"He feels we might need it—as leverage," Angelique said. "Because the Chosen have the mirror the Snow Queen tried and failed to destroy."

The tiny flames Firra had been playing with leaped into roaring fireballs that took her several moments to extinguish.

"But that's impossible—it's in Verglas!" Donaigh almost shook his straw hat loose.

"I inspected the area myself—with Lord Enchanter Clovicus," Angelique said. "And Odette, Misha, and Nadia scouted from the sky. I promise you, the mirror is *gone*."

Donaigh sagged against his horse, his eyes widened.

Firra shoved the fringe of her black bangs from her face, then nodded. "I see. Right. So, you are searching for Foedus, then?"

"Just information on it," Angelique said. "Which is why we were traveling to Ciane. The royal library apparently has one of the most complete collections of references to it. The plan was that I would make copies of the information, and Odette, Nadia, and Misha would take it back to Severin."

Donaigh rubbed his face. "In that case, Ciane's revival is going to complicate things. The library is guarded again, and with his foul mood, King Giuseppe isn't likely to let you in."

Wonderful. I'll have to use a less-than-honest-and-upfront method to get in, then. Invisibility is always an option...

"We'll get you in," Firra said.

Angelique blinked. "Huh?"

When Firra met Angelique's gaze, her eyes burned with determination. "No matter what, we'll get you into the library."

"But if I anger King Giuseppe regarding the library, it's unlikely he'll listen to anything I say about Carbosso," Angelique said.

"It doesn't matter," Firra said. "Our priorities have changed. Getting you that information is now our most important task."

Something in Angelique loosened. "I'm grateful for the help—and for your support—but I have to admit, Firra, I'm surprised you aren't pushing me to set the research aside in favor of helping Sole."

Firra's smile took on a pained edge. "Because if the Chosen have the mirror and we can't stop them, the entire continent will be destroyed."

CHAPTER 26

The ride to Ciane was slowed drastically due to Firra's and Donaigh's horses being, emphatically, *not* constellations.

The pace didn't exactly chafe Angelique, but while it gave them plenty of time to discuss the library, it also gave her too much time to wonder just how much damage Carabosso was inflicting.

Since the smugglers knew Sole and could fly faster than the mages' horses, they offered to fly to nearby villages and warn them of Carabosso, which allayed some of Angelique's guilt.

They also confirmed Carabosso's boast that he had destroyed a total of six villages—though, thankfully, many of the townspeople had fled to surrounding cities.

However, this did serve to remind Angelique that if Carabosso was to be stopped, either mages (*multiple* mages) or Magic Knights would be required.

Keeping that in mind, she sent word to Clovicus and made an official report to the Veneno Conclave requesting help to capture Carabosso. She didn't have much hope reinforcements would arrive in time, but if King Giuseppe was as mulish as Firra seemed to think, she may need help from Conclave mages after all.

This knowledge only served to make her increasingly conflicted by the time they reached Ciane.

I need to speak to King Giuseppe about Carabosso. As little as I like it, he is partially my responsibility. Perhaps doubly so since all mages take vows to confront rogue mages, and *because of my part in countering Rosalinda's curse.*

"My offer still stands."

The comment shocked Angelique so badly she actually jumped a little in the saddle. This made Pegasus stop in the middle of the street, and every muscle in his ethereal body turned taut with tension.

A laundry woman carrying a basket overflowing with dirtied linens eyed the constellation nervously as she scurried past, and a young man carrying a baaing lamb gave them a wide berth.

In fact, though the streets of Ciane were quite crowded, it hadn't escaped Angelique's notice that the citizens packed together to afford her and her mystical mount a large bubble of space.

Angelique stroked Pegasus' neck in an attempt to be soothing. "It's fine, Pegasus." She breathed again when he rocked into a walk, trailing behind Firra's horse.

She glanced down at Odette—who was the only one who dared to walk shoulder-to-shoulder with Pegasus and was on foot. "What offer are you referring to?" Angelique asked.

"Me and Misha and Nadia can research and copy any information on Foedus," Odette said, "so you are free to go with whatever reinforcements King Giuseppe sends against Carabosso."

Angelique quizzically frowned.

Odette shrugged. "It's obvious you're mulling on it. And based on our acquaintance, I can't imagine you sitting still while Carabosso runs loose."

"I'm not entirely selfless," Angelique admitted. "I want him—or Suzu, preferably both, even—captured alive and questioned."

"You could wait until we finish our research to speak to King

Giuseppe—though I don't know how long it will take, and I don't imagine your entrance to Ciane will be a secret for long," Odette said.

"I need to warn the king about Carabosso," Angelique said. "Even with the extra time it took us to travel, we likely have the freshest news about him." She hesitated. "I'd like to keep *your* activities and presence from him, though."

Odette nodded. "In case he gets angry and refuses us entrance to the library? I wouldn't worry overly much. Even if he kicks us from the city, we'll just fly back in."

Angelique slowly nodded.

"It's tough," Odette abruptly said. "Knowing what to prioritize and what to act on. It's one of the things I hate most about being a leader."

Angelique laughed. "I'm no leader. But even as an Enchantress-in-Training, the magnitude of the decisions I have to make..."

"I understand," Odette said. "Just know that the Black Swan Smugglers and I will do our best to offer you backup in this."

Angelique's throat tightened at the kind and unexpected declaration. "Thank you."

"Of course."

Their conversation abruptly ended when Pegasus saw a stand of beautifully ripe pumpkins and—between flattening his ears and snorting sparks—frightened the entire street.

With Firra and Donaigh acting as their escorts, passage to the palace was remarkably smooth.

The two mages led them through the hallways with such purposeful strides, no one—neither the servants dressed in their crisp uniforms, soldiers, or even the occasional fancifully dressed noble—stopped the duo from wandering wherever they wished.

(However, Angelique caught more than a few side-eyed gazes and was fairly certain her presence would be reported to the king within the hour.)

Even the guards standing duty outside the library offered only the feeblest resistance.

Firra and Donaigh strode into the library without hesitation, but it wasn't until Misha and Nadia moved to join them that the guards stirred.

"The Royal Library is off limits to those who do not have the king's express permission," the guard on the left said.

"You'll need to petition his steward," the guard on the right added.

Donaigh made a U-turn and circled around back, throwing his arm over the left guard's shoulders. "Oh, come on, man. Don't you recognize Lady Enchantress Angelique?" Donaigh gestured to her, and Misha and Nadia obligingly shuffled aside so the guards could stare. "She's the champion of Ciane—*and* the one responsible for saving Princess Rosalinda from the terrible curse Carabosso placed on her. It wouldn't be a stretch to call her the savior of Sole!"

"Lady Enchantress." Both of the guards bowed lowly to her. "Thank you for all you have done."

"It was my honor," Angelique said. "But I'm afraid I must ask that you would allow myself and these three—who are my closest of companions—entrance to the library. Speed is of the essence." Angelique could read it in their stances that they weren't going to bend.

It seems a little bit of verbal manipulation will be needed.

"For after this," she continued, "I must speak to King Giuseppe. Carabosso is rampaging through the countryside."

The guards stilled; only their adams' apples bobbed.

"Already he's destroyed towns," Odette added, twisting the knife.

The soldiers stepped aside.

"May the heavens go with you," the soldier on the right said.

Donaigh winked at Angelique as she and the smugglers passed through the doorway.

The Royal Library was a long and narrow room. All bookshelves were pushed against the walls, and the center was a maze of tables, desks, and wooden displays encased with glass and sealed with such powerful magic even Angelique strongly felt it. The room stretched at least three stories high, with bookshelves crowding all the way up to the arched ceiling. Wood walkways wound snug against the walls, giving access to all the tomes, and at roughly three-fourths back into the room, there was a wooden rail that blocked off entrance to the rest of the library, except for one opening located by a giant desk riddled with precariously stacked piles of books, scrolls, and layered with loose paper and dozens of quills and inkwells.

Firra led them through the maze of tables, straight up to the giant desk that blocked the rest of the room. "Benigna!" she called out in a sing-song voice.

There was the scuttling of paper, and after a few moments a tiny, elderly woman wearing moon-shaped glasses that magnified her eyes peeked out at Firra between two stacks of books that were leaning together.

"Mage Firra." The little woman spoke in a wheezy but cheerful voice, and as she gazed out at them, her wrinkle-lined face transformed into a wide smile. "It seems you have brought some visitors to this most sacred of places."

"We need some help." Firra leaned against the desk, propping her elbow on a tiny patch of open surface. "The Lady Enchantress needs to see any and all records and entries you have on Foedus."

Although Benigna's eyes were a little red and weighed down by wrinkles, they were bright with intelligence. "The magical artifact and the dagger of the Robber Maiden?"

"That's the one. Does the library have any references to it?"

Benigna eyed Angelique and the smugglers, her jowls puffing. "You want to use it against the Chosen, don't you?"

Angelique's jaw dropped. "How did you—?"

Even Firra and Donaigh gaped at the elderly woman.

"The King began going through this past year's reports and correspondences that he missed while unconscious," Benigna said. "One of those missives was a report from Prince Severin containing the uncovering of the Chosen. He sought me out to inquire to the validity of the claims."

Angelique attempted an elegant smile. "And what did you tell him?"

"Based on the continent's history and the wise tomes of the library, it was very likely." Benigna coughed again. "But you have not answered my question. You intend to use Foedus against the Chosen?"

"We hope to," Angelique grimly said.

Benigna nodded and tottered off, disappearing behind the books. She reappeared at the other end of the desk and rang a silver bell that tolled loudly in the quiet hush of the library.

A young man and a young lady appeared within moments, both wearing aprons with pockets that burst with papers, writing materials, and cleaning rags. "Pages," Benigna wheezed. "These patrons need to see the *Heart Collection*."

The duo's expressions shifted to shock for the merest moment before they corrected themselves.

"This way, please." The young man strode off, heading to the back-right corner of the library.

The lower level was walled off with paper screens, hiding it from view. The books that were so carefully arranged on the shelves either gleamed and were stiff with the newness of their binding, or were so old the fragile papers were nearly translucent around the edges.

There were scrolls as well, and Angelique espied a few elven-bound books tucked in the corner—obvious from the gold elvish lettering on the spines and the dim light their creamy pages seemed to shed.

Benigna shuffled past the shelves, grabbing seemingly random books and passing them off to the library pages.

The pages then circled around to the single table in the area—a slanted desk raised for convenient reading and a bottom rail for the books to sit upon—and carefully unloaded their burdens.

When finished with her selection, Benigna made her way over to the desk and set a gentle hand on the books. "These tomes contain all known references to Foedus," she said in her paper-dry voice. "Pages, locate these sections..." Benigna rattled off a list that had the pages scrambling to locate the proper books, though they handled them with great care as they methodically paged through them.

Angelique watched, masking her elation. *I thought this research project would take several days, but with Benigna narrowing the search so much for us, we should finish far faster. I don't believe she has a reason to try to hide any information from us, and I think Firra and Donaigh would have said if she wasn't trustworthy. This might be the easiest mission Severin has sent me on!*

The pages finished finding the ordered sections. "Anything else?" the young lady asked.

"No, that is all. Off with the both of you. Go back to book mending!"

The pair bowed and made an efficient exit, slipping around the screens and hurrying away.

Benigna squinted at Angelique, making her sharp, pale blue eyes swim in wrinkles. "I imagine you don't mean to merely *look*?"

Angelique cleared her throat and held up the saddlebag she carried. "Prince Severin requested we make copies."

Benigna briefly pressed her lips together. "Unfortunately, permission to copy the Heart Collection must be given by King Giuseppe himself." She coughed. "It is because of my great trust in Mages Firra and Donaigh, however, that I shall leave you to your work." She winked with such obviousness; her entire body leaned precariously.

She may be elderly, but she's a sly fox. She waited to ask until the pages were gone, and if King Giuseppe hears wind of this, Benigna can't be held culpable.

"How very generous of you, Benigna." Firra patted her hand and gave her a sly grin.

The old woman chortled, then began shuffling for the entrance. "Leave the books where they are when you finish. I'll send the pages to reshelf them." She paused just outside the screened section to give them a measuring look. "You *will* handle these priceless volumes with the care and respect they deserve," she stated more than asked. "For I will *know* if something is damaged."

"You have my word that no harm will come to these books while we use them," Angelique said.

"Very good." Benigna's cheerful smile was back, and she waved as she ambled off, her slight frame weighed down by her heavy robes.

Angelique waited until Benigna's footsteps faded before she opened her saddlebag and began pulling out the necessary paper and writing utensils. She was more than a little surprised when Firra swiped the first set.

"We'll help," the fire mage said when she noticed Angelique's gaze.

Donaigh tipped his straw hat at her. "We're a long way out of the school room, but I'd like to think our handwriting is decent enough that the prince will be able to read our copies."

"Excellent." Odette nodded approvingly as she eyed the stack of books—which was smaller than Angelique liked—and selected one. "With this many hands at work, we ought to finish before King Giuseppe even learns we're here."

Angelique bit the inside of her cheek. "Yes..." She paused

behind Firra—who was already hard at work transcribing one of the books.

It was a short paragraph that gave a cryptic description of the magical dagger and described several of its most famous owners.

Nadia and Misha briefly disappeared, then came back carrying a small table, upon which they spread their recording materials. They also chose a book each, then began the painstaking task of recording the sections.

Angelique waited until everyone was at work to announce, "I'm going to speak to King Giuseppe."

Donaigh blinked. "Now?"

"He has to be told about Carabosso's actions so he can send out the Magic Knights," Angelique said.

"He'll try to wrangle you into capturing him," Odette said.

"I know, but he's not wrong to," Angelique said. "It is the Veneno Conclave's duty to confront black mages *and* rogue mages."

Besides. I'd rather be present when the Magic Knights take Carabosso down. Then I'll be able to take custody of him or *Suzu and question them.*

Odette nodded, seemingly unsurprised. "Good luck," she said before turning her attention back to her work.

"Angelique..." Donaigh paused. "There's a chance he won't listen to you."

"I know, that's why I have to go," Angelique said. "Or his citizens will pay for his actions with their lives."

Donaigh nodded, and Angelique edged past Nadia and Misha's table, smiling as they watched her.

"Thank you, Angelique," Firra called after her.

Angelique nodded, then left the Heart Collection. *I hope this isn't a mistake. If I confront him head-on, it's possible he won't hear about Odette, Nadia, and Misha's presence, and they'll be free to keep researching and copying.*

She left the library and ambled through the hallways, trying to forge her way to the main entrance. Her memory of the palace was a little sketchy, but eventually she found a foyer filled with guards and a footman standing at attention.

They shifted—slightly alarmed by her unexpected entrance into the room from a door *inside* the palace.

"My lady," the footman puffed his chest. "Please state your name and business here," he glanced from her dress to her face and added, "Madame Mage."

"Certainly." Angelique put her charm on maximum and smiled at him. "I am Angelique, an Enchantress-in-Training and the magic user responsible for altering Princess Rosalinda's curse. I'm here to see King Giuseppe, Princess Alessia, and Prince Consort Filippo about the rogue mage Carabosso. It's urgent."

Though her official request for an audience sent the palace into a frantic tizzy, it was over an hour before Angelique was escorted deeper into the castle—to the throne room, to her surprise.

Is he going to turn this into a public meeting? It makes it easier on me—he can't possibly fail to send Magic Knights after Carabosso with his whole court watching. But it makes me suspect he has a plan of his own.

The double doors were opened with great pomp, revealing the Sole nobles in their silk and satin finery, weighed down with gemstone necklaces, rings, and bracelets.

At the far end of the room, King Giuseppe was seated on his throne—his gray eyebrows lowered in anger as his giant gold crown haloed his head.

It was safe to say he was angry with her. *I told Alessia he wouldn't take well to her little sleeping scheme.*

Princess Alessia was seated on a smaller throne set to the side and slightly back from the King's throne. Her husband, Prince Consort Filippo, stood directly behind her.

The princess smiled at Angelique—but it died when she

glanced at her father. Prince Consort Filippo shifted slightly, bowing slightly in respect when he met Angelique's gaze.

It seemed they, at least, were still thankful Angelique had spread the sleeping spell as they had requested.

"Lady Enchantress Angelique," the footman announced.

I SAID *I was an enchantress-in-training!* But the moment was over too quickly for her to object. Already the footman had bowed and backed out of the room.

She almost sighed before she remembered herself, then walked down the velvet runner rug—which split the room in half.

Giuseppe glared down at her from his raised throne—his expression thunderous—but Angelique didn't balk. She'd gone through too much in the past few years to be frightened by a mere *glare*.

Instead, she made her smile sickeningly sweet and only nodded her head rather than bow or curtsey. "King Giuseppe, Princess Alessia, and Prince Consort Filippo—I am glad to see you looking so hale."

"It is convenient you have arrived so soon after the curse was broken." King Giuseppe gripped the armrests of his throne and scowled. "So you can be held accountable for your actions. You expanded the sleeping spell to cover all of Ciane—something I didn't ask you to do."

Oh, no. No, no, no. Alessia was the one who insisted this was necessary. I am not letting them dump the blame on me! "You didn't," Angelique acknowledged. "It was your daughter, Princess Alessia, who asked me to."

"Yes." King Giuseppe glanced at her daughter. "I am disappointed with my daughter that her softness as a mother made her ask such a foolish thing of you."

Angelique, furrowed her eyebrows and tried to puzzle through his answer. "I beg your pardon, Your Majesty...but what are you referring to?"

The King raised his eyebrows in obvious disapproval. "That

you placed an entire city under a sleeping spell because Alessia thought Rosalinda would be *alarmed* to awaken and find the city had changed around her."

What?

Silence smothered the throne room. Angelique slowly moved her gaze from King Giuseppe, to Princess Alessia—who now stared at the floor.

They didn't tell him the truth? They didn't tell him they had me bespell the entire capital because he was acting irrationally? No. No. I am done pandering. He doesn't get to live in this delusion because his daughter is too softhearted to tell him the truth.

It was, perhaps, a bit petty to be airing this ugly truth in the throne room, but Angelique didn't much care. It was his error to think he could publicly shame her.

"I'm afraid you're mistaken," Angelique began. "For Princess Alessia told *me* she wanted the city put under a spell due to your irrational actions—from the shoddy method you were attempting to break Rosalinda's curse to the high-handed way you were managing the country in your fear."

Princess Alessia turned white and sank lower in her throne.

King Giuseppe slowly turned to face her.

Her shoulders trembled a little, but she met his gaze.

"You *what*?" King Giuseppe growled.

"I'm actually not here to discuss the sleeping spell, but rather Carabosso," Angelique continued.

King Giuseppe held up his hand to stop her. "You think we're finished discussing such a misuse of your magic with that simple dismissal?"

"Yes." Unlike Princess Alessia, Angelique unflinchingly met his gaze. "Because things are about to get far worse."

King Giuseppe steepled his fingers together. "I think you fail to see the severity of what I can do to you, Enchantress."

Angelique couldn't help the laugh that burst from her throat. "Please," she said. "I've shouted down the Council of the Veneno

Conclave, slayed not just a basilisk but a wyvern as well, and fished more royals out of foul curses than I thought I'd meet in a lifetime. You cannot scare me, King Giuseppe. All you can do is *continue to disappoint me*."

She wasn't aware that she had dropped the illusion that tinted her eyes so they weren't her natural unsettling shade of silver until she saw the king gulp. In response, her magic brewed.

Steady. I need him to dispatch Magic Knights to take care of Carabosso. There's no sense frightening him. Angelique inhaled deeply and glanced down so she could put the illusion spell back in place, then fixed a smile on her lips and met his gaze again. "As I was saying."

The nobles around her breathed again, assuring Angelique she had successfully hidden the sharp edges of her magic.

"Carabosso is running loose," she continued. "He devastated one village that I saw, and I've confirmed he's destroyed at least five others."

Prince Consort Filippo placed a hand on his sword in alarm. "You talked with him?"

Angelique nodded. "Briefly."

"And you didn't take him into custody?" King Giuseppe asked.

"He had two mages with him. I couldn't have won against such odds. Which is why—when I learned Rosalinda's curse was broken—I resolved to return to Ciane and ask that you dispatch Magic Knights to confront him." Angelique inwardly sighed and stifled the desire to rub her eyes. "Of course, I will accompany them and help in the battle."

"No," King Giuseppe said.

"No, you don't wish me to aid them?" Angelique asked, surprised.

King Giuseppe tapped the arms of this throne. "No, I will not dispatch Magic Knights to fight him."

She gaped at him, dumbfounded by the callous decision. "You

cannot mean that. He is destroying villages and *killing* your people!"

"You know not what matters you dabble in, Lady Enchantress," King Giuseppe growled. "Though my daughter convinced you help her, magic users—enchantresses included—are to refrain from meddling in the affairs of countries."

Now that it is convenient for you, we're going to trot out that particular platitude are we?

Angelique very nicely managed to keep the sarcasm out of her voice. "I know that. If Carabosso hadn't ravaged six of your villages and towns, I wouldn't be here. But as you have not moved, I am forced to come here and plead on behalf of your own people—*do something*!"

A muscle twitched in King Giuseppe's cheek.

There! He's not so uncaring as he appears to be. But what, then, is driving him to such a poor decision?

"My orders stand," King Giuseppe announced. "The Magic Knights will be consolidated and posted in the biggest cities with the army. Our greatest resources must be protected."

Angelique squeezed her hands so tightly, her knuckles turned white. "Your greatest resource is your subjects. If you abandon them, Carabosso will continue his slaughter." Her boiling anger made her stiff as her eyes narrowed.

King Giuseppe wasn't pleasant to deal with before, but now he is the first monarch besides the dead King Torgen to willfully ignore the great danger in his kingdom. How can he be reached? I cannot hope to face Carabosso on my own given how Suzu has joined him! He must *send help!*

"At least allow the Magic Knights to face Carabosso." Angelique kept her chin up as she met the king's steely gaze. "He is gathering companions. If his company continues to grow, even your fortified cities will suffer."

"Sole has outlasted magical attacks before. We will do it again," King Giuseppe rumbled. "Moreover, Carabosso is a rogue magic user—by default, he is the responsibility of the Veneno Conclave."

How very high-road of you—to try and push the responsibility off on someone else—when you just warned me not two shouts ago that mages aren't to meddle with country affairs!

Angelique clenched her teeth so hard she wondered if they would crack. "I have sent word to the Conclave, but it will take time for reinforcements to arrive. During which, hundreds of your people will die."

"If that is so, you and Lord Enchanter Evariste should have taken care of him at Rosalinda's christening," the King spat.

Angelique narrowed her eyes, taking in the way the king grasped the arms of his throne with his granddaughter's name. *Is that his true fear—that Carabosso is going to get to Rosalinda if he moves any of his forces away from Ciane?*

That thought kept Angelique from completely losing it and screaming at the older monarch, but she didn't withhold her fury.

"As you have been asleep for the past year, Your Highness, I shall endeavor to be gracious in your ignorance, but it seems like *I* will be the one to inform you. Our continent is at a war with an organization that has spent *centuries* preparing for the upcoming battle. Every country has faced horrors these last few years. No one—not even Sole with all of its honor and knights in shining armor—can afford to ignore the situation, or their land will be wiped out!"

"Enough!" King Giuseppe shouted, so enraged a vein throbbed in his temple. "You may be a Lady Enchantress, but you will not question how I choose to rule my country. Leave Ciane, or I will have you dragged out."

Angelique almost laughed in his face.

After all I've been through, does he really think I care about making a scene? And does he really think his soldiers could manhandle me? I put all of Ciane to sleep! Heaven help us—or protect Princess Rosalinda.

She ignored the gasps that filled the room and hung in the air like a specter of horror—she didn't care if they were offended on her behalf or not, particularly given that all of them were too frightened to speak out against their king.

She took a half step toward Giuseppe. "The blood of innocents will be on your hands, Your Majesty."

King Giuseppe's face was expressionless as he leaned back in his chair. "Yes, for it will be done as I have said."

It was so quiet, Angelique could hear her own breathing.

This is it, she dimly realized. *Sole will fall—either from Carabosso or the consequences of King Giuseppe's stupidity. Because no one tried to stop it.*

"Grandfather, you are making a grave mistake."

CHAPTER 27

Surprised, Angelique twisted so she could look back at a lovely young lady who had eyes a stunning shade of purple.

It took Angelique a moment to recognize her—for when she had last seen Princess Rosalinda, she had been sound asleep with her remarkable eyes shut.

But though she was King Giuseppe's granddaughter, there was a marked difference between them—and even between the princess and her parents.

Her family was poised and elegant and arranged themselves like statues to be admired.

Rosalinda was graceful—that had been Finnr's gift, if Angelique remembered correctly—but it was not the practiced and controlled elegance possessed by her mother. Rather, it was the grace of someone well assured of their place in the world, an assurance echoed by the stubborn light in her purple eyes.

Really, Princess Rosalinda wasn't like *any* of the nobles present. For she stood with a boldness that could only be inspired by purpose, and Angelique would bet her dress that Rosalinda's purpose was about to clash with Giuseppe's fear.

King Giuseppe seemed to sense it himself, for he stood. "Rosalinda, you should be in your lessons."

The princess offered Angelique a smile as she stopped next to her. As Angelique watched, she rolled her shoulders back, and her smile turned sharp when she faced her grandfather.

"Yes," Rosalinda said. "I'm afraid skipping lessons is just another one of the many weaknesses you'll have to add to the list of my failures."

King Giuseppe narrowed his eyes. "Return to your class—this does not concern you."

"Quite the contrary—it very much concerns me." The princess shook her head like a disappointed tutor. "Not only will I one day inherit this kingdom, but I also happen to be one of your subjects who once lived in the country." Her smile turned brittle. "So, if that were still so, would you mean to let me *die*, Grandfather?"

Angelique barely managed to keep her expression placid. *Oh yes. They are related. They just have* very *different opinions.*

King Giuseppe frowned. "That is enough, Rosalinda."

"No, it's not. Not by half." Rosalinda shook her head. "You are the king. You have been entrusted not merely with land and resources, but with lives. The people pay your taxes and follow your laws because they trust you to guard them. This is how you mean to repay them?"

"You speak of things that you know nothing about," King Giuseppe said.

"Wrong again! Perhaps if I was raised in this *festering* place, that would be true, but I happened to receive a fine education as a child, and I can confidently say that what you are about to decree is *not* what a good ruler would do," Rosalinda said in a strong, *loud* voice.

Angelique wanted to cheer, but she suspected doing so wouldn't make Rosalinda's argument any more persuasive based on the king's body language.

King Giuseppe clenched his jaw. "You dare to speak out against me—to *humiliate* our family in this way—in public?"

"If I had a hope you could be reasoned with in private, I might have waited. Or if someone else had spoken out," Rosalinda let her gaze linger momentarily on her parents before she returned her now steely eyes to her grandfather. "But no one will because you have them too browbeaten!"

Angelique actually snorted in appreciation at that line. Thankfully, King Giuseppe's shout covered up the undignified sound.

"Guards! Remove the princess and take her to her chambers!" he said.

"At least let the Magic Knights go," Rosalinda said. "This is what they were *created* for, to protect the people and react quickly—not to stand by like nursemaids!"

"The knights will do as I say."

"That's not how it is supposed to be!"

"Enough, Rosalinda! You are a foolish child, and you will be held responsible for your careless manners!" King Giuseppe managed to push the anger out of his face as his expression settled into a stony coldness.

"Father..." Princess Alessia quietly started.

"*Silence!*"

Princess Alessia sank back into her throne, looking chastised.

Rosalinda glanced over her shoulder—a move Angelique copied so as to espy the soldiers who were slowly picking their way through the crowd, their faces twisted with dread.

When the soldiers reached them, Rosalinda whipped back to her grandfather and glared at him with eyes the same purple color as his. She lifted her chin and uttered in a voice as cold as winter, "*You*, King Giuseppe, have the same death grip, the same twisted hold the nobility used to have on Sole before the Queen of Hearts. Mark my words, just as she wrested control from the nobles, if you do not change, someone will rip it from you!"

She left in a whirlwind of skirts and chestnut hair, her ladies-in-waiting gliding behind her (with the visibly relieved soldiers trooping after them).

"As for you—" King Giuseppe started, turning his attention back to Angelique.

Angelique didn't even bother waiting to hear more. She turned her back on him and ignored his sputters as she followed Rosalinda out of the throne room and into the hallway.

I have no time to waste on a ruler who doesn't intend to act on behalf of his own people.

Rosalinda didn't seem to notice Angelique was following her, even though the soldiers—who stayed at the throne room door—and ladies-in-waiting bowed to her. The princess was too busy clenching her fists in a way that suggested she wanted to throttle the king.

Angelique followed in her wake, observing the clearly enraged princess for a few moments before she asked, "Where will you go next?"

"To the Magic Knights of Sole. Let us hope *they* can be reasoned with." Rosalinda took several savage strides then blinked and finally looked at Angelique. "Lady Enchantress Angelique!" she yelped.

Angelique smiled. "Indeed. It is nice to finally speak to you, Princess Rosalinda."

Rosalinda slowed down to a normal walking speed. "Thank you for everything you have done—for me and for my family."

"It has been my honor." *Sort of. Actually, no, it hasn't. But it has become an honor to know the person whose life I saved is the one who seems to be intent on saving her own country.* Angelique twitched her skirts as they continued down the hallway. "If the Magic Knights do not listen to you, what will you do?"

"Then I will go myself," the princess grimly said.

Two of her four ladies-in-waiting gasped.

"Your Highness," a third lady-in-waiting said, her voice strained as they started down a staircase.

Rosalinda glanced back at her over her shoulder. "I am not so stupid as to think I can face Carabosso, but I can help evacuate citizens. In fact, whether or not the Magic Knights listen, it is my intention to help."

"Evacuate?" one lady asked.

"They do it for bad weather and floods," Rosalinda explained. "Farmers and those who live in smaller communities will evacuate with their families and livestock and retreat to fortified areas. We evacuated twice when I lived on Sir Roberto's lands. It's a chaotic, hectic time, and any help would be appreciated."

I can see now that the princess received a far...wider sort of education than King Giuseppe may have wanted.

When they entered an empty hallway that made their voices echo, another one of the ladies-in-waiting spoke up. "Your Highness, it's still too dangerous."

"I'll come with you," said the final lady-in-waiting.

"Delanna," one of her cohorts growled.

"The princess is right. We cannot leave those people to die."

The two more soft-spoken ladies—the gaspers—joined arms and exchanged frightened glances, but the third one raised her chin. "Very well," she said in a shaky, frightened voice. "If you believe we can help, we will come, too."

The princess glanced up and down the hallway. "Actually, I would prefer you stay in Ciane, though it will be a great social risk for you."

The lady-in-waiting gripped her skirts with white hands. "You wish for us to cover your flight."

"I do," Rosalinda said. "If King Giuseppe realizes what I am prepared to do, he will have the whole army camped outside my door."

The lady-in-waiting tapped her lower lip. "I think we could arrange something. We will be waiting for you at the stables." She smiled and directed the two quieter ladies-in-waiting up a different hallway.

This left Angelique with Rosalinda and the last lady-in-waiting the others had referred to as Delanna. When Angelique curiously studied her, she faintly recognized the young lady as the attendant staying with Rosalinda when she had first come to see Rosalinda after the curse was set off.

"Firra, Donaigh, and my companions will come with us. I will leave you here so I may go warn them, but is there anything you require my assistance with before I do so?" Angelique asked.

Rosalinda shook her head "No, I don't believe so—" She stumbled and almost walked into a display case of an ancient shield and sword. She corrected herself at the last second, then froze.

"Princess?" Angelique cautiously asked.

"Your Highness? Did something happen?" Delanna asked.

Rosalinda took a shaky breath. "I may have spoken too soon. Lady Enchantress...you know of the legendary weapons?"

Angelique exchanged a look with Delanna before the princess turned to face her. "The weapons of the original Magic Knights of Sole that hang in Aeternum Hall? Yes." Angelique tucked a stray hair behind her ear and offered the princess a polite smile.

Rosalinda licked her lips. "There is a particular weapon from there that I need, the two-handed sword. Do you think you could remove it from Aeternum Hall and smuggle it from Ciane without anyone knowing?"

It seems things suddenly got far more interesting.

Angelique couldn't help it when her smile inched closer to devious than polite. "You know to which knight it should belong?"

"Yes."

Angelique nodded. "Consider it done. My companions are just the people to successfully retrieve it. I will also take my leave so I can explain the situation to them. It seems the stables will be our meeting place?"

Rosalinda inhaled deeply, then started to walk at a much slower pace. "Yes."

"Excellent. Until then, good luck."

Now it was Angelique's turn to branch off from the princess, trying to discreetly route to the royal library—where three smugglers and two mages were sequestered.

A new Legendry Knight will be a great advantage in the battle against Carabosso—and the Chosen. The Legendary Knights were specifically organized to counter mages and creatures of dark magic. We must hope that whoever this knight is, he's a fast learner.

When Angelique breezed through the library doors, the guards, thankfully, didn't try to stop her. When she reached the desk that barred the way to the other half of the library, Benigna smiled in bemusement and waved her past.

I wouldn't be half surprised if she somehow already got word of what happened in the throne room.

Angelique nodded to her and glided to the screened off Heart Collection as quickly as she could. "How goes the progress?"

The mages and smugglers looked up at her arrival.

"Quite well," Firra reported. "Some of the sections are unfortunately small, so it's gone faster than we estimated."

Odette finished copying a crude sketch in one of the books, tracing over the image onto a fragile, half transparent sheet of elven paper Angelique had brought for such a reason. She removed the elven paper from the book and set it with her other notes, but paused and tapped the sketch. "You know, there's something about this dagger."

"Besides being unspeakably hideous according to all legends?" Misha asked.

Firra frowned. "What?"

"Your books didn't mention it?" Donaigh asked. "Every passage I've copied has taken pains to describe how ugly it is, with a bug-like hilt."

"No, it's not its looks," Odette tapped her sketch again, then returned her attention to a new passage. "It just seems...*familiar*."

Angelique studied the Swan Queen with some curiosity. *Odette isn't one to lightly say such a thing. I'll have to ask her about it later—when I'm not off to fight a crazed rogue mage.* She nodded to Odette, then hesitatingly changed the subject. "How much materials are left to copy?"

Misha swapped out the book he was transcribing from (which had a binding that was so clean and new, Angelique could smell the glue holding it together) and exchanged it for an old, dusty book that was faded with age. "I think we maybe have an hour, perhaps two," he said.

Angelique clenched her skirts as they darkened from a pale reddish-purple to a dark green. "And if only three of you were making the copies?"

Odette leaned back in her chair and scratched her side. "Maybe three hours. Did something happen with Giuseppe? Do we need to pack up and flee?"

Angelique shook his head. "It went terribly, but I think you're safe to keep working. I imagine he's so split in his anger—between being enraged with me, possibly his daughter, and for certain Princess Rosalinda—he won't be asking around if I arrived with anyone."

Donaigh fixed the brim of his hat. "How did it go so badly?"

Angelique told them of her shouting match with the king, and that it was broken up only by Princess Rosalinda—who shouted even louder and more fervently—then detailed the princess' plan to leave Ciane to aid those fleeing Carabosso.

"Hopefully she'll convince at least a few Magic Knights to come with us," Angelique said. "But we'll have to leave quickly—Giuseppe will lock Ciane up tight once he realizes what she intends to do."

Odette kept her eyes on the dusty book she was copying from. "You're going with her, then?"

"Yes. And I imagine you two intend to come as well?" Angelique nodding meaningfully at Donaigh and Firra.

Donaigh nodded and sprinkled sand on his copied work,

soaking up the extra ink. "We're with our Briar Rose every step of the way—and we ought to see the job through."

"Through?" Angelique raised an eyebrow. "I didn't think you'd ever leave the princess, even after Carabosso is taken care of."

"Well, at least we'll be free to take a holiday or two." Firra grinned. "Maybe check in with Prince Severin and see if he has any need of us while we dodge summons from the Veneno Conclave."

"If you intend to go with the princess, you ought to leave," Nadia reminded them.

"Firra and Donaigh's exit won't add too much extra work." Misha's quill paused just long enough so he could select a new page to transcribe. "It will perhaps take us an extra hour. We'll still be able to leave early this afternoon."

"Good." Angelique pressed her hands together. "Because I have an additional job for you."

Odette suspiciously glanced up at her. "Why do I suspect it's not going to be something I like?"

"Don't be silly," Angelique winked at the blonde—whom she was truly starting to like as more of a friend than an acquaintance. "It involves your favorite activity: smuggling!"

THE EXIT from Ciane was uneventful—it actually didn't occur to Angelique that the others were nervous about it until the capital was no longer visible and the princess's entourage slumped with relief.

(If they had been that worried about it, Angelique could have cast some alteration magic to change their appearance, but no one had breathed a word of their concern.)

They rode all afternoon, though Angelique had to grit her teeth to keep from groaning over the slow but necessary pace.

(She often forgot how fast Pegasus was in comparison to a normal horse.)

By late afternoon, just when the air started to have a bit more bite to it as the fall sun sank in the sky, they stopped to eat and rest the horses.

"We should decide where we want to stop for the night," said Sir Isaia—Rosalinda's ever-loyal knight, whom Angelique suspected was also the most likely candidate present to receive the Legendary Sword Rosalinda had asked for.

Donaigh settled his straw hat so it cast a shadow across his eyes while he peered up at the sky. "Yeah. I don't fancy sleeping outside in these times."

"We will *not* be sleeping outside." Delanna's voice was firm and gave room for no argument, even as she slipped off her horse and tried—but failed—to take Rosalinda's mount from her.

"I agree—not while Carabosso is loose." Firra dug through her saddlebags and pulled out some food and provisions. "But, then, how much farther do we want to push on this evening?"

Rosalinda took an apple from Firra and nibbled at it. "Do we need to be concerned about meeting up with your companions in a certain location, Lady Enchantress Angelique?"

Angelique was the only member of their little party who hadn't dismounted yet, because she could practically *feel* Pegasus' unbridled energy surging under his coat. "No. I gave them a spell to help them locate me. They'll catch up quickly—they can move faster than you can ride."

Rosalinda's forehead puckered as she tried to puzzle through Angelique's words, but when her apple was only half-consumed, she discreetly passed it off to her horse—who crunched it with great enthusiasm, dripping wet horse slobber on the princess' hands.

She wiped them on the skirts of her gown, seemingly without thinking, and studied Angelique. "Do you need to go somewhere?"

"No. However, I was going to offer to scout ahead," Angelique said. "Knowing if our way is clear might influence how far we decide to ride this evening."

"A splendid idea," Firra said. "Perhaps I ought to come with you."

Donaigh snorted. "You just think I'm going to make you play Rumpelstiltskin's guessing game."

"I don't think, I *know* that if the conversation ever lags, you'll make me play it," Firra grumbled.

"Though I appreciate the offer, I think it would be swiftest if I went alone," Angelique said. "Pegasus can cover far more ground at his usual speed, and your mount needs rest."

"Ah, good point."

Sir Isaia nodded his acceptance. "Thank you, Lady Enchantress."

Rosalinda thoughtfully peered up at her. "Be safe."

Angelique nodded. "Of course, Your Highness."

"Angelique."

When Pegasus turned in a tight circle—his silent declaration that he wished to gallop—Angelique met Donaigh's gaze. "Yes?"

He tossed her a bright red apple, then a hunk of cheese.

Angelique smiled. "Thank you." She took a bite out of the tart apple. "We won't be too long."

Pegasus snorted and pulled away from the group, barely giving Angelique enough time to toss her snack in the saddlebag and cling to him before he was off like a comet, the fire of his mane and tail blazing white hot.

The cooling air stung Angelique's face as the constellation thundered along. They had just rounded a thicket of trees when the potent smell of smoke clogged the air.

Angelique tugged on Pegasus reins, slowing him down.

"Do you smell that?" she asked when she could speak without needing to shout.

Pegasus flared his nostrils and sniffed the air—acting more

like a wolf than an equine. He adjusted their course, then picked up the pace again, and within moments, Angelique could make out the thick clouds of smoke flooding the sky. Pegasus wove around a plowed field and hurdled up a slight hill, pausing when he reached the top.

Flames slowly consumed a village, choking the area in ashy gray smog, but above the hungry crackle of the fire, she could hear the guttural snarls of goblins.

It's Carabosso. He's here!

CHAPTER 28

Angelique's gut reaction was to scream for Pegasus to fly forward, but she made herself take inventory of the situation, recalling that for once she wasn't alone.

Unfortunately, it seemed Carabosso had added to his allies as well.

Goblins, barely visible through the haze of smoke, ran through the streets. A few villagers fled their onslaught, escaping the fire-ruined village and running away.

To the west of the village were four chimera—vile monsters with the body of a lion and three distinct heads: that of a lion, a goat, and a serpent.

Angelique thought she saw Carabosso—his pale skin and dark hair making him rather distinctive compared to the sun-worn villagers—but he disappeared in the swirl of smoke funneled around the village. She saw three other figures. One was the woman whom Angelique was certain was Suzu—for the flames eating the buildings and wooden fences grew higher under her ministrations—the other Angelique recognized as the male black mage that had previously accompanied Suzu and Carabosso, but the last was a new addition—a female black mage who smiled like a snake.

The two unknown black mages disappeared in the smoke, hustling after Carabosso, but Suzu stayed at the edge of the village, fanning the flames.

Yes. That's Suzu alright. And if she's with Carabosso, it's likely they—or their companions—should know where Evariste is.

Suzu raised her arms, feeding the fire's frenzy.

Angelique growled—everything in her wanted to rip away and descend on Suzu.

If I can capture any one of them, I can find Evariste! Her muscles tensed, and her magic stirred at her fingers, but she forcefully turned her gaze to the burning buildings. *However, first we have to save the villagers.* It was torture, but she turned Pegasus back toward their companions. "Fly, Pegasus! We have to tell the others!"

Pegasus took Angelique at her word, for she could have sworn she saw black feathers in her peripheral vision—but it was hard to tell since Pegasus was moving so fast, her eyes teared up and the cold wind froze her nose and fingers.

He reached Rosalinda's company in a few short minutes, spraying dirt and tufts of grass when he halted.

"It's Carabosso," Angelique managed to say around a gasp as she tried to breathe again. "He's here."

Firra jumped up and flames crackled in her eyes. "What?"

Angelique coughed and sat upright when she was able to straighten her fingers after the strain of clinging to Pegasus' back. "He's attacking a nearby village."

"That'd be Tavo." Sir Isaia mounted his hot-tempered horse and looked to Princess Rosalinda. "Do we engage?"

"Yes, but we can't beat them. He has three black mages with him, four chimera, and, somewhere, he acquired a bunch of goblins." Angelique stretched her fingers and tried to hold off the impulse to direct Pegasus back to the village. "There are too many of them."

"But if you used your core magic…" Firra trailed off and at least had the decency to look a little guilty.

Angelique shook her head. *No, Firra, I'll let you talk me into breaking all kinds of laws and will save your country, but I will not risk my soul to do so.*

"We cannot ask that of her," Donaigh said firmly. "Particularly as she has already done so much to help us that will displease the Conclave."

Lady Delanna mounted her horse. "So what do we do?" Once properly situated on the saddle, she loaded a bolt into her crossbow.

Rosalinda frowned. "We could keep them distracted and try to evacuate any survivors."

Pegasus turned in another tight circle, his steps more prancing than usual.

Angelique clutched her saddle and prayed his patience would hold out a few minutes more. "I think he's coming for you, Princess. When I fought with him in the north, he was taking his time moving from east to west," she continued. "To reach Tavo, he must have started traveling south immediately after I got away. I doubt he did so to follow me. As it stands now, he is on a straight path toward Ciane."

Sir Isaia checked his weapons as his mare angrily chewed her bit. "Briar has been his target thus far. I doubt he would change tactics, given that he waited years for her to grow up."

Rosalinda clambered into the saddle. "I'm still going to help with the evacuation."

"Yes, but you cannot help fight," Isaia said.

Rosalinda snorted, sounding more like a commoner than a princess. "Of course not! I might be able to defend myself from any suspicious men in the forest, but I am not so stupid as to think I could face a magic user."

"I'll go with Briar—I can pick off anything that might try to attack us," Lady Delanna offered. "Besides, our horses are the only ones not used to combat. If we get too close to the fight, we might lose control of them."

"Perfect." Firra checked her horse's gear one last time, then mounted up as well. "The rest of us can stand between. Briar, keep your handkerchief over your hair. The last thing we need is for Carabosso to recognize you."

Angelique waited with barely leashed impatience as the group finished preparing. When ready, she loosened Pegasus' reins, and the constellation led the charge to Tavo.

He was the first to reach the crest of the hill—even with Angelique holding him back—and screamed a challenge.

The flames had consumed more of the village, and the smoke had grown thicker. *Suzu is out in the open,* Angelique noted as she saw the sorceress channeling more fire. *But where is Carabosso? If we're to find him, we'll have to stop the fire and get rid of this smoke.*

"Firra," Angelique started to say.

The fire mage nodded. She heeled her horse and shot toward Tavo, shouting barely understandable words of magic as she went. A moment passed, then all the angry orange fires tearing the village apart rippled and turned blue.

Suzu snarled and raised her hands, turning the flames crimson once more.

Firra shouted some more, and Angelique felt a great heave of magic before the flames once again turned the lightest shade of blue, then were snuffed out.

Suzu tried to rekindle the fire, but she only got a few tiny flames going that died moments later.

Firra is a lot more powerful than I realized if she can go head-to-head with a sorceress. But I'm not going to dwell on that now.

"Donaigh, let's go!" Angelique nudged Pegasus after Firra.

Donaigh hopped off his horse then tapped his war magic. He ran so fast, he winked in and out of view, popping up directly in front of a small group of goblins that were on the verge of entering Tavo. He zipped from goblin to goblin, ending them with his daggers and knives.

Angelique directed Pegasus toward where she *thought* Carabosso was. (Suzu was making a beeline in the same direction, with Firra shooting fireballs after her, so they probably meant to meet up and fortify their line of attack.)

Unfortunately, a second band of goblins came pouring out of the city entrance, getting between Angelique and the exiled mage.

Pegasus plowed through the goblins, but though he had no difficulty trampling the creatures, more and more kept attempting to pile on—swinging at his limbs with nail-studded clubs.

"Enough!" Angelique threw herself off Pegasus. She jabbed a finger at the sky, quickly twisting her magic and muttering the right words under her breath as she tied an air and earth spell together. She yanked it tight, then swung her hand down, loosening the spell and shouting a magic command at it.

The ground rippled under her feet, and carefully channeled gusts of wind slammed into the goblins, tossing them head-over-heels.

Angelique straightened, but by the time Pegasus joined her, Sir Isaia raced past them, finishing off the few standing goblins with artful slices of his sword.

Angelique was vaguely aware that Delanna and Rosalinda trotted past on their mounts, heading directly into the village.

"Is it safe to let them go alone?" Angelique threw up an iridescent shield over Firra when a chimera's snake head tried to bite her; instead, it cracked its skull on the shield's surface.

"The village won't burn any more," Firra darkly promised. "The flames are *out*."

If Firra was satisfied, Angelique wasn't going to worry about it. She let herself focus on the fight, rolling her magic through her fingers and into spells in a familiar rhythm.

More goblins marched on the village, but Sir Isaia and his horse stood between them and the closest entrance. The knight with his sword and his mare with her hooves and teeth cut down packs of the monsters. Sir Isaia's expression was determined as he held his ground, defending the burnt village—and Princess Rosalinda.

Firra held the chimera off with walls of fire and threw fireballs at random at the mages—usually whatever one Donaigh was taunting.

The war mage streaked around the battlefield. He knocked over the nameless female black mage—at whom Firra threw an orb of fire. The enemy mage rolled away, but the fire spell passed so closely to her that her hair caught on fire.

Angelique shuffled through her repertoire of magic, creating craters in the ground, smashing the mages with boulders, splashing their faces with water and then flash-freezing the moisture to their faces, and doing everything she could to harry them. (She tried hitting them with lightning, but apparently her previous strike had greatly offended Carabosso, for he roared with wrath and produced a thick shield that protected them from the strikes.)

The battle raged on as Angelique twisted her magic, creating innocuous-appearing puddles around the black mages.

"Firra," Angelique called. "Give me some fire!"

"On it!" Firra's brow puckered as she threw at least half a dozen molten fireballs. They slammed into Angelique's puddles, sizzling and producing hot—and noxious-smelling—steam directly around the black mages.

It technically gave them a chance to scheme while out of sight, but Angelique didn't think it was likely given that they couldn't see each other, much less Angelique, Firra, Donaigh, and Sir Isaia.

It's worth the gamble, she thought, noting the strain that was starting to show in the tense muscles around Firra's eyes and the tightness of Donaigh's smile.

The two mages slumped with relief—though Firra strengthened her firewall around the chimera.

"Brilliant job thus far!" Donaigh declared.

"I don't know about that," Angelique muttered. "Once Rosalinda and Delanna get everyone out, I think we need to flee. We don't have enough forces to win."

"I agree," Firra said.

A quick check on the mist revealed the hazy shapes of Carabosso and the two less-powerful mages that accompanied him, but Suzu was missing.

Where could she have gone? Angelique carefully traced the battlefield, but the purple-robed sorceress was nowhere to be seen. Instead, she spotted a few villagers—an old couple, an injured man, and parents with two children—mounted on horses, fleeing south.

Rosalinda must have found them.

Carabosso reclaimed her attention when the mist faded enough that he could see again, and he threw an orb of raw magic at her.

She hastily raised an iridescent shield. When the red orb hit the defensive spell, it shed sparks and filled the air with the foul smell of singed hair. It was persistent, shoving into the shield with such strength, Angelique's palms ached as she held the shield up, funneling more magic into the spell.

Donaigh zipped back and forth between the male and female black mage, stabbing at them with daggers. His strikes never made it past their shields, but it kept the pair occupied. "Firra, help Angelique!"

Firra was still holding off the chimera with walls of fire, but she swiveled and shot a fireball the size of a boulder at Carabosso.

Carabosso blocked it, but it shattered his concentration,

breaking the red orb. His face froze in a snarl as he stretched out his hand, and red and black flames gathered in his palm.

As Carabosso chucked the spell at Firra, Donaigh barreled into him, making the spell go awry.

Firra still had to leap out of the way and ended up flopped on the torn-up ground, loosening her grip on the fire that held the chimera back.

With roars, the multi-headed animals bounded into the fight.

Angelique turned toward the beasts, but the female black mage snarled and threw a ball of angry red spellwork at her. Angelique couldn't tell exactly what the attacking spell was, but it felt dark and ancient.

Panicking, Angelique loosened a bit of her raw magic, which enveloped the spell in silver before slicing it to pieces.

Sir Isaia's horse screamed in rage as the knight hacked off the snake heads of two of the chimera, then swung around and retreated back to Angelique, Donaigh, and Firra, closing ranks with them. "If something doesn't happen to change the tide, we're going to get overrun," he said.

Angelique saw movement out of the corner of her eye and turned in time to see a woman mounted on a horse, leading a second horse, which carried two boys on its back. They fled the battlefield and the village, safely outrunning the battle.

More survivors...

Carabosso roared in anger, spurring Angelique back into action. She twisted her magic and pulled a bolt of lightning from the sky.

Again, it hit a shield that Carabosso barely managed to form in time, but this time Angelique twisted the spell so small sparks of electricity broke off from the strike and surged over the edge of the shield, zapping Carabosso with audible cracks.

It couldn't have hurt him much, but Carabosso's even louder snarl of rage brought a smile to her lips.

Encouraged, she peeled back a layer of the earth and tried to smash the female black mage between the layers, but she fled—smacking straight into one of the charging chimera in her panic.

Feeling the faint trace of magic behind her, Angelique turned back to the village just in time to watch Briar—mounted on her horse—come flying out of it.

The princess pulled her horse to a stop and seemed to take inventory, not noticing the sorceress who chased behind her.

"Look out!" Angelique shouted.

The princess didn't hear, and Angelique watched with horror as Suzu charged a spell and chucked it at Rosalinda, hitting her and her horse with a ball of orange lightning.

Angelique tried to throw a shield around the princess, but a chimera took advantage of her distraction and rammed her, slamming her into the ground.

"I've got her." Sir Isaia ran past, sliding his shield off his back.

She'll be safe with Isaia—he won't let her die.

Using magic, Angelique threw the chimera off her, then spun an illusion of three goats. A flick of her fingers and the illusionary goats went running away from the battlefield with loud bleats, the chimera chasing after them.

Carabosso stormed in Suzu's direction, his eyes fixated on Rosalinda, who was pressed against Sir Isaia as he braced his shield.

"Oh, no, you don't!" Angelique rapidly twisted her magic into as many spells as she could, going for power over precision.

Lightning bolts clapped with deafening volume, spraying singed earth into the air as a small whirlwind harried the rogue mage. Next, she set off bursts of light, hopefully blinding the enemy, and softened the ground so the chimera and mages alike started to sink.

Carabosso bared his teeth at her, but at least she managed to stop his progress.

Unfortunately, the more she wildly fired her magic, the more her core powers stirred, winding around her legs and purring in her ear, tempting her.

No. Angelique stubbornly shoved it off. *It was one thing to use war magic against a wyvern, but we need these mages alive so they can be questioned!*

Donaigh ran past Carabosso with his speed magic, narrowly missing the rogue mage's face with the edge of a dagger.

Donaigh darted back behind Angelique and her shield and made a face at Carabosso. "Almost got you there—though any mark I left wouldn't be half as pretty as that fetching brand of yours."

Carabosso's face twisted in his rage. "Get rid of the war mage!" he roared.

Donaigh chuckled and tapped his magic again.

The male black mage from Carabosso's company threw up a thick ice wall which Donaigh rammed into while using his speed magic. He ricocheted off it with a yelp of pain, landing on the torn ground with a groan.

"Donaigh!" Firra screamed.

Angelique moved to help, but a chimera leaped at her from the left. She raised an ice wall of her own that tilted so the chimera landed on top of it. A push of her magic and she flung the ice shell into the sky, throwing the chimera through the air.

When she turned back to Donaigh, the war mage was wrestling with the male black mage. Blood leaked from a wound on his head, but he tapped his magic and slammed his skull into the black mage's nose, who flopped and fell with a gurgle.

Donaigh had barely enough time to grin before his eyes rolled back, and he slumped to the ground.

"Donaigh!" Firra screamed again. Her flames grew in size, and she blasted a path to her longtime friend and partner, burning to cinders anything that dared to venture near the war mage.

The male black mage scrambled to his feet and fled Firra's hot anger, blood dripping from his broken nose.

Angelique threw up a shield, blocking a red bolt of magic from Carabosso as he covered his minion's retreat to their side of the battlefield. "How bad is it?"

Firra was silent for too long as Angelique flung ash over the roaring chimera, temporarily blinding them.

"He's not dead," Firra finally said in a shaky voice. "But he needs help. We need to retreat."

"Should we back up to join Sir Isaia?" Angelique craned her neck, looking for Pegasus.

A brilliant white light ignited, catching her attention. *Please don't be more enemies.*

She carefully shifted, spinning her magic as fast as she could.

Before she could make out the newcomers, five notes were blasted on a horn. Some of the light subsided, and Angelique could make out a band of approximately twenty mounted Magic Knights.

Off to the west, another group of Magic Knights came galloping over a hill, their golden armor gleaming in the light of the falling sun.

The knights swept past Rosalinda and Sir Isaia in an organized formation, and as one, the knights roared. "*For Sole—for the Briar Rose!*"

A knight dressed in fancy armor pulled ahead of his squad and flung a dagger at a pack of goblins.

When the dagger struck the ground, it flooded the area with an explosion of light. Goblins shrieked and pawed at their eyes, smashing into one another as the blinding light faded and the knights pounced.

The other squadron of knights that came riding in from the west fell upon the chimera, instantly easing Angelique's load so she didn't feel quite so cornered. Leading them was a knight with a lance that shone a bright gold color and radiated magic.

He and the one with the dagger must be legendary knights!

Angelique hadn't seen them in action before, but as she watched the knight of the lance thrust his weapon at a pouncing chimera—and throw the monster backward with enough force Angelique could hear its skulls crack—she dimly realized why Severin had despaired over Sole's absence from the Summit.

"You irksome wretch!"

Angelique spun around and saw Carabosso throw an oily liquid at Donaigh—who was still sprawled on the ground and out cold.

Angelique shouted, sweat dripping down her temple as she threw up an earthen wall, shielding Donaigh from the strike.

Queasiness boiled in the pit of her stomach, but Angelique tried to ignore it. *I can't give up—the knights just got here! Surely we can win and capture Carabosso and Suzu!*

The female and male black mage joined forces, attempting to create what looked like tar-covered black vines.

Angelique smirked for a moment—for the male was still holding a hand to his broken nose—then tapped her magic and pulled a geyser of water from the ground that shoved the duo apart and drenched them in water.

An angry hiss made her look up, and Angelique's heart lightened at the sight of three swans circling overhead. "Rosalinda!" she shouted, eyeing Suzu as the sorceress threw a few black orbs onto the ground—each one erupting into another chimera. The Legendary Knight of the Lance plowed one over before it even had time to uncurl to its full size.

In one frenzied moment, Angelique flung a small ball of lightning at Suzu, waved her thanks to the swans, and then yelled to the princess, "Look up!"

She pointed to Odette and her companions who—with an ingenious hookup of ropes—carried the Legendary Weapon Rosalinda had requested: the two-handed sword.

As they came closer to the fight, light surrounded the swans—cutting straight through the ropes.

The sword fell free of the hook up and struck the ground, blade first.

The three smugglers fell like miniature meteors and hit the ground with a loud crack that raised a gust of dust and debris. When the light faded, Odette, Misha, and Nadia remained.

Odette looked somewhat murderous as she stood barefoot on the battlefield. Nadia danced around her, snatching a rudimentary spear from a fallen goblin and attacking the nearest creature.

Odette ignored the chaos of the battlefield and glared at Angelique. "That was beyond dangerous. We are never doing that again! Angelique, do you hear me? We are smugglers—not thieves!"

"Technically, it was not stealing, as the princess has a right to the sword." She threw a ball of flames at the female black mage—which she dodged.

Yep, it seems I have more luck with weirder spells. Angelique poked a finger at the male dark mage as he chanted and tried to loop chains of black magic around her. A spark from her alteration magic, and a rock became a slippery fish that smacked the mage in the face—hitting his now-twice-broken nose and making him flop to the ground in shock.

Odette was not impressed by the show. "Oh, is that why you told us under no circumstances could anyone find out what we were doing?"

I feel like Odette might understand my jaded personality if I ever chose to let it show. It seems like she has similarly been put through ridiculous situations.

Angelique grabbed a handful of grit and blasted it with alteration magic before flinging it at the fallen dark mage. As it hit him, the grit transformed into a bunch of angry, *swarming*, red ants that slipped under the mages' clothes.

"Princess," Angelique—ever dutiful even in the middle of

battle—began, "meet Nadia and Misha of the Black Swan Smugglers, and their leader, Odette, the Swan Queen." Angelique crouched, missing another chain of black magic.

"Stop calling me that!" Odette caught the three daggers Misha tossed to her, then waded through the goblin pack—still barefoot—after Nadia.

Briar sprang on the legendary weapon and pulled it from the ground. "Isaia!"

Yep, just as I thought.

Sir Isaia did not share her sentiments—or Rosalinda's—for she heard him say, "No. Briar—Princess Rosalinda—you can't!"

Uninterested in a lovers' argument, Angelique glanced at the Black Swan Smugglers. "Could one of you watch my back for a moment? I want to attack a chimera, but I need a moment to cast the right spell."

Odette was at her back in an instant, carving a trail through the goblins.

Misha scooped up a goblin club from a fallen foe. "Which chimera?"

Angelique nodded at the closest monster, which was tangling with Firra.

The fire mage managed to keep the beast back with white-hot fireballs, but she was stretched thin—she still stood guard over the unconscious Donaigh. The monster tested her reach, striking at her with its snake-headed tail and then batting at her with a clawed paw.

"Right, then." Misha flung the club, which cracked the chimera on its lion head, then whistled.

The chimera whirled around, locked eyes with Misha and snarled.

"That wasn't really necessary." Angelique yanked on her powers—wincing as more magic slammed into her than she could safely use on this one spell. She hurriedly twisted it into the necessary structure and muttered in the language of magic.

The chimera stalked forward, closing in on them.

Angelique threw her work at the creature, creating a massive chunk of ice that froze around the beast's paws and torso, freezing it in place.

Before she could do anything more, a magic knight charged up and slew the monster.

Firra waved her thanks and traced a circle of fire around herself and Donaigh.

Angelique relaxed marginally, then glanced back at Rosalinda and Sir Isaia, hoping they had made the exchange,

They hadn't.

In fact, they were still arguing.

"I'm not worthy—it won't accept me," Sir Isaia said.

Angelique allowed herself a rare treat and rolled her eyes. "You can tell this is Sole," she announced, "because a knight is willing to argue about something like worthiness in the middle of a battle. This country could do with a good dose of common sense."

"Yeah," Odette agreed. "They've got almost *too much* honor."

"Could be worse." Angelique gestured and stabbed a cluster of goblins with stakes of ice. "They could be arguing about love."

Odette blushed, and Misha snorted with laughter.

"Oh dear, was love a frequent discussion during battle for the Black Swan Smugglers?" Angelique asked—not *quite* caring that she was betraying her image.

"It came up when we fought Rothbart," Misha said.

Odette was a whirlwind, spinning with her daggers as she struck low and jumped high, untouchable as the goblins scrambled and failed to keep pace with her. "We discussed it *after*."

"If that makes you feel like a better leader, I'll not nay-say you." Misha ducked a goblin making a clumsy grab for him and instead tripped the creature so it fell into one of its cohorts, knocking both of them flat.

"Angelique!" Fright paled Odette's skin as she pointed across the field at Suzu.

The sorceress stood with the female black mage—they were teaming up on the Legendary Knight of the Lance. (The male mage Angelique had thrown fire ants at was now screaming and rolling on the ground.)

Angelique inhaled sharply. She gestured, calling down a bolt of lightning—an attack that was swiftly becoming her favorite spell. Suzu blocked it with a shield of tarry black magic.

Do I use my powers? she wondered, the magnetic pull of her core magic tickling her. *But it'd be in front of so many people...what if I hurt one of them?*

"Blaze...*Faro!*" Briar shouted.

Light lambasted the battlefield, casting white on everything.

Angelique vainly held a hand up to block the light as she squinted through barely-open eyes.

Sir Isaia now held the two-handed sword Odette and the others had retrieved from the palace. As she watched, the sword sucked up the intense light.

The knight turned toward Suzu and swung the sword—which released the white-hot light it held in its blade and sliced through the earth. It carved a path through the ground, creating a deep gouge, then hit Suzu with such force, the sorceress was flung off her feet. She hit the ground with a splat and appeared dazed as spasms wracked her body.

"Well," Rosalinda blithely said. "That worked nicely."

Angelique watched long enough only to confirm that Sir Isaia jumped on his horse and urged it into battle.

The new Legendary Knight changed the morale of the battle.

While the arrival of the Magic Knights had turned the tide, the fight was still dark and grim. But with his two-handed sword still glowing like the sun, every time Sir Isaia leveled his weapon, enemies toppled like flies.

Angelique breathed easier—there was no question who the

winner would be now. She scanned the battlefield, looking for signs of Carabosso and—more importantly—Suzu.

I can't let her escape!

She saw the sorceress—still shaking and unable to stand.

Angelique pushed her magic into the ground, and roots shot out of the earth, encasing Suzu in a tangled root system that held her fast.

Angelique started to smash her way to the sorceress when she barely heard Firra shout above the din of battle, "Angelique!"

Angelique spun, quickly locating Firra, who was holding back a hoard of goblins as the Magic Knights rushed to take care of them.

Her face was pinched with worry. "It's Donaigh—can you take a look at him?"

Angelique glanced back at Suzu—who struggled feebly against the roots—then looked to Donaigh.

The war mage was still splayed on the ground, pale and bleeding.

Angelique wanted to scream. But Donaigh had always treated her with respect and understood the toll of what the continent asked of her.

With a tortured growl, Angelique shifted her path and instead joined Firra. She threw herself to her knees, already twisting her magic into one of the most powerful healing spells she knew.

Donaigh was worse than she had thought. He had a hidden wound on his back, in the left shoulder, which had been bleeding out into the torn earth beneath him.

Angelique sucked air in through her teeth as she concentrated on her magic.

Healing magic is so very difficult because I can't let even a whiff of my core magic survive it—it would kill whomever I'm trying to heal.

Her palms grew clammy and her hands shook as she focused on the war mage, tuning out the goblins' savage battle cries and the roars of the Magic Knights.

Odette and Firra guarded Angelique as she slowly dribbled healing magic into Donaigh's shoulder wound—cleaning it and starting to staunch the blood flow.

Donaigh moaned in pain and winced.

Angelique leaned closer, carefully studying his face. "Donaigh? Donaigh, can you hear me?"

"Angelique?" His forehead wrinkled, but he didn't open his eyes yet.

Firra smiled tightly. "At least he can recognize your voice."

Angelique tilted her head to the side as her healing spell spread through Donaigh's body. "I don't *think* he has any injuries besides this shoulder one."

Firra let out the breath she had been holding and nodded. "Thank you, Angelique."

"Capture them! Don't let them get away!"

Angelique looked up as a squad of Magic Knights thundered past on their blood-thirsty mounts.

Suzu and the two other black mages—who must have freed her from her bindings—ran, almost tripping on their robes.

They're trying to escape!

Angelique stood and grappled for her magic, throwing the first spell she could think of at the trio, calling out for help.

Three hawks screamed and shot out of the nearby forest, diving at the mages and scratching at their faces with their powerful talons.

The male black mage's face was twisted in a snarl and he tried to engulf one of the hawks in flame—but the bird was too smart and veered out of reach while its brethren swept in.

Suzu ignored the uproar and pulled out a black diamond, which she flung at the ground.

"*No!*" Angelique screamed.

A door of light bloomed in front of Suzu. It started as a rectangle of golden light, but blue magic swirled around it so it hardened at the edges, turning from light into gray rock. Chipped rock dusted with snow formed the frames of a door. The inside danced with light before blue fire roared to life, then abruptly faded, leaving a portal to what looked like the base of a mountain.

Her heart squeezed as she could feel the familiar pulse of Evariste's magic. It struck her heart with such strength, she almost collapsed.

Then the first black mage hopped through the door.

CHAPTER 29

"No!" she repeated.

She didn't measure her magic and didn't carefully twist a spell. Rather, she let her unyielding power slam into her and ripped out the first spell it could form.

The ground in a twenty-foot circumference around the door peeled off of the earth like a giant was picking at it, then curled in on itself with a thud.

But Angelique was too late. She saw the second black mage and Suzu jump through and collapse the portal just before earth slammed into place.

Suzu had escaped.

And her method only confirmed Angelique's fears. She was with the Chosen, and it seemed they were milking Evariste for his powers.

Angelique finally did drop to her knees, her disappointment and relief vying for attention.

She was glad it was over, glad they had won, and glad Tavo wasn't entirely destroyed.

But Evariste...

"Donaigh, are you all right?" Firra crouched next to him and helped the war mage sit up.

"I'll be fine in a bit. I can feel Angelique's magic at work." He chuckled. "That will teach me not to overestimate my own speed. Thank you, Angelique."

Angelique stared at the ground, but she raised a hand to signal she had heard.

"Where's Briar?" Sir Isaia twisted in his saddle and scanned the battlefield.

"I heard her calling for her horse after she dropped your legendary weapon on you," Firra said.

Sir Isaia's mare threw her head, expressing the nerves her rider wouldn't show. "Did she go back into the village?" he asked.

"Probably." Firra glanced up at the knight. "I'll sweep the southern half if you check the northern half."

Sir Isaia nodded and nudged his horse, who pounded toward the village.

Angelique finally raised her eyes and scanned the battlefield. "I don't see Carabosso, and he didn't flee with Suzu and the others. Either he slipped away when we weren't watching, or…"

"I'll hurry." Firra ran for Tavo, jumping a dead chimera on her way.

Angelique rubbed at a streak of grime on her hands. "Call me if you need assistance."

"Sure thing!"

Angelique sighed and stared at the nearly set sun. She wanted to sound happy like the others, but she couldn't quite muster it with Suzu's exit fresh in her mind. Though she ached with the sight of Evariste's magic and was frustrated with the sorceress' escape, she was still able to gather a flickering flame of hope.

She used Evariste's transportation magic. Magic can't be stolen or ripped from a person if they're dead, which means he must *be alive!*

Her eyes glazed with tears, and she blinked only when someone stepped between her and the sun.

It took a few moments before Angelique realized it was Odette. *That's right. I can't just sit and sulk.* She inhaled, and she mustered every ounce of her will to smile up at the Swan Queen. "Sorry, I stared at the sun too long. Thank you for retrieving and delivering the Legendary Weapon."

Odette studied Angelique for a long moment, then shrugged. "You paid us well," she reminded her.

Angelique snorted as she stood, her legs a little shaky from both the sheer emotion and the riptide of the day's events. "It was a far riskier job than the one I originally hired you for."

"I can see why it was necessary."

"How bad was Ciane when you left?" Angelique asked.

Misha laughed. "It was a total uproar. The King is hopping mad—I don't think he expected his precious granddaughter to be even half the firecracker she is."

Angelique tiredly rubbed her face. "I imagine so. He's grown distinctly crotchetier every time I've seen him. You brought the transcribed pages about Foedus?"

Odette nodded. "Nadia has the copies."

"Excellent. I'd like you to take them to Prince Severin of Loire. By now he should have returned to his home at Chanceux Chateau," Angelique said.

Odette balanced a dagger on her finger as she watched the knights sweep the battlefield, slaying the last chimera and killing the few remaining goblins. "You don't wish to show him yourself?"

Angelique bleakly stared at the smashed earth she had dragged up. "No. That magic Suzu used belongs to the Lord Enchanter who is my master. That she had such a spell means she and her cronies are the ones who captured him. I have to find her."

"She seemed to be working with Carabosso," Misha said. "If we can track Carabosso, I imagine he'll have useful information."

Angelique perked. "That's true. And unless he has a teleportation spell of his own, he can't have gotten far. Thankfully, I happen to be abnormally skilled in tracking spells." Angelique fanned her fingers open, and just as her magic started to wind across her fingers, three fireballs shot straight up from Tavo and disappeared.

"The fire mage?" Odette guessed.

"Yes." Angelique scrambled across the mess of the battlefield and into the still-smoking village—the smell of ash was so overpowering, it made her eyes water.

Odette, Misha, and Nadia hurtled after her, exchanging murmured bits of conversation as they fell into a V formation.

"Firra?" Angelique yelled when she thought she was near the street from which the fireballs had erupted.

"Over here!" Firra shouted.

Angelique darted down an alleyway, popping out on a street and stumbling upon a rather surprising image.

Delanna sat next to a bruised and unconscious Carabosso. He bled from one shoulder and looked more disheveled than even Angelique felt as Delanna poked his neck with a crossbow bolt.

Rosalinda leaned against a building, her eyes closed, her head tilted toward Firra.

The fire mage smoothed Rosalinda's hair back from her temple and stood. "Briar Rose is hurt. Delanna said Carabosso used a nasty spell on her. I don't think he mortally wounded her, but I'd like you to heal her. I'll secure Carabosso."

"I understand the sentiment, but I'm not going to take any chances." Angelique briskly crossed the street, already twisting her magic into a sleep spell. She gave it triple the power it required and stretched out her hand, intending to tap his head to transfer the spell. It was then that her spiteful side got the best of her, and she instead chose to lay it on him by delivering a swift kick to his side.

"What's that?" Firra asked.

"A sleep spell. I'm sure the Magic Knights will have proper tools to subdue him, but the other mages already slipped through our fingers. I'm not taking any chance that will give Carabosso the opportunity to escape."

Angelique narrowed her eyes and watched for a moment, but nothing changed.

Carabosso's handsome looks were somewhat muted by the already forming bruises on his face, making his skin look more ashen than fashionably pale. His shiny black and silver-threaded hair was torn out of the low ponytail he had fastened it in. The brand that marked him as an exiled mage was still an angry red scar on his forehead, but he had it partially hidden beneath feathery bangs.

It's disturbing. He doesn't look like a practitioner of black magic—if you ignore the brand, he looks like a Veneno Conclave Mage that went through a rough battle. That, more than anything, bothers me. Black mages are usually quite easy to pick out—the dark nature of their magic stands out next to the beauty of even the most average mage.

If Lovelanna is correct, and there is a mole among the Conclave... would we even be able to tell?

Abruptly, Carabosso's mouth dropped open and he snored. Loudly.

Firra rubbed one of her eyebrows. "That must have been some spell. How long do you think he'll be out of it?"

Angelique swiveled and approached Rosalinda. "A day. At least." Her gaze slipped back to Carabosso, and she felt her magic stir within her like an angry wolf.

No. Not here.

She set her shoulders, but it took two tries before her magic correctly wove into a proper healing spell. Once finished, she set a hand on Rosalinda's shoulder, letting the spell slowly seep into the princess' body. "You said Carabosso used a spell on her?" Angelique frowned as she felt the last few flickers of the spell before they disintegrated. They were bitter like poison and *strong*. Even though they weren't doing the princess any harm at the moment, the bits of spell tried to flare to life. The spell didn't die entirely until Angelique's silver magic roamed across Rosalinda's body, effortlessly swallowing the last bits of dark magic.

"Yes," Delanna confirmed. "It was red-ish strings of what I assume was magic. They wrapped around her body and held her captive."

Angelique nodded, disturbed on behalf of the princess and what the spell signified. Whatever it had been, it was *dark* and powerful. *The Chosen must have recruited Carabosso almost immediately after the Veneno Conclave exiled him. How else could he have such power in a magic discipline he was not taught as a student?*

Hooves pounded on packed dirt, and moments later, Sir Isaia and his mount appeared in the smoke.

"Briar?" he asked, his voice tight with worry.

Firra looked to Angelique.

She forced a smile for appearance's sake. "She'll be fine. She needs to rest—we should take her to someplace safer—and more comfortable. But it's good that she sleeps. Carabosso, however…"

Sir Isaia sprang off his horse's back, a pair of manacles dangling from his hands. Two swift strides, and he was on the snoring black mage, securing his arms behind his back.

"He won't go anywhere," Sir Isaia said. "Not with two squads of Magic Knights and two Legendary Knights around."

"Three," Lady Delanna said.

Sir Isia blinked and frowned slightly in confusion.

"There are Three Legendary Knights present, now that you are the Knight of the Two-Handed Sword," she gently reminded him.

Angelique remained by Rosalinda for a moment longer. She was less concerned about the princess—she survived the torture of the black spell, now it was just a matter of relieving her pain—and more concerned that her magic (still oozing from her and swirling invitingly in Carabosso's direction) might unwind and turn into something that could harm Rosalinda.

"Once Carabosso is restrained, we need to think where we should take Rosalinda for the night," she said.

"The village of Ippari is just a bit south," Firra said. "I imagine the villagers who escaped were fleeing there. It will be safe for tonight."

Angelique rested her hands on her hips and tried to discreetly stretch her back. "Then that's where we'll go. Sir Isaia?"

He stood tall, though his eyes rested on Rosalinda's sleeping face. "Yes?"

"I assume you will be the one to bear Rosalinda to Ippari?"

He swallowed and was silent for several long moments. "Yes."

Angelique nodded, then shifted her gaze to Odette, Misha, and Nadia. "You three will come to Ippari to rest for the night?" Though it was a question, she put enough weight in her gaze to make it into a statement.

"I suppose it would be wisest," Odette agreed. "Flying while fatigued is never a good idea. Although..." she flicked her eyes to the side. "Misha?"

"Yes?"

"Could you run and inform the other Magic Knights of our location—and that we have Carabosso?"

Misha was gone before she finished her request.

Odette nodded in satisfaction. "The battle was a bit hairy, but everything will settle down with this much help around."

"Yes," Angelique said, genuinely surprised by the realization. *I've fought alone for the past few years...I have forgotten what it's like to have help.*

"Where are you holding him?" Angelique barely kept the snarl out of her voice.

Carabosso smirked and said nothing.

Angelique dropped the quaint illusion that colored her eyes and revealed their eerie silver shade. "Where is Evariste?"

Her magic flowed across her shoulders and swirled at her feet like a predator looking for something to devour.

"Where indeed?" Carabosso laughed. "All these years, and you *still* haven't found him, little apprentice."

The burning fury of rage pulled at Angelique, pillowed with the promise of violence as her magic unfurled hopefully.

Stop it, Angelique told herself. *I will not behave like a monster. If I unleash my powers on him, I'm no better than the Chosen—as tempting as it may be.*

Still, the allure was there.

Carabosso's smirk flickered when a tiny bit of her cold magic brushed him, and a muscle in his cheek jumped.

How much would it take to make him talk? Just a few weapons pressed into his gut? Perhaps another arrow digging into his scabbed shoulder wound?

Enough. Angelique shook off the pesky bits of her magic like a housewife cleaning cobwebs from the kitchen.

She studied Carabosso with a tilted head. "It's over, you know. Reinforcements are on the way."

They should have been here before I arrived, but that is a separate complaint.

"They won't just seal your magic this time," Angelique continued. "And I doubt you'll ever see the sky again once you arrive at the Veneno Conclave—and that's only if King Giuseppe doesn't rush a death sentence for you before Conclave representatives arrive. You have nothing to gain by hiding Evariste's location. And even if you don't tell me, there are mages with the Conclave who can *make* you talk."

Angelique held his gaze until he looked away.

He stared at the wall of the inn's wine cellar where they had stowed him. "It surprises me," he said abruptly.

Angelique quirked an eyebrow.

"How you continue to work with and serve an organization that has so wronged you," Carabosso said. "You lack the will to stand up for yourself, it would seem, and the courage to take what is already yours."

Angelique narrowed her eyes. *There is danger in speaking to him. But in this area, I think I'm safe enough.* "I stay because before I was an apprentice—before I was a *mage*—I knew that honor and duty are important." She paused for a moment, remembering her father, a valiant soldier, and his warm bear hugs and his unshakable sense of integrity.

His heart would break if he were alive and I turned from this path, and that says nothing about Evariste...He'd be disappointed, and—

Angelique savagely cut the thought off. It didn't matter—because despite what everyone said about her, she wouldn't sway. Not *ever*.

She waited until Carabosso's dark eyes met her gaze. "I took a vow to protect the people of this continent, and I'll *die* before I break my word."

Carabosso's head snapped back as if she had physically slapped him, and for a breath pain swam in his eyes, but faster than she could identify it, rage swept through him. He clenched his jaw and glared at her, his upper lip curled back in a sneer.

There was something in her words, something in what she had said that upset him—a thing worth noting given the grim future she had cheerfully reminded him of numerous times.

"Go ahead and struggle," he spat. "It will end in failure! The Conclave will break, and these lands will be plundered!"

Angelique kept her expression cold, though a shiver traveled up her spine. Knowing she wasn't going to get anything useful out of him unless she resorted to torture, she nodded to the four Magic Knights guarding him, then climbed the creaky stairs out of the cellar.

"All your struggles will be for naught," he shouted after her, his rage building so it made his voice hoarse. "And then where will your shining honor be? What good will your *duty* be to you in a world as black as night!"

Odette—her forehead creased with worry—waited for her at the top of the stairs. "Did he say anything useful?"

Angelique shook her head as she walked into the kitchen. "No. Just more ranting."

Odette chewed on her lower lip and followed Angelique behind the bar of the inn and outside. "Do you think he's speaking the truth? That the Chosen have some kind of plan to bring the darkness of night to the land?"

That's exactly what I fear. But there's no use letting terror fester in our hearts. Angelique smiled pleasantly. "The night doesn't bother me," she said. "I've *ridden* it."

Odette released a deep breath. "That's right. Pegasus." She grinned. "Someone ought to remind that git that the darkness of night has stars."

Together they left the inn, stepping out into the afternoon sunshine. Brightly colored leaves fell off a giant oak tree and dizzily twirled through the air, which held the bite of cold.

"I don't know that we're going to get any information out of Carabosso very soon," Angelique said.

Odette caressed one of her daggers in her thigh bandolier. "Should Misha, Nadia, and I fly out to Severin, then? I know this morning we decided to wait and see if Carabosso said anything helpful, but..."

Angelique nodded. "I'm not willing to inflict any torture to get him to talk. If he's taken to Ciane, I imagine the Magic Knights will get him to sing, but I don't want to delay sending Severin the information on Foedus. And while I'm certain that by now he's been informed that the Sole princess is awake, your firsthand account will be useful."

"Now that Carabosso is taken care of, do you think King Giuseppe might agree to send the Magic Knights to help the rest of the continent?"

Angelique sighed. "I don't know."

"Angelique!" Donaigh zipped down the main street of Ippari with his magic, grabbing his straw hat when it almost fell off his head after he skidded to a stop. He looked markedly better than he had the previous day just after the battle. His pep was back, and his wound was almost entirely healed up. (Rosalinda also showed no ill effects of her tangle with Carabosso, thank goodness. Angelique didn't want to think of how King Giuseppe would holler if Rosalinda returned to him injured.)

"Is something wrong?" Angelique asked.

"Not at all! The reinforcements you requested from the Veneno Conclave—they've arrived."

I must have heard him wrong. She folded her hands together. "I beg your pardon...what did you say?"

"The Council received the message you sent and dispatched Master Weather Mages Blanche and Rein—they've got four war mages with them," Donaigh said. "Firra sent me. They want to talk to you."

Angelique was so shocked, her jaw almost dropped.

She had requested backup from the Veneno Conclave on at least a dozen different occasions—her journey to Kozlovka to face Rothbart and his wyvern, fighting Clotilde the witch queen in Arcainia, the storms that had isolated Ringsted—the list went on and on.

And now they finally *decide to help? Frankly, I'm shocked—I had given up all hope. Although it is likely The Council is all too aware that if Sole falls, the rest of the continent will rock. Perhaps this is a sign that the Conclave will be more active in our battle against the Chosen?* She tried not to get her hopes up—after all, it was very possible Clovicus had finally harassed the Conclave into doing something, and the organization had no intention of doing anything else at all helpful or useful after this.

"Where are they?" Angelique asked.

"At the Magic Knights' camp." Donaigh led the way—limiting

himself to a fast walk rather than disappearing with his speed magic.

"Coming, Odette?" Angelique called over her shoulder.

"Are you certain I should?" Odette asked. "Won't this meeting be just for mages?"

"I'd prefer if it wasn't, actually." Angelique beckoned for Odette to follow. "Besides, we might learn an interesting tidbit."

The knights' camp was just outside Ippari. They had tents of Sole red and gold pitched in rows so orderly, they could be used to draw straight lines; and every knights' horse that was picketed out on the lawn didn't nibble at the dying grass but rather observed Angelique and the others with the eyes of watch dogs.

It smelled faintly of sweat and leather, but Angelique found the scent more pleasing than the stilted and heavily spiced scent of the Veneno Conclave fortress.

Blanche and Rein were standing under the largest of the knights' tents. All but one side had been rolled up, giving its occupants—the mages, Princess Rosalinda, and the three Legendary Knights—a view of the camp and the village.

"Master Weather Mage Blanche, Master Weather Mage Rein," Angelique called out to the pair when she also stepped under the tent. "What a pleasure it is to see you."

Blanche gave her a friendly smile. "Greetings, Apprentice Angelique."

Behind her, Rein gave a little wave as he chugged water from a waterskin.

"We were sent by the Conclave to capture Carabosso, but it seems you have things handled," Blanche said.

Angelique shook her head. "I fought in yesterday's battle against Carabosso, but it was actually Princess Rosalinda and her lady-in-waiting who captured Carabosso." She gestured to the princess.

"Really?" Rein raised his eyebrows. "How did you manage that, Your Highness?"

Rosalinda smiled beautifully, her purple eyes making her look extra striking as she set a hand on her cheek and said, "Why, Delanna beat him senseless, of course!"

Next to her, Lady Delanna bowed her head. "I could not have done so if you hadn't stabbed him in the shoulder, Your Highness."

Rein's jaw dropped, but Blanche chuckled a little. "Both of you were terribly brave to confront him," she said.

Rosalinda shrugged a little. "It was more a reaction. We only won the battle because of Angelique and the Magic Knights."

Sir Isaia and the other two Legendary Knights who were present bowed deeply.

"You honor us, Your Highness," the Legendary Knight of the Lance said.

"I apologize for our tardiness—it sounds like we missed out on a good fight." Rein waved to the four war mages—three men and a woman—who strode through the Magic Knights' camp, stopping just outside the tent to bow.

Blanche's smile was part exasperation and part affection. "What Rein means to say is we apologize we didn't arrive in time to aid in the battle, but at least we'll be able to take Carabosso off your hands."

The Legendary Knights shifted and exchanged glances.

"We'd like to take him to Sole first," the Legendary Knight of the Lance said. "So that he might be tried in our courts."

"I understand your desire to see him punished, but as an exiled mage, he is our responsibility, and he falls under our jurisdiction," Blanche explained. "It is the duty of the Veneno Conclave to mete out justice on those with magic."

"That's interesting," Sir Isaia said. "It seemed he wasn't under your jurisdiction when he attacked Ciane last year and spent months terrorizing the Sole countryside. Lady Enchantress Angelique is the only one who helped us."

Rein furrowed his brow. "Angelique is an apprentice."

Angelique almost rolled her eyes at the expected response, but it seemed those present not only shared her exasperation but were angered by it.

Gone was Princess Rosalinda's smile as she stared the younger weather mage down. "Really? *That's* what you have to say to that complaint?"

The Knight of the Lance crossed his arms over his chest. "Indeed. I find myself stunningly unimpressed that you wish to quarrel over a title when the lady in question has done more for Sole in the past two decades than the entire Veneno Conclave organization."

Rein frowned. "I understand Angelique has attended to Sole, as is her duty. But elevating her above her title is wrong."

Delanna made a scoffing noise and stared Rein down as if he were a miscreant stable boy.

Angelique looked from the weather mages to the others, worry plucking at her eyebrow. *While this is somewhat gratifying to know that others outside the mage community notice my work and value it, it's also a bit dangerous. I don't want Sole—or any other country for that matter—rubbing the Veneno Conclave the wrong way. The Conclave still has a great number of honorable mages, and we could use their help, as much as the Conclave's overall attitude frustrates me.*

"Rein." Blanche set a hand on her companion's shoulder and shook her head. "We are in the wrong. We arrived late and—as the knights said—the Conclave has relied solely on Angelique and previously Evariste to look after Sole when it seems the situation was a much bigger problem than one rogue mage."

The knights nodded and settled down a little.

"Regardless," Blanche turned to face Rosalinda. "All we can do is give our condolences and ask for the opportunity to right the situation."

Rosalinda eyed her. "And take Carabosso to the Veneno Conclave for trial?"

Blanche bowed her head. "Exactly so."

Rosalinda looked from Blanche to the four war mages. "Are six mages enough to safely escort Carabosso back? His associates fled. They might try to free him."

"We came prepared, Your Highness," Rein assured her. "We have equipment that will seal Carabosso's powers, and the war mages who will accompany us are skilled in the art of stealth and battle. Carabosso's allies won't be able to find us as long as the war mages keep their magic going."

The war mages bowed deeply. "If it pleases Your Highness to know," the woman war mage stated, "we belong to the Council's personal guard and are among the top-ranked war mages. There is only one war mage who ranks higher than the Council's guard."

Angelique could *feel* their puppy-like gaze—most war mages seemed to bestow it upon her whenever she was in their proximity. She fidgeted her feet—safely hidden beneath the skirts of her dress—but kept her slight smile on.

I feel like an imposter whenever they look at me like that.

"Very well," Rosalinda finally said. She glanced at the Legendary Knights. "I'm not wholly certain what we would do with Carabosso in Ciane, anyway."

The knights reluctantly nodded.

"*However*," Rosalinda added. "I request a detailed report once you arrive at the Veneno Conclave and again after he is put on trial. My grandfather will be *greatly* interested to hear how your justice system works, and as I know the Conclave will punish Carabosso with all due diligence, perhaps it will restore his faith in the organization."

Donaigh whistled at the princess' daring, and Angelique glanced at Firra—who was smirking openly.

Blanche glanced at Rein and raised her eyebrows. He frowned before the lines around his lips softened. "That is a fair request," he admitted. "We will fulfill it."

Rosalinda's smile was back. "Excellent! I must thank you in advance."

Blanche folded her hands in front of her and shifted to Firra and Donaigh. "I assume you both will journey back with us?"

Donaigh shook his head, but it was Firra who nonchalantly said, "Nope."

Blanche blinked. "*No?* But your assignment is over—Rosalinda has both fallen asleep and awoken, and Carabosso has been captured."

Firra smiled, and Angelique could almost feel the heat of fire radiating off the mage. "We'll be staying here in the interim, until *Lady Enchantress* Angelique dismisses us. Unless, she will be traveling with you back to the Conclave?"

Blanche's expression lost some of her benevolence and was replaced with embarrassed surprise. "Um, that is to say..."

Angelique frowned slightly as she weighed the possibilities.

If I go with them, I might be able to learn more about Carabosso—maybe. *Or maybe the Council will block me out of spite due to my little tirade last year. But Carabosso is the most valuable asset we've retrieved in years.*

She nodded. *I'll send word to Clovicus. He'll not only be able to get whatever information they pry out of Carabosso, but he'll be able to put forth his own questions. The Veneno Conclave also wants to find Evariste; they won't fight him on this.*

Though she was able to defend her answer, a part of Angelique couldn't help but wonder if she was being a coward. Carabosso was a chance to find Evariste, and that's all she had wanted for the past five years.

But she was smart enough to know that her abilities didn't lie with information extraction—or rather she couldn't stomach the kinds of spells and charms that would be used on Carabosso to get him to talk.

We have him, she thought. *He's not going anywhere. And there are better uses of my time. Winter isn't too far off, and Odette will make a delivery to the elves then.*

"Unfortunately, I have other duties that I must see to that make me unavailable for the journey. Sorry." She used an apologetic smile, but it was a bit hard to keep up the farce when she could see Blanche's relief—though the war mages looked a little disappointed.

"I perfectly understand," Blanche said.

Rein, surprisingly, frowned a little. "That's unfortunate—your particular core magic would be a great reassurance, but it seems it can't be helped."

The conversation died, leaving an awkward silence.

"Shall I take you to see the prisoner?" Donaigh asked.

"Yes, please," Blanche said.

"I ought to come as well, then," Firra sighed.

"You just can't stand to be parted from me, sister," Donaigh laughed.

"You've found me out, brother." Firra tugged on the brim of his hat and stepped out of the tent.

Rein followed behind them. "I didn't know you two were related."

"They're not," Blanche said dryly.

"We're siblings of the heart," Firra said.

"Which is merely a romantic way of saying you are cohorts who understand each other's humor," Blanche chuckled.

The four war mages bowed before trotting after Firra, Donaigh, and the weather mages.

As soon as they disappeared behind a large tent, Rosalinda heaved a sigh of relief. "I'm glad they came," she said. "Grandfather isn't going to like that he doesn't get to punish Carabosso, but I don't know that we're prepared to deal with his brand of darkness."

"There's something unsettling about him," Odette agreed, speaking up for the first time since they joined the mages. "Can't say I'm sorry I don't have to hang around him any longer." She rested her hands on her hips and turned to face Angelique. "I take it I am to tell Prince Severin that Carabosso is being taken to the Veneno Conclave Fortress?"

"Yes, please," Angelique said. "I'll ask my contact at the fortress to send Severin updates once the trial begins." She sighed and rubbed her temple. "I cannot wait for the magic mirrors to be finished so these endless courier messages become unnecessary."

"How long do you think it will take?"

"A few more months," Angelique said grimly. "Magic mirrors are expensive because they are difficult to create. The only reason it's even possible is because GrandMaster Craftmage Rumpelstiltskin is doing the bulk of the work."

"If you would pardon the interruption." Rosalinda took a few steps closer to them and nervously smiled. "Firra and Donaigh told me about the Summit and the effort led by Prince Severin to fight against the enemy that is stirring up trouble continent-wide."

"The Chosen, yes," Angelique said.

Rosalinda grabbed the skirts of her dress and clenched it. "Please allow me to be extremely forward—and quite possibly go against the wishes of my grandfather—and ask that Sole be included in these efforts." She hesitated. "I spoke with Carabosso a bit when he had me under control with his black spell... The Chosen have obviously been planning this, and they *want* Sole to be crippled. I cannot allow that."

Behind her, Delanna smiled with pride, as did Sir Isaia. (The other two Legendary Knights started to nod but awkwardly changed into a shrug and a fidget when they realized what they were doing.)

"Severin will be pleased to hear from you." Angelique met Odette's gaze. "You don't mind passing that message along as well?"

"Nah," Odette said. "This will be an easy run. As long as no overly zealous forester tries to shoot us down, that is."

Rosalinda's eyes bulged. "Has that actually happened?"

"There have been a few close calls," Odette said. "But if you'll excuse us, Misha, Nadia, and I ought to head out. There's still plenty of the afternoon left, so I'd like to get a start on the trip."

"Of course," Angelique said. "Thank you, Odette."

"Yes, thank you, Swan Queen Odette," Rosalinda said.

Odette rolled her eyes at the title but gave the princess a slight bow and a quick smile before she strode off.

"I imagine you will leave today, Angelique?" Rosalinda asked.

"Yes," Angelique said.

She paused, deliberating for a few moments. *I intend to travel to Farset before Odette and Severin join me there, but if I leave now, I'll be months early. Are there any other loose ends I could attend to in the meantime?*

After a moment, a plan came to her. "I'm headed off to Farset," she announced. "Riding Pegasus, I'll get a fair distance in a few hours."

She relaxed a little, pleased with her decision. She would return to Tylis to ask the smuggling sisters Neely and Farraige if they had heard any news of the mage that had attacked her in Zancara. As an added bonus, given their occupation, she'd see if they knew anything of Foedus while she was at it. *It doesn't hurt that meeting with them will give me an excuse* not *to face King Giuseppe again.*

"I cannot thank you enough for all you have done—both for my country and for me," Rosalinda said.

Angelique smiled. "It was my honor—I am glad to know that the boon I gave you when you were a babe in a cradle has helped you. Though I am sorry this all turned into such a mess."

Rosalinda shrugged in a very un-princess-like manner. "I don't know that it could have been any different—though I do wish I could figure out *what* has happened to my grandfather. When I lived as a peasant, he was a very good king. And now..."

"He has always been very concerned for you, Princess Rosalinda," Angelique gently said. "And fear causes people to make impulsive and often unwise decisions."

Rosalinda slightly pursed her lips. "I suppose," she said. "Regardless, we owe you a great debt of gratitude. Thank you—and please, I must insist that you call me Briar Rose—or just Briar."

"Very well, Briar. I wish you luck with your return."

"Thank you," Rosalinda said glumly. "I rather think I will need it."

"Everything will be fine, Your Highness," the Legendary Knight of the Lance said.

"It will be," Rosalinda agreed. Though she smiled, there was steely determination in her eyes.

King Giuseppe doesn't know what he's getting into, Angelique thought. *Serves him right. Can't say I'm at all sorry that Rosalinda—that is, Briar—doesn't toe the line with him. I don't really enjoy getting shouted at whenever I come to help.*

"Take care, Angelique, and safe travels," Rosalinda said.

"You as well, Briar." Angelique started to curtsey but was surprised when Rosalinda instead threw her arms around her in a quick embrace.

They parted with smiles, and Angelique headed to the inn one last time—intending to inform the other mages of her departure.

Things will change, she dared to hope. *Catching Carabosso is the exact sort of leverage we need. Now we'll finally have an edge—even if we have a lot of clean up to do.*

CHAPTER 30

"So you haven't heard of it at all?" Angelique asked.

"I'm 'fraid to say it, but nope." Neely shook her head as she walked shoulder-to-shoulder with Angelique through the city of Tylis. "Of course, I haven't come across many artifacts in my business. But I do know a few smugglers who specialize in 'em. Have you heard of the Black Swan Smugglers?"

"Yes, actually," Angelique said. "I've interacted with them quite a bit."

"Odette's crew are the most famous for sticking their thumb in the magic pie," Neely said. "They've got all sorts of unusual customers—rumor has it they've even done a few jobs for the Verglas Assassins' Guild." Neely shuddered openly.

So the Black Swan Smugglers have served elves and *assassins. That is quite the clientele.* "I have talked to them about Foedus, but they didn't know anything about it, either." Angelique ducked under a low branch of a tree that had claimed a spot for itself in the middle of the street—though traffic parted effortlessly around it.

"Given its ancient history, finding it is going to be difficult," Angelique continued. "There's a good chance it's been lost in history."

"Farraige and I will keep our ears open," Neely said. "If we hear anything, we'll send word."

"Thank you." Angelique hesitated to ask her next question as they turned a corner and wove through a residential street, forcing them to dodge clothes lines, laughing children, and a fox that followed traffic patterns as it trotted down the street. "Have you heard anything more of the mage that followed me into Zancara?"

Neely scowled. "He must have magicked himself in somehow—everyone swears they've never taken a living soul to Zancara. Farraige and I are the only two with that distinction."

Angelique sighed. "Thank you for asking."

"Of course." Neely stopped when they reached an intersection and nodded to the city gates—which crouched at the end of the perpendicular street. "You're leaving?"

"Yes," Angelique said reluctantly. "I have no other business here."

Given that I was able to speak to Neely faster than expected, it's still weeks before Odette and her crew will meet with the elves. I suppose I could reconnect with Severin and Elle—they should receive news from Clovicus soon about Carabosso's questioning.

"Then I wish you luck in finding this magical dagger," Neely said. "And I must take my leave here."

"Thank you, Neely," Angelique said.

Neely bowed. "It's always my honor, Lady Enchantress." She winked, then disappeared into the swirl of the crowd.

Angelique exited Tylis through the gates—pausing to give the soldiers guarding the entrance a properly generous smile.

She followed the broad dirt road into the forest that sprouted just outside the city, a smile fixed on her face as she passed the farmers with loaded wagons, merchants, soldiers, and others who made their way down the road.

I ought to call Pegasus and get a real start on my journey, except I don't rightly know where to go. Perhaps I ought to travel down to Torrens and check on Evariste's house. I could stop in Ciane and see how King Giuseppe has reacted—the fastest route to Torrens would be to pass through Sole anyway.

It felt good to walk. In the rare weeks there wasn't an emergency, Angelique still tried to train in the mornings, but she had slipped a bit since her years with Evariste and Puss badgering her.

Half an hour passed, and through the brilliantly colored forest canopy, Angelique could see gray clouds forming. She had long ago stopped seeing other travelers as the road had split multiple times, and she had consistently taken the smallest road that cut deeper into the woods rather than the more-traveled roads that ventured out to farmland and other nearby villages.

Looks like rain is rolling in. I should probably make haste.

She had just decided to call down Pegasus when she rounded a bend in the road, revealing crumpled bodies.

Angelique ran to them, her magic already activating in her worry. She crouched by the closest body, relieved to see that his chest moved as he breathed, but his eyes were shut.

He—and his unconscious companions—all bore wounds. It appeared to be dagger and sword stab wounds, but it was tough to know for certain.

During her investigation, Angelique realized the group of five —three women and two men—was a band of Farset soldiers.

Given that forests occupied most of Farset, the uniform for soldiers was rather unique in comparison to other countries. Soldiers were dressed in muted greens with leather boots. Every warrior had a bow and a belt quiver and was equipped with a few hunting knives and a short sword.

Their uniform was designed to blend in with the forest, and soldiers received special training from the elves themselves so they best knew how to fight amongst trees.

Farset also emphasizes teamwork, which makes taking out an entire band a difficult thing. So what got them? It couldn't be a troll or a wraith. The soldiers have stab wounds; they weren't savaged. But goblins wouldn't leave them merely unconscious, so...thieves? But they still have all their weapons.

Goosebumps broke out on Angelique's skin. The silence of the forest was oppressive—not even a bird dared to sing or chirp. But what made her most nervous was the way her magic gushed around her in a bigger and bigger spiral, searching for whatever threat was near.

She could physically *feel* someone watching her like a dagger in her spine.

I can't let on that I know.

The pitter-patter of raindrops falling on leaves filled the air. Angelique forced herself to place a healing spell on each soldier, attending to them as if she didn't feel anything wrong.

She tugged them over to the side of the road and flashed her magic a bit more in a few more healing spells as she swallowed, her mouth dry from the anxiety of being *hunted*. The rain finally slipped past the forest canopy, and a few drops spattered Angelique's shoulders. She shivered—the water was icy cold in the fall air.

A branch cracked, but she didn't react.

I need to time this perfectly.

She stood and started to move as if she planned to inspect the next soldier, but abruptly thrust her arm up in the sky. "Pegasus! It—"

A dagger was chucked at Angelique. She threw up the shield spell she had prepared as soon as she saw the fallen soldiers, catching the thrown weapon. The dagger was obsidian black—it didn't even gleam in the dim light of the forest.

That looks like—

An axe went hurtling over her head, missing her completely. Angelique threw more magic into her shield before she realized she was not the intended target. The weapon tore horizontally through the trunk of a tree just behind her. The tree groaned and toppled, falling in her direction.

Angelique leaped out of the way, then realized with a strangled gasp that the thick tree trunk would fall on top of the unconscious soldiers and crush them.

She dashed forward, spinning her magic into a wind spell. Releasing it made the tree bend back the opposite way. She threw more magic into the spell, relaxing only when the tree fell into the woods and not out on the road.

"It seems I won't have a problem proving my mother wrong."

Angelique whirled around, her magic blazing to life when she saw the familiar man standing on the road across from her.

It was the black mage who had attacked her in Zancara—the one who had spoken of Evariste.

He leaned against a tree, his glossy hair perfectly in place as his red eyes glowed in the shadows of the forest. When she met his gaze, he smirked—an expression that underlined his handsome features and made them cruel.

"I knew that even if you could stop me, I could still find a way to beat you." He pushed off his tree and strolled across the dirt road. A careless gesture at the soldiers and a head tilt expressed his bottomless confidence. "And it seems I have."

Oh, blast—no! Angelique loosened the magic she'd been hoarding up since she saw the mage.

A gust of wind blew dust and grit into his eyes, and a tree groaned as its branches swooped low and narrowly missed whacking him in the back of the head. Angelique threw a dagger-sharp shard of ice at him, but an iridescent green shield sprouted into place, protecting him just as it had during their first encounter.

Undeterred, Angelique moved the ground beneath his feet, turning it into mud, then flash-freezing it with ice. As he fumbled to stand, she threw a fireball at him—which was again stopped by his shield charm.

A twist of her hand, and water dumped over him in a thick

waterfall. When it hit his shield, she dropped its temperature, turning the water into an ice glaze that encased the shield.

She could barely make out the black mage's swearing above the racket she raised. She shook off the few raindrops that had hit her and glanced at the sky as the rain picked up from a light trickle to a downpour.

Is this his doing?

She felt the unpleasant whisper of his magic. *Nope. But that is.*

She whirled around, looking for more shadowy weapons, then spotted the black arrows hovering over the soldiers. "No, no, no!"

She raised a magic shield over the fallen soldiers just in time to block the storm of arrows. Her magic tugged at her senses, drifting longingly toward the black arrows.

Angelique savagely yanked her powers back and crafted her next spell. *His charm will block a physical blow, but what about something intangible?*

The spell weave was a tricky one, but Angelique finished just as the black mage crafted a massive lance out of shadows. She lobbed the spell at him, then reached out with her magic and used tree branches to snatch up the lance midair. Using the trees made them drop a bucketful of rainwater on her, plastering her hair to her skull and shocking her with the cold even though the charms on her dress kept her skirts dry.

"Hah," the black mage laughed when Angelique's spell hit his face. "You still think some low-level sleep charm will work on *me*?"

"Not a sleep spell," Angelique spat through gritted teeth as she wrestled to hold the lance back.

"What—" He sneezed before he could finish his words, then scowled. "You—" More sneezes cut him off.

Channeling her magic, Angelique pulled down the branches that cradled the shadow lance so low that the trees creaked and groaned, then she abruptly released them. The trees snapped upright, catapulting the lance far away.

Behind her, the black mage rapidly sneezed five times in short succession. "Blast it!" He popped open a corked vial and chugged it, then tossed it aside so the vial shattered on the road—which was starting to turn soft in the rain. "A sneezing spell? That's childish."

"But effective." Angelique considered tossing up a spell to shield her from the rain before realizing she didn't have the capacity to attack *and* defend *and* block out the rain. If she used her core magic rather than twisting it into separate spells she could, but she wasn't going to cross that line.

She ignored her magic as it screamed at her and instead automatically threw up a shield.

The black club, however, hit her from behind, cracking her in the skull.

Angelique saw stars and fell to her knees, splashing mud everywhere. She tried to breathe but heard the squelching of the mage stalking closer, so she blindly shoved her fingers into the muck and shook the ground beneath his feet with a rapidly formed spell.

He swore and slipped, giving Angelique enough time to throw a healing spell on herself and stand. She staggered but was already twisting her magic in a new spell, which she tossed at him.

In midair, the spell clicked, turning into a spattering of yellow-green acidic liquid—heavily inspired by her tussle with the wyvern.

The black mage dodged the attack and zipped past her, using his shadows to form a scythe.

Angelique fumbled to strengthen the shield protecting the soldiers.

The scythe made a jarring, cracking noise when it collided with the defensive spell and broke into tiny—*sharpened*—shards that dug into the shield. One piece actually managed to partially lodge through it.

Angelique's heart pounded as she yanked up her skirts and delivered a brutal kick to the black mage's gut. *His charm blocks physical magic attacks, but not purely physical assaults. And the sneezing spell got through just fine as well. Maybe that's why it's so strong—because it has a limit.*

He bent over, wheezing in pain, but when she tried to jab him in the throat—her hand laced with electricity—he blocked her with his forearm and threw a saber at the soldiers' cracking shield.

Angelique retreated to strengthen the spell but threw a wad of ice as a parting shot—which, of course, his shield blocked.

She was at her limit in terms of twisting and slinging spells. She couldn't go any faster than this, and unfortunately, he was right about the soldiers—she had to protect them in addition to dodging his attacks herself.

She impatiently pushed her sopping hair out of her face. *I can't focus enough on attacking. Do I grab the soldiers and retreat?* The thought was bitter as bile in her mouth. *But he obviously knows where Evariste is! I can't just retreat! Maybe I can put a tracking spell on him?*

Angelique eyed him and tried to mentally sift through the potential charms she could make, but the mage shot off slender black pins with enough force to drive them into a tree. She threw her magic in a large shield—protecting herself and the soldiers.

Again, her core powers tugged at her as they brushed her senses and longed to be used. (It wasn't quite so tempting now; rather, it was almost painful—like stubbing her toe or stepping on a rock with a bare foot.) She shook off the feeling and started twisting her magic.

She noticed the black mage was smirking, so she glanced around, looking for more of his weapons.

Polearms topped with spears and thin, crescent-shaped side blades jutted out of the ground.

Angelique tapped her magic and dredged up rocks from deep within the ground underneath the soldiers. The rocks surfaced in a pile, raising the fallen warriors above the ground, cracking the road and moving them out of reach. She simultaneously turned the sloppy, wet ground beneath the polearms into a sort of quicksand mixture that sucked them under.

The icy cold rain was starting to get to her. It was extreme and persistent enough it was starting to make the charms on her dress fail. Her teeth chattered, and she was having a hard time feeling the magic at her fingertips as her extremities numbed. *I need to do something, fast.*

The black mage narrowed his eyes and studied her. "Why don't you use your core magic?" He waved his hand at the broken earth that marked out their battlefield. "You could have stopped my weapons with your war magic, but instead, you scurry around like an insect. All of this is child's play compared to the power you have in your core magic. Enchantress or not, your core magic will *always* be more potent and powerful."

"I don't need it to fight you!" Angelique snarled. Gathering her magic, she threw a blazing flare of light at him, hoping to blind him.

Unfortunately, he ducked and shielded his eyes as the light sailed over his head, then popped back upright. "I get it." The red light of his eyes was almost maniacal now. "You don't *want* to use your core magic." He laughed so hard he actually bent over and slapped his thighs. "After everything you've been put through, you're still standing...but you regulate yourself so you're only at a fraction of your strength? That's hilarious!"

Angelique struggled to swallow as her magic buzzed at her fingertips. "I don't know what you're talking about." She tapped one of the magic disciplines she rarely used—music—and mimicked the sound of a cathedral bell tolling directly above his head.

He staggered at the noise and cursed, but his dratted shield charm held up when she batted at him with a tree trunk.

I have got to get that charm off him if I hope to take him. And I have to take him. I can't forge a strong tracking spell that would be subtle enough to escape his notice—it would be too intricate to make while trying to both attack him and protect the soldiers.

"But you do." His smirk was back again. "You're not curled up in a corner like Mother and the others thought you would be after the brutal treatment you've had—not by a long shot. You're even *worse* off. You waltz around free and strong…but you won't use your powers. You've willingly neutralized the strongest weapon you have at your disposal." He laughed and shook his head. "Everything would be so much easier for you if you just *used* your magic, but you're such an idiot, you won't! Instead, you'll let your own master sacrifice his life for yours."

Angelique staggered as if he had physically hit her. (If he had, it probably would have hurt less than to hear the truth.)

He's right. I've known it from the start—if I had been faster, Evariste wouldn't have been caught. Even though Dream Evariste insisted it wasn't my fault, it was.

"But that's not going to be a worry for you much longer." He extended an arm and pointed to Angelique. Shadows withered around him, forming hundreds of black hiltless daggers. "Because I'm going to kill you and prove once again that I'm powerful. Though, it's not nearly as impressive now that I know you're an idiot. In fact, I can't believe you bested me the first time."

Angelique put an iridescent shield in place and grimly held her ground, but he didn't appear at all bothered by the prospect.

Instead, he bared his teeth in a feral grin. "And it's going to be *such* fun when I tell your master that I slayed his precious student and that your blood dripped from my hands. It will *kill* him."

Evariste.

Rain spattered Angelique's face, a shockingly cold sensation.

It won't matter if I did my duty like a good apprentice or if I helped a thousand people if I can't find the one person who offered me friendship.

Numbness crawled up her legs as the beautiful fabric of her dress grew even more drenched in the downpour.

I'm scared. Of what I'm capable of. Of what I've done. The steady thump of her heart filled her ears, and she stared unseeingly at the mage. *And I'm sick of losing those closest to me.* The thought made her pause. *My parents are gone...but Evariste isn't. He's still alive. This mage just said he would speak to Evariste. He's out there somewhere. I can still find him. Just how much is that worth?*

"Done fighting?" he sneered. "Wise decision. You look like a bug struggling for life."

"Five years," Angelique said abruptly.

He squinted at her. "What?"

"You've had Evariste for five years. I'm going to get him back."

The war mage scoffed as he forged another batch of daggers out of shadows. "You're not in a position to say that." He nodded at the soldiers, where black swords hovered directly above them.

Angelique raised her gaze and felt the moment her illusion that colored her eyes evaporated. "And I'm not going to let you escape, either."

"Turning your back on those in need after all your high-and-mighty words?" he laughed. "It seems you've finally cracked."

"No," Angelique said.

He finally met her steady gaze. The muscles at the corner of his mouth twitched, and he stood taller. "Haughty words from..." He trailed off as he tried to pull his weapons back, but they didn't budge.

Angelique felt her magic drift restlessly like fog as it held his swords and daggers anchored in the air. She tilted her head back and studied the war mage, her eyes at half-mast. "For Evariste," she said, her voice just above a quiet whisper.

The war mage scoffed. "As if you could—"

Angelique released her war magic, flooding the area with silver light. Its release stirred up a wind and pushed the trees back.

The shattered glass of the broken vial and the soldier's weapons rose into the air. Angelique felt her magic surround every individual shadow weapon. The war mage's angry magic spit black sparks that burned at her senses.

A nudge to her powers made them slide tighter around the weapons. Then, like a dragon devouring its prey, it clamped down on the weapons, swallowing the foreign magic.

Angelique smiled as she felt all the shadow weapons—from the polearms in the ground to the needles protruding from the shield she still had in place over the soldiers—fall under her control.

Slowly, they floated higher and higher in the air, but Angelique's magic wasn't done. It skulked around the war mage, drawing closer and closer to him.

He took a few staggering steps through the mud, his eyes wide with panic as he forged another saber from the shadows and pointed to Angelique.

The saber didn't even get a chance to move. Angelique's magic pounced on it, taking control so it floated with the other weapons.

The way the world looked *changed*. Everything grew a silvery overtone, and she could feel so much more. In fact, she could even see his magic clustering at the palms of his hands.

She was also vaguely aware of her war magic.

Freed, it invaded the forest, flowing outward and leaving Angelique at the epicenter. Soon, she could feel rusted weapons, branches with sharpened or pointed edges—anything and everything with a sharpened edge that had been left in the forest.

It was *enthralling*.

"No!" the war mage shouted, drawing Angelique's attention back to the clearing.

Angelique shifted her gaze to him, and all of his shadow weapons, the soldiers' weapons, and everything under her control shifted to get a clear shot at the panicking black mage.

Silvery strands of her raw war magic twined around him, slithering toward his hands.

He tried to create more shadow weapons, but before he could

even finish making them, Angelique's magic snatched them up, drawing them under her control.

When he started to create a bow and arrow, her magic latched onto his hands—bright and unforgiving. As she watched, her magic *devoured* his. It didn't overpower or push back…it floated over it, swallowing it whole.

Angelique thoughtfully watched as he screamed, and her magic slowly crept up his body. His legs were stuck, trapped under the swamp of her power.

His hands were clumsy as he fumbled with a pouch at his waist. Her stardust magic covered his fingers as he plucked a black gem from the pouch. He dropped it and shouted something.

A portal sprang to life—this one was gold with creamy white marble. The blue fire inside it flickered before displaying a vision of golden dunes.

Baris.

Between the heady feeling her magic produced and the thrill of feeling *fully* free, it took Angelique a moment to realize what was happening. "No!" she shouted.

The war mage flung himself through the portal with a grunt. The portal snapped shut behind him.

He'd gotten away. Again.

"NO!" Everything in her control launched at the spot where he had stood, savagely stabbing the ground. She screamed—half-enraged, half-broken-hearted. "Not again!" She grabbed the sides of her head and howled in the rain.

Charged by her rage, her magic built—and that was when she snapped out of it.

Through the silvery sheen of her magic, she saw the lances and sabers shoved hilt-deep into the ground, the arrows that had been so ruthlessly shot into the ground they had snapped in half, and the ugly claw marks left by the glass Angelique had taken control of.

She swallowed, almost choking herself, and finally realized dimly: the war mage hadn't been afraid she was about to capture him...he thought her magic was going to eat him alive.

And in that moment, Angelique wasn't certain she *wasn't* capable of such a thing.

Her stomach rolled, and this time when she wretched, it had nothing to do with the price of her magic and more with self-loathing at the disgusting realization.

The Council, her Instructors—everyone was right about her.

She wasn't just dangerous; she was a monster.

PAIN HAD BECOME Evariste's world. Not red-hot stabs of a mortal wound, but rather a cold, endless pain that made every joint ache and wore away at his mind.

He was being drained every moment that passed. The mirror was pulling on his magic and using it to power itself. But instead of getting his magic yanked from him in the painful episodes Liliane had implemented, it was a slow, constant, and torturous pull.

It was a wound that wouldn't heal, a constant bite that ate away until all he could do was breathe and stare into the dark void of the mirror.

Everything was cold—not like frost and snow but rather the cold of a black cavern with no end in sight.

Sometimes he could see glances out of the mirror into the bedroom it was positioned in. He tried to puzzle out what country he was in—mostly to serve as a distraction from the constant pain, but his only clues were the room, which wasn't much to go by. The floor was tiled with a priceless pink rock, and the frame of the canopy bed was richly decorated with sparkling jewels and ornate goldwork.

However, Evariste was willing to bet it was a northern country based on the thick, crushed-velvet material that formed the bed's canopy and the plush rugs laid on the ground.

He tried to escape, tried to learn anything he could about his surroundings, but the mirror was an unforgiving prison.

Time had passed—he wasn't sure how much due to being unable to see much more than haze—and as the pain wore away at him and the endless *whisperings* never ceased, he collapsed.

He couldn't sleep with the mirror whispering hateful words to him, and the few times he did, his dreams were inescapable nightmares.

I think...I'm dying.

It was a grim thought, but it was almost comforting. The pain was too much. He had no memories to fortify him. His escape attempts had already failed. There was *nothing*.

The faint click of shoes on tile drew Evariste's attention. Some of the haze covering the front of the mirror had decreased a little. He could make out the faint shapes of the bedroom furniture, but it was the form of a human that made him scramble to his feet despite the pain.

A young lady with silky black hair and lively blue eyes peered into the depths of the mirror. Her eyebrows furrowed slightly as she stared at the mirror, and she took a step closer.

Does she see me?

Evariste's breath was ragged at the thought. "Hello?"

She tilted her head, then pulled the cuff of her long-sleeved dress up over her hand and scrubbed at the mirror, roughly where Evariste's face was. Once finished, she squinted and didn't look any less perplexed.

"Can you hear me?" He ignored the putrid whispers of the mirror and tried to take a step closer, but found he couldn't. "My name is Evariste—I'm a Lord Enchanter. Send word to Enchantress-in-Training Angelique—"

"Snow White?" a woman called out of Evariste's vision. "Are you ready for the meeting with the Cabinet?"

"Yes, Stepmother." Snow White turned and glided away, though she paused at the very edge of Evariste's view. "Stepmother, do you remember who gave this mirror to you?"

"I'm afraid not, dear. Was it your father before he passed away?" asked the second, unseen female.

Snow White shook her head and started walking again, this time disappearing entirely. "No, for I know you received it during the first birthday celebration you had after he died." The young lady's voice faded as she walked farther away, but whether she knew it or not, she had given Evariste a shred of hope.

Snow White was the oddly-named princess—and sole heir—of Mullberg. And Mullberg was the home of the Veneno Conclave.

Evariste doubted the Conclave would find him...but Angelique might.

Surely it will be easier for her to locate me in a country—much less a palace—than whatever forsaken place the Chosen's cavern was. Right?

He sank to the ground again when the pain became too much and glanced at the cracked corner of the mirror.

I just have to hope she can push through the haze and find me...even if I'm sitting in the very mirror that the Snow Queen unsuccessfully tried to obliterate.

But this is Angelique. She has the strength—if only she'll use it!

ACRI PANTED. His sweat made his hair stick to his skull. His heart thundered in his throat, and even though he was now half a continent away, everything in him screamed to run.

Angelique hadn't just stopped his shadow weapons...her magic had *devoured* his.

It was impossible. It was unheard of.

She should only be able to wrestle control from him or maybe overpower him. But she hadn't.

No, instead her magic had nearly eaten him alive. And in

those moments when he was in its thrall, he felt the bottomless abyss that was her magic, and he *knew* she was capable of great and terrible things.

What was, perhaps, the most terrible part was that Angelique didn't know just how powerful she was.

She's a monster!

Acri shivered and sank lower in the golden sands of Baris—cold despite the heat of the desert. In that moment, he feared her—more than he feared his mother's cruel love, more than he even feared the creepy mirror she had dumped Evariste in.

Because it was *impossible* for a person to be able to channel that kind of power and not crack. No human was valiant enough to be able to stand against such a tidal wave and survive.

And if she breaks...she might take us all with her.

The End

A CONSTELLATION'S DILEMMA

Pegasus, equine of the sky, bearer of the Luck Star, whose hooves had crossed skies older than most realms...was stuck.

As had been his custom since the air turned cool in certain lands, Pegasus had left his spot in the heavens to investigate a certain pumpkin patch. It pleased him to inspect the bright orange squash which reminded him of growing stars. The scent of the dirt and growing things was pleasant, and the emerald green of the vines was not a color he often saw in his realm.

But.

Today the green vines did *not* please him, for they had wrapped around his legs, and despite his legendary strength, he hadn't been able to yank free.

He lowered his muzzle and sniffed the vines that had crept around his hooves and legs. The faint metallic whiff of gold filled his nostrils. He eyed the vines, finally spotting the faint, glittering lines that spiraled through each leaf like a vein.

Gold.

He snapped his head back and snorted, outrage and fury making his stars burn brighter. Already knowing the outcome, Pegasus again tried to charge free. The vines held, making him stumble. He would have pitched sideways and fallen if he hadn't maneuvered his wings to counterbalance.

The roaring fires of his powers still burned, but it was separated from him, as if someone had cut them from him.

Because they had. A mortal must have noticed his frequent trips to the pumpkin patch and had fashioned this trap for him—a very *stupid* mortal who clearly didn't understand his or her limits.

As a constellation, Pegasus had great powers, near immortality, and could make and destroy nations. His only weakness...was gold.

It had the ability to cut him off from the powers his stars gave him, and it could capture him—he couldn't break free of anything veined, lined, or forged with real gold.

It could not, however, control him.

It could not keep him from bucking a mortal off and cracking their spine. It could not keep him from plotting their death.

Who, after all, was so proud they thought they could own the stars? An idiot, that's who.

He tried to paw his front left hoof, but the gold-threaded vines held fast.

The patch grew unnaturally dark as his rage built, and he flapped his massive black wings. The heavens rumbled, but, cut off from magic as he was, he could do nothing but protest.

Pegasus was the horse of the heavens. He was not meant to be contained, and he would *not* bow to some arrogant mortal who thought he could be captured!

He sneered at the sky and tossed his neck, the situation rankling him more by the moment.

Begrudgingly, Pegasus was forced to admit that he was perhaps also angry because Ursa the bear had sent whispers through the galaxies that someone was trying to trap the constellations.

It was a warning he had ignored. With good reason—Ursa was

the most dim-witted constellation Pegasus knew. A trap made for the bear would *never* be clever enough to hold him.

When Pegasus freed himself, he was going to be the laughingstock of the stars for the next century—and that was only if he was able to swiftly kill whatever individual had planted this trap for him. If the mortal was smarter than he estimated, he may be stuck in service for decades.

Pegasus flicked his flaming tail and was able to pull against the gold-veined vines just enough to kick a small, unripe pumpkin.

He snorted at the next closest pumpkin—a hulking monstrosity that was as large as he was. The enormous squash was not unusually sized, for this was a giant's pumpkin patch—and *no*, it was not a giant who had done this. (Giants made Ursa the bear look brilliant.)

Pegasus pinned his ears at the pumpkin and considered trumpeting his anger.

The vines slowly climbed higher up his legs, curling so high they started to slither across his belly, reminding him of the embarrassing and frustrating severity of his situation.

There was the hum of magic, and Pegasus turned his head toward it.

A door of light bloomed at the edge of the pumpkin patch. It started as a rectangle of pure golden light, until blue magic swaddled it, solidifying the edges into weather-worn stone veined with precious metals and gems.

The inside of the magic door blazed for a few moments longer, crackling like flames, before the blue magic turned into flames and ate the light away, granting Pegasus a look inside, into a realm of red and gold.

A mortal fled through the magic portal—a human boy by the looks of it. The hemline of his tunic was singed, the laces of his boots were on fire, and he reeked of burnt hair.

A dragon's roar echoed from the open portal, and the human

hastily flicked his wrist, dismantling the portal just before a blast of fire escaped through it.

The boy heaved a sigh of relief and leaned against a giant pumpkin. "Master Clovicus is going to box my ears for that jump." He wiped sweat and ash from his forehead, then ruefully inspected his tunic. "That's if he doesn't kill me for ruining my clothes."

On closer inspection, Pegasus could see that the scorched human was not actually a child—nor was he a man. He was in that gawky, gangly stage—all legs and limbs and very little control or sense.

And yet, he could walk through realms, judging by his powers. That sort of magic was rare and potent. And luck had bequeathed it to a sneezing man-child who kept wiping his nose off on his sleeve.

Figures.

Pegasus danced in place—or attempted to—when he felt one of the vines slide its way up his chest. He tossed his head and snorted as he tried to rip free—to no avail.

His snort must have captured the runt's attention, for the human twisted so his side leaned against his pumpkin perch, and he squinted in Pegasus' direction.

"Are you stuck, poor boy?" The human pushed off the pumpkin and started in Pegasus' direction.

Pegasus tucked his chin, then bugled—a deep sound that resonated in his chest like the beat of a thousand drums. The flames of his mane and tail flared as stars on his coat burned brighter.

The human stopped so fast he tripped over his own feet and fell with a gasp. "Y-y-you're a constellation." Still on the ground, he scrambled back in the direction from which he'd come, stopping only when he rammed into a giant pumpkin.

He stared at Pegasus with bulging eyes and gulped. "You must be...Pegasus?"

If he were free, he would have kicked a pumpkin at the simpleton's guess.

There was only *one* equine of the night sky. Anyone who couldn't recognize him immediately, as far as Pegasus was concerned, was unlearned.

Pegasus tested another vine as he sneered at a pumpkin—which, as an outlet for his anger, had been upgraded from something of interest into a sworn enemy.

"I...I could get you out."

Pegasus swung his head around to stare at the perhaps-not-quite-a-simpleton.

The human rocked to his feet, his legs positioned so he could flee in an instant. "I mean...you're stuck, aren't you?"

Pegasus cocked his head.

"I can use my magic and cut you free of the vines. I'm an enchanter."

Pegasus sucked air in, making his chest puff and his nostrils turn red.

"It's true!" the mortal rushed to say. "Or almost—I'm taking my test soon!"

Pegasus considered the gangly boy and twitched his nose.

He could stay here and kill whoever had planted this trap, but it was possible that might take time if they were prepared enough —as much as it irked Pegasus to admit it.

It would mean he owed the snot-nosed brat—as a constellation he could never accept help even if it was freely offered. There was *always* a price.

But it had taken the human several moments to recognize him, which meant there was a very good chance he didn't know much about Pegasus. Besides, he called himself an enchanter. There was only one realm that commonly used that term, and constellations had not frequented it since days of yore—which meant he was even less likely to be learned in some of Pegasus' more...*potent* powers.

Pegasus huffed, for it wasn't much of a choice.

He folded his wings and dampened his power so when he spoke directly into the boy's mind, it wasn't quite so deafening. *YOUR TERMS?*

Pegasus' hopes of ignorance were realized when the boy scrunched up his face in perplexation. "Terms?" the mortal said. "What do you mean?"

WHAT DO YOU WANT IN RETURN?

"Oh, um... nothing?" He sheepishly scratched the back of his neck. "Master Clovicus is forever telling me that with my teleportation magic, I have a duty to help those in all the realms since I'm in a unique position. I don't think it's quite fair because he also endlessly lectures me that I should stay in *our* realm, but when I reminded him of that last year, he turned my hair purple for a month."

Pegasus swished his tail in frustration. It was possible the boy was an idiot *now*, but in the future, he might realize just whom he had saved and demand something then. No, it was better to settle this now. *YOUR TERMS*, he repeated.

The boy squatted down, frowning in thought. "So, you want an exchange? Must be something like craft magic."

Pegasus almost bulged his eyes that a human would compare him with his powers and domain to a mere *human* with magic, but the boy didn't notice.

"Hmm, okay, I've got it. Sometimes I can't use my portals—if it's too dangerous, it just won't work. Then I have to travel like everyone else, which I can say is *dead slow*. How about, if it's an emergency, I can call you for a ride?"

Pegasus gnashed his teeth. This brat expected him to carry him through the skies?! Forget it. He'd rather wait and kill whoever set the trap.

The boy, seemingly unaware of his anger, squinted at him. "I mean, I assume you can gallop really fast?"

Pegasus froze, his ears pricking forward despite himself.

Gallop? Did...did he mean he wanted Pegasus to carry him over land? Like a horse?

Frankly, Pegasus wasn't sure if that was insulting or not, but it was much better than flying the brat. He wouldn't fly anyone ever again; he'd vowed that long ago.

YOU WISH TO BE CARRIED ACROSS LAND, OF YOUR REALM?

"Oh, yikes, I hadn't thought of outside my realm, but you bet. I really *shouldn't* be realm-hopping. The rules of my magic are a bit different outside my realm, so I can only randomly hop realms and hope I don't land somewhere dangerous. So, yeah, staying in my realm sounds good!" The mortal smiled with the confidence of a human used to being liked.

It made Pegasus want to bite him out of principle.

But it wasn't a terrible trade. A human life—even one of magic—was a flickering candle to a constellation like Pegasus. Being ridden like a horse didn't sound appealing, but it was better than letting the rest of the constellations hear of it. Besides, no one important visited the realm of enchanters and mages—actually, it might be interesting to occasionally tour it.

And, if the boy turned out to be a real brat, he could "accidentally" kill him.

Pegasus exhaled deeply. *I ACCEPT.*

The boy hopped to his feet and approached Pegasus at a trot, pulling a dagger from his ash-streaked belt. "Great. I'll get you out in a jiffy. Do you mind telling me where we are?"

YES.

"Oh, right, then. I'm Evariste, by the way."

I DON'T CARE.

"Nice to meet you, too!"

EVARISTE DID GROW up to learn more about Pegasus—or rather

he most likely researched him—after the first time he got a ride to a destination that should have taken almost a full day in less than an hour.

Thankfully, the snot-nosed mortal turned into a decent-enough adult, for he rarely ever summoned Pegasus, and usually only did so in emergencies. (Or what passed for an emergency to mere humans.) And his realm was interesting enough—though Pegasus no longer frequented pumpkin patches, even when they were in season.

Yes, Pegasus would never call himself *fond* of the Lord Enchanter, but he didn't ponder killing him anymore. However, Evariste managed to surprise him when Evariste summoned him just outside the elves' Alabaster Forest.

"Pegasus!" Evariste called with a smile that was too eager. "It is so good to see you again. I'd like a ride to my home in Wistful Thicket in Torrens, please."

Pegasus arched his neck and studied the enchanter, trying to discern what had him so happy.

Eventually he decided it wasn't worth the effort. *FINE.*

"Wonderful, thank you." Evariste bowed his head with proper respect. "I have another passenger I'd like you to carry—she's my apprentice, actually. Please allow me to introduce you. Angelique!"

Pegasus blinked at the news—Evariste had never called him before while toting along a traveling companion—but the mystery of the enchanter's good mood was solved when said traveling companion stepped out from behind a tree.

He supposed she was beautiful for a human, and though she smiled sunnily like her teacher, Pegasus could see there was a haunted look in her eyes, and there was something about her smile...

Evariste grinned at him. "Pegasus, this is my apprentice, Angelique." He looked down at her, his smile softening considerably. "Angelique, make your greetings."

"Good day to you, Pegasus." The apprentice spoke in a husky but soothing tone that didn't falter as she met his gaze.

Curious, Pegasus snorted and tossed his head.

She curtsied but didn't shrink back in fear, nor did her expression change.

That's what it was—her expression was pleasant enough, but it was clearly practiced. Not many could hold his gaze without flinching. That she had, said much about her—potentially.

He extended his neck, maneuvering his muzzle close enough to her face to get a good whiff.

There. She didn't smell false, even though she had a flavor of power to her. But that meant she'd been forced to endure a lot to learn how to keep up such cheerful stoicism.

Pegasus glanced at Evariste—who had an idiotic look of affection on his face.

Ah.

Pegasus had lived long enough to recognize the stirrings of love. It wasn't anywhere near to flowering right now. But given it was Evariste-the-simpleton and a female mage of power that was perhaps greater than Evariste's, it was only a matter of time.

Which meant Evariste had probably summoned Pegasus for the girl's sake.

When Evariste looked at him and renewed their eye contact with a tangible undercurrent of joy, Pegasus' suspicions were confirmed.

Very well. An extra person didn't matter to Pegasus. But Evariste looked like he was ready to settle in for a chat, which *did* matter. So, Pegasus turned his rear to the enchanter without speaking and moved across the clearing.

"How perfect," Evariste said in his annoyingly-bright voice. "Pegasus approves!"

"*That* is what his approval looks like?" the apprentice said, clearly stunned.

"Oh, yes," Evariste nodded. "If he hadn't liked you, he probably would have broken one of your limbs."

Pegasus supposed Evariste might be a stupid twit for the possibility of love, but at least he had grown more intelligent as he aged—which was more than could be said for the majority of mortals.

But if the Lord Enchanter thought Pegasus was going to prance sedately across the lands like a good pony, he was sadly mistaken.

Besides, it would be good to see just how much courage the student had. Yes, Torrens was no small distance from the elves' forest, but Pegasus would make it a *short* trip.

PEGASUS FLEXED his wings in the soothing silence of the sky realm. It was mostly dark, except for the soft glow of neighboring stars and the glittering dust of galaxies.

He settled his legs—or rather, the stars that made up *him* moved into proper alignment, for in his home, he didn't need to confine himself to the body most realms required—and flicked his tail, sending an asteroid off on a careening path.

Then, he heard it.

"Pegasus! It is I—"

Ah, Evariste. He would—

"Enchantress-in-Training Angelique, student of Lord Enchanter Evariste of the Fire Gates."

Pegasus paused in surprised. *Angelique?* That was Evariste's apprentice, wasn't it? Why was she calling?

"I summon you from the skies to carry me across the lands. Come!"

Pegasus considered not answering. He owed the apprentice nothing. But the apprentice—in their limited meetings—had never struck him as a fool, and it seemed unlikely she would call on a whim.

Very well. He'd answer. It didn't mean he would help, but he wished to see what she wanted.

He pawed a hoof, igniting his powers and making his stars blaze. Once he had gathered all of his constellation close, he stretched out his wings and leaped into Evariste's realm, settling into a corporal form during the shift.

He emerged into a blue sky and spotted the apprentice on the ground, surrounded by a crowd of people. He shed the feathers of his wings as he dropped, but he did not go so far as to soften the crash that shook the ground when his hooves touched the dusty road.

His power crackled, eating up the dirt so he made a small crater when he fully landed, his stars burning the ground.

A glance at the apprentice confirmed she looked pale but grimly determined. So, for the showmanship of it, Pegasus reared up and trumpeted loudly. (It greatly satisfied him the way the mortals rapidly backed up and gaped at him in awe and fear.)

The apprentice spoke with another mortal and awkwardly held a saddlebag before she fully turned her attention to him.

Smugly, Pegasus pawed at the ground, creating a thundercrack.

The apprentice visibly swallowed but cautiously approached him. "I know I'm not Lord Enchanter Evariste." Her voice was grim and resigned—what happened to the cheerful act she usually put on? "But I'm desperate enough that I'll try to make you yield as you do for him. Now will you test me, or shall we fly?"

It took Pegasus a moment to realize she had essentially challenged him. Foolish, stupid mortal.

He lunged at her, his powers making his stars flare.

The student thrust her arm out and shouted a spell.

Pegasus froze when he heard the rolling words of magic.

Similarly, the student clamped her mouth shut, cutting off the spell before speaking the final syllable that would set it into motion.

Did...did she just nearly cast a spell that would summon *squirrels?*

Confused, Pegasus danced backwards.

She was Evariste's apprentice. She was capable of far more than attacking squirrels. But why, then, did she challenge him?

Pegasus didn't like being puzzled, so he flicked his flaming tail in irritation and stretched his neck out, trying to work through the student's thoughts.

The student fumbled with the pack, flicking it open as she held it out. "It's for Roland." She showed the motionless black-and-white cat tucked inside.

It took Pegasus a few moments to place the feline. He'd met him when he dropped off Evariste and the apprentice on occasion. Roland was a mouthy cat capable of magic and another sign of Evariste's infatuation with the girl.

But whenever Pegasus saw the apprentice with the big-mouthed cat, the light in her eyes turned brighter. The animal was important to her, that much he knew.

He huffed and looked away from Evariste's hopeful apprentice.

It was official: he was growing soft in his old age...or perhaps turning senile. Grumbling in his chest, Pegasus lowered his front-half down, making it easier for the apprentice to slip on his back.

If he had known he was going to end up serving as a courier for not just Evariste, but his student as well, Pegasus would have said no out of spite the day the mortal offered to save him.

Because this was intolerable. Obviously. Completely.

She was crying again.

Seasons had passed—*years* had passed since Pegasus helped

Angelique cross into Mullberg so she could cast healing spells on Roland. She had eventually explained to him about Evariste missing and the manner in which he had been taken.

Initially Pegasus carted her across the continent more to scope out the state of the place than for any real reason—though in the privacy of the sky, he would perhaps admit he was marginally concerned for Evariste.

But somewhere along the journey, Angelique's manners had transformed from frightened reverence to something warmer and more familiar.

She kissed his muzzle, patted his neck, and leaned against him in moments of weakness.

Really, it wasn't a way a constellation should ever be treated... but Pegasus *liked* it.

And the person that made him enjoy it was crying, again.

Pegasus considered rousing her. She was sleeping, tucked against his side, her cheek pressed against his shoulder, making it so her tears trickled down into his coat. But waking her wouldn't take her sadness away.

All he could do was stay there for her. And he did. He spent most of his time in this realm now—and it seemed like the rare occasions he *did* leave, Angelique would get herself in more trouble, which made him *more* inclined to stay.

The stars in Pegasus' coat stirred.

If that war mage hadn't used Evariste's magic to escape...he would have ended him in the most painful way possible. How *dare* he attack Angelique, and—

Angelique shifted in her sleep, mashing her face in his coat.

Pegasus had to twist his head and neck awkwardly to gently press his muzzle against her hunched shoulder.

He hadn't spoken much to her. He didn't really *want to* either. Not because she wasn't worthy, but because his voice couldn't disguise his power or near limitless existence.

If Angelique knew exactly what he was capable of, he

suspected the nights of her sleeping splayed across his back, snoring loud enough to rouse nearby wildlife, would be over.

Pegasus swiveled his ears, finding the thought distasteful.

No, he'd hold back. Maybe, after enough days of treating him like a pet, Angelique wouldn't retreat from him even if she did learn of his powers. Surely a decade or two would be enough...right?

The thought made Pegasus pin his ears, ill at ease.

He wasn't certain he had two decades before she found out. Things were growing more dangerous. And while Pegasus wasn't going to extend himself on behalf of others—he couldn't really, for if he used too much power, he could collapse the continent—he would certainly use it to protect Angelique. And find Evariste, too.

But he had a suspicion that, in the future, much of the battle against the enemy that held Evariste would rest on Angelique.

He didn't like it, but he didn't know what he could do to defy it when his powers were, frankly, too *much* for this particular realm. Not to mention it still was a little taboo for constellations and other beings of great magic to frequent this realm with all their power.

So he would stay.

He would let Angelique cry on his shoulder, and he would carry her wherever she wished. And whenever she stretched out her hand for him, he would be there.

And when they finally retrieved Evariste, Pegasus was going to give him a good kick for making Angelique cry so much, rescuer or not!

The End

OTHER BOOKS BY K. M. SHEA

The Snow Queen Series:
A completed Epic Fantasy series of two books and an anthology of short stories

Timeless Fairy Tales:
Beauty and the Beast
The Wild Swans
Cinderella and the Colonel
Rumpelstiltskin
The Little Selkie
Puss in Boots
Swan Lake
Sleeping Beauty
Frog Prince
12 Dancing Princesses
Snow White
Three pack (Beauty and the Beast, The Wild Swans, Cinderella and the Colonel)

The Fairy Tale Enchantress:
Apprentice of Magic
Curse of Magic
Reign of Magic

The Elves of Lessa:
Red Rope of Fate
Royal Magic

King Arthur and Her Knights:

A complete historical fantasy series of seven books

Robyn Hood:

A compete historical fiction series of two novellas

The Magical Beings' Rehabilitation Center:

A complete urban fantasy series of two books and an anthology of short stories

<u>Other Novels</u>

Life Reader

Princess Ahira

A Goose Girl

<u>Second Age of Retha: Written under pen name A. M. Sohma</u>

The Luckless

The Desperate Quest

The Revived

ABOUT THE AUTHOR

K. M. Shea is a fantasy-romance author who never quite grew out of adventure books or fairy tales, and still searches closets in hopes of stumbling into Narnia. She is addicted to sweet romances, witty characters, and happy endings. She also writes LitRPG and GameLit under the pen name, A. M. Sohma.

Hang out with the K. M. Shea Community at...
kmshea.com

Printed in Great Britain
by Amazon